The Kanta Chronicles

Nick Sutcliffe

The Kanta Chronicles
Copyright © 2017 by Nick Sutcliffe

No part of this publication may be reproduced, distributed, or transmitted in any form or by any means, including photocopying, recording, or other electronic or mechanical methods, without the prior written permission of the author, except in the case of brief quotations embodied in critical reviews and certain other non-commercial uses permitted by copyright law.

tellwell

Tellwell Talent
www.tellwell.ca

ISBN
978-1-988186-64-1 (Hardcover)
978-1-988186-63-4 (Paperback)
978-1-988186-65-8 (eBook)

Bolfodier

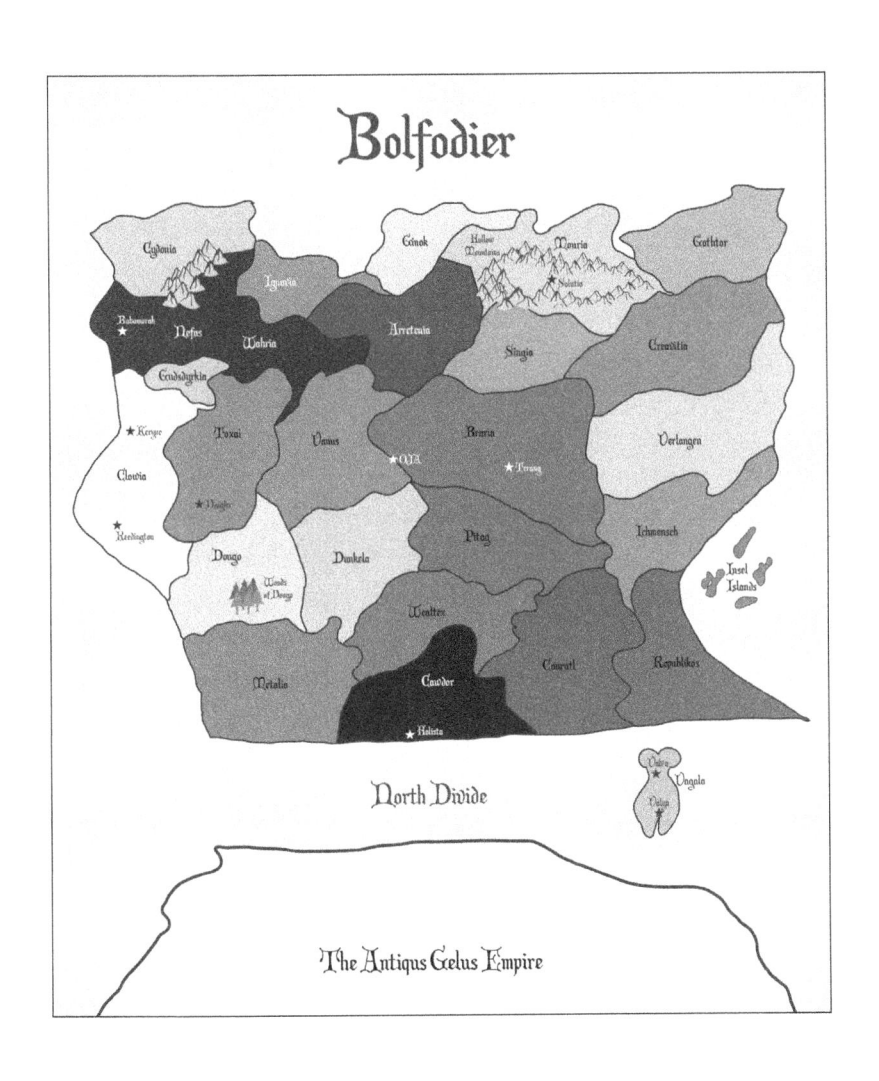

Thank Yous:

Frist and foremost to my wonderful parents Maureen and Brian, whose patience with this project is only surpassed by their patience with me. Secondly, my siblings Chris, Val and Pam, for without them this book would never have been possible. Thank you to my many aunts and uncles including but not limited to Dave and Dolores, Val and John, and Barry and Chas. I've got too many of you to name everyone, but I thank you all nonetheless and appreciate your support throughout the years. To my cousins Greyson, Lyle, Greg, Erik, Rachel, Cameron and so many others who helped promote, finance and create this book, I'm truly grateful for your support through this entire endeavour. To my teachers, especially Mary Philp, whose guidance and encouragement have helped not only mould myself as a writer but as a man as well. To the various artists (visual, musical or dramatic) who have helped inspire my works. Bolfodier would not exist if it wasn't for your profound impact upon my life, and I cannot express my deepest gratitude, appreciations and love for your works that not only bring life to Bolfodier, but to all those who experience them on a daily basis. Every word I write creatively can be traced back to one of you, and I'm truly grateful to have you in my creative conscious.

To my friends, Stu, Shaun, Devo, Gilbert, Bilal and all my Windsor crew, thank you for being my friends and loving me despite of how much of an asshole I can be. Thank you to all the readers who loved this story online enough to read it and read it again in print. I'd be remised if I didn't thank all the others who helped support this book by donating to the Kickstarter campaign online; without you all, this truly would not be possible Thank you to everyone in my life who has been antagonistic towards me, for you helped bring me to the infinite realms of fantasy. And thank you to you, reader, who have taken the time to read this book in its true entirety. Lastly, but certainly never least, I'd like to thank my Heaven-sent grandparents, Jim and Rosalie, for their unending love, devotion and pride in me. The two of you keep me going when I'm at my lowest and have made me (as well as the rest of our family and friends) a better person simply just by being in my life.

About Bolfodier:

The world of Bolfodier is quite different from our own. Most importantly, it has magic and the existence of their divinities is never in doubt. But what really sets Bolfodier apart are these facts: the sun rises in the north and sets in the south; the days are 25 hours long, each hour still being 60 minutes, all other units of time are the same, with the exception of there being 14 months in a year and each month is 30 days long; and finally, the more north you go the warmer it gets, and vice versa with the south.

Part One: Panken

Chapter 1:

What Do I Choose?

All alone he sat in his cave; he looked out from his favourite thinking chair, a rock that had been warped by all the times he and his ancestors had sat on it. Panken looked at nothing in particular, but took in the hidden path that led to the small clearing in front of the forest caves. He didn't notice that the sun was shining, nor that nature was in perfect harmony around him. He only thought about what it'd be like to be a care-free man, like those back in Terang who called him 'Prince'. But out in his family's private forest of the first outer ring of his home, care-free he was not.

Just when he thought he couldn't decide, he heard a noise - someone was coming. Looking to see who it was, Panken noticed a flash of sky blue in the green of the forest. The woman, for he could tell by the way she constantly had to untangle her dress from the shrubs covering the path that she was a woman, clearly didn't know the path very well. But Pan could tell that she had been down it at least once before, for she was heading right towards him. When she finally did step out into the clearing, he recognized the dark haired, skinny form of his mother. Surprised to see her away from his father's side, he asked her what she was doing here and offered her a spot on his thinking chair once she'd reached the cave's entrance.

"I couldn't take being in that room right now; so I decided to go looking for you. I've been to that shop Shade's been carving wooden figurines for, his and Marina's house, the Nosiop Inn, your room. I should have figured you'd be here; the males of the Kanta bloodline have always been drawn to these caves." She paused before she continued, her dark hair blowing in the wind. But her blue eyes weren't on her son as his expression darkened and a disgusted shudder ran through him at her last comment. "I came to apologize."

"Really…for what?" he asked in distracted confusion. Was his family's darkest secret the answer to his problem?

"All this fighting we've been doing these past few months. Your father and I want you to be happy, even if that means abandoning the throne for a girl."

"But I want to rule as well! Why can't I take Sabrina as my wife and queen; we love each other and the only thing that seems to be stopping you from letting us be together is some prophetic 'curse' that's ages old! 'Danger will arrive with the red emeralds; the only way to escape this curse is to remove the red from the sight of green.' What does that even mean? It makes no sense!" Panken argued the same argument.

"I don't know what it means. Over the years the family has hired knowledgeable wizards, prophets, sorceresses and anybody with a fragment of a guess. While on occasion one idea has been agreed upon, no one's been able to say with certainty. And until we know for certain, we aren't taking any chances."

"So I'm being denied my happiness because of a stupid riddle no one understands!" Panken yelled, his anger now rising.

"No, we're denying that so that we may continue to serve this wonderful land we call home." His mother's patience was clearly running thin.

"But why do I have to give everything for this problem? Why must I suffer to become king? Did you ever think that this ultimatum you've given me is how the 'curse' will be completed?"

"Yes we have thought of that. But do you think your father and me to be heartless, that we don't care if you suffer as long as you deny your love and take the throne?" She was yelling at him now. "It pains us to have to do this to you. We're positive that Sabrina is a lovely woman; we just don't want you to get hurt when we're gone. We want you to be forever happy with your life."

"But then why do you forbid that from happening? I am happiest when I'm with Sabrina; can you not see that?"

"Yes we do, but-"

"Then let me love her!"

"We are! Don't you think that if we didn't want you to be happy we would've killed her by now to ensure you take the throne?!"

Pan sat in stunned silence for a moment before he could react to this comment. "I hadn't thought of that. Thank you for that. But this choice is impossible for me to make. What would you do if someone made you choose between me and Dad to die? That is the choice the two of you have given me."

"First of all, no it's not. Second, I'd choose your father

- he's lived his life and you have only just fallen in love; you still have lots of life to live."

"I've lived more than you think I have."

"You are just twenty-four, Panken. Lying with a woman for the first time is not all there is to life, my son." His mother smiled at the small look of horror that quickly crossed her son's face.

"That may be, but I know I haven't lived long enough to make this decision. Only a wise man can make it, and I'm no wise man - I'm just a smart lad." His mother smiled at his cheek, which made Panken smile; a rare occurrence of late.

"I know, but might I suggest that you talk to a wise man who was a lover and a ruler; someone whose opinion you can count on and trust."

"Father will be dead by the end of the week and I-"

"I was talking about your father."

Panken looked to be struggling with something. "But he'll try to get me to take the crown - it's what he wants!"

"Not if you ask him to tell you of love and rule separately; he's always been able to balance points from different perspectives." Pan could see how she hoped this would get him to talk to his father.

"And he is renowned for that fact." Heaving a sigh, he continued, "You're right; I'll be forever mad at myself if I don't try to break this fight before he dies, and I could really use his advice right now." He stood to go.

Standing as well, and giving him a comforting hug, his mother said, "OK, let's go see him and hear what he has to say." They left the cave arm in arm and headed back for the castle.

Chapter 2:

Bloodline Web Curse

Back at the castle, Panken and his mother entered from a servants' entrance at the back that led to the cellars. From there, the pair climbed a set of stairs that led to the kitchen before parting ways. His mother stayed with the cooks to ensure that the king's midafternoon meal was being prepared, while Pan took the servants' stairs and went straight to his chambers. He, like his mother, loved to take the servants' stairs simply for the company and the tales they heard the servants tell one another.

Upon reaching his room in the Royal family's private quarters, Pan dressed himself in his most modest attire - a pair of old mud-covered and faded brown pants and a green shirt that was more patches than shirt - before he fixed his appearance in the mirror at the back of the room. His brown hair was getting too long for his liking as it was starting to cover his ears and matching brown eyes, but Sabrina had requested that he grow it out a bit; she'd thought it would make him look like the fabled old kings of Ginok, the birthplace of hereditary royalty. While walking to his parents' chambers, he bumped into a petitioner.

"Oh, I'm sorry."

The petitioner, a girl, was no more than twenty, if that, and had shoulder length brown hair. "It's OK, I wasn-" The girl's pale blue eyes had fixated on a point behind Pan which he knew to hold a portrait of him and his father in Brarian ceremonial robes. "Prince Panken!" She immediately fell to her left knee, crossing her left hand to grab her right ankle, while her right hand wrapped around her back in a fist, her head bent forward to give what was known as the Brarian Salute.

Knowing that the position was uncomfortable in itself, not to mention being awkward when wearing a dress, Pan tried to get the girl to stand immediately upon seeing her take this position. "Please miss, get up, there's no need for this. We're alone; you don't have to do this," he said as he tried to lift the girl up, but she would not budge. He hated it when people did this sort of thing; the Brarian Salute was an ancient practice from before Pan's family had come to power in Braria and it was meant to denote the weak and pathetic. It was a barbaric practice adopted from the position prisoners in Ichmensch accused of treason were executed in.

But she wouldn't move, so Panken resigned himself to what must be done. "Rise, but remember your place." Finally, she stood but kept her head bowed. "Miss, please lift your head - I wish to speak with you. And I request you tell me your honest opinion, even if that means yelling at me and/or speaking ill of my family, ok?"

"My Lord-" The girl shied away from his touch as he tried to lift her head, and still wouldn't raise her head to look at him. It was then that Pan noticed the girl's hair was wet in places, as if she'd washed it quite recently; and that her clothes, though clean, were more tattered and torn than his. Her pale yellowish brown dress looked as if it had been retailored at least a dozen times and was of a style Pan hadn't seen worn since he was a young child. The shirt she wore under the dress was the colour of dried out dirt and her sleeves were cut a little too short and too frilly for women in Terang. And her corset, somehow, seemed to be too loose on one side of her body but too tight on the other.

"I wish to know your views on how my family runs Braria. Please tell the truth, not what you think I want to hear."

"Yes Prince Panken," she said in timid voice, meekly accepting the task he requested of her.

"Simply Pan will do, miss"

"Sire," she said finally looking at him, allowing Pan to see the resignation in her eyes. But there was also the tiniest hint of resentment; whoever this girl was, Pan had to admire her inner fire. "I'm part of a very insignificant family from the border town of OJA; I couldn't call you as your friends do."

"Wait, you're from OJA? Are you a Lex?" How had Sabrina described the family she'd spent a year with?

"Yes that is my family name. Why do you speak it with respect, rather than disgust like everyone else?" The look in the girl's eyes told Pan that nobody outside of her family had ever spoken to her with even the tiniest amount of respect.

"About two years ago, your family gave shelter to a woman from Vagala, her name was-"

"Sabrina!" Her eyes absolutely shined at the mention of the name. "You know Sabrina, sire?"

"Yes, I know Sabrina."

"Really? H-how is she? Is she ok?"

"Well, she's a little upset right now, Kailee but she's fine."

"She told you of me? What troubles her, maybe I can help."

They were still standing in the archway that led to the private chambers of the Royal Couple. There was a small table nearby surrounded by chairs which Pan now led her to. "Yes, she told me of you, Kailee. She spoke most highly of you and your family; she says you became like her sister. As for her troubles, that would be me-or more accurately my family. You see, Sabrina and I wish to be married but my parents won't let us due to an old legend. Which brings me back to my original point: how do you think my family has ruled and treated its inferiors, such as yourself and others in OJA?" Pan thought he saw a frown cross the girl's face as he mentioned that he and Sabrina wished to be wed, but once he again asked his question there was only a small smile on her face.

"My Lord, I offer my sincerest congratulations and sympathies at these events. As for my views, I hear nothing but praise for how the House of Kanta rules Braria. But sire, I live in poverty because of my family's history and how people think we earn the little money we have."

"But why is that such a hindrance, Kailee?"

"Do you not know your own family history, Prince Panken?" she asked with an unbelieving look on her face.

"No I don't actually," he replied knowing she didn't mean the history he did know of.

"Well about a thousand generations ago my family was a wealthy one. The head of the house had worked very hard to get where he was: a royal adviser and suitor for the then princess. Rumours at the time said that the then king was going to remove his family from power and give it to one of his three trusted advisers."

"A thousand generations ago, my family didn't rule Braria. So how does this deal with my family?"

"I'm getting there, sire. When the time came to choose which adviser would rule the country, my ancestor wasn't chosen, but yours was. This greatly upset my ancestor, but at the request of both the former and new king he and the other adviser stayed on to be advisers.

"But my ancestor wanted to rule. So he schemed how to kill the new king and steal the crown for himself and his new wife; who, by the way, wasn't the old princess. Someone found out his plan and told the king. The king was very surprised to hear of this treason; the two had apparently been friends since they were children.

"He told the informant to try and join my ancestor, so as to know when he would strike. My ancestor was caught; many demanded his death but your ancestor had a more, er, interesting punishment in mind. His wife was to become a whore and be the only source of income for the family. He was also forbidden to be with his wife, as man and wife, except for every five years on their anniversary. To ensure he didn't pleasure himself without his wife, the rest of the time he was forced to wear a chastity belt." The way she said the punishment in a monotone voice made it seem so much worse.

"My god, I'm so sorry, that's really harsh."

"Don't go trying to re-write the past, it's impossible. Besides," she said with a tentative smile, "the score was settled, for they had a son. The son grew up in the aftermath of his father's mistake and seeing that his parents were only happy every five years. He grew angry and resentful about what had befallen our once great family. He saved his life's earnings and paid a credible sorcerer to enter the servitude of the Royal family and curse them, so they would lose their rule. A year later, the sorcerer was executed for cursing the family."

Pan couldn't help it, his anger boiled over and he lost control. "WHAT?!" he bellowed. The small wooden table they were sitting at exploded as his anger unleashed a surge of magic into it, causing splinters to rain down on the two of them. Kailee shrieked out in fright, crawling away. "That's why we were cursed? That's why I can't…?"

"W-what's wrong, sire?" Kailee asked in such a weak voice that Pan could barely hear her. Her hands were covering her face from the falling pieces of the table.

Seeing her cower in fear brought his senses back to him. "That curse is what troubles me and Sabrina, it's the reason my parents won't let us wed," he said calmly, but the anger was still present.

Still very frightened by the outburst, Kailee spoke, nearly pleading, "Prince Panken, please forgive me; I didn't mean to bring up what is now clearly a sore subject with you. Perhaps I should come back at another-" She stopped at feeling Pan's gentle hands on her shoulder, lifting her back to a standing position.

"It's ok, Kailee," he said calmly, looking into the girl's pale blue eyes. "It's not your fault nor is it your problem. You answered my question like I asked you to: honestly. Now answer this for me in a similar fashion. Since the curse was placed, has my family ruled fairly - in your opinion and that of your family?"

"Sire, my family has accepted we've fallen from grace;

we are happy. Yes, there is the odd one of us who gets mad and ends up dead. But it seems our luck is changing; shortly after Sabrina left, the mayor's son began courting my sister Jayne, and she seems to like him as well."

"Well it's now I, who offers congratulations. But that doesn't answer my question exactly."

"No it doesn't," she said with a thoughtful look. "Like I said, we are occasionally angry at what has become of us; which I think understandable, considering. But we seem to agree with most everything the House of Kanta does."

"No complaints at all?"

"Well, taxes are a little too high; my mother has had to take a job as a courtesan at times for us to just get by." She shied away from his gaze as she revealed this.

"I'm sorry, but I've tried to talk to my father about that; trying to make him change it from a certain amount to a certain percentage of a household's monthly income. But he never does anything about it."

"Everyone complains about taxes; don't lose sleep over it."

"That's true."

"Have I answered satisfactorily, my lord?"

"Please call me Pan. And if you answered me honestly, then yes, you have."

"Sorry…Pan," Kailee said shyly.

"It's ok; most people take a while to get used to it. Now I believe you came from the public entrance, which means that you came to visit my father. What is it you need?"

"Well, I heard that there was strife in the Royal family due to 'the past coming true.' I wondered if it had anything to do with the curse. So I came to offer my assistance in removing it."

At hearing these words, Pan's face brightened. But then he remembered what he needed. "And how do you plan on doing that? I was under the impression that to remove a curse as strong as this one we needed a few things that are a bit hard to come by now, it being so long since it was cast."

"There's one more part to the story. The night before the curse was cast, the sorcerer wrote to the son who hired him and explained what type of curse he was placing on the Royal family. The letter says he placed a Vicetz Curse on your family."

"Are you sure, a Vicetz Curse?" Pan asked, thinking that a Vicetz Curse wasn't nearly strong enough. Vicetz Curses were used to cause one's deepest desires to drive them mad. And while this could lead to a loss of power, it would have no effect on Pan twenty-five hundred years later.

"Yes I'm sure; I have the letter right here." She handed a small worn piece of paper to him. It was a short letter, but its impact on Pan was much bigger. Face fallen, he sunk into a nearby pillar. "Is everything alright, Pan?" Kailee asked with a worried look.

"No. The curse place upon us wasn't a Vicetz Curse; it was a Bloodline Web Curse. Something that is much worse." Bloodline Web Curses were certainly powerful enough to still be troublesome after twenty-five centuries. Like a spider spinning its web, this curse was patient, working through the generations, causing the cursed to be led to its conclusion.

"But the letter said it was a Vicetz Curse."

"I know, but sorcerers have a certain way of writing that sheds the truth of their words. Few people besides sorcerers know this and fewer know how to read it. You see the two threes and two in the signature, that's how you know which words to read to understand the truth of what the sorcerer has written. I'm thankful your family has kept this letter for so long, but this complicates things to the point that it might be impossible to remove the curse."

"Why is it impossible?"

"It's *nearly* impossible. We now need a descendant from that sorcerer that happens to be a witch. Yes, it has to be a witch; the complications of magic," explained Pan.

"But why can't you use another sorcerer?"

"Because the Spell of Undoing requires the gift that is opposite to the one who cast the spell in the first place. That's why it's extremely rare that spells are undone. And Bloodline Web Curses bind the families of the cursed and caster so that only the caster's descendants can remove the curse."

"So you need the caster or one of their descendants?" the girl asked.

"Yes, very good Kailee." She smiled at having understood all this. "Again, thank you for bringing me this letter, even if it brought bad news."

"You're welcome Pan, I think."

"Now I ask you to go visit your friend. Sabrina is staying at the Nosiop Inn; it's just inside the part of town that looks like you're going to get attacked if you enter it. Don't worry, you won't get attacked; I'll give you a small entourage. Once you two have caught up, tell her all that has happened here and that she must meet me at the caves - she knows which caves. It has been a pleasure Kailee, but I must go. Hopefully this will be over soon and we can meet each other properly. Now go!" And with that he left for the castle's Blackreich; its magical armoury and storage area.

Chapter 3:

Kailee and Sabrina

Kailee just stood there stunned; confused by the sudden dismissal and order to go visit her friend. But just as she made up her mind to go and follow Prince Panken, two men appeared at her side. They were clearly castle guards, judging from the matching leather armour dyed a deep blue, metal helms and arsenal of handheld weapons strapped to their bodies. She thought she recognized them from when she'd entered the private chambers of the Royal family.

"Ms. Lex?" the one on her right asked. He was the bigger of the two, but had a kind face about him. His partner simply looked at her with the same look she'd seen men give her mother: lust, as if she were just a tavern whore. It was men like this that had made her turn to the charms of her own kind.

"Yes…?" she asked nervously.

"My name is Gideon Vanto, and this is Freddie King. Prince Panken asked us to escort you to the Nosiop Inn. Please follow us."

Reluctant, but eager to see Sabrina again, she agreed.

They led her out of the castle, taking her out of the Royal family's private chambers, down the grand staircase that spiraled down into the centre of the entrance hall, and finally out the large wooden doors to a small stable at the side of the castle courtyard. There they convinced her to get into a small carriage. Its door was engraved with the Kanta family crest: two intertwined 'K's. If Kailee hadn't known better, she would have thought they were meant to appear to be made of broken bones. Kailee had never ridden in a carriage before and was inwardly impressed at the gesture Panken was making - even after she had given him a complete shock and made it nearly impossible for him to be completely happy.

The trip was quite comfortable and short; people obviously didn't bother the Royal family, or those in their carriages. The door opened and there stood Sabrina, a look of surprise on her face. Kailee jumped out and gave her friend a hug.

"What-how-thought Pan…" Sabrina stuttered after she was released from the hug.

"It's good to see you too. I will explain everything after we've caught up with each other," Kailee said with a huge smile. Sabrina's long red hair still came to the curve of her bottom. Her emerald eyes matched the simple dress she wore perfectly. Her skin was still marble white, and her lips were still as red as her hair. She still looked so beautiful.

"Yes, it is good to see you too, Kailee." The smile Sabrina gave her made Kailee's stomach flutter and heart ache. "And I should hope you explain, you have a Royal escort, and knew I was here. But you're right, we should catch up first."

So the girls went inside and up to the room that Sabrina

was renting. It was big for an inn this size, with a fair sized bed, wardrobe and writing desk; apparently being the paramour of the prince came with good accommodations. Sitting the both of them down, Sabrina and Kailee told each other what had happened to them since Sabrina had left the Lex home and OJA. Sabrina was thrilled to hear about Jayne being suited by the mayor's son and what this could mean for the Lex family. Kailee was astonished to hear about Sabrina meeting Pan and falling in love with him, how they had been with each other on several occasions and the trouble they were now having. Hearing of her friend's trouble reminded Kailee of the other reason she was here.

"Sabrina, I believe I owe you an explanation of my being here."

"Yes Kai, you do."

"Well I left OJA because I heard that the House of Kanta was in an uproar about 'the past coming true.' As it turns out, it was you this strife was over. When I arrived at the castle, I literally bumped into Pan. He asked me what I thought about how they rule. I told him and then he asked why I was here. I told him I came to help with the strife if I could. I told him of our connected past and showed him a letter from the sorcerer who was behind the curse. After he read it, he claimed that his family was under a Bloodline Web Curse. This greatly upset him as he thinks it nearly impossible to remove. He gave me an escort so I could get you and tell you this and that he wants to meet you at the caves. He said you knew which caves."

"Did he say when?" Sabrina asked with sudden seriousness.

"No."

"Thanks Kai. But I must go, Pan is surely waiting. Stay here, I'll be back to talk more - I just don't know when. Wait for me please, sister. Go wherever you wish until I return." Walking over to the writing desk and opening a drawer, Sabrina produced a pin Kailee had seen her wearing in OJA that looked like a crude drawing of a fish. Handing it to Kailee, she said, "If you leave, wear this pin - it'll protect you. I love you and we need to talk more. I'll be back as soon as I can." With that Sabrina gave Kailee a quick hug and a kiss on the cheek and left.

Chapter 4:

Desperate Measures

Following the hidden path by memory, Pan studied the book he carried as he walked to the clearing outside the caves. Pan had barely gotten there with his spell book and pouches of black and white sorcerer's sand when Sabrina arrived. After a brief embrace, Sabrina gave him a worried look; she'd seen the book he brought: *The Mantras of Power*. The half-moon gave off enough light for them to see each other clearly.

"Pan? What are you doing? You can't use those spells; they're the oldest spells in history! The spells Nina taught to the Ancients, Lilith's chosen few! You, you don't have that kind of power, my love."

"Sabrina, I'm trying to rid my family of this curse, so we can be together. I've read this book and it tells of a power that will allow the one who uses it to make all those he knows do whatever he wants. I just have to make it my own."

"Are you talking about *Erised Mamagneta*?"

"Yes," Pan said, bracing himself.

"Are you *insane*?! NOBODY can handle that spell! That

power is even stronger than love! And how do you 'make it your own'?" she asked in a shrill voice that was much higher than normal. The moonlight made her moist, green eyes shine, both with concern and exasperation.

"I'm desperate! Prophecy tells of one who'll be able to control that power - and it sounds a lot like me. I just don't know how to make it my own."

"Panken, I know you're desperate; I am too! The prophecy only speaks of a ruler in love - there are many of those. And if you don't know how to make it your own, how do you plan on using that spell? Besides, you can't force someone you don't know to do your bidding. You need a descendant who is a witch. There are very few witches in this world and most live below the North Divide in the Antiqus Gelus Empire or in Vagala: two places you can't or won't go. Please find a different way, love. I can't help you if you do this."

"It doesn't say the person bent to my will has to be living," Pan said with a manic voice. "I can dig that bastard who cursed my family up and force him to remove it. And I would go to those places, you need only ask. And you can help me: you can cast the spell on me."

"I-I couldn't. I'd turn you into a monster. Panken, please don't do this. Not even for me. I love you, but you're scaring me with this talk of using *The Mantras of Power*. Just come to me and love me…I need you."

Panken walked over to the woman he loved and held her to him. Sabrina had started to cry when she realized what he was contemplating; but within his loving arms she calmed down. He kissed her fiercely.

"Pan, I want to be rid of this curse just as much as you, but I don't want to destroy you to get it. If I can only love you from afar then that's what I'll do, even if it kills me."

"My dear, you don't have to love me from afar. I won't use the spell, but I need to find the witch descendant, if she exists."

"You don't even know if she exists?" Sabrina shrilled. "Yet you'd kill yourself in an attempt to find out if she does?"

"No, I'd kill myself in an attempt to have our love be approved by my parents."

"Why can't your parents be dead - then we wouldn't have this problem?"

"Sabrina?!"

"I'm just kidding. But you know it's true."

Panken heaved a sigh. "Yes, I know it's true. But I won't kill my parents just to settle this. You know, they actually seem to really like you - besides the fact you bring a curse."

"Really? We've only met once and I thought that I'd left a bad impression."

Thinking back to the first and only time Sabrina had met his parents, Pan realized that it wasn't the greatest first impression. The night had started out well enough with Shade and Marina joining him, his parents, and Sabrina for dinner, but had quickly deteriorated when his father had laid eyes upon Sabrina. "Well, I think it has more to do with the fact that they think I'll fall in love with someone likable."

"Only likable?" she asked with a raised eyebrow.

"They only have to like you; I'm the one who *has to* love you." At this jibe, she gave him a look of mock shock and poked him in the shoulder. He was glad to see her restrain her smile, knowing she could smile at a time like this.

"*Have to?*"

"OK, choose to. But I also choose to be rid of this curse.

It's all I can think about; I'm obsessed. Help me please."

"My love, you know I'd help if I knew how to, but I don't. But what if…" she trailed off.

"What if what?"

"Now, don't judge me on this but, what if you stepped down as Prince and I…"

"No! I've wanted to be king since I was a child. And besides, that would bring the curse to fruition. I couldn't put my parents through that; it'd kill my father prematurely. I-"

"Your father won't see the next moon. I know you don't want him to die but Hados is calling his name - and nothing can stop that. Go spend his last few days with him. I'll be fine, I've got Kailee."

"I can't; he's so angry with me. He-"

"He's your father. He won't want the last memory between you to be a fight. Trust me, it'll be fine. Now go!"

"You're right. I've got to ask him a few things anyway."

"Women usually are right, you know," she joked.

Rolling his eyes, but giving her a hug nonetheless, he picked up his spell book and sorcerer's sand. With one last kiss, he left for his father's bedside for the second time that day.

Chapter 5:

The Foolishness of King Leo

When he arrived back at the castle it was midnight. Considering it was so late, Pan decided his talk with his father could wait until morning. They both needed their sleep.

Inside his room, Pan took off his clothes and flopped onto his bed. Having had little sleep over the past few weeks had finally caught up to him and he was asleep before his head even touched the pillow.

Panken woke the next morning to the sound of banging on his door. After a second set of bangs, the door opened to reveal Shade, Pan's best friend. Dressed in black pants and a burgundy shirt, Shade shut the door before turning back to Pan. His blackish brown eyes, which matched his close-cropped hair perfectly, leveled at Pan as a smile pulled at the edges of the goatee he was struggling to grow. And as always, in his hands were a small piece of wood and a small curved blade that he used to carve the wood in his hand. "Oh, it's nice to know that the future of the kingdom cares so much for it that he's spent the entire morning sleeping, rather than at the bedside of his dying father. Has his highness reached a decision yet?" Shade asked in his unique mixture of joking sympathy, as he had every day for the past few weeks since that fateful dinner.

"No," Pan said, rubbing the sleep from his eyes. "Wait, did you say it was midday?" Pan asked in a panic. Shade simply nodded his head. Realizing how late he'd slept, Pan immediately got out of bed to get dressed. "Thanks for waking me," he said to Shade as he rushed to get dressed. "Make sure you pick up your shavings when you leave."

But before he could exit the room, Shade called him back. "Pan, wait. There's something I need to say: I'm sorry, I never meant for all this to happen. I didn't think that your father would actually get so upset when I mentioned the curse. You know I'd never try to hurt you, right?" Gone was the cheerful banter, and only sincere remorse was in its place.

Pan simply nodded with a hand to his friend's shoulder and a small smile to say that all was forgiven. Seeing Shade's returning smile, Pan left his room and rushed to his father's. Upon entry, Pan noticed only his mother was there, sitting at her husband's side, holding his hand and looking like she hadn't slept in days. The energy she'd had yesterday was gone; seeing her husband so ill had taken its toll.

"Mother, you look exhausted. Why don't you go get some sleep; I can look after Father for a while."

Jolted out of her thoughts by his sudden appearance and voice, the queen silently agreed and left for the master chambers.

"Father, can we speak?" The king's eyes opened as he weakly beckoned his son to his side. Leo Kanta, his father, once so strong and energetic, had been reduced to something so feeble that a conversation was the extent of his energy. His mother had comically attempted to have the king look his best; she'd cut his greying brown hair and trimmed his greyer beard. Taking his mother's chair, Pan rushed to say all that he could before he was interrupted. "Father, I'm so, so very sorry for what I've done. I know the curse can't be lifted but I want so much to rule with Sabrina as my queen. Why do you ha-" His father raised a hand to stop Pan's babbling.

"My son," he wheezed in between coughs, "I know how you feel. It pains me so to make you choose between your two greatest desires. I'm sorry too. I know Sabrina is a lovely woman and that you are quite happy together." Seeing his son's look of curiosity, he explained. "I keep a very close eye on the things that are most precious to me. I also know that you'd love nothing more than to rule. I can only imagine what the battle inside you right now is like: the Prince and the romantic. If only you had siblings, we wouldn't have this problem." His father was visited by a strong fit of coughs now.

"We don't need to have it in the first place; you can let Sabrina and me rule together."

"I've always considered that option, but I fear for the future. Forgive me, but I don't want my grandchildren growing up in an uncomfortable home."

"Just because it's not a castle, doesn't mean it's uncomfortable; look at Shade's and Marina's house."

"I know, but why risk it."

"So I can be happy!" He was getting tired of trying to get this point across.

"People everywhere suffer!" Anger had crept into his

father's voice but he shoved it away before he next spoke, still with regular coughing fits. "Pan, I love this country and I don't want to give it over to someone who'll run it to the ground. I know you'd never let it come to ruin, you care more fiercely about it than I do! Am I to assume you're here because you've made a choice?"

"No, I haven't made a choice yet. It's too hard."

"My son, I'm sorry but you're acting like a child: '*it's too hard;*' life is full of hard choices, no matter who you are. It's time you come to terms with life."

"What do you want me to do, Father? Both paths lead to disappointment with myself; and you know how much I hate disappointing people."

"Yes I know. And I want you to choose before I die. I still have to appoint the next king, and I'm running out of time. I want so much for it to be you, but I can't force the crown to your head. But I also want to personally wed you to a woman you love. I know I'll never get to do one of these things and that is half the pain I feel at this ultimatum."

"We don't have to feel this pain, Father. Release me and give us what we all want." Pan was now grabbing at straws.

"I won't jeopardize the rule of the House of Kanta over a girl!" his father shouted. The force of his voice startled Pan the slightest bit, as it gave him a glimpse of the man his father had used to be; the man Pan had loved all his life.

Pan stood to leave and walked to the door. There he turned back. "Our rule will eventually come to an end. We've already angered our subjects into cursing us. Your spies should have told you that if Sabrina ever becomes angered with us that we could be dead in a heartbeat. But she'd never do that because she has more respect for life than anyone

I know. She won't force you out of this ultimatum for she respects that she can't have people do only her will. She'd make an excellent queen in war or peace! I know the threat is credible but you're acting like a scared, old fool. Last night I nearly killed myself trying to grab the last hope I had at ending this curse. I'd be dead now if she hadn't stopped me. So I ask you, Father, does a woman like that seem worth the risk of our rule?" Without waiting for an answer, Pan left.

Once he was gone, the queen came rushing in. She had tears in her eyes. "Why?! Why did you have to make him angry at you *again*, Leo? He came here to ask for your help and forgiveness and you gave neither and called him a child! He's your son and he's in a position none his age should be in. You're dying, Leo; do you want his last memories of you to be this argument?! He knows that he has to make difficult decisions in life, but he can still ask for help!" She started to cry and couldn't finish her outburst.

"Evelyn, come and sit," he said kindly, a pained expression on his too pale face. "I know I'm dying and that this fight isn't what we want our last memories of each other to be. He can ask for my advice, but I fear even I am too biased. I know he loves this girl but I won't have him throw the crown away for her! He is right though: ending this ultimatum would make us all happy."

"Then why don't you?"

"Even if I did, he couldn't marry her - she's a commoner. And she's Vagalian!"

"So? Who cares where she's from? She's a good person; surely your spies conveyed that to you! And what does it matter if he loves her? Being of 'royal blood' is just something the fabled old kings of Ginok made up so people would go along with their takeover - you know that!"

"Yes I know that! But the public doesn't! What would happen if they saw him marry a commoner; they'd see the truth, that's what! And then riots would break out all over. Nobody wants that." Saying this reduced him to a fit of coughs.

"You know your son is right: you are an old fool. Sabrina is a damelin! Even you, the most magically ignorant person ever, know that means she comes from a long line of magic, which was once the basis for rule; so she has a form of 'royal blood.'"

"Why do you support him? Don't you like being a queen?"

"Yes, I like being a queen. I've spent my entire life in castles and palaces, but that doesn't mean I find the idea of not living in one repulsive. I'm not going to sabotage my baby's chance at happiness or love to stay queen and live in this castle! That's why I support him: because he's my son; and he's yours too!" With that, Evelyn made to leave but was stopped by her husband grabbing her arm. For a dying man he had a strong grip.

"I love my son! I've always supported him in everything he's done, even if I've disagreed with it. Being his father I think I should be able to…to give him a test so that I can rest in peace knowing my boy is a man, a good man. Being able to make major decisions is my way of testing him. We have always been people of authority, and I won't go to Hados and tell thousands of my ancestors that we no longer rule or have any political sway!" He released her arm but she didn't go to leave; she just stood there staring at him with a look of shocked horror and incredulity.

"Goodbye, Leo. I hope your pride helps you tell your ancestors what you want to, and not the truth: that *you* threw away the crown!" And with that, she left her husband king to the pains of death.

Chapter 6:

Feeling Better

Kailee had spent the past hour pacing back and forth across the room, awaiting Sabrina's return. She'd been gone too long; surely these caves weren't hours away. Just as she was about to go out and look for her, Sabrina walked in the door and heaved a sigh.

"What are you doing up, Kai?" she asked when she saw that Kailee was standing in the middle of the room.

"Making sure you're all right. What happened?" She could feel the worry on her face. Taking Sabrina's hand, she led them over to the bed where she sat them down.

"Pan wanted to use *The Mantras of Power*." Seeing Kailee's blank look, Sabrina elaborated, "It's a spell book that contains the most powerful and oldest spells in the world. Few copies exist and fewer can use the spells inside. But Pan wanted to use a spell no one knows how to even work," she said, her disbelief at it all still on her face.

"No! You did-"

"I talked him out of it, thankfully."

"Thank the spirits."

"Indeed," Sabrina said with another weary sigh. "He's probably trying to find another solution. We're both desperate but I can't imagine the pressure he feels. He hates leaving people unsatisfied, and this will definitely do that."

Kailee leaned over to Sabrina and gave her a sympathetic hug. "I'm so sorry. I can't imagine how *you* are feeling. To have left home and fallen in love with someone only to have his parents try to shun you out of his life; this must be killing you."

Sabrina gave Kailee a kiss on the cheek. "Thank you, but I don't need your sympathy. I just need to feel better."

Kailee froze for the briefest of seconds at hearing the phrase Sabrina had used. "I feel your pain, sister. But I can't help any more than I have; I can't force the king and queen to do anything, I'm a simple commoner. Nobody ever listened to me, nobody except you."

"No Kailee, I need to *feel better*," Sabrina said as she put her hand on Kailee's back.

Surprised by what Sabrina was doing and its meaning, Kailee looked at her with a mixture of alarm and longing. Then she remembered they weren't in OJA anymore. "I can't make you *feel better* anymore, Sabrina. You love Pan and I don't want to make him angry with me for what you're asking me, and not him, to do." No matter how much I want to, she thought.

"Oh please, Kailee. I can see the longing in your eyes. Besides you make a different kind of love to me than Pan; and it's you who I need now."

"Even if I want to Sabrina, I-I couldn't." She crawled to the other side of the bed and sat down; this was using all of her willpower. Sabrina came and sat beside her, a little too close for Kailee's willpower.

"Kai, how long has it been, since you *felt better*?" Kailee mumbled something that she knew Sabrina couldn't hear. "I didn't hear, how long?"

"Too long - since you left," Kailee said meekly. Sabrina was surprised; it'd been over a year since she'd left OJA.

"Oh-oh my Kailee, tha-that's too long! I know you don't like men, but even still."

What Kailee said next was even more shocking. She'd wanted to say it to Sabrina before she'd left but couldn't find the words. Now they came without her wanting them to. "I love you, Sabrina. It crushed me when you left, just as we were getting close. You were my first and only and I can't think of anything without thinking about you! Every night I've dreamed of you on top of me, trusting and licking. And while I'm happy you found someone, I'm devastated it wasn't me! You're right that I do want to, but I can't now that I know you love another as I love you and that he fights to love you!"

It took Sabrina a few moments to react to this with more than a blank face. Every passing second that she didn't say anything seemed an eternity to Kailee, who grew closer to tears. Just as she was about to cry, Sabrina cupped her face with a hand and lifted her chin and pressed her mouth to Kailee's. Taken aback for only a second, Kailee was soon kissing Sabrina as passionately and fiercely as she was being kissed. As their tongues met both women let out a moan of pleasure they hadn't felt in over a year. Within minutes they were lying on the bed, wearing only each other.

Sabrina had locked the door, but people still tried to get in. The men wanted to join in and the women wanted quiet;

the two of them were moaning quite audibly in pleasure, screaming the other's name as they agreed with each other.

It was well past dawn before they collapsed, finished and relieved like never before. They fell asleep in each other's arms; peaceful smiles on their faces.

They awoke hours later, tired but content.

Kissing Kailee's cheek, Sabrina asked what had clearly been on her mind the whole night. "Kailee, did you mean what you said last night?"

Kailee's face went red from embarrassment and she wore a look of horror. "What - I don't know what you're talking about." She tried to hide her face, hoping that Sabrina would drop the topic.

"You know exactly what I'm talking about," Sabrina said turning her around so they were facing each other. "That little outburst you had right before I kissed you. The one where you said you loved me, that I was you first and only and how you wished I wasn't with Pan but with you."

"Oh, that." Kailee was uneasy about exposing herself like that. "I actually said that?" Sabrina nodded solemnly in response. "Yes I meant it. I'm so, so, so, so sorry for springing this on you; I can't have you, I know, but you have to know how I've felt all this time." She was close to tears as she laid out her heart.

"Why didn't you tell me? Why have you bottled it up inside for the past year?" Sabrina asked, her concern palpable in her voice.

"Why? Because you were so anxious to leave for here, Terang the near centre of Bolfodier, a place your mother would never go, that I thought I meant so little to you I couldn't bring myself to tell you and have you laugh at me."

The words came out angrier and with more venom than Kailee had intended. She couldn't help it; it was just there. And the look Sabrina gave her at the mention of her mother; how had she just confessed to loving this woman and the next second used her greatest source of pain against her? "Oh I'm sorry for that I-"

"Don't apologize for feeling - it's what we women are good for. And how could you think I didn't care about you? I spent as much time as I could with you; I spent the nights silencing our passion. I told you of what my mother made me do in confidence, to show you that I still had nightmares about things in my past too. If I didn't care, then why would I have done those things?" Hurt was visibly strewn across Sabrina's face.

Kailee got up from the bed and walked away a bit. "Maybe so you could stay with us longer!" She covered her mouth as soon as she said it, but there was that anger and venom. Maybe repressing her feelings hadn't been such a good idea after all.

Sabrina walked over to her and, cupping her face in both hands, kissed her. "Kailee, I love you. Maybe not like I love Pan, but I still love you. You are a lover and sister to me. Saying you think I don't care about you, pains me. To have you think I left without a reason or that I wouldn't miss you, is hurtful and insulting. I have also thought of you during the night, as you've thought of me, and I've missed you too." Saying this, Sabrina looked into Kailee's pale blue eyes and saw only love. She leaned in once more to feel the light brush of lips; a more passionate kiss than either had ever known.

Chapter 7:

How Do I Choose?

Seething, Panken had run from his father's death bed to the caves that had always drawn him in close. He wanted to bring the castle down onto his father! He had heard his parents argue and had narrowly avoided detection. So, this was all a test to his father? Hadn't his father said he was a man years ago, upon the completion of his Reckoning? Angry and confused thoughts swarmed Pan's head, like being in the middle of the market on sale day.

"Arghhh!" Panken screamed. Everything in the vicinity took to the opposite direction of the clearly painful and angry scream. He unleashed a ball of nightfire onto the large stone near the entrance, the nightfire burning the stone into nothingness leaving only the distinct smell of burning rotten eggs. He regretted this immediately as it was his thinking chair.

He heard a noise behind him. Turning to see who the intruder was he ignited another ball of nightfire in his hand, ready to be unleashed at a moment's notice. When he saw his mother approach, he immediately extinguished it.

"Was that nightfire?!" she demanded in a scandalized tone.

"Not now; I'm in no mood!"

"Nor am I." Her tone and face agreed completely. "But after that bloodcurdling scream, I'm surprised to find everything intact."

"You know, just because the men of our family have always been drawn to these caves, doesn't mean the women have to be as well."

"Excuse me, young man? I am your mother and the Queen of Braria and I will not be talked to in such a tone; especially after I just pleaded your case to your father! But you knew that, of course." Apparently he'd been caught after all.

"Well, now we know how obtuse he's being, what am I to do?"

"I don't care what you do; just make sure you don't do anything stupid. Follow your heart," she said with what he guessed was meant to be an encouraging smile but only served to dampen his spirits.

"That's the problem! It's telling me to do three different things that will leave me miserable. If I knew what my heart was saying to do, I would've done it already!"

"What's the third thing?"

"Kill Father." Seeing the look of horror on her face he added, "Don't look so surprised! Like you didn't think of it?"

"He's still my husband and your father, not to mention the king!"

"I'm not going to kill him, Mother. But I do think he should act like those things he is to us and not the pompous fool he's being now!"

"Yes, but men who can't see reason won't want to, even to save their lives." The look she gave her son as she said this made Pan think that she was warning him against the same action.

Casting this thought aside, Pan only half seriously asked, "True, but can't we beat some into him?"

"Panken?!" said his mother, offended by his suggestion of violent behaviour; he'd always been a level headed and peaceful person. "Maybe you should talk this over with Sabrina. She might calm you down and clear your head enough to possibly make a choice."

"Yeah, I should do that. I'll see you later." He left without hearing or caring about her goodbye.

Panken put his hood up and closed his cloak as he entered the part of town that housed the Nosiop Inn. He didn't want to be recognized. He knew that the back door was open and less popular, so that's where he went in. Climbing the steps, he met Jensen, the Nosiop's owner, and gave her a quick hello as well as a finger to his lips to let her know to keep his being here a secret. As he neared Sabrina's room, he heard an angry snarl and a calming, soothing voice he was sure was Sabrina's. As he unleashed a small thread of magic to unlock the door, he entered the room.

Upon entry, Pan's mind was made up.

Ten Years Later

Chapter 8:

A Dangerous New Partner

It had been nearly ten years since Pan's father had died and he'd become the Nifehan of Braria. Even though his father had been king, Pan had become the Nifehan because of his wizarding abilities, and his queen-less bed. How he hated that name.

Much had changed in those ten years. After the death of his mother five years previous, Pan had developed himself a new power. Upon reading countless volumes of ancient wizarding texts, he finally was able to find out what people thought of him and his choices - and her.

This power, called the Time Wind, allowed Pan to see the life of everyone he met through their eyes. Then he could take them back to an emotion they'd felt, no matter how far away from them he was. The only drawback to this was that he wasn't the only one who Saw; all he saw, the victim saw. It was for this reason that Pan was known as the Memory Thief. This nickname, he did not mind.

About a year after the death of Pan's father, a woman had moved into the cottage across the lake the castle was on.

She always wore a very form-revealing dress that was the colour of blackblood. Her name was Selina, and she was who Panken desired above all else.

He'd spent many days, months, and years watching her, learning her daily routine, who her friends were and anything else he could learn about her. He never learned of her family, nor where she'd come from. Most of this was learned by his powers as the Memory Thief; bringing in those who knew Selina and bathing in their memories of her. Her voice was as sweet as the juice from an apple, her hair as black as nightfire, and her eyes the perfect colour of amethyst. How Panken wished he could gaze into the real things, not the memories he stared at for hours on end.

Pan was suddenly brought back to his senses by the giggling of at least two girls. He knew just who was to blame for this: Freddie King. And no sooner had he thought this than King came around the corner with two girls on each arm and another on his back. Pan was amazed at how nearly all of Braria knew that Freddie King was barely a step above a male prostitute, and yet nearly every week he had a different girl in his bed - and there was usually more than one. Why did he allow those soldiers who were stationed in the castle to have nighttime visitors? Which of his predecessors had thought that allowing guards to be housed in the same area as the Royal family was a good idea?

Realizing he was tired, and that he didn't want to hear the exaggerated moaning, Pan got out of his plush throne, walked to his private chambers, and readied himself for sleep. Just as he got into bed he started to hear the moans. Tonight they were extremely exaggerated, and Pan knew that he was going to have trouble sleeping. Blissfully sleep found Pan before the calls of ecstasy got louder.

No matter how much he wished it, or how much he tried, this one moment would not be buried. With every step he took, Pan felt the dread build; he hadn't felt dread on that day ten years ago, but he knew what awaited him at the end of the hall on the other side of that door; closed by magic for a very good reason.

This time though, was different. Every few steps he took, something else took the dread's place in his attention. At one point it was a celebration he could barely remember, but he didn't want to remember that night. At another, it was the words his father had spoken, crowning him Nifehan. And when he was but a few steps away from that dreaded door, it was a moan; the moaning of a woman that he still, to this day, could not remember the name of.

And then his hand was on the knob.

It must have been nearly dawn. He'd woken from a most vivid nightmare; one that had plagued him for the last ten years, always resurfacing this time of year. He saw them kissing, without even a sheet between the two of them. He was thankful he'd woken when he did; he usually shot a ball of nightfire if he saw much more.

But then, he heard the cries from the hall. At first he thought it was the women with King, but then he heard the male cries. It sounded as though a woman had broken into the castle looking for someone and the guards were trying to stop her. Pan got out of bed and dressed in a simple cloak to see what was going on.

Upon entering the hall, Pan saw the guards: Vanto and a new recruit he couldn't recall the name of at this moment had finally captured the woman and were forcing her out.

Then she saw him standing there.

"My lord! Sire please, may I speak to you?" the woman pleaded. Realizing that the Nifehan was in the hall, the guards tried to explain but Pan just raised a hand for silence.

The 'girl' was more a woman closer in age to Pan, and he thought he recognized her but he couldn't remember where from just then. "Release her, Vanto. What she has to say must be important if she sneaked in at this hour." Upon hearing his words, visible relief exploded on her face. There were shadows under her grey eyes due to her clear lack of sleep and her blonde hair was a mess. Her clothes weren't much better: a rust red dress that was a bit too long for her and her shirt was on backwards, though it did match her eyes.

Flinging herself to the floor at Pan's feet, she said, "Thank you, sire. You're as kind as I've heard you were. My name is Vivian." She looked up into his eyes, activating his power. Panken felt the familiar sensation of being ripped in half and shoved into her eyes. He saw her life; saw she was friends with Selina; he took his time bathing in her memories of her. Then he saw the one thing he had never expected. And then Selina was gone and he heard Vivian's voice: "My lord, I know you care for Selina, and I'm sorry I have to show this to you, but I fear for her life. She's missing and her cottage has been completely torn apart. I know it is awful to think, but I believe my brother did it - I think he's taken Selina." And then he was shoved out and forced back together.

"Sire? Do-do you agree with me?" She seemed to be holding her breath, like she expected him to yell and scream.

"Ms. Vivian, I'm sorry, but I do not. How long since you last saw either of them?" Vivian looked scared when he said he didn't believe her.

"Three days, my lord. Why?"

"I'm sorry miss, but I think Selina is just fine. Your brother, on the other hand, I believe to be dead." Vivian's face paled at what he said, and then she started to cry. "I'm sorry to have to tell you this, Vivian, but you must not think about that right now." He unleashed his power, bringing her back to a calm moment in her life. "Now, can you tell me if you remember Selina ever mentioning why she was in Braria?"

After thinking for a moment, she said, "My lord, she said once that she wanted help with something. But I don't know what it was. Although, when she was asleep, she would sometimes cry out 'I'm coming mama...I'm trying.'" She saw Pan's quick look of fear, but before she could ask what was wrong, he turned to the guards.

"You will escort Ms. Vivian to the kitchen and make her whatever she wants to the best of your abilities. Then take her home and make sure she goes to sleep. Then you'll find King - try the tavern, you know how he is in the morning. Send him to me immediately and tell him to prepare for imminent departure for Cydonia. Now, leave me!" he shouted.

Vanto and the other guard, Alan (that was his name), were shaken by the Nifehan's tone of voice; he hardly ever spoke with such authority, but when he did, his order was to be followed and he was to be left alone. So they left to do what he told them to do in silence.

Panken returned to his room unnerved by what he'd seen in Vivian's memory. The thing he'd never expected to see. The burn-like mark on Selina's leg shaped like a screaming skull, the mark of the Dark Union. The child of Zelda the Tortress and Isabelle the Nercomerc.

Zelda was a cold woman. Eyes colder than ice, it was

said. She had been taught the art of torture by the best in Gudsdyrkia as it was at war with Wahria; but as the war ended, Zelda's love for her victims' screams grew. She was exiled from Gudsdyrkia and never looked back. She had enjoyed befriending communities then taking them one at a time and ripping their insides out, laughing manically as they screamed in agony. She'd torture anyone - men, women, young, old - it didn't matter to her and her heartless shell of a body.

Isabelle was just as insane. She was also a sorceress trained as an assassin by the Intunerica, the 'solution of the Hollow Mountains' in Mouria. As death's mercenary, Isabelle was effective, if brutal. It was said that she'd only kill men, claiming they were everything wrong with the world. But like Zelda, Isabelle too, was exiled and thus began her mission to rid the world of the poison that was Man. The difference was that she would walk into a village and kill three quarters of it, then leave. She forced quick but painful deaths to all males above the age of manhood; she left the women and children.

It was said to be chance that the two walked into the same town. Their reputations preceded them, of course, but before Isabelle could unleash her power, Zelda had stopped her. Realizing who the other was, they killed their way to Vagala, and then disappeared, never to be seen or heard from again. But not before the rumour spread that they would bring a child into the world who would forever continue their work. This child would eternally be known as the Dark Union.

Everything made sense to Pan now. Selina's sudden appearance after a series of unexplained deaths of notable historians in the surrounding countries, her blackblood dress, everything.

But how was this possible? The Crusaders had captured and burned the Dark Union nearly eight hundred years ago. There was no way anyone could have lived that long, even if she somehow survived the burning. Immortality was a trait only the dead had, and Selina was most certainly alive.

Then he remembered Zelda's mark - besides the countless dead - was a phoenix feather in the houses of the first and last victims in every town. Perhaps the Dark Union could never die, without being reborn; just like the phoenix whose feathers Zelda was quite fond of as her calling card.

Now another thought occurred to Panken: how could the two women conceive a child? They would need powerful magic, magic not present during the time of the Taint. The Taint was a half century near to a millennium ago where magic had nearly disappeared from all of Bolfodier, before an unknown hero had righted it by sacrificing himself in the Sanctuary of Darkefyre in Ignavia.

And then the answer came to him: the Temple of the Goddess. The mythical colossus beneath the island of Vagala, that had to be what the two of them were looking for. The Temple of the Goddess was as old as Bolfodier itself and its magic, Pan knew, would not have been affected by the loss of magic the rest of the world had experienced during the time of the Taint.

This day was not going how Pan had hoped it would. The prospect of a voyage to Vagala was intriguing; was the ancient text he'd read three years previous correct? However, Pan was not happy about this development, now he'd definitely have to see *her* again. Sitting at his desk he started to write the letter that he hoped would allow King to help convince Sabrina that he was true. Every word, every pleasantry he wrote ripped open every wound Sabrina had left on his heart that he'd spent the better part of a decade trying to forget. His apology was a lie; smiles, even false ones, made things much smoother than a scowl he found.

> *Sabrina,*
>
> *I know you're not likely to help me with this unless I apologize, so I'm sorry I practically banished you and Kailee. Seeing the two of you like that was not pleasant for me and I may have acted a bit harshly and stupidly.*
> *As to the matter for which I write, I need safe passage to Vagala, for I fear the Dark Union and must find a way to prevent her from harming my people. I know the only place to find answers to my problems is in Vagala and you are the only one I can think of who will lead me across the North Divide. I ask this as the Nifehan of Braria.*
>
> *Hoping you'll help,*
> *Panken*
>
> *P.S. Beware the man I send this with, he has a certain way with women.*

Pan had just finished sealing the letter when King arrived with a knock to Pan's open bedroom door.

Walking in and over to where Pan awaited him at his desk, King gave a fist to his heart. "You summoned me, sire?" King asked in a flawless voice that hid what his breath could not. Likewise, his clothes couldn't hide the fact that he was drunk. His jacket had stains on it from where he'd spilt and it was buttoned up incorrectly. His mahogany hair was a mess and his black eyes were bloodshot from the drink.

"Yes, King, I have a mission for you." Pan recoiled at the smell of his breath. He was thankful that King's ten-year conscription was up; Freddie King may have been a fantastic fighter and an exceptional negotiator, but his vices were too much for Pan to handle any longer.

"What is it? I'll do it!" The way he smiled and nearly fell over as he said this nearly made Pan change his mind about sending him.

"I need you to go to Cydonia, to a small mountain village called Hockley, and find my old friend Sabrina. You remember her, yes?"

"Of course, sire. I'd never forget a woman like that, sire," he said with a leer of a grin.

"Good to know," Pan was a little unsettled by the grin but blamed it on the drink. "I need you to get there and back as quick as you can. We'll be attempting to cross the North Divide and we'll meet you in Holista - that's in Cawdor. I don't want you stopping for your nightly distractions, King. No matter who you run in to." Pan wanted that last point really emphasized.

"Yes, sire!" King said with a bow of his head while taking the letter, then sped off to the stables. Pan thought he looked disappointed by this last order.

Heaving a sigh, Pan flopped back into his chair. He was very tired and he had a headache. He'd barely gotten any sleep that night and the sun was just coming up. Rubbing his temples with both hands, he decided he'd wait two weeks before he left for Cawdor; for now, he needed sleep. As he stood from his chair, there was a knock at the door. Not in any mood to see anyone at this early hour, he wondered what they wanted.

"Who's there?" he demanded to the door.

"My name is Iselda," the voice, clearly female, answered. He didn't know anyone named Iselda.

Pan had taken one step when the door burst open. Selina walked in. Shocked by her sudden arrival, Pan took a step back while gathering his magic. He knew she could kill him in an instant, but he wanted to be ready.

"Put your magic away, I'm quicker than you!" She avoided his gaze. Despite his fear, Pan couldn't stop himself from looking over the woman in front of him. She was so much more beautiful in person than in the memories he'd violated to look at her. Her hair was a silken wave of nightfire, complete with the hints of purple that flecked the deadly substance of the underworld. Her skin was so smooth, and possessed perfect complexion. Her lips looked so soft and their flawless strawberry pink colour called to Pan like nothing he'd ever known. And her dress, her beautiful blackblood dress, the way it hugged each and every one of her body's curves from her shoulders to thighs where it loosened to allow her to walk, was the most arousing piece of fabric Pan had ever seen.

"The few guards I ran into, they aren't dead; they're either in complete pain or pleasure," she explained. "I figured you'd discovered who I was when I saw Vivian run here, crying over her rapist of a brother."

"He tried to rape you?" Pan asked with concern, before finally remembering who he was talking to.

"Yes, and he's a pile of ash because of it." A clearer warning, Pan could not imagine. "He's caused me a fair amount of trouble. But I can't wait anymore. For nine years I've waited for you to introduce yourself to me. When I first heard the 'Memory Thief' rumours, I nearly left. Yet you never discovered who I was, so I stayed, hoping you'd come to visit me. But you never did. Now, all that's in the past." The way she said all this, like it was entirely his fault, reminded him of Shade's berating his not introducing himself to Selina. She still hadn't looked him in the eye.

"Why did you want to meet me so bad? Why haven't you just come as a petitioner or something, if you were so desperate to meet me?" Pan's caution flared as soon as he heard her explain she'd wanted to see him.

"I figured it would be better if we met on your terms, rather than mine." Finally, she looked at him. And as he felt himself being ripped in half, Pan was drenched in her memories, a millennium's worth of memories. And now Pan understood: she was just a lost girl, looking for her mothers. Never knowing them had led to an eternity of searching for any trace of them. Pan felt a stab of pity for her.

"I need your help, Panken." He could see the fury she felt at the truth of this statement. "Twelve years ago, when I lived in Dunkela, the country was still so fascinated by the prince who had discovered the lost library of the Valin Twins: Valintina and Valentani. He'd done this with only a map with no names, a shovel, and his wits. The library was rumoured to be a treasure trove of ancient volumes, as well as some less ancient texts. There was even one rumoured to be written by the twins themselves, about the darkest souls from the beginning of time to the time of the Taint. But no one knows for sure if these rumours were true, for the prince took each and every book in that library for himself.

I know you're that prince." Pan was slightly alarmed that she knew this, for he'd gone to great lengths to keep his identity hidden while on his Reckoning.

"You're probably the most knowledgeable about me. I want to find the graves of my mothers and I'll do anything to find them! Even if I have to live for thousands of more years, I'll find them!"

"Selina-"

"I told you, my name is Iselda!" she chastised, causing Pan to pause for a second.

"Iselda, I understand your yearning to find where your mothers are buried. But, you know better than I how long it's been and your guess as to where they are is as good as mine. I'll try to help you as best as I can, but I make no promises as to success. Oh, can you release my guards now - I'm tired of being surprised for one day." She just nodded and within seconds Pan heard footsteps rushing towards the door of his chambers.

"My lord! Intruder-there's an-" they rushed to inform him.

"Relax friends, I have everything under control." Seeing that he was being serious, the guards left, bowing silently.

"Thank you for agreeing to help me," Iselda said with a very quiet and sincere voice.

"Your welcome. Although it's not like I had much of a choice."

"You had a choice! You could have denied me any help; in which case I would have given you a long dose of unendurable pain. If you were still unwilling, I'd kill you, leaving your throne to the people."

"Like I said, I didn't have a choice. Now if you don't mind

I'd like to get some sleep. You-"

"We're not leaving now?" There was a hint of a threat in her voice.

"No. I've sent for help, which will take a while to reach us. In two weeks we'll leave for Cawdor, where we're to meet this help," he said in an equally stern voice. "In the meantime, I suggest you get some rest and, if possible, fix your friendship with Vivian. Tell her the truth, but be gentle about it. You don't have to tell her who you are, but you owe her the truth about her brother."

"I think I can do that. Thank you, again." And with that Iselda left.

Once she was gone, Pan relaxed. He informed the guards that she was allowed to come and go from the castle as she pleased but she couldn't enter the Blackreich and was to be watched at all times when she was here. On a different note, he informed them that the gates were to be closed for the day, and no one but Shade was to be allowed into the private chambers of the Royal family. Then he returned to bed, falling into a fitful slumber.

Chapter 9:

The Journey to Holista

"I don't like this," Shade said as he curled his thick goatee around his finger; a nervous habit he'd developed once the goatee had grown in.

Walking out onto the small window balcony, Pan looked out. From here he could see the majority of Terang, as well as the lake that both the castle and city surrounded. And as he watched the sun set in the south, Pan released a weary sigh. "I don't like it, either. But I don't have much of a choice."

"No, it doesn't sound like you do," Shade agreed as he joined Pan on the balcony. "But I still think you could have put up more of a fight, resisted slightly."

"Every single guard who saw her said that she barely looked at them and the most indescribable pain followed. She only gave pleasure to three of the fifteen men that she encountered. Pain may be your thing, I don't want to know, but it's not mine," he said with a smile to his lifelong friend. "No, agreeing to help her was probably the best thing I could have done."

"Oh, I totally agree that agreeing was the best thing you

could have done. But it also made you look like the lovesick puppy you've always been when it came to this woman." The smile Shade gave Pan as he said this made Pan know that while Shade meant what he said, it was meant to be a joke. "Besides, you don't know if she would have given you pain if you resisted a little. Knowing how you feel about her, as everyone does, might have convinced her that the carrot was a more effective tactic than the stick."

"No; she told me that she'd used the stick, and I believe the look I saw in her eyes as she told me this. Besides, I'm pretty sure that I repulse her; when she spoke of my Reckoning, the amount of contempt that came from her was palpable."

"How did she know that the one who found the Valin Twins' library was you? I thought you said that you took every measure to ensure that you weren't implicated?" Shade asked, voicing one of Pan's many concerns.

Giving his friend a grave look as this question was raised, Pan simply said, "I'd thought I had. And the fact that she knows it was me is one of the many things about this whole thing that makes me uneasy. She's been roaming the world for nearly a thousand years; there's no telling what she's learned in that time." Turning away from his friend, Pan once again looked to the setting sun as the sky started to turn the indigo of twilight. For a long time, the silence expanded between them as they took in the sunset. "You know what I'm going to ask."

It wasn't really a question, but Shade answered it anyway. "Yes."

"And will you do it?"

As Shade didn't answer immediately, Pan turned away

from the sunset and looked at his best friend. "I've never wanted that," he said to which Pan nodded his understanding. "But I know that you trust no one else. So yes, reluctantly, I will do it."

Pan smiled a small smile to his friend's acceptance to his unspoken request. Shade, however, turned and returned to the room as he headed for the door. Just as he got there, Pan said the two words he knew would stop him from leaving. "Thank you." Shade stood with his hand on the latch to the door for a long moment before his head fell. When it came back up the next second, Pan could see the ghost of a smile on Shade's lips. And then, Shade was gone. Slightly surprised, Pan turned back to the southern sun, as the last sliver was being swallowed by the distant horizon.

The following two weeks passed too quickly for Pan. He still didn't know how he felt about helping Iselda. So far she was obeying his wish that she wasn't to go into the Blackreich; although, she seemed upset that there was a restriction.

It was now time for them to leave. Pan had left his trusted friend and adviser, Shade, in charge; declaring him temporary king, until his return. That was, if he did return. He'd be taking two guards with him. With Iselda none were necessary, but the guards gave him an illusion of protection. Once the time had come for them to leave, Iselda was thankful they were finally leaving; even though Cawdor was only a three to four-day journey, she'd stayed and waited for Pan to get prepared. He thought it was because she was finally happy to have travel companions, despite her stating otherwise when Pan had brought this up.

Departing just after dawn, they rode hard, only stopping to eat at midday. They didn't stop again until nightfall when they set up camp. They were all extremely tired from the long day's ride that had taken them passed the Brarian border and into Pitag. Pan didn't like the idea of sleeping in Pitag as it was full of thieves and cutthroats and worse, but it was the most direct route to Cawdor. Pan had ordered that they make camp in a secluded area, but his order that a fire be avoided went ignored.

Sitting around the fire, Pan once again judged the wisdom of his agreeing to help Iselda in her quest to find her mothers' graves. He also thought of the lives he'd put at risk by bringing them along with him. Vanto and the other guard, who Vanto had introduced as Remus Shaw, seemed quite capable and were more alike than he thought either noticed. He knew that by bringing these two good men along, he'd put their lives at risk; but both had volunteered for the job and had been made aware of all the risks involved in taking it.

As he contemplated all this, Pan stared into the flames of the fire, barely eating any of his food. It wasn't until he noticed that Shaw and Vanto were unrolling their travelling pillows and blankets that he noticed how late it had gotten. The guards did try to not fall asleep after being reassured that Pan was able to protect himself if needed. Although Pan was tired, his curiosity got the better of him.

"Not to be rude, but, um, how old are you?" he asked as he sat down across from Iselda at the fire. The glow from the embers and dying flames cast mysterious shadows across her face, making it difficult to read the look she was giving him at his starting a conversation in such a way. Although she had come to the castle every day since revealing herself to Pan to the time they'd left this morning, their few conversations hadn't been very personal, or conversational for that matter. It was more her checking to make sure he wouldn't go back on his word.

So when she tilted her head before a faint smile dusted across her lips and she replied, Pan was quite surprised. "Since my creation, I've lived to be an old woman about ten or eleven times. Plus, there was that life that the Crusaders killed me; I was about as old as I am now when that happened."

"So you have to grow up again and again?" That wasn't how Pan thought immortality worked. But it did explain why after memories of her being grown up there were memories of her as a child, when he had seen her life.

"Yes, but thankfully I remember the previous lives and I know when to expect changes." Her voice seemed to carry a hint of sadness.

"Sounds fun. But don't you just ever want to stay dead?" Pan asked without thinking. When he realized what he said, he looked to apologize, but stopped in his tracks when he saw the way the Dark Union was looking at him. The low light and dancing shadows made it difficult to tell, but Pan thought it was surprise, a pleasant surprise.

"Only every time I die; immortality isn't all you mortals make it out to be, it gets boring after about the third lifetime." She gazed into his eyes as she said this piece of wisdom, judging his response to the secret.

Pan's gaze didn't falter. "Good to know: mortality's the way to go." He looked around the dense forest that concealed their camp; Pitag was a land of thieves and he didn't want to attract too much attention. After a short pause he again couldn't ignore his burning curiosity. "So how long…how long have you known who you are, who your mothers were?"

"Since I was fifteen in my first life, so a while. Ever since then I've worn blackblood, even as a baby."

"Yeah, how do you take care of yourself when you're young?"

"I live with a family until my powers manifest, then I run away and start my quest again."

"You just leave?"

"I have to; otherwise I'll kill my 'father'. I leave them a note explaining myself. I sometimes return; they seem to understand."

Pan was struck with sympathy. "I'm sorry."

"For what?" she asked with a hint of protectiveness.

"For the fact that you have to live like that, and that you had to find out so early as to whom you really are. To think yourself normal and then find out you're not must have been difficult."

"It was a relief, actually," Iselda said with a faint smile, turning away from the fire. Pan thought that she didn't even see her surroundings as the hauntings of her past demanded they be experienced once again.

But her answer to his question took Pan by surprise. "What?!"

Startled out of her memories by his voice, she turned back to him. "It was a relief," she repeated. "It explained why I was always wanting to gouge my 'father's' eyes out with a white hot fire poker every time I saw him - a trait I'm sure my mothers would be proud their daughter possessed even when she was so young. Thankfully my powers didn't come to life until I was twenty and had learned to control the hatred." She seemed a bit disappointed by this last point.

"A-A-Wow! I-I guess it's safe to say you've never been with a man, isn't it?" Pan immediately regretted saying that and braced himself for the pain. But it never came.

Opening his eyes, he looked over to her. Even in the poor light given off by the fire, he could see her facial expression. She was smiling, but the smile only scared Pan more. "There's a reason I look like this, Panken," was all she said.

A shiver ran through Pan. "Care to explain?" he asked with an unusually high voice.

"I found out who I am through a letter from my mothers," she explained with that unsettling smile still on her face. She was clearly enjoying making him uncomfortable. "Apparently I was found with it. It explained who I was and who my mothers were. It told me I was to be immortal and gain power over pain and pleasure and life and death. It also said I was to be the most beautiful woman of all time so I could lure men to my bed and torture and kill them. So you see Pan, I have been with a man - many men. But if I were you, I wouldn't want to join that list." To emphasize her point, she licked her lips while drawing a long fingernail across his throat.

Pan couldn't speak; he couldn't make a sound. All he could do was nod his pale face up and down slowly. Iselda gave a small laugh at his reaction to her story. Finally, Pan found his voice, but it was that weak squeak he'd had before. "How long, how long since you brought a man to your bed and killed him?" Why did he have to ask that; it surely would make her kill him.

Iselda simply regarded him as if he asked how she was enjoying the trip. "Not since my third life. But that hasn't stopped people who know of my existence from calling me the 'Dark Union.'" The way in which she said her nickname gave a clear indication that she didn't like it.

"That's where that name comes from?" Pan asked, relieved that his voice was back to its usual pitch. "I thought it meant you were the union of two of the darkest women of the time."

"Yes, that is the origin of my nickname. Although, your way of thinking makes sense too." The fire had died too much for Pan to see, so he got up and got some more wood for it. Pan was thankful for the excuse to remove himself from her sight, if only briefly. He wasn't tired anymore, though. "What about you, Pan? How long has it been for you?" Iselda asked, clearly trying to make him relax.

Despite the fear and unease he felt towards her, Pan sat down next to Iselda when he finished putting the wood he'd collected on the fire. "Too long. Why - you interested in relieving the stress I've built up over the years?" Hadn't she just warned him about that not five minutes ago?

Too busy reprimanding himself, Pan hadn't heard Iselda gasp at his saying 'years' and not 'months' or 'days', nor had he noticed that she discreetly looked him up and down and then quickly shook the thought out of her head. "Not unless you want to die. Although, I'd still like your help, so you'd have to wait awhile longer," she said to clarify, for the both of them, that the offer wasn't part of this journey. Her tone was the same as when she had 'asked' for his help two weeks ago; there was a coldness that hadn't been there a few moments before.

"It's been ten years, with no end in sight. I think I can wait."

Finally, he'd made her speechless. The moment was short lived, but it was long enough for him to properly see and appreciate her shock. "Ten years?! How have you never just ordered some girl to you?" Her cheeks flushed red from the asking of such a brazen question.

"Oh, I did; ten years ago. She was willing enough; but after I realized what I'd done, I swore to myself that I'd never force anyone to my bed again, no matter what. I want to care for the woman in my bed. That promise has not been easy to keep, but I've kept it." There was a trace of pride in his voice as he boasted about keeping his promise.

Suddenly Iselda was kissing him. Taken aback at first, he soon returned the kiss, releasing a bit of his tension. All of a sudden, reason seemed to return to both of them and they pulled away from each other.

"Um…"

"Goodnight, Pan," she said shyly, red with embarrassment.

"A-right, goodnight." They fell asleep on opposite sides of the camp as Pan unceremoniously extinguished the fire.

The next two days weren't as long or hard of a ride as the first, but the Nifehan and Dark Union didn't speak a word to each other at all. They slept on opposite ends of the camp, barely making eye contact and went to sleep as soon as they stopped for the night. It was also starting to get colder the further south they went.

By the time they reached the small fishing village that was Holista, both Vanto and Shaw were a little suspicious. They confronted Pan about their worry.

"Sire, we don't mean to press, but what happened between you and Iselda that first night?" asked Shaw.

They were avoiding his eyes, which is what Pan was doing to them. "Nothing," he lied.

"Look, sire, you two were acting like friends that first night and now you go out of your way to ignore each other. Something happened. You don't have to tell us anything, but as your guards, we think you should tell us if there's anything that might lead to a problem in the future," continued Vanto.

Pan knew they were sincere and only trying to do their job. He decided to tell them the truth. "We just opened up a little too much and now it's a bit awkward. It's nothing of importance, trust me. If there's any problems about to be had, it'll be when Sabrina sees me - don't react, I can protect myself from her." No sooner had Pan finished talking that both Iselda and King approached them.

"My lord, Ms. Selina found me and told me to follow her to you. I found your friend, sire, she's waiting just outside town for me to return with you," King reported.

"Thank you, King. Did anyone accompany you two here?" he asked, fearing the answer.

"Yes sire. A woman named Kailee came with us."

Resigned to the fact he'd have to see them both again, Panken sighed. "Take us to them, King." King turned on his heel and led the four of them out of town and into the nearby woods. About five minutes in they came to a clearing.

And there she was: the woman he'd loved all those years ago. She was still so beautiful, having barely aged. Her red hair was a bit lighter, but she was exactly how he remembered her. Beside her was Kailee, who seemed to have finished maturing and stopped ageing completely five years previous. Pan's heart rose into his throat and his stomach turned over, making him queasy. He paused briefly to compose himself before stepping forward. Iselda, he noted, took notice of this with what he would have thought was concern was it not coming from her.

When Sabrina saw him, she got up, walked over, and gave him an awkward hug. He barely returned it when she pushed him away, saying an uncomfortable hello. Pan returned the awkward greeting in kind.

"So, um, is this your queen?" she asked indicating Iselda and avoiding his eyes.

"What?! No, no; that's Iselda, the Dark Union." At hearing who was among them, Sabrina raised her hand to attack, but there was an outburst of motion. Pan and the three guards moved between the two women, then Iselda shot a small but potent dose of pain at Sabrina which brought her to her knees and Kailee running to her lover. "Everyone calm down!" Pan shouted. "Now, Sabrina, let me explain." Both Sabrina and Kailee looked up at him from the ground and he was shoved into both of their memories. He rushed to the end so he could explain. "A new power I acquired in your absence," he explained, seeing their twin looks of confusion. "Now, after I wrote you that letter, Iselda burst into my room and explained herself. She is simply looking for the graves of her mothers, and I've agreed to help her as best I can. I simply ask you help us by giving us safe passage to Vagala."

Sabrina looked completely taken aback by this turn of events. When she finally found her voice, she exploded on Pan as she stood back up. "Help you, help her? Are you CRAZY, Pan? You know as well as I do what she is! And even if I wanted to help you, I can't; you can't enter Vagala!"

"Yes, Sabrina, help us. And no, I'm not crazy; I'm smart enough for she hasn't shot me with pain like she just did to you. If I hadn't agreed to help her, I'd be dead. And yes I can get into Vagala!" Pan responded calmly to her outburst. His last statement was met by shocked faces from the women; the guards didn't seem to be listening.

"H-How? I thought it was impossible." Her voice was finally back to a normal level.

"It's quite simple, actually. All you have to do is invite me in. Just say 'It is the wish of (your name) that (my name) be allowed access to Vagala.' That's it."

"Are you sure? How can the three of us not know this and somehow you do?" she asked with doubt.

"I've had ten years of sleepless nights. So, to fall asleep, I read; I read every book in the castle. I continually bought more to the point I think I've read every book in Braria."

"It seems rule was a good choice for you, Pan," mumbled Sabrina. Pan heard this and gave her an angry look, but didn't say anything.

"So why do we have to go to Vagala? I've never been there," questioned Iselda, trying to change the subject back to the mission.

"Because," Pan said, finally making eye contact with her, "you were born there. It's also the last place your mothers were known to be."

"Ok, so let's go," she proclaimed, but nobody moved.

"There's a problem, Iselda. It's nearly impossible to find Vagala unless you've been there in living memory. That's why Sabrina and Kailee are here: to lead us there quickly and safely, but only if they choose to. And they must choose to do so without our help." He added that last bit so Iselda wouldn't force them.

There was a brief and tense silence, and then Sabrina spoke. "Pan I only rushed here because I thought you were in trouble. When I left Vagala, I swore to myself that I'd never go back there unless it was to save lives. Now that I see what the problem is, I'm not sure I want to help you." These words prompted Kailee to speak for the first time.

"My lord, I know I've hurt you. I'm sorry about that, but I don't regret my actions ten years ago. I know you didn't punish my family for my failures and I thank you for that. I've wanted to go to Vagala ever since Sabrina first told me about it. Ma-"

"Kailee, what are you doing?" Sabrina asked with an unbelieving look.

"Trying to right a wrong, my love. I think we should help them. Besides, you've been promising to take me to Vagala for years now. I-I think we owe it to Pan." She gave Pan a weak smile.

"Ow-Owe it to him? If we owe him anything, it's a simple explanation, not safe passage to an island *magically fortified against male entrance*!" Sabrina shrilled.

"Then do it for me; it's our anniversary. We'll take them there and have a vacation." It seemed like Kailee was pleading.

"I-I…fine!" A flash of pain crossed Sabrina's face as she

relented. She turned to Pan, "We'll take you there, but that's it, Pan, I swear it! If you try to get-"

"Thank you, Sabrina, for agreeing to this. And thank you Kailee for convincing her. I just might let you two back into Braria." This time, his words were sincere and not as painful.

"Ok, now can we go? I may have a millennium's worth of patience, but it's starting to wear thin!" exclaimed Iselda.

They all left the forest and returned to town. They found a large ship that had enough rooms so that everyone would have private quarters and paid fifty gold marks to take it into the North Divide. Then they were out at sea. Sabrina cast a spell onto the ship that made it steer itself and said the journey would take about five to ten days, depending on weather, so they all grabbed rooms and went to sleep for the night. Pan, as the Nifehan, insisted that he take the captain's quarters; both Sabrina and Iselda fought this, but eventually relented.

Chapter 10:

Rumours

Iselda couldn't sleep, not that she now felt so close after centuries of searching. It all seemed so surreal to her; she was heading to her birthplace, her real birthplace, and she was being led there by someone who may have known her better than she knew herself. She didn't know how she felt about that fact, though she did know that she was relieved to not have to be the leader of her centuries-long quest. But with all her excitement and relief also came doubts: not about the others who had joined her, but about herself. Why hadn't she thought of Vagala? Why had she waited nine long years to seize this opportunity, despite having everything to manipulate the Nifehan into saying yes from the first day she'd stepped foot into Braria? Wasn't that why she'd come to Terang in the first place? But the doubts that weighed at her heart the most were why she had kissed Pan, and why she had wanted to comfort him and chase away the pain she'd seen in his eyes before they'd talked to Sabrina and Kailee. She couldn't, and wouldn't, start to have feelings for a man who was in essence her prisoner.

She got out of bed to go for a walk along the deck, hoping the salty air would clear her head of everything that was marinating her mind. But as she stepped up onto the deck and the chilling wind hit her face, the only thought that was in her head was thankfulness that her dress was deceptively warm. She was surprised to see that Kailee girl leaning against a rail. "Hello, what are you doing? Aren't you cold?" The sudden noise made the girl jump and give a little shriek.

"Oh, it's just you."

"Sorry for scaring you," Iselda said as she joined her against the railing.

"Don't be. I've always been easy to scare. And after ten years of living in the Cydonian mountains, I think I should be able to take this wind. I wasn't really doing anything. You?"

"Relishing the fact that I'm so close after so long." The smile she gave as she said this was genuine and serene.

"I'm sure it's been a long time." She paused before asking her next question with caution. "Are you really the daughter of those two women?"

"Yes, I am. They were the evilest women in two millennia and I'm still proud to be their daughter."

"I'm sorry," Kailee said which took Iselda by surprise. Nobody reacted that way when she said she was proud of her mothers.

"For what? You've done nothing to me."

"You never met your real mothers; it must have been hard living without knowing what they were really like." The sincerity in her voice shocked Iselda; no one was ever this kind to her, especially not another woman.

"Oh, I know what they were like - history tells me all I need to know. I just want to tell them I love them and that I wish we could have been together." There was a long silence during which they just looked out at the sea. Finally, Iselda's curiosity got the better of her; she'd heard of the scandal, but she wanted the truth. "So, what happened ten years ago? You know, between you, Sabrina, and Pan."

"That's a long story," Kailee answered turning her reddening face away.

"I have all the time in the world. And besides, I think I'm the only one that doesn't seem to know - I've only heard the rumours."

"What rumours?" the girl asked with obvious curiosity.

"Well when I first arrived in Braria nine years ago, the story was that Pan and Sabrina were engaged but the king wouldn't let them be married, threatening Pan with the crown if he thought to do it in secret. Loving the crown more than her he chose to rule, leaving his heartbroken lover to seek comfort from the first person to offer it. Over the years, the story has gotten crazier and crazier. I think my favourite version is the one where Sabrina has a lover on the side and kills the king, hoping this would make her queen, but her plan backfires as Pan finds out and banishes her and her lover."

Throughout both versions, Kailee had kept her emotions a mystery. "Well, there's truth to both of those." She took a breath, to steel herself Iselda thought. "But since you've only heard the rumours, here's what really happened, as best as I know it. Twelve years ago Sabrina walked into my hometown of OJA. My family gave her lodging for about a year. Over that year, I fell in love with her, but I never told her how I felt. She left and wound up in Terang. There, she met and fell in love with Pan. When Pan tried to introduce her to his parents, they broke out into a fight. When all was said and done, the king declared an ultimatum: Pan was to choose between love and rule, before the king died. That didn't leave much time for Pan to make a decision. As it turned out, the reason the argument broke out was because a sorcerer had cursed the family to lose their rule. I don't know all the details but it had something to do with Sabrina's red hair and green eyes. I went to the palace to try and help, for my family had once hired a sorcerer to curse the Royal family. After explaining this to Pan, he led me to the open arms of the woman I'd loved silently. I was so happy to see her again, I nearly kissed her right there, but I knew I couldn't for she loved Pan now.

"Pan had thought he'd found a way to have the curse removed and to wed Sabrina as his queen, but his plan was too dangerous and Sabrina talked him out of it. When she got back to the inn she was staying at, I was waiting, and I confessed myself to her. Instead of shunning me like I feared she would, she did the exact opposite: she made love to me. The next morning, she demanded the truth about my confession. I gave it and all she did was kiss me.

"And that's when Pan walked in and decided he wanted to rule. He practically banished us from Braria and left us to find a new home, with only our love for comfort."

Iselda felt complete sympathy for this woman. She also felt anger towards Pan, but she couldn't understand why. "Oh my, I'm so sorry. If I had known the two of you were the help we were meeting here, I would've suggested we find someone else to take us to Vagala. This must be so hard for you two."

"Thank you for your sympathies. I think it's only hard on Sabrina and Pan; but they're both strong and can look past it. She'll see you to Vagala safely, don't worry."

"I appreciate that, thank you. No one's this kind to me, knowing who I am."

Kailee turned and looked fully at her, giving her a look of such compassion that Iselda gave a gasp at seeing it directed at her. "Just because your mothers weren't exactly the nicest people, doesn't mean their daughter shouldn't be allowed kindness." Hearing these words filled Iselda with a feeling of such elation she gave Kailee a hug and felt a few tears flow. Kailee just cooed and comforted her. So much for the head clearing power of the sea.

"I'm sorry; I shouldn't do things like that. It's just that nobody's ever been this nice to me," she said as she pulled away and wiped her eyes.

"Don't mention it; I know the feeling." They fell silent, simply enjoying the comfort of a friend. "Ok, I told you my story, it's your turn. What happened between you and Pan? I saw the look you gave when Sabrina asked if you were his queen; and then I heard the guards talking about you two 'opening up too much.' Care to explain?"

"He told the guards?!" She knew why she was mad this time.

"I don't think so - they were trying to guess what that meant." Kailee was quick to make this comment.

After taking a calming breath, Iselda returned the favour to Kailee. "Well, I guess it's only fair. The first night we left Terang, we got to talking. The conversation moved to how long it'd been since…well you know." Kailee gave a nod she understood. "He said it'd been ten years. I was surprised he hadn't ordered a woman to him. He said he did, ten years ago, but that he would never do it again because he wanted to care for the woman in his bed. I don't know why exactly, but this struck a chord within me and I kissed him."

"Really?!" Kailee asked with a look of glee at new gossip.

"Yes. It didn't take long for him to return it." A strange pause overcame Iselda as she thought of the kiss, it hadn't seemed like a kiss from someone who hadn't had one in a long time. When Kailee nudged her and gave a knowing look, Iselda pushed the thoughts from her mind. "After about thirty seconds, logic seemed to come back into our heads and we pushed each other away. It has been too awkward ever since."

"I'll bet." There was the gleam of a secret in the girl's pale blue eyes; but what secret, Iselda couldn't figure out. "So, how long has it been for you?"

This girl had some nerve, Iselda had to admire that. "With a man, centuries; a woman, a couple of weeks." Iselda wondered how Kailee liked the question. "You?"

"A couple of hours." Her face turned red and she turned away, looking down at the water hitting the ship. "Sabrina was a little upset about how I made her do this," she explained.

An awkward silence followed. Then a question came to mind for Iselda, one she'd wanted to know the answer to for a while now. "What's it like…being in love with someone like you are with Sabrina? Having a true lover?"

Kailee turned to look back at her, her eyes searching hers. "It's amazing; I can't put words to how it feels to love someone and have them love you back." Her voice had become impassioned when she said this. Then her voice brought back the compassionate quality. "You've never had a true lover, have you?"

Iselda just shook her head as a series of memories flooded her mind of a time when she'd thought she had. "Being me isn't all people would think it is. I'm too scared to look for someone because I think they'll turn me in or won't love me. And when I die, I'm reborn and they'd be dead." Her voice was a little higher than usual as she spoke rapidly. She calmed herself before continuing. "I can't love anyone even if I wanted to."

"You can always love someone. Maybe Pan will find a way to make you mortal or your lover immortal. With all that reading, surely there's been something of that nature." This caused Iselda to smile, but it was short lived.

"Why would he do that? He's only doing this because he knew I'd kill him if he didn't agree to help. Why would he show me any type of kindness after this?"

"Because Pan is different, and a good person. Most men would love if their girlfriend willingly kissed another woman, but Pan was disgusted by the thought. Yet he didn't kill me to get rid of his disgust, as another would have. And I think he likes you. I'm sure he'd help if you asked nicely, and didn't threaten his life in the process." The smile on her lips hinted at a wisdom that was beyond the girl's years.

"He does like me - it's common knowledge that he's lusted after me ever since I came to Braria. Did you know he used that power of his to find out things about me?"

"That one where he makes us see our life?"

"Yes. All you see, he sees. And after he's done, he can make you feel any emotion you've ever felt, no matter how far apart you are. Everyone calls him the Memory Thief. And, come to think of it, I bet he used it on you when you convinced Sabrina to help us. From what I hear, it's quite subtle and you think it's your own thinking that is controlling these emotions."

"Would he really do that?" Kailee was a little scared at the prospect.

"I don't know; you seem to know him better than I do."

Just then Pan walked out of the captain's quarters and walked over to the pair of them. They both stared at him in fear that he'd heard their conversation and searched for something in his posture that shouldn't be there. They didn't find anything.

"Hello, what are you two doing up so late?" His voice was casual.

"Talking," Iselda said simply, still searching him.

"Ah," he said with a small, knowing smile. "Care if I join you?" He was acting too relaxed considering who he was talking to, Iselda figured.

"No."

"Yes."

"I mean, yes, we do actually. It was just girl talk that we wanted to finish. It's nothing you'd be interested in," Kailee quickly covered up, keeping her eyes on Pan's.

Pan got a curious look on his face. "I see," he said with suspicion, "I'll see you girls in the morning then. Goodnight." With that he returned to the captain's quarters.

When they saw the light go out, the girls let out a breath they didn't realize they'd been holding. Looking at each other with fearful looks, they silently parted ways and went back to their separate quarters.

Chapter 11:

Vagala

The next morning Pan didn't bring up the night's events with the girls. But he was still suspicious; Kailee had first not seemed to mind if he joined their conversation, but had quickly changed her response upon hearing Iselda's. Pan had instructed the guards to watch for anything the girls did that wasn't just girls being girls. They weren't to make their watching obvious, and they were to tell Pan if they saw anything. They never saw anything.

The rest of the trip went by without further incident. Thankfully, Pan was able to talk to Iselda again without it being awkward. Hugely relieved that he'd managed to do so, Pan was looking forward to conversing with her again; the guards weren't all that good at conversation.

When they reached the island, they docked at a large shipyard. Getting off the ship, the group of seven made their way through the maze of docks to the shore. As they got closer, Pan could physically see the barrier that guarded the island from any unwanted guests. Unseen to those without magic, the barrier looked like a heatwave with sparks firing off all over it. When they reached it, the girls entered without a problem. Turning back, they said the incantation to allow the guards and Pan in; Sabrina was slightly surprised that it actually worked. When they reached the nearest town, which was only a twenty-minute walk from the shipyard, Pan was surprised to see Iselda and Kailee hug each other goodbye. By the look on Sabrina's face, she was equally surprised. Pan was happy to note this.

Now that Iselda was the only woman among them, she did all the talking in getting them horses, rooms, and possible directions. The only problem was that none of these women had heard of the Temple of the Goddess. After asking what seemed like the millionth person about the Temple and getting a look of incredulity, they decided to look for a woman of magic. After some more asking, they found that the nearest was a sorceress by the name of Jessica who lived in a town a day's ride from the town they were in.

"So, we'll leave at first light for where exactly?" Pan asked. He and the guards had stuck to the shadows and let Iselda run around looking for the answers. During this time, he'd taken stock of the situation in which he now found himself: one of the first four males to set foot on Vagala since the dawn of time. He didn't know why, but he'd always thought that Vagala was the one hot spot in southern Bolfodier. Then he remembered that it was Sabrina who'd given him that impression, and Sabrina had always had a greater tolerance for the cold than him. Thankfully they were back at the inn they'd rented rooms in, where the wind couldn't get to them and a fire was lit in each of their rooms for warmth.

"The town's called Valva," Iselda said matter-of-factly, but with a hint of annoyance.

"Ok. Alright, get some sleep everyone." They had three rooms; Iselda was alone and Pan and King roomed together. Pan didn't trust King with so many women near, and sleeping in the same room insured that their secret was maintained.

Pan was asleep as soon as his head hit his pillow. He hadn't got much sleep on the boat and walking around all day had tired him out.

The next morning Pan was the first one awake and he immediately roused the others and started to get everything ready to go. They were off for Valva in a matter of minutes. Not even twenty minutes out of the town, and the vegetation started to disappear; the island had become a desert as far as Pan could see. He didn't like the prospect of the entire island being a desert, especially one where there was little heat and little shelter from the cold. At least the roads were marked and kept clear.

"So, what was that hug about between you and Kailee yesterday? I didn't think you two were that close," Pan asked of Iselda about an hour after they left. The two of them were riding ahead of the three guards.

"You don't know everything that went on during the ship ride here," Iselda answered secretively.

"You're right, I don't. For instance, I don't know what the two of you were talking about that first night when I interrupted you."

"Why so curious?"

"Bad habit; once something peaks my interest, it won't leave me alone."

"So I've noticed. But it's none of your business what we were talking about; it's between us and doesn't concern you." Iselda had a bit of a warning in her tone.

"I don't care who it's between!" Pan's voice was a little more forceful, more authoritative. "I want to know, so spill."

"We're not in Braria anymore, Panken; you've no authority here. And remember who you're talking to," Iselda said in a clear threat.

Realization lit his face. "Fair point," he said. He urged his horse forward and started to trot ahead of her.

His horse hadn't gotten two feet in front of hers when she called him back. "Did you use your power to control emotions on Kailee to make her convince Sabrina to help us, Panken?" Now he knew what they'd been talking about.

"No, I didn't," he answered truthfully, keeping his face blank from what he now knew.

"Have you ever?"

"How do you think you know of it? Of course I've used it!" Pan started to trot ahead.

"On me?" Iselda demanded in a threatening voice. "You wouldn't dare use it on me, would you Panken?"

"No. I haven't used that part of my power since I talked to Vivian. She was upset, as I'm sure you know, and I wanted her calm. As for using it on you, do you think I'd try? I'm not too fond of pain. Although, I wouldn't mind a less edgy version of you right now. You seem a little tense today."

"Is that a threat?" The anger and menace in her voice made Pan's blood freeze and caused him to stop his horse.

"N-No; just a simple observation." His voice had that

high pitched quality to it again. "What's wrong, Iselda? Why are you acting all hostile?" Thankfully, these questions were asked in his regular voice.

Iselda looked around with a thoughtful look on her face. The guards were a bit of a ways back now. She took a deep breath and calmly answered, "It's the island; it's heightened my hatred of men. I'm sorry."

"It's not your fault. Just please, try to control yourself." Pan hoped that came across as sympathetic.

"I am!" she screamed.

"OK!" He let her continue on ahead while he waited for the guards. "Whatever you do, don't do anything to upset her," he whispered in warning to the three of them.

By the end of the day, they'd reached Valva. Panken and the guards had their faces covered to hide who they were. Iselda went around asking where they could find this Jessica, and learned that she was living in the forest just outside of town. They decided to wait until morning; the day's ride through the desert had made them tired.

They got a couple of rooms at the local inn. There were only two left and the guards insisted that four in one room was overcrowding it. That meant that Pan and Iselda were to share a room. They weren't happy about it, but agreed it was better than King sharing with Iselda.

"How is this island a desert? Shouldn't that be impossible?" Iselda asked as she furiously loosened her dress and sand spilled onto the floor.

"It's the Temple; it must literally have to draw energy from the island to have such strong magic." He was about to go over and help her, then thought better of it.

"Then how is there any vegetation at all?" she asked in wonder.

"That I don't know. Perhaps being so far from the Temple allows the energy drain to leave gaps of island as it would be, were the Temple to never exist."

"Do-Do you think that if we find this Temple, we'll find my mothers' graves?" Iselda asked as she got into the bed. Pan had taken the floor without complaint; she had let him have the captain's cabin after all.

"I don't know; it's the last place I know them to have been. I don't even know if they died there. Just remember it's been nearly a thousand years; they'll be completely decayed by now. We may not be able to tell it's them."

"Right. Look, about earlier, I'm sorry. I didn't mean to be threatening or hostile, I just couldn't help it. I haven't felt like that in hundreds of years and I'm sorry." Her voice was very timid and quiet.

"It's alright, Iselda. You're getting closer to where you were created; it makes sense you're turning into who your mothers intended you to be. I'd be surprised if your magical aura didn't start to glow like a heated fire poker within the next few days."

"Really, I'll be that powerful?" she asked with incredulity.

"I suspect that by the time you're inside the Temple, assuming we find it, you'll be able to kill everyone within a few leagues of it."

"Seriously? That powerful?" Her face wasn't eager, but scared. Pan wondered what it was she was afraid of: the power or her enjoyment of it.

"It's only a theory, but most magic works something like that. If it works like that for you, I or the others will have to ride behind you so you won't be able to see us. That way we won't get killed."

"Oh!"

"Yes. These next few weeks will have to be taken carefully by the five of us." Pan looked at her and saw she still had the scared face mixed with what he could only guess as hesitance.

"If there's nothing at the Temple, or we can't find it, what will you do?"

"I don't know; it kind of depends on you. In the disappointment of finding nothing you might become so angry you kill us. But if you don't, I'll most likely go home." Pan tried to judge her reaction to this but she'd finally brought her face under control.

"I'll try to control myself, I swear. But if I do kill you, I'm sorry." She seemed sincere in this sentiment. "But no matter what happens, unless I kill you, can you do me one more favour before you go home?" Iselda asked shyly.

"Provided you don't kill me, I'll try. What is it?"

She didn't answer. After a few moments he sat back up to see what was taking her so long in answering. She was taking long, deep breaths with her eyes closed. When she opened them she asked her question so quickly Pan didn't understand. Seeing his look, she repeated herself more slowly: "Will you make me mortal and remove my powers?"

This greatly surprised the Nifehan. "Why would you want to be powerless and mortal?"

"So I can be normal! I don't want to travel forever, fearing someone will discover my secret. I told you I'm tired of living. And I have always wanted to start a family." She looked near tears, but Pan doubted that she'd actually cry; she was too tough.

This response made him rethink Iselda; she wasn't a lost girl, she was a desperate and sad woman. But he knew the answer to her question. "I'm sorry, but I don't think I can. That would have to be done in the Temple, most likely. You'd kill me if you saw me. I can't even enter the Temple. The magic that guards the island stems from the Temple, and the barriers are hugely magnified - not even Sabrina's powers could allow me access. I'm sorry, Iselda, but I can't help you with that, even if I wanted to. But don't give up hope; maybe this Jessica will help you."

"Thank you. Kailee was right: if I asked nicely, you would help. Goodnight Pan."

"Goodnight." With a wave of his hand, Pan extinguished the lights, but not his curiosity at what else Kailee had told Iselda about him. He fell to sleep quickly.

Chapter 12:

Jessica

When they reached the house that was supposedly Jessica's, it was mid-morning. The faces of the four men were again covered as Iselda knocked on the door. A few seconds later, it was opened by a short woman who looked to be a few years older than Pan.

"May I help you?" she asked in a voice that was like two stones being scraped together. She could not be considered pretty: her eyes were too close together and an off shade of hazel that almost looked like a baby's feces. She was frumpy looking and her dress didn't do her any favours.

"Are you the sorceress Jessica?" Iselda asked.

"Yes, I am. What do you want?" She didn't seem to be a very pleasant person either.

"Well, we were wondering if you could help us find a place on the island. A place nobody really knows about-"

"What makes you think I'll know of it, then?" Jessica demanded.

"Because you're gifted! And the place we're looking for is a place of magic."

"Where are you trying to go?"

"The place we seek is called the Temple of the Goddess." Upon hearing this response, Jessica's face became unreadable. She looked Iselda up and down, and then gazed at Pan and the three guards.

"Who are you, child?"

"My name is Iselda. And I'm not a child."

"I see. And you, wizard, who are you?"

Pan removed the covering from his face, revealing his small smile. "I'm the Nifehan of Braria, Panken Kanta." Pan now looked into Jessica's eyes and felt the familiar sensation of being ripped in two and shoved into her eyes. He saw her life.

When he was done, Jessica raised a shaking finger at him. "What have you done to me, wizard?" she demanded with as much venom as he thought she could.

"It's called the Time Wind. It allows me to see the memories of everyone I meet. It's nothing to worry about, there are no after effects." Iselda gave Pan a discreet raise of her eyebrow at this. Jessica didn't notice.

"We'll see about that. I don't trust you, wizard. If you somehow found out how to get yourself and three other men onto the island and didn't announce yourselves; well, there's nothing trustworthy about a sneak."

"Never mind if you can trust him or not," Iselda chimed. "Do you know of the place we seek?"

"Yes, I know of it. But I can't take you there."

"Why not?" Iselda demanded with a note of anger that gave Jessica pause.

"Because I don't know where it is. I've looked everywhere on this island and there doesn't seem to be any indication that such a place ever existed."

"Oh, it existed."

"And just how do you know?"

At this, Iselda just gave a smile and lifted her dress up so that the mark of the screaming skull that was on her leg was revealed to Jessica. Jessica paled immediately at the sight of it.

"No! It-It can't be! The Crusaders killed you hundreds of years ago! It can't-just can't be!" Jessica mumbled.

"Oh, trust me, it can. Now will you at least give us a general direction?"

"I told you, milady, I don't know anything about its location. But I have seen that mark before!" she wailed, pointing at Iselda's now covered leg.

"Where?" Iselda demanded harshly.

"In a city three days southeast of here, the capital city! It's called Valya. The mark was on the wall to an ancient looking building that looked like it hadn't been used in centuries. It's really strange because it looks like a mansion, but is in the middle of the city square."

"Thank you, Jessica."

"Don't kill me, mistress. I'm your servant; all hail your power," Jessica whimpered at Iselda's feet. Pan was giving her a confused look, which Iselda ignored.

"Do you know anything about the tomb of my mothers?"

"No, mistress," Jessica said looking up, "I only know that they disappeared after they came here and then about twenty years later rumours of you started to circulate. That's it, I swear that's all I know, mistress! Don't kill me." She had resumed grovelling at Iselda's feet.

"Stop your whimpering! You are a highly regarded

sorceress!" Jessica stopped, but Pan could still hear a quiet sobbing. "Get off the floor - you're coming with us. You're going to show us where you saw my mark."

"Yes, mistress," Jessica said meekly. She got up and went to pack for the trip she'd just been ordered to take.

Once they had left, Pan tried all day to get Iselda alone so he could have her explain Jessica's actions. Every attempt was thwarted until they set up camp for the night.

"Finally!" he muttered under his breath. This caused Iselda to give a brief smile, before suspicion clouded her features. "Have…have you ever got that, um, reaction before?" Pan asked cautiously.

"Only once. I woke the next day to find she'd stabbed herself in the night. That was centuries ago, though." Iselda acted like this was a regular occurrence.

"Why did she react like that? Why was she so submissive?" All the caution had left Pan, leaving him to the mercy of his curiosity.

"She's a descendant of the sorceress who first found me. She was sympathetic to my mothers for wanting a child. When I was created, she cast a binding spell over her family to me; I'm forever their master. I don't know why exactly she did this," Iselda explained with a hint of frustration; clearly she wanted to know as well.

"Well, you seem to have the potential of an army on your side that is scared into servitude. So why do you need me?"

"Because, you have access to more resources, and it's

only a coincidence that Jessica is a descendant of sorceress blood - yes it must be sorceress blood. That army I supposedly have is only twenty strong at most."

"Well, you better make sure our guide doesn't kill herself, or this trip can become a lot longer than it needs to be."

"She can't die; she's a pure immortal, now. Your nightfire will scar her, but it won't kill her. She's under my spell." The smile she gave Pan as she said this looked like she was daring him to try to see the validity of her words, but her eyes begged him not to.

"Does she know all this?" Pan asked, trying to ignore both her smile and eyes.

"She only knows that she can't end her servitude to me prematurely. I don't know if she knows what that entails, though I doubt it. She doesn't seem to think outside that which she is told."

"I'll have Shaw watch over her just in case she's fooling you."

"There's no need. I can read her thoughts, so I know if she's up to something."

"Now, that's a useful power to have," Pan commented, having more than once wished for that power.

"It also means I have to listen to her whimper in fear in her mind," Iselda countered. "Not exactly what I want to listen to all night long."

"Two sides to everything, I guess." This wisdom was greeted by silence.

"I think you were right."

"About what?" Pan asked, puzzled by the sudden change of topic, and the fact that she'd just said he was right.

"Me and the thing about my power getting stronger the

closer I get to the Temple," she said calmly.

"So, am I being stupid by sitting here? Or am I okay?" There was a hint of fear in Pan's voice which gave Iselda a small smile.

"You're fine. But by this time tomorrow, we should be over halfway there, and then we shouldn't talk. If I'm thinking correctly, by midday the next day is when you'll have to stay out of my sight."

"Ok, thanks for the timeline. If it changes, could you let me know, before you kill me please?" Iselda gave a small laugh at this. Pan liked her laugh and wished he could hear it again.

"I'll try. The waves vary in strength and come at random intervals; it may be a bit hard to give clear warning."

Pan gave a nod of understanding. "After midday tomorrow, we'll try to stay clear. How exactly do you plan on not looking at us at night? Or when we leave in the morning?"

"Blindfolds. After we get to Valya and are sure the Temple is there, Jessica and I will continue while you and your men start back to her house. That way you should be far enough away that when I rejoin you, I won't kill you."

"Ok, but what if the Temple isn't in Valya, or you need my help with something?" Pan asked with genuine concern.

"Then we keep searching, or I come and get you for your help. We will find it and I'll stay blindfolded if I have to, until we do. And you will help me until I find it."

"Don't worry, I won't abandon this," he said with a smile that seemed to catch Iselda off guard. "But I may need to send someone back to Braria to make sure everything is in order."

"That's fine; I really only need you."

"Oh, really," Pan said with a sly smile, "you need only me?"

Iselda, seeing his smile and catching his tone, simply said, "Tread cautiously with your next words, Panken. I'll still shoot you with pain if I feel like it."

"Right," Pan said, losing his gusto but not his smile. "You could at least give me Jessica." Suddenly his body was on fire, every nerve was screaming in agony. He couldn't get a breath to make a sound; it was like nothing he'd ever experienced. Then it was gone and he could breathe again. Choking for a breath, he met Iselda's eyes. Anger was mixed with something he thought was sadness, but he choked on the fury he saw.

"You know, that first night, I felt sorry for your situation. But now I can see why you were in it!" she said with a voice that shook with the anger she seemed to be feeling. She stood to leave but Pan caught her hand, gently.

"That was a joke. You know I'm not like that." His voice was gentle and soft. But when he continued it grew a roughness he'd never used on her before. "I'm still a man, though. I may have chosen my path but it's still been ten years. I think I can at least make a sly remark every now and then. What you did was uncalled for." He let go of her hand, but she just stood there. She silently demanded entry to the truth behind his eyes. He gave her entry.

"Yes, I suppose you are, but not about me or my servants. There are a million other women on this island; be sly about one of them. Otherwise, that second of pain will become longer and stronger." And with that, she left.

"I'm sorry!" Pan shouted to her. She didn't acknowledge it.

They didn't talk the rest of the way to Valya. A journey that was slowed and made worse by a ceaseless rain that turned the cold desert sands into even colder mud. Iselda was unfazed; she was immune to the effects of the cold waters; and the surprising cold shoulder from Pan she was receiving. Despite the growing hatred she felt towards her prisoner-companions, she found herself missing the conversations she and the Nifehan had shared. If nothing else, they'd provide her with a respite from having to listen to the mental whimpering of her newest servant Jessica.

Thankfully, though, the rain stopped the night they arrived in Valya. Jessica was to show them the building with the mark the next day, so they found an inn for the night. Iselda had been blindfolded since that afternoon; according to Pan's theory, they were getting close. The strongest surge yet had come when they entered the city; it was so powerful it was like thunder, the rain had bounced twenty feet into the air, her outline had darkened and her magical aura had hummed loud enough for everyone nearby to hear. She could now sense every living thing within a few leagues of her. She knew she was more powerful than Hados now.

As she'd recovered from this powerful surge, Iselda noticed that her blindfold had become askew. Taking the momentary opportunity to get a sense of her surroundings, Iselda was shocked to find the city surrounded by green. Could Pan have been wrong about the Temple's need to siphon the energy from the island, or was he wrong about her and the closer she got to the Temple. Fearing the answer to either question was yes, Iselda quickly fixed her blindfold before she killed one of her male companions.

At the inn, she removed her blindfold once she was alone with Jessica. She was taken by surprise at her new sight: Jessica was translucent and she could see the blood flowing all through her body.

"Mistress, is everything alright?" Jessica asked timidly.

"Wha-Yes, Jessica, everything is fine. Why, I haven't felt like this since, well a long time ago." Iselda wore a large smile. That long time ago had been her first twentieth birthday, when her powers had first manifested themselves; how powerful she'd felt, and how scared.

"Yes, mistress." With that, Jessica took her spot on the floor and went to sleep. Iselda soon followed suit in her bed.

Chapter 13:

The Temple of the Goddess

Pan was just about ready for bed, but one thing remained that he still had to do. He gathered the guards in the room he was staying in. "Friends, a word." The three guards made their way to his side with confused looks on their faces.

"Sire?" asked King.

"I have important matters to discuss with you, gentlemen. And what I say will not be questioned and will be followed to the letter." The three nodded their solemn agreement and snapped fists to their hearts. "Tomorrow, I will go alone with Jessica and Iselda; you are to remain here and await my return. If I don't return by nightfall, return to Braria and give Shade my regards and best wishes as he is the new king."

"Sire, no we-"

"You can't-"

"Friends, quiet! Please don't object to what I tell you. I don't know what Iselda will do when she finds what she's looking for, if she finds it tomorrow. I do know, though, that I don't want to jeopardize the lives of my last messengers if something goes wrong. She's now more powerful than

Hados, and I don't want her angry at you three. I have a feeling that what she's looking for is in this town and that means her power might be felt everywhere. With a single drop of Jessica's blood Iselda could raise the dead, or kill us all. I'll go alone and you three will do as I say."

"Yes, sire," they chanted in unison, fear evident on their faces.

"I don't think she knows all this, but don't take my word for it. Good luck friends - to us all. Now, sleep!" And so they went to sleep. Pan couldn't though, for he was too nervous about what the morning might bring.

Iselda woke at dawn. She woke Jessica immediately and sent her to wake the others while she dressed. She had just put her blindfold on when Jessica entered the room.

"We're ready, mistress."

"Well, don't just stand there - take me to the Temple!"

"Yes, mistress!" Jessica hurried to her side and led her downstairs. They left the inn and headed for the building with her mark. Jessica led her through a maze of streets and alleys to what sounded like a town square. "We're almost there, mistress." As soon as Iselda heard this she felt herself get excited. But then something was trying to calm her down. This made her angry.

"Stop messing with me, you." The calming presence left immediately and she got excited again. Apparently, the emotional half of Pan's powers wasn't subtle at all.

"This is it, mistress. We're here!" Jessica said after they'd climbed a small set of stairs.

"And the others?"

"Stopped abruptly halfway through the courtyard."

Iselda ripped off her blindfold and looked all over the wall for the screaming skull. As Jessica has said, the building looked like an ancient mansion. "Where is it? Where's my mark?" Iselda screamed, grabbing Jessica by the throat and slamming her against the wall after not seeing the burning skull anywhere.

"Mistress?" asked the scared sorceress. Iselda unleashed a highly potent dose of pain to Jessica's chest. Jessica let out the most bloodcurdling scream Iselda had ever heard. Others turned to see what was happening, but she ignored them.

"Where is my mark?" growled Iselda in a deadly voice after she stopped the pain and Jessica had recovered.

"Mistress, I swear - it's right there," she said pointing to a brick with writing on it.

"That's only…" Iselda looked closer. "That's Gothtorian!" She released Jessica's throat and she fell to her knees. "Get me a pen, some ink, and something to write on. Now!" Jessica rushed into the square, looking for the writing utensils. Iselda had never learned Gothtorian, it having been a dead language for a century by the time she'd been born, but maybe the others had.

Five minutes later, Jessica returned with everything. "Mistress, here." She handed over the pen, ink, and paper. Iselda scribbled the stone's contents onto one side, recognizing her own name at the top; clearly it was meant for her.

"Take this to the others and see if they can translate it. Have them write on the opposite side."

"Yes, mistress," Jessica said as she ran off into the crowd in search of Pan.

Pan was leaning against a house wall looking out into the square, remembering doing this same thing often enough in his own city, when he saw Jessica run from the steps of the mansion she'd said Iselda's mark had been on. Her scream a few minutes previous had drawn the attention of the entire square, and Pan feared that Iselda might find herself in an unpleasant situation if she wasn't careful. Jessica, he noticed, had the piece of paper Iselda had just written on with her. Suddenly she was before him.

"Master Pan, mistress wants you to translate this." How different this woman was under Iselda's control. Pan took the paper and was surprised to see Gothtorian.

"Really, I'm to translate *this?*"

"Yes."

"Ok, but I'm a bit rusty, and this is very old and pure."

"Write the translation on the back."

Pan did as he was told. He was disturbed by what it said. Written directly to Iselda from Jessica's ancestor, the note provided instructions on how to enter the Temple and call her mothers' spirits. Then Jessica's ancestor apologized for not raising Iselda herself. When he was finished, Pan handed the note to Jessica and she ran off back to the Temple with it - to her death, Pan knew.

Iselda was about to go and see what was taking Jessica so long when she came back into view. She noticed that the townspeople were all cautiously watching both herself and Jessica ever since she'd shot Jessica with pain. They watched as Jessica returned up the steps and handed the piece of paper over to Iselda. And then they returned to their daily lives.

"I'm sorry, mistress. They're a bit rusty on the language, but they got it." She smiled with pride at completing a task and handed the note to Iselda.

With the tiniest bit of hesitation and a shaking hand, Iselda read the paper.

> *Iselda, congratulations! After all your searching, you've found the place where you were created. Welcome to the Temple of the Goddess. Now, I'm sure you want in so here's how: put your left hand on the stone with the inscription and declare who you are and who your mother - or in your case mothers - is(are). Then enter the doorway and you'll be inside.*
>
> *You'll have been led here by one of my descendants, so have her do the same. Now with both of you inside, take her blood and properly draw a Star of Death and Moon of Life in the room with all the statues of regal looking women. Draw these in the centre of the room. Again declare who you are, the same way as you got in, and call the names of your mothers: Zelda Kanvice and Isabelle Megta. Their spirits should appear within*

a few seconds. Talk with them - they want to talk to you.

I'm sorry, dear child, that I left you with those people. They had wanted a child and I only told them not to take you here; you had to come here yourself. Please forgive my goodhearted gesture to my friends. I'm happy you've finally made it home.

As Iselda finished reading the letter, she smiled, stood up, and put her left hand onto the stone with the inscription. "I'm Iselda Ness, the Dark Union, daughter of Zelda Kanvice and Isabelle Megta. Do the same," she instructed Jessica.

Jessica raised her left hand to the inscription and said, "I'm Jessica Khantik, sorceress, daughter of Helen Khantik."

Suddenly, the stone with the writing on it vanished into an ever-expanding hole that soon formed a doorway. Taken aback by its sudden appearance, both Iselda and Jessica hesitated briefly before they walked through the door and down a long flight of stairs. At the bottom was a large, open room containing a massive statue of the Goddess Lilith with a snake wrapped lovingly around her. The statue was a grave marker for Lilith's daughter and creator of the entire human race: Nina, the first woman. Iselda and Jessica knelt at the base of the statue and offered an ancient prayer that all women instinctively know to both Lilith and Nina. They then took the small hallway to the right of the statue with doors on both sides at random intervals.

"We're looking for a room with a bunch of regal looking statues of women. We need to be in the centre of that room." They walked the hallway, Iselda checking the doors on the right, Jessica the left. The interior structure seemed to be quite different from what the exterior suggested, Iselda thought as she walked along the hallway.

"Here, mistress," Jessica said pointing to a room two rooms ahead of where Iselda was.

"Get me a basin, a deep one," Iselda said as she made her way over to the room Jessica had indicated.

"Of course, mistress," Jessica said with a look of obvious confusion. She was back within a moment with a deep basin. She placed it at Iselda's feet.

She was about to stand when Iselda shot her with a pain that brought her to her knees. "Hands over the basin - NOW!" ordered Iselda. Jessica stuck out her hands which shook from the fear she felt.

"Mistress…?"

"I'm sorry, Jessica. I need your blood, and I need lots of it." Without even bothering to hear her protests, Iselda took a knife from her belt and slashed the sorceress' wrists. Her blood flowed into the basin like a red waterfall. Jessica's body slumped to the floor, dead.

Iselda went to work on the Star of Death and Moon of Life; drawing the swirls and lines at the correct times, in the correct order. She had been taught these magic circles in one of her childhoods, and had continued to practice drawing them so as to never forget. Her practised hand had her finished in mere minutes. Her hands and the skirt of her dress were covered in Jessica's blood.

She placed her left hand into the centre of the overlapping spellforms and declared, "I'm Iselda Ness, the Dark Union, daughter of Zelda Kanvice and Isabelle Megta. And I call their spirits from the world of the dead." She stood as she removed her hand from the spellforms and they caught fire - fire that looked a lot like nightfire. There were suddenly two flashes of light and her mothers appeared; not clothed, but not naked either.

"Daughter," said Zelda in an eerie voice.

"Mother," Iselda said with a shaky voice. There were tears in her eyes.

"Our darling, what's wrong?" Isabella asked in an equally eerie voice.

"I never thought I'd see you in this world."

"Child, how long has it been?" asked Zelda.

"Nearly a thousand years. I'm so sorry it's taken me this long to find this place, mothers! I've looked everywhere, asked millions if they knew where you were buried, but they never did. I finally forced a king into helping me - and so he has."

"Why do you regret forcing this king, Iselda?" Isabelle asked in a voice that betrayed her hatred of men. Her black eyes were seething with anger.

"I don't regret forcing him, Mother! He's led me to you!"

"Do you care for this man, Iselda?" Zelda asked in a gentler voice than Isabelle.

"No I-" Iselda had to think. Did she care for Pan? She couldn't care for him, she'd sworn she wouldn't; but yet she'd opened up to him, kissed him, gotten angry - no *jealous* - in response to that comment about giving him Jessica. She had come to regret forcing him rather than asking him to help her. "Oh my," she gasped with a hand to her mouth as she sank to the floor. "I do; I do care for him!"

Isabelle's face contorted in shocked anger. "How could-"

"Easy, Belle. She isn't completely you. We may both hate men, but it's obvious our daughter feels differently about them. If she chooses to love this man, I think we owe it to her to be happy for her and leave it at that."

"Leave it…You've gone soft, Zelda! I used to have to control you! What happened?" Isabelle was livid.

The look in Zelda's icy blue eyes at this was almost terrifying. "Soft?! Yo-"

"Mothers, please! This is our first reunion and we're arguing! I had no idea until now how I really felt about Pan, but somehow I've come to care for him. I'm sorry that I've destroyed the work you tried to complete with me. I had no intention of this happening, it just did. Please stop yelling at each other; I can't stand to have this happen like this!" Iselda started to cry tears of sadness, and hung her head.

"Iselda, look at us." Isabelle's voice was so soothing, that in surprise, Iselda looked up. "I'm sorry, daughter for reacting like I did. It took me by surprise that you love a man. Please forgive me, Iselda. Zelda is right, you aren't me - or her - and we have little right to force our beliefs on you."

"Thanks, Mom," she said with a small smile.

"I'm sorry, Zelda. You're not soft, you just accepted our daughter quicker than me."

"It's alright, Belle; I was surprised too." She leaned in and gave her lover a kiss, which Isabelle returned.

"Mothers, I've known who I am for a long time and I've dreamed of this moment for ages. I have a few questions, if that's ok?"

"Ask away, daughter," Zelda cooed.

"Why did you have to die? I never even knew what you looked like until now! Where are your graves? Why did you leave only that one-page letter to tell me everything?" she asked as she produced the letter from the inside of her dress.

"Well, I guess we deserve that," Zelda said. "We had to die to give you life. We knew our mission would end one day when we died. So we tried to convert other women to our cause; only one sorceress, Viola Khantik, was able to sympathize with us. She led us here and helped us complete our dream in creating you. We had to pay our lives so you would be immortal. You are ten times stronger at your weakest than we were at our strongest. We have no graves because our bodies were fused to give you yours. We only wrote that brief letter because we thought that Viola would raise you and tell you everything the letter didn't. We're sorry we didn't write more, but we had little time before the magic of your birth was to start."

Iselda was shocked to hear what her mother had just told her. She was her mothers' graves; she was what she had been looking for all along. "I've searched a thousand years for…me?"

"Apparently yes, child," comforted Isabelle. "Do you have any more questions?"

"I'm tired of living. Life gets boring after a while and I want to die. Not now, but at the end of this life. Is there any way I could give up my powers?"

Their faces were shocked. "I don't… know, Iselda. We can't do anything to help you. But I've heard stories of a certain type of stone that sucked magic out of those gifted with it if they were too close. See if your king knows of anything of the stone," offered Isabelle.

"Thank you. I'll see if such a thing exists." There was a howl from some unearthly creature that sounded as if a dragon was trying to howl like a wolf. "What was that?" Iselda asked, looking around.

"Hados; or more accurately, Zotz." The look her mother gave at the mention of the feared guardian of the Pits made it clear that she was not afraid of the beast. "It is time for us to go," Zelda said.

"No! Don't go! I want you to stay!" Iselda cried, sounding like a child.

"We're sorry, dear. But we must. You can always return and talk again."

"I love you!" A thousand years of waiting and searching said in three words.

"And we love you. Now, go love your king, this Pan," cooed Isabelle.

"Yes, Mother, I will," Iselda said with a smile. They smiled at each other. There was a flash of light and they were gone, as was the Star of Death and Moon of Life. Only the basin of blood and Jessica's body remained. A tear rolled down her cheek at the sudden departure. She always thought she'd have more time.

Iselda hid the blood; not that it was necessary, she just wanted to be the only one able to use it. Then she picked up Jessica's body and walked out of the Temple, saying a prayer for Jessica at Lilith's statue, where she'd laid the sorceress' body.

Chapter 14:

Expressions of Love

With the use of sign language and a very unconvincing attempt at a female voice, Pan had convinced a woman to go and tell Iselda that he'd returned to the inn they'd stayed at. Once he got there, he saw to the quelling of the fear he'd put in his guards. They were alive, and that was a good sign.

"What do we do now, sire?" Vanto asked, after they'd cheered his return.

"Well, we should get some sleep. I want to get home before too much trouble piles up on Shade."

"Yes, sire! But what of Iselda; is she coming back with us?"

"I don't know; that's her choice. If she does, I'll have to give her some limitations, although I'm not sure how that will go over," joked Pan.

Just then there was a knock on the door. "Pan, it's me. Can we talk?" came Iselda's voice from the other side. It didn't sound angry; it sounded nervous.

"Alright, just a minute." Pan got off the bed he'd just flopped onto and went to the door. He opened it with caution. There she stood, without a blindfold and biting her lower lip. She smiled when she saw him.

"Wha-"

"I can control myself. Besides, I wouldn't hurt you; you fulfilled your promise to me. Can we go to my room?"

"Ah, ok. Sure." Pan was still confused. The last time they'd talked, she'd been angry with him. Was all forgiven? "We're going to talk; I'll be back when we're done," he informed the guards.

Once they were inside her room, Iselda shut the door. Then she gently took Pan's hand and led him over to the bed. "What-what are you doing?" asked Pan, who was very aware of how close she was to him.

"I want to thank you. You helped me, somewhat willingly, find my mothers and I'm very grateful for that. Now, if you don't mind, I'd like to ask you one more favour, Nifehan." The use of his title caught Pan off guard and made him raise his caution. "I'm looking for a certain type of stone; I don't know what it's called, but I hear it can remove the magic from somebody. Do you know of such a stone, Panken?"

Pan was taken aback by this approach; it seemed she was petitioning him for something. But he nodded his head and answered her question, "Yes. What you're looking for is called quillum. It's very rare. There is some back in Braria. But before I let you use it, I want you to tell me why you need it."

"Haven't you asked that already?" she asked with a small smile. "I would like to be as normal as possible, and I don't want people fearing me everywhere I go."

"That's right, I did ask that already. We'll see if it works on you; but if it doesn't I don't know of anything else that would." Pan noticed she was treating him differently, with more respect and…compassion?

Now Iselda did the most bizarre thing yet: she gave him a hug. "Thank you, Pan, thank you so much." Pan was too shocked to reply. His face was covered in his incredulity. Iselda released him from the hug and gave a small laugh at his face. This made both their faces turn red from embarrassment. "Pan, even if the quillum doesn't work…can I still stay in Braria?" she asked in a small voice.

"Ah - of course. But if you do, please don't kill anyone; I don't need any more disturbances in the night, thank you."

"Of course."

"Where's Jessica?" Pan asked, knowing the answer but wondering what she'd say.

With this, Iselda got a sad look on her face. "She's dead. In the Temple, some rituals needed doing and through the course of those rituals, she died," Iselda said, bowing her head.

"Ah," Pan said, surprised she had told the truth, mostly. "You're acting differently, Iselda. What else happened in there? What did your mothers say?"

Iselda took a deep breath, steeling herself for what she now had to reveal. Letting the breath out, she said, "As I was explaining why I took so long in finding the Temple, my mothers made me realize something - something that surprised all of us. Isabelle was furious at first, but she warmed up to the idea and eventually even encouraged me to go for it when they were leaving."

"What was it they made you realize?" Pan asked in a whisper.

She looked into to his eyes. Seeing those beautiful eyes of amethyst made Pan remember why he was first attracted to her. Her eyes were wet, tears just starting to form. "They made me realize that…that I love you, Pan."

Pan waited for the butterfly to fly by, for this was surely a dream. She couldn't really have just said she loved him. His face felt incredibly embarrassing, so it probably was. Realizing that this wasn't a dream, Pan responded, "You love me? I-I don't understand." He regretted saying those words as soon as they'd left his mouth and registered in her ears.

Her hopeful face turned to one of heartbreak at those words. "Well, I don't know how it happened. All of our talks have been quite personal, and I guess the more I found out, the more I cared. I didn't intend for this to happen, and I can see it was a mistake to tell you. I'm-I'm sorry." Tears were flowing freely from her eyes now as she got up to leave.

Pan grabbed her hand to stop her. Looking into her tearful eyes he saw she was clinging to this last shred of hope. "Don't go," he said gently. He stood up and brought her close to him. "I'm the one who's sorry; I shouldn't have reacted like that. It was insensitive and I was caught off guard. You weren't wrong to tell me. Now, let me tell you something." Wrapping his arms around her back, he brought her the rest of the way to him. Leaning in, he felt more pleasure than he'd ever felt before.

Gideon Vanto was starting to worry. The Nifehan had been gone a long time; too long for his comfort. He knew the Nifehan was quite capable of protecting himself from most any enemy, but Iselda was different. Her magic was unlike anything else in the world, and that meant that his leader was in trouble. But what troubled Vanto the most was that he was even less able to defend against Iselda. After three hours of his silent deliberating, his companions finally seemed to realize that their Nifehan was taking longer than he should have been. They had started to discuss what sort of action was needed in this situation.

"We need to storm the room!" King said, ever lustful even if it was for blood.

"No, first see if he's ok. If we can hear his voice from the hall, we'll know if he's ok," Vanto argued.

"She could be torturing him; but we'd hear his voice if she were," reasoned Shaw. "Unless she had Jessica place a spell on the room that makes it impossible to hear what's happening inside." Gideon knew that when he'd chosen Remus Shaw to accompany himself on this mission, he'd chosen a young soldier with great potential, and this only furthered that opinion.

"If she wanted to torture him, she'd have done so by now."

"Maybe she just killed him and left."

"She'd have killed us too, if that were the case," Vanto reasoned. "And why wouldn't she have just killed us when she knocked on the door? No, she's not that secretive about killing, nor is she a liar for that matter. If she said they were talking, that's what they're doing."

"Storm the room!"

"No!" both Shaw and Vanto yelled, finally shutting King up.

Unfortunately, it wasn't for long. It was like Vanto could see the new idea pop into King's mind before he said it. King argued, "You know, they may want to be alone." This statement was met by twin confused faces. "Look, he's wanted to meet her since she first arrived in Braria; maybe they're being, er, a couple."

"Leave it to you, Freddie King, to insinuate something so vulgar," Vanto muttered loudly. "No; she wouldn't do that, she's not too fond of men, remember?"

"Is it vulgar to suggest something so natural? They're both lonely and have just succeed in this quest, why not celebrate? She may not be fond of men on a general scale, but even you, Gideon, have to admit she feels positively towards him. I'm going over there and seeing what's keeping him," King stated, getting up.

But before he could take a step, Vanto stood and blocked his path. "No, not you; you'll only end up getting yourself hurt or worse, killed. I'll go." And before his comrade could respond, he was out the door. Walking down the hall to Iselda's room, he tried to turn the knob, but it wouldn't turn. He knocked on the door, hard. There was no answer. Again he knocked hard; this time the door opened slightly.

"Yes?" the Nifehan asked, clearly annoyed.

"We…we just wanted to make sure you were alright, sire." Vanto's voice was a little weak at seeing his leader annoyed; never a good sign.

"Well, I appreciate the concern, but what would you have done if I hadn't answered the door?"

"Attempted to break it down, sire; to ensure you were alright."

"Ok," the Nifehan said with a small smile. "I'm just fine, Vanto. You can tell the others that I possibly won't be back until we leave tomorrow. Now, GO AWAY!" And with that, the door was shut in Vanto's face.

"Just fine?" Iselda asked from the bed. "I had the impression you were more than 'just fine.'"

Pan just smiled. Taking his shirt back off he said, "No; I'm just fine. I think you'll have to try harder to make me more than 'just fine.'"

"Is that a challenge?" Iselda teased as she sat up. The sheet that had covered her fell away, revealing her perfect body. Her black hair was a tangled mess, but that only added to her exquisite beauty. Her eyes shone with mischief at the challenge she'd just been given. As she glided over to him, she noticed Pan couldn't help but stare at her; this caused her to smile. As she roamed her hands over his tight chest, his pants hit the floor. She didn't know why Sabrina had left him for Kailee; Pan was a near perfect specimen.

He walked her over to the bed, but a step away she stopped. He turned to see why she stopped, confusion on his face. This was exactly what she wanted. She pounced. Knocking the breath out of him as they fell onto the bed, she stifled the complaint she anticipated by turning up the pleasure: she slid him into her womanhood. They moaned in unison.

She sat up, as if she were mounting a horse, and started to thrust her hips in every direction possible, squeezing herself around him. Iselda was soon leaking her sweetness, adding more lubrication, panting Pan's name with every single thrust of her hips.

Pan couldn't sit still any longer as he sat up and let loose his tongue on her very sensitive breasts. She shrieked in the pleasure of it all. They couldn't hold it in anymore as ultimate, blissful pleasure took them. They fell apart but managed to stay together as the pleasure submerged them into the realm of unconsciousness.

When Pan woke the next morning, he felt completely exhausted. The thought of he being the only person in existence to experience this feeling amazed him; he being the only one to survive the Dark Union. He realized the sun wasn't up yet, so he closed his eyes and relived the night's events. Just as he was finished, Iselda rolled against him with a smile.

"Good morning," she said sleepily.

"Good morning yourself."

"Did I win?"

"Win what?"

"The challenge. After that you have to be better than 'just fine.'"

"Well, I don't know; I'm kind of tired." At this remark she bit his nipple. "OW!"

"That's what you get for being annoying," she said with a mock pout to emphasize her point.

"Ok, fine! I was better than fine as soon as I kissed you."

"That's better." She snuggled next to him to show all was forgiven.

He kissed her forehead, enjoying the moment. "I love you."

She looked up into his brown eyes, eyes she had confessed

to adoring, and searched to see if his words were true. Seeing that they were, all she could do was kiss him with more passion than she'd felt in a thousand years. "And I love you, Panken."

They sat there watching the sunrise, enjoying the silent intimacy. After the sun had risen for an hour, there was a knock on the door. "That will be the ever-so-concerned guards." He was annoyed that the moment was over.

"I told you they were unnecessary, but you brought them anyways." He knew she was annoyed too, but there was a sense of pride in her statement. Women always had to be right, he thought.

"Right, I know I should have listened." There was another knock on the door. "We'll be right there! Just give us a minute!" he shouted to the door; no more knocks came. "We should get dressed." He saw the reflection of his reluctance in her eyes, but they both got up and started to dress.

※

They left the room and found the three guards waiting. They'd packed Pan's things and silently handed them for him to carry. They all averted their eyes as Pan led Iselda down the stairs. Pan didn't care; he was still living the night's events. They paid the innkeeper and saddled the horses. They left two because Pan now rode with Iselda and Jessica wouldn't be making the journey back.

It would be another week or two before they were back in Braria, so they took their time. Iselda wasn't in a hurry anymore; she just wanted to spend time with Pan.

The first night away from Valya, the guards cornered Pan. "Yes, friends?" Iselda was out hunting for firewood.

"Um sire, we were just wondering, forgive us, but what, um, happened last night?" King asked. As an afterthought, he looked around. "And where's Jessica?"

Pan could only smile at the mention of the previous night, but that quickly disappeared at the mention of Jessica. Not wanting them to worry for his safety needlessly, he said, "Jessica was released from Iselda's control after they entered the Temple yesterday. And as for last night, she told me she loves me, and then she thanked me for helping her. That's all."

"And that took all night?" Vanto had been around Pan for far too long.

"Well, it was a little hard for her to confess herself," the Nifehan said with a sly smile.

"Ok, so you telling me to stop knocking and bothering you was because that woman was trying to tell you she loves you?" demanded Vanto.

"Yes." They were seriously pushing the boundaries of their station.

Looking at the faces of King and Vanto, Shaw spoke for the first time. "Forgive us, sire, but we don't believe you. What you're saying would take an hour at the most. And it was not before three hours of your absence that we started talking of what to do. Unless she thanked you in the manner of lovers…" Maybe this kid was worth keeping after all, Pan thought.

"Alright fine! We did, OK? Happy?" Pan wasn't happy about having to divulge this.

"Yes, sire. Thank you for being honest with us, sire,"

Vanto said with a bow and left. The others quickly followed suit, sensing their leader's distress.

"What was that about?" Iselda asked, appearing at his side. "What's wrong?" she asked again, seeing the anger in his eyes.

"Nothing," he said, pushing down the anger, "Our unnecessary friends just wanted to know about last night."

"And what did you tell them?" To Pan, the question seemed to be asked out of curiosity, not anger. This surprised him.

"The bare minimum, no details; only that which would make them stop asking questions to which they have no right to the answers."

"Well, if they're so curious…maybe you could show them what happened." Her voice was timid, but the glint in her eyes spoke of the true thoughts behind the suggestion.

"Sorry, I'm not one to have an audience." Seeing her face fall, he took her hand in his. "Just because I said 'no' to having an audience, doesn't mean 'no' altogether." This brightened her face. They said goodnight to the guards and Pan cast spells to make it look like they were asleep, and to keep the noise in. Then they continued from where they had left off the night before.

This pattern lasted until they got to the shipyard. They found their ship and Pan reversed Sabrina's spell so it would take them back to Holista. As he did, he explained the difference between undoing and reversing a spell to Iselda:

the difference being that undoing a spell required one to remove magic whereas reversing caused the magic to still be present, just working in the opposite manner than originally intended. Then he instructed the guards not to bother him unless there was absolute need, or they'd arrived. He and Iselda then entered the captain's quarters, locked the doors, cast noise-cancelling spells, and jumped each other onto the bed.

They lost all track of time. They'd closed all the windows, so they couldn't see the sun. Candles were spelled to last until they arrived; they provided the only light and added to the intimacy of the journey.

By the time they reached Holista, Pan had used up all the reserves he'd built up over his ten-year hiatus. He was glad for the break, but never dared mention this to Iselda. Leaving the ship, they noticed it was midday; the bright sun blinded their sensitive eyes.

Chapter 15:

Lullaby Falls

By the end of the half day's ride, they were about another half day's ride to the border between Cawdor and Wealtez, one of the two countries constantly at war with Pitag which both lay to its south. They'd ridden hard most of the day. Pan was anxious to get home; Terang was still at least a couple of days away, but he had many things to do at home and couldn't wait to do one in particular.

Iselda was a little upset when he said he couldn't love her that night. She said she was tired as well, but Pan could tell that it was a lie. But if he had one more night's indulgence of her indescribable love, he'd die. When he said this was the reason why they couldn't be together that night, she got the biggest smile, but only kissed him and said goodnight.

But before Pan went to bed, he saw to one thing more. Gathering his guards, he instructed them to ride ahead of him and Iselda to Braria to inform Shade that he was on his way home, but would be taking his time. He also told Vanto to tell Shade that he had a surprise for him. And then he went to bed. He got the fullest night's sleep that night since he couldn't remember when.

Pan and Iselda slept in the next morning as they both recovered some of the energy that they had spent over the past week and a half. When they finally did wake, Iselda was surprised to see the guards had left. "I sent them ahead so that I could inform Shade that I was alive and well and would be home soon. I thought that we could take our time, and possibly catch a sunset at Lullaby Falls," Pan suggested as he drew her into himself for a deep kiss.

When they had finally pulled apart from each other, Iselda's eyes shined brighter than he'd ever seen them shine. "Lullaby Falls? That's a bit out of the way, isn't it? A little more west than we need to go?" she teased. Lullaby Falls was located in the southwest of Wealtez, near its shared border with Metalia. It was also one of the most romantic places in all of Bolfodier. It was said that the falls were so quiet, the panoramic view so beautiful that even the hardest hearts would be moved. And sunset was said to be the most romantic time to experience it all.

"You sound as though you've been."

"I have." Seeing the look of confusion on Pan's face she elaborated, "I was alone, and it was nearly six hundred years ago. It really is the most beautiful sight you've ever seen."

"I can think of one or two more," Pan said as he looked at her meaningfully. She just looked at him with the most heartfelt smile that made Pan's heart melt. "There's another." At this, Iselda pulled him in for a very passionate kiss. "So, should we go?" asked Pan as Iselda released him from the kiss.

"Yes," she said. "Yes we should." And that being settled, the two of them packed their things, saddled their horses, and departed to the west and to Lullaby Falls.

It took them a day and a half of riding to reach Lullaby Falls. But when they did, Pan was stunned by the sight before him. The waterfall was shaped like a crescent moon that flowed its pure waters soundlessly into the small lake below. Surrounding the lake was a field of grass that gradually rose to the plateau that the falls rested upon. It looked to Pan as if his definition of paradise had been made real as he looked upon the most beautiful thing created by nature.

Sliding from his saddle, Pan helped Iselda from hers, and with her hand in his, he led her to a spot a couple of feet from the waters' edge. Positioning her so that her back was to the water and the sun was directly overhead, Pan ran his fingers through her silken nightfire hair, scrunching strands together and placing others delicately in place. During all of this, Iselda had a confused look on her face, to which Pan only smiled cryptically. "Stay here and don't move," he said as he stepped back ten paces. "Now," he said as a light breeze pulled at Iselda's hair, "I want you to smile that beautiful smile of yours." When she did, Pan had found his memory of the most beautiful sight in the world.

When he returned to her, he could tell that his actions had confused her. "What was all that about? What were you doing?"

Hugging her close, Pan whispered into her ear, "Close your eyes." Assuming she had, Pan started to whisper magic into her ear. He spoke words he knew she wouldn't, or couldn't, understand; but when he heard her gasp, he knew she saw the memory he'd just etched into his mind.

Feeling her go weak in the knees, as he knew she would, he picked her up in his arms and walked her to the edge of the lake before setting her down.

"Wow," she said, her eyes fluttering as her mind tried to cope with what had just happened. But before she could, Pan leaned down and kissed her. Startled at first, Iselda eventually pulled him in tighter to herself as she deepened the kiss.

They spent the rest of the afternoon swimming under the falls and enjoying the fact that they were alone at one of the five Romantic Wonders of the world. As the sun started to set, they got out of the water, dressed, and walked to the northern part of the field. From here, they had a fantastic view of the sunset as well as Lullaby Falls and its surrounding field. As they waited for the sun to touch the horizon, they ate a dinner consisting of the wild berries from the field and bread they had remaining.

As they ate, Pan looked over to Iselda, her hair still wet, and saw that she was happy. Seeing him stare at her, she got a slightly worried look on her face. "Pan, is everything all right?" she asked.

"Of course, my love," he responded as he lost himself in her amethyst eyes. "It's just, I'd started to believe that I'd never feel this way again."

"Try never feeling that way for a thousand years," she said, as a look of pain flooded her eyes. "But now, we never have to be without love ever again." She leaned in and gave him a loving kiss.

Pan returned the kiss, but pulled away before his passion started to demand what his body could not give at that moment. To distract himself, he asked a question that had gnawed at his curiosity since they'd met. "Darling, what I'm about to ask is asked out of simple curiosity; I just want to know the answer, regardless of what it is." Seeing her nod her understanding, he continued, "How did you know it was me who found the Valin Twins' library?"

At hearing his question, Iselda got a look of embarrassment. "It was an accident, really. I'd heard of the library in my first life, but before I could leave home to go and find it, it was destroyed. Or so it was believed; people said that the earth ripped open and swallowed the entirety of the Valin Twins' stronghold. I'd all but forgotten about it until I overheard some men in the local tavern saying that some fool they'd met earlier that day was looking for the lost Valin Twins' library. So I went to them and asked if they knew where this person was digging. They pointed me towards the hills about two days from town that many suspected was the former sight of the stronghold.

"So I set out to find this 'fool'. But when I got to the hills, I didn't see a fool; I saw a wizard using his magic to remove the earth until the library had been revealed. He walked in and after a few minutes of him not returning, I followed him inside. As stealthily as I could, I made my way into the rows upon rows of shelves packed full of books. Some of the titles I saw I'd only heard whispers of: *The Lost Goddess, The Disappearance of the Vigmece Clan, The Mantras of Power*." She saw the look of shock that crossed Pan's face as she mentioned these volumes.

"I thought I felt someone else in there with me that night," Pan commented as he recovered from his shock at hearing her admit she knew he had these books in his possession.

"As I searched the shelves for anything that might contain

information pertaining to my mothers, I saw the light from your lantern and hid myself in the shadows. That's when I saw you; you looked like a child on his birthday as you gazed at all the books within your find. You left and shortly returned with a trunk that looked as if it was made of keyholes, there were so many, and a clanging ring of keys that I assumed matched the locks on the trunk. Making sure you weren't coming back any time soon, I left and hid myself up on the hills that now covered the library. And then I waited until you exited and left before I re-entered the library, only to discover that you'd taken every single book.

"I furiously tracked you down, finally catching up to you at the border between Dunkela and Vanus. From there I followed you all through Vanus and Wahria, and Arretenia all the way to Ignavia where you stopped at the Sanctuary of Darkefyre, and then back through Arretenia into Braria to Terang. When you didn't emerge from the castle after three days, I figured this was your home. I returned to Dunkela, finished what I was there to do, and relocated myself to Terang."

She looked up at him as she finished with a small smile. "That's why I never complained about your using of the Time Wind to essentially spy on me; I knew that you would never know, but my knowing what you'd done was a kind of trade we made. For all I knew, you may have known who I was the moment I moved into my cottage; there were a couple of times when I thought you saw me following you and you may have recognized me. Plus, how many other people wear blackblood religiously?"

Pan gave a small laugh at her last comment, as she had a point. "You don't need to apologize for following my very long path back to Braria. It was the first step that led us here, and I'm enjoying myself too much to have a complaint," he said as he drew her into himself with her back to his chest. They sat like this with their eyes closed for a few moments as they enjoyed the closeness of the other and everything that seemed perfect in their lives. When Pan finally did open his eyes, he saw that the sun was inches from touching the horizon.

Nudging Iselda to look, the couple looked out at the beauty before them. Once the sun touched the horizon, the water that fell from Lullaby Falls turned a deep red and the lake turned a soft, romantic pink. Both Pan and Iselda gasped from the beauty of it all, as the indigo of twilight closed in around them like a pack of wolves surrounding its prey. The lower the sun set, the closer in twilight came until it drove the red from the falls and pink from the lake. And then the stars were out, reflecting off the surface of the lake and sparkling in the falls.

Turning herself in his arms so as to face Pan, Iselda leaned in and kissed him as pleasure flooded his body.

Chapter 16:

A Friendly Explosion

By the time they'd returned to Terang three days later, Pan was well rested and ready. But before he could be with Iselda, he had duties to attend to. He had to deal with the problems that Shade couldn't have dealt with, he had to relieve Shade of his duties of being king, and he had to secretly organize his wedding. He didn't want Iselda to know of the last item on his list; it was to be a surprise.

"My lord and good friend, I'm overjoyed you've returned. Being king isn't all people think it is," Shade said as he and Pan hugged each other in greeting upon meeting in the large entranceway of the castle. Shade didn't look very surprised to see his good friend walk in with Iselda's hand in his; apparently more than just Pan's survival had been reported to him.

"Finally, someone who agrees with me," Pan joked. "Have any major problems, friend?"

"Just one: Vivian wanted you to pay for and go to her brother's funeral or whatever. I told her I couldn't pay right now - you'd decide to pay or not when you returned - but

I went in your stead. It's not that major, but it's the worst thing that happened."

"Sounds like you're a better leader than me; care to keep the job?"

"Tempting, but no. it's yours until you die, old friend."

Pan gave a look of mock disappointment. "I'll see Vivian later. I have another job for you, Shade." At this, Pan drew him aside, away from the crowd that had gathered in the entrance lobby of the castle. Having informed Iselda to give him and Shade a moment alone before they'd entered the castle, Pan saw her hold herself back.

"So, what's this surprise you have for me?" Shade asked, with a look on his face that Pan couldn't understand. "I mean, besides you wanting me to plan your and Iselda's wedding?"

"How did you know that's what I was going to say? I haven't mentioned that to anyone, including Iselda." Pan was flabbergasted that his friend had known this.

"You think that after thirty-four years I don't know you?" Shade asked with a look of incredulity. "I knew something wonderful had happened the moment Vanto said you were alive, but you wanted to take a couple more days to take your time. You've been gone nearly a month, even though you knew how I didn't want to be king. So you taking your time, purposely, was the biggest tip off. Although, truth be told, I half expected you to *finally* try to have something happen between you two now that you were to be spending so much time with each other."

The smile Shade was giving him as he said this was his best teasing smile, but also showed that he was happy that Pan was happy. "Well, since you know me so well, you'll know to have made this a very private event and told Alix to make a *small* feast. Oh, and invite Vivian as well; Iselda should have at least one person there that's her friend."

To Pan's great annoyance, Shade just nodded. "Well, congratulations! I'll continue to look after everything and I'll keep it as quiet as possible. I can't guarantee about the feast though; you know how Alix gets at the very mention of a feast. But I'll do my best, my king!"

"Thank you, friend. One more thing, I'd like for you and Marina to do it. Now go, this will take a bit of work." Shade was clearly ecstatic at the news and rushed away to see to its completion.

"What was that about?" asked Iselda, who'd sneaked up on him.

"Wha-uh, nothing, just a small meeting between me and my councillors I'm organizing. It's nothing of importance, just a formality."

"If it's just a formality, why does Shade have some work to do? And why is he so happy about doing it?"

"He has some work to do because he's gathering all the councillors, and he's happy because he wasn't entirely happy being king. He gets to give that up now that I'm back," Pan lied seamlessly, with an internal sigh.

"Why did he call you 'king'; you're not the king?"

This made Pan stumble. "How much of our *private* conversation did you hear?"

"'…how Alix gets at the very mention of a feast. I'll do my best, my king.' From there on."

"Well, he was giving me a taste of what he's 'endured' over the past little while, during my absence," Pan quickly recovered. To try to get her off the topic, he gave her a gentle kiss, pulling away just as she was getting into it.

"Tease; I hope you plan on finishing what you've started," Iselda said, clearly irritated.

"I'm sorry my love, but I'm still too tired. Maybe in a few days I'll have my strength back." He heaved a sigh to make his point.

Iselda completely pouted at this. "It's been five days; haven't you rested enough?"

"I would barely last a night; you're that good, my love. I'm trying to save my energy so I can love you fully for longer than one night. Is that not worth the wait?" He just kissed her, not letting her respond. Again he pulled away too soon for her liking.

"Stop doing that, it makes me want you more," she said with closed eyes, eyes that emphasized her point clearer than her words ever could.

"Come on, I apparently have to go see your friend Vivian. You should come too."

"Ok, it'll be good to have some girl time; too many men this past while," she jibed at him. Pan just nodded his agreement, which made her even madder.

As they walked to Vivian's, the memories of Pan's and Iselda's first meeting came back to him. "Ah, darling, how much did you tell Vivian about how her brother died?" He feared the answer.

"I told her the truth. Robert came over and tried to force himself on me and I killed him in self-defence. Then I burned his body and trashed my house so nobody would suspect

I was anything but the victim. I gave her his ashes to bury and told her not to dwell on his last hours but remember the years they had together. That calmed her down; although she did have me leave quite quickly after that." At the mention of her leaving, Iselda got a look of uncertainty on her face.

"You burned his body?" Pan asked trying to hide his shock and disappointment at how he knew this was now going to go. He'd forgotten this detail and regretted inviting Iselda now.

Sensing Pan's disbelief at this point, Iselda explained. "You do know he tried to rape me!"

Keeping his true thoughts to himself, Pan simply said, "Yes. Well, maybe she's forgiven you." There was much scepticism in his voice.

Suddenly the door opened to reveal Vivian; she'd obviously heard them.

"Hello Vivian. How are you?"

"My lord?! Fine - I'm fine, thank you." She was obviously surprised to see him. Then she saw Iselda and her mood darkened immediately. "What are you doing here, Selina?! I thought I'd made myself perfectly clear that I *never* wanted to see you again." She hadn't moved to let Pan in.

"Ah, Vivian, she's with me. May we come in?" Pan asked in a tense voice, fearing the explosion he knew was bound to come.

Turning her attention back to Pan, Vivian stepped aside to let them in. "I guess I can't deny the Nifehan, now can I?" She didn't look too happy about having to allow Iselda into her house. "So… to what do I owe this…pleasure?" She asked as she led Pan and Iselda into her slightly messy kitchen where she offered them a seat at the simple table.

Pan and Iselda sat as Vivian attempted to clean up. Her forced attempt at civility was much appreciated by Pan, who didn't want a fight.

"Well, I came to apologize for the aftermath of our last meeting. It occurs to me I may have been a little insensitive. I am sorry about your brother and I'm sorry I couldn't attend his funeral. I'm also sorry that it had to be me to tell you of his fate," Pan said with a bow of his head.

"Thank you, my lord. But do not burden yourself with those pains, it's not *your* fault he's dead," she said with a look of such loathing and hatred towards Iselda, that Pan was positive that if he wasn't there Vivian would try to kill Iselda, slowly.

This look was not lost on Iselda, who bowed her head in shame. "Vivian," she said softly, "Vivian, I'm sorry for what I did. But I didn't exactly want to be raped. I told you I did what I did in self-defence. How-"

"I understand why you killed him, Selina! I don't understand why you had to burn his body! That was unnecessary!" Here was the explosion. "And then you wait *four days* until you tell me what you've done! I can forgive you for killing him; it's what you did afterwards that I can't forgive! You were like my sister, Selina; I loved you!" Vivian shouted. The look on Iselda's face as Vivian yelled at her was one of deepest regret.

Pan had to get Vivian to think about him again, so as to minimize the explosion. He rushed to speak before Iselda could retort. "Vivian, Shade told me you wanted me to pay for the funeral; I will. I hope you were comforted by the presence of one who is practically my brother in my stead." He placed a pouch on the table in between them. It landed with a heavy thud. "That's twenty gold marks. It should cover the expenses. Please, don't be foolish with the extra."

Both women stared at the pouch, and then shifted their gazes to him; they wore identical expressions of incredulity. "Thank you," was all Vivian could say, she was so shocked by the gold.

"Iselda, could you give me and Vivian a moment alone; I have some things to discuss with her." She looked confused at this, but left anyways. Once she was outside the door, Pan continued. "Now, Vivian - Vivian!" he said, snapping his fingers to get her attention back. Finally, her attention shifted back to him from the pouch. "Sometime soon, my friend Shade will be coming by to invite you to mine and Is-Selina's wedding." At this her head snapped to full attention. "I know it seems odd to you, and I understand and am fully aware of her crimes, but we make each other happy. But if you don't want to come to the wedding, that's understandable. I just thought Selina would want some of her friends there. Although, that was before I knew she'd burnt your brother's body and you had said you never wanted to see her again. If I had known, I wouldn't have brought her here. The wedding is a surprise, so please don't tell her. Thank you, Vivian. Goodbye." Without waiting for her answer, he stood and left.

He was just about to open the door when she called him back. "My lord, wait!" He waited as she came running from the other room. "Please, my lord, take your gold back. It's too much, way too much. The funeral wasn't even three gold marks. I can't take this," she said handing the pouch to him forcefully.

"Think of it as compensation. I'm sure you need it more than I."

"It's still too much." She took out five gold marks and forced them into his hand. "Here, take these as…as a wedding gift."

Realizing he wouldn't win, Pan nodded. "Thank you, Vivian. Goodbye."

"Goodbye."

"I see you two made up nicely," Pan said as they made their way over to Iselda's cottage. Smaller than Vivian's house, it was made of wood.

"I never said we made nice; in fact, I said she kicked me out of her house," Iselda defended.

"True, but you did fail to mention that she would become hostile if she saw you again."

"And you failed to use your powers to make her calm so she didn't bite my head off," she retorted.

"That explosion of pent up emotion was going to happen the next time she saw you, no matter what. I simply allowed it to happen, but allowed my presence to keep it from getting violent, as I'm sure it would have had I not been there," Pan explained with a meaningful look to her.

"Fine; I didn't mention that she hates me," she said as she opened the door to her home. "But it's not a secret; most women do just because of my beauty. And I did kill her brother, don't forget."

"Nice, and very modest of you," Pan teased.

"Oh ha-ha! I may be a thousand years old, but it would appear I still have things to learn." She pulled him close to emphasize her next point. "Like how not to overuse my lover."

"Yes, you do need to learn that. That would be most useful."

"So, what do we do now?"

"What do you want to do?" He already knew the answer, of course.

"You. I want you to take me up that castle to your bedroom, seal the doors, and make me moan in pleasure so that all of Braria can hear me."

"That's quite a mental picture. But I, unfortunately, am still tired. Why don't we gather the things you absolutely need and then go and see if you're affected by quillum?" he proposed, starting towards the second room which he assumed to be her bedroom.

"Fine. But that was a once in a lifetime offer," Iselda said with a pout.

Turning back, Pan raised an eyebrow. "Oh, really? I highly doubt that." He stepped back so he was tight against her, reached around and grabbed her buttocks, and pulled her closer into him. Iselda let out a small moan at this action. "Something tells me you'll be offering that to me and more, soon. Very soon."

"What are you planning?" she asked, searching his eyes.

After a moment's pause, Pan answered, "I'm planning on taking you into my Blackreich and seeing if the quillum inside affects you. That's my plan."

"Fine. But you are hiding something from me, Panken Kanta, and I intend to find out what it is," she swore solemnly.

Pan just smiled, released her bottom, took her hand, and led her towards her bedroom.

Chapter 17:

Quillum

There wasn't much that Iselda found essential from her cottage home. A couple of dresses and a small wooden box, which she seemed to regard more preciously than the dresses, was all she brought. Upon their return to the castle, Pan had a maidservant bring the items up to his chambers. And then he led her to the throne room to take her to the Blackreich. From the throne room, they climbed the raised dais and walked to the staircase that was behind the thrones. Taking Iselda's hand, he led the two of them down into the bowels of the castle.

It had been many years since Pan had been in the Blackreich. There was no door, but the frame that led into the vastness that was the Blackreich was made of the rarest substance in all of Bolfodier: white shadothyst. Carved delicately into the white shadothyst were magical enchantments that barred anyone without magic from entering. As always, everything was dusty. Shelves upon shelves lined the walls; books of magic on the left, magical items on the right, and tables with attached benches in the centre ran the length of the vast room.

Walking in Pan pressed his palm to a metal plate on the wall to the right of the doorway, activating the magical lamps and illuminating the room.

"Wow! This place is huge," exclaimed Iselda, looking at the vast room before her. "It's dusty, too. How long has it been since someone's been down here?"

"I check on it every so often, but nobody's really been in here since I became the Memory Thief."

"Why so long?"

"Because there's been no need. No one can get in here without the required amount of magic and I haven't needed restrained magic in years."

"So this place has just been gathering dust for the past five years? How do you know everything still works? And what's restrained magic?" Iselda asked.

With a flourished wave of his hand, Pan eliminated the dust, making everything sparkle as if new. "Nothing of magic stops being able to work the way it's intended to. It can be weakened, but never will all the magic be completely non-functional. And don't be impressed by the dust trick; everyone can do that. As for restrained magic, restrained magic is a form of magic, usually in the form of an object, which is meant to perform a certain function. Quillum, for example, is restrained magic."

"Ok, so where's this quillum; that's why we're here isn't it?" Iselda demanded impatiently.

"Yes, it is. The quillum is that crystal obelisk over there," Pan said pointing to the middle shelf of the third set of shelves. Iselda went to go grab it but Pan held her back for a second. "Before you grab it, reach out and tell me if the air around it is warm."

Clearly confused by these instructions, Iselda walked over to the shelf and reached out her hand. When it was about six inches away from the obelisk, she shrieked and pulled her hand back. "That's burning hot! Not *warm; burning HOT!*" she yelled at Pan.

"Excellent," Pan said with a smile. He reached under the table and pulled out a glove similar to a blacksmith's. "This will work if the air is 'burning hot.' I don't know how it will affect you, but affect you it will." He put the glove on and walked over to Iselda and the quillum. "Go and sit down, my love," he said with a kiss to her slightly glaring face. Iselda went to the nearest table and sat as he grabbed the quillum.

"Do I… do I have to say some incantation or something?" she asked tentatively.

"Yes, you need to dance around the obelisk naked while shouting 'hallelujah' at the top of your lungs for an hour." Seeing her look of complete horror, he laughed. "No, you don't have to say anything. You just need to cut open your hands. Magic flows through the blood and the quillum drains it from the blood." Pulling a knife from his belt and handing it to her, she realized he was serious this time. "Here, use this." He set the quillum down in front of her on the table. The obelisk sprouted from a pewter pyramid carved to be identical to the ones found in Nefas, where quillum was mined. "Make sure you let some blood fall on the crystal; it allows for quicker withdrawal and wakes the quillum up," he said, sitting down beside her.

Taking the knife, Iselda cut the inside of her palms. At the motion, she felt a curious sensation as she thought of Jessica and how a similar action had led to her death. The sensation wasn't guilt, as Jessica's ancestor had all but told her to kill Jessica, but having been the one to do it and as harshly as she had didn't sit well with Iselda. Putting her hands above the crystal and the centuries she'd spent as the Dark Union behind her, she let three drops fall and hit the obelisk.

Her reaction was instantaneous: her body became limp and her eyes glazed over. Her breathing slowed. She was in the grip of the quillum.

Iselda was somewhere between consciousness and unconsciousness. As soon as the first drop of blood had hit the crystal obelisk, she could no longer feel herself. All she could see was that the quillum glowed in flashes of orange. Over time she realized that the time between flashes was shorter. She was feeling tired, but she did nothing about it - she couldn't look away from the quillum's eerie glowing.

She didn't know how long it'd been since the spell had taken her: an hour, a day, a month? Time was meaningless in her current condition. She eventually noticed that the glowing didn't fade but only grew brighter. Now she was really tired. It felt like minutes, but she somehow knew it had at least been hours since she'd cut her palms.

There was a strange sensation on her leg, but she didn't notice this.

The light from the quillum was extremely bright now. It also seemed to be glowing more of a greenish colour.

Suddenly her eyes were covered and there was whispering

in her ear. At least, she thought it was whispering. The light seemed to be getting dimmer and she seemed to be regaining control of herself.

All of a sudden, she was extremely aware of how tired she was. Someone was holding her and panting. Or was she the one panting?

"Wh-Wher-I?" Iselda tried to speak but was too weak. There was a soothing sound in her ear. It was Pan, she knew, but she couldn't understand him. Then everything went black as she fell into unconsciousness.

When Iselda woke, everything was dark and blurry. When she noticed she was in a bed, she tried to get up. Suddenly a flame appeared out of nowhere, making her blind from the sudden light.

"Stay down," a deep, slow voice said. It came from the flame; well behind it.

As her eyes adjusted, she realized it was Pan and her foggy brain had only made his voice slow and deep. He looked as if he hadn't gotten any sleep. There was a relieved smile on his face. "Pan…" It hurt to talk, her throat was so dry.

"Easy, love. Drink this." His voice was normal now. He handed her a small goblet. She drank the liquid, it tasted awful, but she drank the whole goblet without complaint. At this, Pan raised a surprised eyebrow.

She didn't feel tired anymore, but she still felt weak. "Where am I?"

"Where you've wanted to be since we got back home: you're in my bed."

All she could do was smile at this completion of her wishes, even though there was a loophole between her idea and the reality. "How long have I been out?"

Pan's face got a saddened expression at this. "I'm sorry, my love. I left you too long with the quillum. When I got back, I immediately broke the spell. That was dusk, it's nearly dawn now."

He grabbed her hand and tried to kiss it, but she pulled it back. "You-you left me?!" Iselda shrilled.

"Yes. I know the speed at which quillum works, so I left you for a few hours to do some minor tasks. I couldn't touch you, or I'd be trapped same as you, and we'd both die. But when I got back, I realized that I'd taken too much time. That's why you are so weak now." Pan bowed his head in sorrow and contrition.

"Good, now I know who to blame for taking all my energy!" She was a little mad that he'd left her side, leaving her to the mercy of the quillum.

"Payback for the boat ride." His small smile and the mention of the boat ride cracked her armour. She couldn't help but smile.

"So, now what?"

"You go back to sleep. I'd like it if you were strong for tomorrow night," he said with a wink.

"What are you planning?" she asked with a moan.

"Nothing, my sweet," he said with a kiss to her forehead. "Now, sleep. And when you wake, eat something."

Too weak to resist, Iselda just nodded and let sleep take her.

Chapter 18:
Can You Take a Hint?

Iselda woke to the sun high in the sky, blazing in on her. Pulling the covers off, she realized she was in a loose, purple nightdress. Looking for her dress, she found it by a large mirror. There she also found a note from Pan.

> *I thought it would look nice with your beautiful eyes. It was my mother's. Now get something to eat.*
>
> *I love you,*
>   *Pan*

Iselda checked herself in the mirror. Pan was right; the nightdress did go with her eyes. But she liked her dress better. She changed and went to the kitchen.

"Ah, Ms. Iselda! I've been expecting you," said the head chef Alix with a thick accent. He was short and stocky and had a very thin moustache that curled at the ends.

"What time is it?"

"About midday. Here, mangez, eat this," he said handing her a plate. "C'est rabbit with cooked carrots." His accent eliminated the 't' from rabbit and 'ts' from carrots.

Iselda hadn't had rabbit in a long time and so she dug in eagerly, not caring that she took up counter space and was in everyone's way. "This is delicious, Alix." The chef merely nodded, knowing that the food he cooked was good. Finishing the rest of the plate and handing it back to Alix, Iselda said, "Thank you; that was just what I needed. Now, do you know where Pan is?"

"I'm glad you enjoyed it. And I'm sorry; I don't know where he is. You might want to try the throne room though; he spends a lot of time in there."

"Thank you, Alix. I'll see you later." With that, she left to find her beloved.

Pan was waiting for Iselda in the throne room. The room had a raised platform that held the Royal thrones. The room was circular, but very large and had columns all around the walls and beside the raised dais. Behind those was a staircase that led to both the Blackreich and to the balcony that overlooked the lake adjacent to the castle as well as the castle's courtyard. He was lounging in his throne when he saw her come in. Both thrones were made of some dark wood with thick arms and tall pointed backs. Of course, the seat, back, and arms of both chairs were covered in plush cushioning. Pan immediately sat up straight and gave her a huge smile. "Glad to see Sleeping Beauty is awake, finally."

"Well I've been awake for about an hour now."

"Excellent. That will mean you've eaten and should have

your strength back. Time to see if the quillum really worked."

"How do we do that?"

"First you try to give me an intense dose of pain," Pan said simply.

"No, I won't," Iselda declared.

"It's either that or killing me; pleasure is too easy for you to give me. Besides, it only has to be for a few seconds. It's just a test, love."

"But I don't want to hurt you; I love you," she whined.

Pan stood from his chair and gave her a hug. "I'm nearly positive the quillum worked; you probably couldn't hurt a fly. If you do this, I'll do something for you…" Pan took her ear into his mouth to give her a few ideas of what he was hinting at.

She just smiled. "Ok, fine," she caved.

"Excellent. Now gather all your energy, focus - do whatever you do to cause pain. Now, release it into me." Pan's eyes exploded open and he fell to one knee. Iselda was beside him in an instant, her face white with horror. "You know, pale isn't a good colour for you; I prefer you blushing," he said with a smirk.

Comprehension dawned on Iselda's face. "Don't EVER do that again! You scared me; I could slap you!" Her voice was angry, but her eyes were relieved. Pan just laughed. "It's not funny!" she yelled at him, but she was smiling now, too. Oddly, she felt a twinge of sadness at the loss of her powers and immortality, but her relief at finally being rid of their burden greatly outweighed her regret. With an over exaggerated sigh, she leaned forward and kissed him.

"I'm sorry," Pan said with tears of mirth in his eyes, "I couldn't help myself. I've wanted to do that all morning."

He wiped his eyes of the tears.

"It's ok, because I've decided to up the ante. I want more pleasure than you've ever given me. And I want it NOW!"

"Well, I can't have you waiting forever." Her face lit up with giddy excitement. "But, I'm sorry I cannot - you are still too weak. Maybe tomorrow."

Her face fell, utterly disheartened. "If you don't want to-" Now she had tears in her eyes.

"My love, I do. Forever, I do. But trust me, patience is a virtue. I promise that tomorrow you'll be so overwhelmed with pleasure and joy that I'll hardly be able to keep up." This cheered her up a bit. "Did you like your present this morning?"

"I loved it; and you were right, it does match my eyes. But I think I like my dress better, sorry."

"Well, we'll just have to get you some in blackblood, won't we?" Realizing they were still on the floor, Pan gave her a hint at what was to come. "Come on, off the floor. You can sit in the queen's throne, at my side." He caught the questioning look she gave as she got up.

"I'm not the queen; I've no right to sit there," she said.

"Ah, but me being me, I can allow you to sit there. I just have to say the words, which I have," Pan said with clearly over flourished gestures. This made her laugh.

As Iselda sat, the chair reformed to be comfortable to her. The throne's arms became skinnier, the back bent back, and the cushions became a tiny bit stiffer. "I never knew it did that," Pan whispered in awe. This phenomenon had shocked both of them.

"It's quite comfy," she stated simply.

"No one has sat in that chair for years. It must-" he

covered his mouth when he realized what he was saying.

"It must what?" The suspicion was in her eyes again. "Panken Kanta, you're hiding something from me and I want to know what it is - now!" Iselda demanded.

"Oh, it's nothing of importance. Just my friends Shade and Marina want to meet you properly. They were going to stop by tomorrow night," Pan seamlessly lied.

"But you said tomorrow we could be together!" complained Iselda.

"And so we shall, my love. They'll be over and gone so we can be together before it's too dark out. I promise you, you'll not be disappointed with the way tomorrow's set to go." He leaned over to seal his promise with a kiss, which she returned willingly and passionately.

They spent the afternoon talking about anything that came up, with Pan trying to avoid the topic of tomorrow as much as possible. Iselda could clearly tell, so she tried to avoid it as well. But she couldn't figure out why.

So she brought up another topic that had itched at her for a while: the whole story, from his perspective, of him, Sabrina, and Kailee. She could tell he wanted to avoid this topic as well, but for a different reason. Despite the hurt still present, he told her everything she wanted to know.

This part of the conversation took most of the afternoon. Iselda swore to herself that she'd fix the pain that Pan still felt after these past ten years; she'd do all in her power to make him forget it. She was going to make him focus on his present and future with her.

The sun had set before they'd realized the time and their hunger, so they headed back to the kitchen to see what Alix had left over.

"No, no, no! You can't have scraps for dinner, my lord. I'll whip you and Ms. Iselda something fresh," Alix pronounced.

"Will you relax? I'm saving room for tomorrow's dinner with Shade and Marina. Somehow, I know that's being blown way out of proportion."

"Out of proportion?! Shade said-"

"Alix, I don't want to argue with you in front of *Iselda,* it's improper." Both Alix and Iselda caught the inflection on 'Iselda' and understood she couldn't know about what was happening.

"Very well, my lord. *Scraps* it is!" The Head Chef was clearly upset by this fact.

Once he was gone, Iselda turned to Pan. "Why can't I know about tomorrow's dinner? It's clearly more than the four of us; spill!"

"Very clever," Pan said. "But if you figured that much out I'm surprised you couldn't figure out that whatever is happening tomorrow is a surprise for you. Hence why you can't know."

"A surprise? For me? But I hate surprises," Iselda said, confused he hadn't lied again.

"Clearly. Because you keep asking about it - ruining the surprise. Maybe I should have told you about it from the start."

"Yes - there's an idea I like!"

"But that would take away from the magic of it. So I won't tell you."

"Why not?" Iselda put on her best sad face. Having never needed it, it wasn't that great. "You can tell me about Sabrina, but you can't tell me about this?"

"I can tell you about this. I was just trying to be romantic, so I didn't, and I won't until tomorrow. So please, stop asking about it; it's less than a day away!"

Seeing that Pan was being sincere, she let it drop. "OK, I can wait. But it better not be anything like that stunt you pulled earlier, or I'll hurt you for real," she threatened.

"Yes ma'am. Now, let's eat our 'scraps,'" he said, mimicking Alix's tone of disapproval for the word 'scraps'. This made her laugh.

"I love you," she proclaimed.

"And I love you," Pan said. She leaned over and kissed him with all the passion she could handle, which right then, was a lot.

They went up to bed not much later. Pan flopped into bed and Iselda snuggled up to him. They fell asleep holding each other close.

Chapter 19:

Last Minute Changes and Gifts

Pan woke very early the next morning; he was so excited. The sun hadn't come up yet. Quietly getting out of bed, he got dressed and went to the writing table.

> *My sweetest Iselda,*
>
> *I am sorry that I can't watch you sleep, as I usually do, but I have some things to attend to before tonight's surprise. No I won't tell you what it is, so don't bother; it's only a few hours away. I can't wait! If you don't see me today, that's ok; we'll see each other at the surprise.*
>
> *Remember what tonight means!*
>
> *I love you,*
> *Panken*

Pan placed his little note on his pillow, so that she was sure to see it. Then he silently and gently kissed her lips; lacing it with magic so he would be able to track her all day. It was unlucky for the bride to see the groom the day of, even if the bride didn't know she was a bride. Then Pan took his leave to see if everything was going according to plan.

He first went to the kitchen where he found that Alix had indeed gone over the top. For less than ten people, Alix had cooked enough duck and pheasant to fill twenty people for three days.

"Alix! I said 'SMALL!' This," he said indicating the kitchen full of food in varying stages of preparation, "is a regular sized feast. Didn't Shade tell you there were only ten or so people coming?!"

"No, he just said you were marrying Ms. Iselda tonight, it was a secret, and you wanted a small feast. And I've made a small feast!" Alix answered with his thick accent.

"This isn't small!" Pan said pointing to all the food. "You cooking all this means that I have dinner for the next week." Pan knew the effect these words would have on Alix.

"My lord…you can't eat *leftovers*," he said the word as if it was the vilest word in existence, "c'est a crime against your station! You never saw your father eat leftovers, did you?!" The question was rhetorical and Alix's face was livid with anger and exasperation.

"No, Alix, I didn't. But what am I to do with all the extra food?"

"Give it to those beneath you. That would be an amazing first act as king. Show the people you still care."

Pan was caught off guard by this response; he'd never thought to do that. "That's actually good advice, Alix, thank you. I think I'll do that."

"You're welcome, my king. Now, out of my kitchen before the bride sees you," Alix said, shooing him out with his hands.

Next Pan went and saw Shade to see how everything else was going. He was decorating the throne room in white with three maidservants.

"Ah, good friend, how goes your decorating?"

"My king, all is well," Shade answered, dropping what he was doing to talk with Pan. "All will be ready for tonight. What time are we starting?"

"Well, I told Iselda that dinner would be over by nightfall. So I guess we have to start a few hours after midday, which is a few hours away. We should get ready, my friend."

"I have a couple of hours to spare. You have to go get ready; I have to keep decorating if we're starting in a few hours."

"Thank you, Shade. You're like the brother I never had. Thank you for everything you've done for me over the years; it's meant a lot."

Shade put his hand on Pan's shoulder. "Anytime, brother." Then they hugged each other, brothers of the bond. "Now brother, you really must go and get ready. It'll take a lot of work to make you look half as good as Iselda, or me for that matter."

Pan laughed at his brother's joke. "Yes, thanks for the reminder. I'll see you at the altar," Pan said and departed to get ready for his wedding.

Iselda awoke a few hours after Pan had left. She found his note immediately and was saddened by the fact that she might have to wait all day to see him. She had wanted to wake up in his arms, like she had on the ship. The boat ride was easily the best time of her many years of life. And after they'd left Lullaby Falls was quickly becoming one of her least favourite.

But Pan had said tonight they could be together again. She suddenly felt a small pang of empathy for Kailee, who'd had to endure this silently for a year over Sabrina.

She stretched once out of bed, changed, and went to get something to eat.

Down in the kitchen, there was a lot of commotion. People were running in and out with trays of meat, fruit, and bread. She could hear Alix yelling instructions in what she assumed was his native tongue. Once he saw her, he immediately rushed to her side.

"Ms. Iselda, 'ow are you zis beautiful day?"

"I'm sad, Alix. Pan said he had a surprise for me today, and I hate surprises. Then I wake up to a note that says I won't see him until our dinner with Shade and Marina, and whoever else is coming. That's hours away. I'm starting to think he doesn't like me anymore." There were tears in her eyes.

"Don't be sad, Miss. I happen to know the Memory Thief cares deeply for you, and that you'll love his surprise for you. That you're questioning him only proves I'm right," he said as he wiped away her tears with one of the rags he kept in the many pockets in his apron.

"You know what the surprise is, don't you?" The tears were gone, but the sadness still clawed at her voice.

"Yes, Miss, I do. Nearly the entire castle knows, but the Nifehan has asked that we not tell you; he doesn't want the surprised ruined. He likes to see the surprise in peoples' faces." This comforted Iselda slightly.

Just then, Shade came running in. He wasn't that much taller than Iselda, if at all, and he was quite skinny. His eyes were a dark brown, nearly black - a shade that matched his hair and thick goatee perfectly. He came to a halt beside Alix and Iselda. "I just spoke to him about scheduling. We're starting in an hour, so the food should be ready in three." Then he braced himself for the explosion he seemed to know was about to happen.

"Oh, Nique-moi!" yelled the chef. "Three hours, c'est impossible! What does he think me to be, a miracle worker?! What happened to beginning at dusk?"

"Alix, calm down! Everything will be fine. He wants dinner done by dusk because he promised the night to Iselda; which is fair, considering what today is."

"Ok, fine! But why am I just hearing this now? He-"

"Because I'm just hearing it now. Things don't always go according to plan, Alix. Now, stop yelling at me and get it done!" Shade now turned to Iselda. "Iselda, Pan has a small gift for you in your room. It's only part of the surprise, but he wishes to see you with it when we begin in an hour. You must please hurry; he's very anxious to start. My wife, Marina, will help you find us. Now, away to your room!" He gave her a little push to get her moving. She ran as fast as she could to see what Pan had gotten her. Her heart leapt with the knowledge that she'd be seeing Pan in an hour.

When she got to her room, she saw it. It was spread out on the bed. It was the most beautiful thing she'd ever seen.

It was a blackblood dress, the likes of which she'd never seen. It was simple, yet elegant. It looked as though it wouldn't be as form revealing as her usual dresses, but her figure wouldn't be hidden either. There were small floral patterns all over stitched in white. She went to touch it and found it to be made of silk: the smoothest and finest silk Iselda had ever felt.

A knock on the door brought her out of her reverence for the dress. "Who is it?" she asked.

"Iselda, it's Marina, Shade's wife," came the reply from the other side of the door.

"Oh, come in." Marina came in. She was a little shorter than Iselda, but that was all. Her hair was strawberry blonde, almost pure pink; and her eyes were a dazzling blue. She was every bit as beautiful as Iselda, who couldn't help but be a little jealous. The two women stared at each other in open awe of the other's beauty.

"Dear spirits," Iselda said, "you're beautiful. I have new respect for Pan."

"Wha-Thank you, you too. And what?"

"Thank you. And I was just complimenting Pan on his mental strength."

Marina got a sad look of happiness on her face. "Yes, his resistance has been sorely tested every day for the past ten years, even when Sabrina was here. I'm glad you've come along; for the longest time I was afraid I was going to have to let him do what he surely wanted to do. But that's in the past, now." Marina's eyes next found the dress, and the look of awe returned to her face. "That's a beautiful dress."

"Yes, it is. Thank you. Can you at least tell me what it's for?" Iselda asked, a little frustrated that she was still in the dark about the day.

"You'll see in a bit," Marina said with a small smile. "I just saw Pan walking downstairs; he looks better than I've seen him in years. I'm sure that you'll both be breathless at the sight of each other. Now, into that dress; we don't have much time."

"This is more than just a dinner, isn't it?" Iselda asked as she started to undo her dress.

"I would've thought that would be obvious. If it was just a dinner, would I be here? Would you not have seen Pan yet today? Yes, today is more than a dinner. Now hurry up and get that dress on, before I take it for myself!" Marina demanded.

"OK, OK, I'm going. But it would go quicker if you helped."

Marina stepped behind Iselda and helped untie her dress. Changing was ten times easier with someone's help.

Throughout the next forty-five minutes, Marina helped Iselda into her dress and brushed and styled her hair so that she looked like a statue of beauty and femininity come to life. Iselda did the same for Marina, who insisted that she look worse than Iselda. When they were done, Marina took Iselda's hand. "Now, follow me; I'll take you to Pan," she instructed. Iselda followed her without complaint.

Chapter 20:

Wedding

Pan was waiting at the makeshift altar at the top of the steps in the throne room. His hands were sweating and he couldn't take his eyes off his feet. He was dressed in the traditional Brarian ceremonial robes: black pants and shirt, a white jacket with gold embroidery along its neck and down along the edges, and a black, floor-length cape with the blood red 'K's of the Royal seal. Shade, who was standing beside Pan, put a hand on his shoulder and urged him to look up.

Walking into the room were two women. Marina, who looked absolutely dazzling in her purple dress, was leading a teary eyed goddess into the room. No, not a goddess - it was Iselda! She looked indescribable! There were no words that could even scratch the surface of the beauty she had at that moment.

And suddenly, she was there, standing before him. His breath was caught in his chest; his heart felt like it was about to erupt, beating like it wanted to create a rhythm for all of Braria to hear.

"Pan…" It was barely a whisper, but she covered her

mouth as if she'd shouted.

"Will you marry me, Iselda?"

"…Yes!" This time she did shout.

Shade and Marina had climbed to the top of the platform and were now facing the crowd, a crowd that seemed well over the ten or so people Pan had planned on. Between the four of them was a small marble table that held a single goblet made of pure Brarian silver. "The sacred covenants of marriage are not to be entered into lightly," declared Shade.

"They are an eternally binding agreement between two willing parties. Love must be present in their hearts, yet sacrifices are required to prosper. Panken and Iselda understand the requirements of this world and of the spirits in the next, and they are ready to pay the debts required," Marina told the gathered masses.

"Iselda, as Panken's wife, you would be the Queen of Braria. That title brings heavy burdens; none as heavy as the clause to the people stating you will do all in your power to protect and lead them to prosperity. Can you lead and protect us in such ways, giving your life if necessary?"

"I-I can. I will give my all for the betterment of this country and her people. I give my word as Iselda Ness."

"Good. Now do you forever promise to love Panken; to make him happy and peaceful to the highest degree?" asked Shade.

"Yes, I will please him in every way I can," she declared with a wink to Pan.

"Give me your hand," Shade demanded. Iselda gave the hand closest to him. Taking an ornate knife from his belt, Shade sliced her palm open. She let out a gasp and turned to glare at him. He turned her hand over and let the blood flow into the goblet that rested between the four of them. "As proof to your words, the crown demands blood payment." Iselda simply bowed her head to his explanation.

"Panken, for the past ten years, you have ruled as the Nifehan of Braria. You will have no real changes to your duties, only your title. As king though, you must put your people above yourself or even your queen. Can you live with the terms as set down by the first king?" demanded Marina.

"I'm still dedicated to my country and I will always do what is necessary for my people."

"Good. Now do you promise to forever make Iselda happy and peaceful to the highest degree?"

"Her happiness will always be the most important thing to me; save that of my people," Pan declared.

"Give me your hand." Marina took the knife from Shade. Pan handed her his closer hand, which she sliced the palm of and let the blood drop into the silver goblet.

"Iselda," Shade said, "by your oath, your love, and now your blood you are forever bound to Panken Kanta."

"Panken," said Marina, "by your oath, your love, and now your blood you are forever bound to Iselda Ness.

Now they spoke in unison. "Take the cup with your blood and feed it to your spouse." The bride and groom did as instructed, drinking their fill. "Now, by our power, and in the presence of these witnesses, we declare you wed! Let the world know: Braria has a new king and queen!" There was an uproar as the ceremony concluded. The crowd roared louder as Iselda flung herself at Pan and kissed him.

When she finally pulled away, there were tears in her eyes but she was smiling the biggest smile Pan had ever seen her wear. That smile alone made his heart skip a beat.

"You look…beyond verbal description," he whispered in her ear over all the noise. She just held herself tighter to him as he led her to the ballroom where tables created an empty space big enough for half the guests to dance in, and musicians playing all kinds of instruments started playing an upbeat piece that told the surprisingly true story of a certain Clowian maiden and the unusual relationship she had with a bear.

Taking her hand, Pan led Iselda out onto the dance floor as the music changed to something slower and more romantic. Pulling his bride in tight to himself, Pan led Iselda as they danced alone for the entire five minutes of the song. As the music ended, the crowd began to clap as partners were forming and joining them out on the floor. Then the music started again.

Chapter 21:
Unexpected Forgiveness and Congratulations

After an hour and a half of ceaseless dancing, in which Pan thought he'd danced with every female present, he finally had to take a break as his feet were in a fair amount of pain. It was during this respite that Pan saw Iselda dancing with Shade and laughing at the things he was telling her. No doubt it was something embarrassing about his childhood. As he thought of all the possible stories Shade could be telling his new bride, Pan noticed Marina making her way over to the table at which he sat. "Don't worry, I made him promise not to tell her the more embarrassing ones until at least tomorrow," she said with a smile as she sat down beside him.

"Well, as long as it's not the more embarrassing ones, then it's ok." The smile he gave her made them both laugh. "Thank you, by the way; not just for today, but for everything you and Shade have put up with these past ten years. I know it wasn't easy to be my friend, and I'm sorry for anything that I did or didn't do that upset you in any way. You've made Shade one of the happiest people I've ever known, and I'm very thankful for that."

At hearing this, Marina just smiled bashfully. "Thank you, but you've never needed to apologize to or thank me for anything. There's no one Shade loves more than you, Pan, not even me." Upon hearing this, Pan looked at her in surprise, but her smile stopped him from denying this. "I've known about that for nearly as long as I've known him, and accepted it long ago. The point, though, is that we do any and everything we can for the people we love, no matter what it is. I love you Pan, as I know you love me, and I know that you weren't yourself these past years; I long ago forgave you for any and all things that you may or may not have done to me." Standing up, Marina pulled him up by his hand and into a friendly hug.

It was at this point that Shade and Iselda came over to the table they were standing at. "I hope we aren't interrupting anything," Shade said with a smile. Releasing Pan from the hug, Marina went to her husband and kissed him. By the look on Shade's face, Pan could tell that Shade wasn't expecting this kind of greeting. When he was finally released from his wife's embrace, Shade had the most bewildered expression on his face. Turning back to Pan and Iselda who were silently laughing at his face, Shade said, "Um, I'm hungry; anyone else hungry? Where is Alix with that feast?"

As if on cue, members of the kitchen staff entered the ballroom with carts full of food and drink and tables to set it all upon. Alix had laid out a huge feast as a buffet. As the aromas of the food let everyone know that dinner was served, the music came to a halt and everyone rushed to their tables and the food. All throughout dinner people came up to congratulate them, wish them well, and say the random things that came to their minds. Despite Pan's worries, there seemed to be little leftovers. Either Alix hadn't gone over the top as feared, or the extra guests had compensated nicely.

Once everyone seemed to be settled, Shade stood and commanded silence. "I would like to say a few words. As the one who represents King Pan's family, and the one who's known him the longest, it's time to bring out the embarrassment." There were small amounts of laughter to this. "Just this morning, Pan called me the 'brother he never had'. I couldn't agree more, for we've been brothers since we were kids. And as your brother I get to make this speech." The smile Shade gave him as he said this made Pan realize that he had to endure the full thing to get to the point that awaited him at the end. With a slight nod, he acknowledged to his brother that he could continue.

"Ten years ago, as we all know, Pan was in love with a very different woman." There were nods of agreement to this by those who remembered. "The then king - rest his soul - was dying and had forced Pan to choose love or rule. I thought for sure that he'd choose love, for he loved her more than anything. I also knew he'd wanted to be king since he could remember his thoughts. To this day, that is the only time I've been surprised by what he did: he chose rule.

"Since then, while he is still the same man I call brother, I've felt a part of him had been taken. He wasn't the same youthful man full of wonder.

"Then, a month ago he left to help a woman that he's been attracted to - but been too chicken to do anything about - since he first saw her. Three days ago, he came back; and *all of him* came back. I saw it immediately. It took all of two seconds for him to tell me what had brought him back. It was Iselda.

"So, Iselda, I'd like to thank you; you brought back the lost part of my brother. I'd also like to welcome you to our makeshift family." He lifted his glass and drank to her. Everyone followed his lead and there was applause. Pan stood, turned to his brother, and embraced him as such.

When he sat down, he could feel the tears on his cheeks. He looked to Iselda, who wiped the tears with her thumb and kissed him. The crowd roared.

Suddenly there was a blinding light and a wail of unearthly horror that shock the room. When the light faded and the wail ceased, there were faded silhouettes of two women who weren't naked, but not clothed either. Many people, including Pan, had stood in a panic at the noise and light, but all of them froze at the sight of the two women in the middle of the dance floor.

"We are Iselda's mothers," said Isabelle.

"We've come to congratulate our daughter," Zelda declared.

"Mothers!" cried Iselda as she ran to the centre of the room.

"Hello daughter," Isabelle said as she reached them. "Congratulations! We're so happy for you!"

"How did you get here? I thought that-only in the Temple-How?"

"Hello to you, too. And Hados has allowed us to breach

the veil, so we only have a moment," explained Zelda. "Like Belle said, we're very proud of you. Now, bring Pan to us, we must talk to him." There was an edge of danger in her voice as she said this. Pan rose, strode to the centre of the room, and put his arm around his wife's waist.

"I am Pan."

"Yes of course," Iselda's mother said with a knowing smile. "Be warned, wizard: you know who we are and who she is. We've accepted you as the one for our daughter. Betray that trust and you'll wish you'd never left that other woman; we have an eternity to punish you," Isabelle warned, a new smile forming at the thought of the torture to be had.

"I've no intentions of hurting her. And I know all too well the consequences if I do. And that other woman chose another path."

"That may be," snarled Zelda, "but don't be stupid and forget your place."

And to show his humility before her mothers, Iselda was shocked as Pan assumed the position of the Brarian Salute. The room gasped as everyone saw the king perform the very thing he'd decreed never be done again. Looking from Isabelle to Zelda, Pan saw the small smile that crossed Zelda's lips upon seeing this. As he stood, he asked, "Is that all? Just the warning?"

"No, we also carry a message from your parents," Isabelle said in a serene voice. "They offer their congratulations as well as their love. They braved the Pits to bring you that message. Don't let that ordeal be for nothing: honour that sacrifice. We'll see them to the Gates, as a gift to you." The underworld was divided into three sections: the Pits, the Gates, and the Fields. Most people ended up in the Fields;

those deemed to have lived better lives went to the Gates; those who lived evil lives were sentenced to the Pits. That Pan's parents had willingly journeyed into the Pits showed how much they loved their son. And the fact that Iselda's mothers not only would, but could, escort them to the Gates showed just how much favour they'd garnered from Hados.

"Thank you. If it's not too much to ask, could you pass along my thanks and love?"

"Of course, son," Zelda said peacefully. Then the threat returned: "Don't let our love for our daughter, and thus you, be taken advantage of. Hados has been very kind to us." As if beckoned by its master's name, an ear-splitting howl beckoned the two women back behind the veil.

"I love you," Iselda said to them before they left.

"And we love you, sweet daughter," they said in unison. There was a flash of complete darkness and they were gone.

A tear rolled down Iselda's cheek which Pan wiped away with a gentle swipe of his thumb. He then leaned down and kissed her gently as he led her back to the table. "Back to your meals, everyone," he said to the guests who were all staring wide-eyed and open-mouthed at them.

The rest of the meal passed without further interruption. As Panken stood to leave, the room fell silent. "Friends, thank you all so much for celebrating this joyous occasion with us. But I hope you'll understand when I say I have to go. I have some vows to fulfil. But please stay, eat, and party for as long as you want; just because we leave doesn't mean you have to! Also, we'll not be seeing any petitioners tomorrow - we're busy! Goodnight!" He led Iselda by the hand away to his - *their* - chambers.

Unfortunately, they were stopped before they got there

by a guard. Pan recognized him as the guard whose name he couldn't remember, his name still a blank in his slightly intoxicated mind. "Forgive me, your Highnesses, but there are three women at the door who would very much like to see you." The guard seemed very uncomfortable in delaying them their wedding night.

Pan was a little confused; why hadn't the three women just come and joined the party? Alan! That was the guard's name. "Who are they, Alan?"

"Ms. Vivian from across the lake, and two other women from out of town that I don't know," the guard replied.

"What do they want?" Iselda asked, puzzled and slightly annoyed at the delay to her wedding night.

"I don't know, they just said they wanted to see you. They said they didn't want to come and join the party. But the other two women aren't with Ms. Vivian."

"What do these other two women look like?" Pan asked, anxious for this to be done with.

"One is quite petite with very thick, shoulder length brown hair and blue eyes; the other is nearly the complete opposite: voluptuous with long red hair and gr-"

"Green eyes," Pan finished the description.

"You know them, sire?" Alan asked.

"Yes," Pan answered in a constricted voice. "Bring them here, Alan. And don't let anyone else see them."

"Right away, your majesties," Alan said with a bow of his head as he sped away.

"What are they doing here?" Iselda asked. He could tell that she was hiding the smile she wanted to give at seeing her friends for his sake and was grateful for it.

"I don't know. I thought they were honeymooning

in Vagala."

"Me too." It was clear she didn't like this interruption, despite it being her friends. But before they could say more, Alan came back into the hallway leading Vivian, Sabrina, and Kailee towards them. Vivian was the first to speak.

"Your Highnesses, please forgive us; we know what we're interrupting. I just wanted to say congratulations again." Now she turned to Iselda. "I know we haven't been on the greatest of terms recently, Selina, but I'd like it if we could go back to normal. I'm so-" She was cut off as Iselda stepped forward and gave her a hug.

"I'd like that very much, Vivian. I'll come over as soon as I can!"

"Thank you, your majesty," Vivian said with a large smile. Then she bowed and left.

But before she got too far, Iselda called her back. "Vivian!" Seeing the other woman turn around, Iselda continued, "If you want, you can have my cottage; I don't need it anymore," she said with a smile to Pan.

"Thank you, your majesty," she said with another bow before departing with a smile.

Turning to the other two, Pan put on an impassive face. "Why are you two here? I thought you were in Vagala."

Sabrina gave a small smile. "Forgive us, Pan. Like Vivian, we're here to congratulate you. I'm happy for you, I truly am." Pan couldn't tell what it was, but Sabrina seemed different somehow.

"Thank you. Now if you'll excuse us, my wife and I have some unfinished business to attend to," Pan said with a thin veil of malice lined with annoyance.

Just as he was about to turn away, Kailee spoke, but it

wasn't to him, "Forgive me, your majesty, but I beg a favour." Pan turned to see her head bowed to Iselda. "For the past ten years, I've been banished from my home and my family for the crime of loving someone. But if it's ok with you, your highness, I'd like to be able to move back home with my lover so we can spend more time with my family." Pulling Sabrina with her, Kailee knelt on the floor, head bowed to Iselda.

There was a moment's silence as the new king and queen gazed down at the two women in twin poses of supplication. Pan had decided as soon as he wasn't asked that Iselda would be the one to grant or deny the request. "It's for you to decide," he whispered in her ear.

Iselda knelt down opposite Kailee. Lifting her face with her hand, Iselda gazed into the girl's eyes. "You showed me true kindness, even knowing who I was. None before you have done that - not even Pan. For as long as I live, I will never forget that. You do not need to kneel before me, Kailee; I should kneel before you. Go back to OJA, and see all your loved ones. I just ask you do two things: always ask me if you need help, and let me visit whenever I'm in town." When Kailee nodded her head in agreement to her queen's terms, Iselda kissed her forehead as a sign of the forgiveness given. Then the two stood and hugged.

"Congratulations, Iselda! I hope my description lives up to your experience," Kailee said with a smile. Sabrina now rose with a cautious grin. She gave a small nod towards to Pan.

"It already has, friend. It surpassed it even." Iselda was also smiling.

"Kailee, we should go; you remember our wedding night…" Sabrina gently said to her lover.

"Oh! Yes, right. We'll leave you two to whatever you have planned," Kailee said. "I'll see you when you're next in OJA!" With one last one-armed hug, Sabrina and Kailee took their leave.

Pan and Iselda were finally able to reach their bedroom and enjoy each other. They wasted no time in making up for what time they had lost during the past week.

Chapter 22:

Family

Iselda had been in complete bliss the past four months since her wedding. The people seemed to love her as their queen and she was really getting back on normal terms with Vivian. But the best part had been learning she was pregnant with twins. The news that she was to be a mother to Pan's children had made her the happiest woman in all of Bolfodier.

She had decided to go and visit Kailee and Sabrina in OJA. It was a day's journey to the west of Terang. She had told Pan what she was doing and that he should stay behind; she knew he was uneasy about her friendship with Kailee, but understood the connection the two had. Iselda hadn't seen Kailee since the wedding and was anxious to actually talk to the girl.

Before setting out, Pan had insisted that she take a guard with her, for not only her protection but that of their unborn children. She had agreed to have Vanto accompany her to the border town. He was one of the longest serving guards and he would protect her as well as she ever could, had she her powers still.

When she had found out she was pregnant, Iselda had sent a letter to Kailee to explain the good news and that she would be coming soon for her visit. Kailee had sent her entire family's congratulations at the joyous news and said she looked forward to her visit, but that she was busy for a few months so it would have to wait. That had been three months ago.

This was Iselda's first visit to anywhere in Braria as its queen, so she was very anxious to see what the rest of her new responsibility looked like. When she arrived in OJA it was late, but she wasn't tired. As she got out of the carriage, she told Vanto to wait while she was inside. Looking at the little of the town she could see at this hour, she was happy to see that it wasn't a complete dump. She supposed that being on the border had its advantages. She could hear the ruckus of singing from the tavern, the hammering of metal in the blacksmith's shop, and the whining of horses at the inn as she walked through the streets towards the modest house Vanto had informed her was Kailee's and Sabrina's.

Walking up to the door, Iselda saw the light in the window. They were clearly having supper. Iselda hadn't sent word ahead because she wanted the visit to be a surprise. She knocked on the door and heard the shuffling inside.

The door opened to reveal Sabrina holding a frying pan she was in the middle of washing. Drawing back the hood she'd had up to hide her identity, Iselda smiled at Sabrina. "Hello, Sabrina! How are you?"

"Iselda? Fine, please, come in," she said stepping aside to allow her room to come in. The home looked to be quite cozy with the living room leading directly into the kitchen and dining room.

Kailee had come around the corner to see who was at the door and let out a squeal when she saw who it was. Running up, Kailee gave Iselda a friendly hug before saying, "I wish you'd told me you were coming; we would've cleaned. The house is a mess. I can't believe the queen is in my messy house!" She then gave Iselda another hug before releasing her. Sabrina then led the three of them to what was obviously the dining room, frying pan still in hand.

"I hope I'm not interrupting anything," Iselda said as she sat down.

"Not at all; we just finished dinner," responded Sabrina who was at the sink washing the dirty dishes. "We were actually just wondering when you'd stop by. Is Pan with you?" There was a hint of unease in the question. Clearly there was still hurt here as well.

"No, it's just me," she assured, "I thought it better if I came alone." Sabrina just nodded her head, but Iselda knew she was quite grateful. "I've got so much to tell you."

"Really? Like what?" asked Kailee with a gleeful look in her eyes. Hearing this, Sabrina left the dishes and quickly sat at the table beside Kailee.

"Well, as you know, Pan and I are going to be parents. What you-"

"You know what it is, don't you? You know if it's a boy or a girl?" Kailee was clearly excited about the news.

"No, we don't know the sex yet. But we know something just as important." Here Iselda gave a pause for dramatic effect. Only when both women gave exasperated sighs did she tell them the news. "What you don't know is that we're having twins!"

This was met by a brief silence but then they both let out

cries of delight and ran around the table to give her a hug. The giggling and hugging lasted for another ten minutes before they were able to calm down. Sabrina went to a shelf and pulled down a bottle of milk mixed with cocoa. She poured three glasses and raised her own. "To the future of Braria; to your children, Iselda!" The others raised their glasses and Iselda blushed a little.

"Thank you, Sabrina; it means a lot coming from you."

"Iselda, please, it's the least I could do after what you did for us."

"I know, but still. I know that you don't exactly like me, and I understand, but you still invited me into your home and toasted my children. If there was ever someone who had a right to hate, it's you, but you-"

"Iselda," Sabrina cut in, "I do like you. I apologize for how I first acted when we met but I am not lying when I wish you well and hope your children grow to help the world grow. And I have no right to hate you, nobody does. You've been an excellent queen these past few months and I'm sure you've been a good wife. Pan always wanted children; I'm sure he's never been happier. And all I want for him is to be happy."

Tears choked all the words that Iselda wanted to say so she settled for a heartfelt hug. Sabrina seemed to understand and returned the hug. Out of the corner of her eye Iselda saw Kailee smile and she was happy that everyone seemed to be happy. When the two women finally released each other from the hug, the three of them went to the couch in the living room.

"So, do you have any names? Or have you not thought about that yet?" Kailee asked as they all sat down.

"Of course we've thought of that! We talked all night about names the first night we learned we'd be parents!"

"And what are they?" Kailee asked eagerly.

"Well if they're boys we were thinking Nicklaus Shade and William Leo. And if they're girls: Nikki Kailee and Evelyn Isabelle." Kailee's face was only a smile as she beamed at the honour of having her name given to the Royal Princess.

"What if it's one of each; you know, one boy and one girl?" asked Sabrina as she rubbed Kailee's shoulder.

"We don't know. We have so many people we'd like to honour with the names, we don't know which names to pick. We know one of them will be named either Nikki or Nicklaus. And we've agreed that we want you two there when they're born. It would mean a lot to us if you came." This was greeted by shocked looks on both their faces. Iselda had to hold back a laugh. Then the hugging and giggling started up again.

Pan paced the hallway as he waited for permission to enter. Iselda had gone into labour seven hours ago and was giving birth to their twins right then. He couldn't believe he was a father.

The door he was pacing in front of opened to reveal a sweaty Sabrina, who as a healer had been Iselda's first choice as a midwife. He looked up, unable to bear the silence she was giving him. She smiled at him. "Congratulations, Pan! You have a beautiful son and daughter. I'll go get the others."

She left the doorway so that he could enter.

Rushing in, he saw them. The three people he loved the most were all snuggled together in his bed. His beautiful wife laid her head against the headboard as she rocked the two bundles in her arms. She smiled up at him as he looked at her relaxing from the pain of childbirth.

"Would you like to hold your son first, or your daughter?" she asked him. He knew she was tired but she wouldn't sleep for a long while. Terang had waited decades for a new heir to be born; the celebration for the two newborn heirs would last at least a week.

"My daughter; let me hold my baby girl first." She gave her over and he got the first glimpse of his family. As he gazed lovingly at the sleeping bundle in his arms, Pan saw that his daughter looked a lot like how he thought his wife would have looked as a child. As he held her, Pan felt the wave of love that he'd felt whenever he'd rubbed his wife's belly these past few months. "She has my mother's eyes!" he shouted when she opened her eyes and he recognized the blue looking back.

Iselda smiled and said, "Nikki Evelyn and Shade Leo, meet your father." Pan smiled as he let loose the tears that had threatened to come since he found out he'd be a father.

When the door opened and his brother and sisters walked in, Pan couldn't believe the luck he'd had in life as the fruition of all his dreams came true.

Part Two: Iselda

Chapter 23:

An Unexpected Letter

The past five years for Iselda had been hectic. Raising twins had its challenges, but the rewards were far greater. Nikki and Shade seemed to be growing up so fast, despite being only four and a half. Pan was constantly telling her that both pouted just like her and that he had to hold back laughter whenever he saw it; he found it too adorable. But what she loved most about her beautiful children was how much they both tried to be like her and Pan; they would take turns sitting on the thrones and pretending to be petitioners and answering how they thought their parents would. It was a little scary to see how well the two of them answered.

Much had changed in those five short years that had passed since she had become queen. To everyone's great delight, Pan had given up his Time Wind abilities with Sabrina's assistance shortly after Shade and Nikki were born. She had requested, so as to not frighten her children, that any record of her as the Dark Union be erased, save those in the Blackreich that couldn't be destroyed. Her friend Vivian had also passed away shortly after the birth of her children, apparently from the same sickness that had killed Pan's father all those years ago. The strangest thing about the whole thing though was the fact that after Vivian's death she had felt waves of sympathy from her newborn children. When she had mentioned this to Pan, he'd told her that she was imagining things; Shade and Nikki were barely five months old and didn't have magic.

As Iselda walked to the kitchen for a late night snack, she was approached by Shaw, one of the guards that Pan had taken to Vagala. His wife had also recently given birth to a son, Romulus, a few years ago. Romulus, Shade, and Nikki had become playmates and good friends. After giving a fist to his heart, Shaw asked, "Your highness, do you have a moment?"

"Of course, Shaw, what do you need?" she answered, wondering why he seemed so nervous.

"I know that we're not supposed to do this sort of thing, but this little girl came up to me today and wanted me to give you this letter. She seemed really adamant that you get it when you were alone, and I know I should have reported her but she was just a little girl and-" he rushed to get out before Iselda cut him off.

"It's OK, Remus. If she was just a girl, I'm sure it's nothing of harm. Show me the letter." Shaw handed her the letter, but she could not grab it. She backed away from the acid green sealing wax, running out of room when she hit the corridor wall. "It's-it's not possible!"

Now Shaw was really nervous. "My lady, are you OK?" he demanded as he rushed to her side; the letter dropped on the floor. "Dear spirits, what have I done? Forgive me, majesty; what can I do?"

Iselda had to forgive the man; he couldn't have known who the girl was. Calming herself, she said, "Get Pan and tell him to meet me in the throne room. And then try to have our court artist Lykane create a likeness of this girl - I want her found NOW!" Shaw raced to do as his queen commanded. Iselda tentatively picked up the letter, saw her name on the envelope in the flourished, yet compact, handwriting of the woman who she'd once thought she loved, and opened it.

> *Greetings Iselda,*
>
> *When I heard that my old friend was the new queen of Braria, well, I was oddly puzzled. I could have sworn this old friend had sworn off men centuries ago; that she had vowed to remain a chaste immortal, like me. And when I consider how this friend tried to kill me the last time I saw her, well, let's say I have the upper hand.*
>
> *Fair warning, friend,*
>   *Empress Annabelle*

Iselda reread the letter, feeling the bitter sarcasm that she associated with Annabelle radiating from the declaration, as she waited for Pan in the throne room. When he saw her sitting on the steps to the raised platform, he ran to her. Encircling her in his arms, he held her tight. "You're trembling; what's wrong? Shaw came running in right when I was getting to the best part of story time. Your children are very worried, as am I. What's going on that you're organizing a search for a girl?"

His brown eyes pierced hers and calmed her. She handed him the letter and he read it over. When he was finished, confusion was clearly marked on his face. So she explained, "That letter is a formal declaration of personal war against me by the Empress of Toxai. There's still a part of my life you know very little about."

Before Pan could ask for further explanation, the sound of footsteps drew their attention to the room at large. Holding each other's hands, and with identical expressions of worry, were Shade and Nikki walking towards their parents. "Mommy, what's wrong? Mr. Shaw said you were scared, why are you scared?" Nikki asked.

Iselda's heart found its way to her throat as tears came to her eyes. "Nothing, sweetheart. I got a letter from an old friend, who I thought had died; Mommy was just shocked by it, that's all. Come give me a kiss goodnight you two, it's way past your bedtime and Daddy still has his story to finish." The children went to their mother and gave her a hug.

"I'll protect you, Mommy," Shade whispered in her ear. "Me, too," whispered his sister in her other ear. And here again, she felt waves of love and worry crash into her as she held her children.

Iselda had to hold back the tears at the pureness of her children and their innate ability to tell when something was wrong. "I know," she told the two of them, squeezing them a little more for love. "Now, off to bed; Daddy still needs to tell me my story." This made them giggle as they each took one of their father's hands and dragged him to their chambers.

Chapter 24:

A Forgotten Tale

Pan was quite worried about the letter the Empress of Toxai had sent Iselda, but for the sake of the ruse she'd told the children, he put on an impassive face. When the two of them were in their beds, he asked, "Where did I leave off? What just happened in our tale?"

"The brave prince was rushing to the castle to face the beast and save the princess," Nikki reminded him.

"Of course. Now, the beast had placed the princess under a powerful spell that made her do its bidding. As a trick, the beast let the prince find his princess in their castle, lying on the ground." Panken acted as the prince, feigning surprise and rushing to a point between their beds. "'Oh, sweet princess, please don't be dead' he cries to her. As he leans in to kiss his love, he sees the impossible: her eyes are open, but black as night. He jumps back and draws his sword. 'What have you done to her, beast?!' he shouts at the now floating body of the princess.

"'Foolish prince,' says the beast in the princess' voice, 'You will never defeat me; the kingdom is mine!' The beast then raises his hand and with his now superior magic, pulls the prince's sword from his grasp. 'I shall kill you with your own sword,' claims the beast. 'And when it's too late to stop, I will release your love, so she can see how it was she who killed you.'" Pan paused here for dramatic effect as his children gasped at this new wickedness.

"Daddy, no, the prince can't die!" Shade yelled at him, his sister strongly nodding her head in agreement.

"I know he can't die, my son. But the beast swoops down upon the prince, who stands tall to what he knows to be coming. And when he sees his princess' eyes return to their natural colour of blue, he can only smile at seeing her beauty returned to her. 'I love you,' he whispers to her as his heart is pierced by his own sword.

"Realizing what she has just done, the princess cries out in pain. 'No, no! I couldn't stop; stay with me, my love!' The prince's eyes close as he takes his last breath in her arms. 'No!' she screams." Pan saw the tears that fell from Nikki's eyes, as she and her brother looked to each other. But he couldn't stop here, for he knew his next piece would dry up her tears.

"The beast appears behind her in his human form, laughing at the princess' suffering. 'Cheer up, princess; you'll see him soon - in the underworld!'

"Upon hearing these words, the princess spins to face the beast, filled with the most righteous of hatreds and the prince's sword in hand. With a cry that freezes even the beast's blood, the princess lunges at the beast, kicking his chest. As he falls to the ground, she climbs his body, raises the sword over her head, and plunges it into the beast's skull. And not even the beast's unholy powers could save him from this death-dealing blow. His body explodes into darkness and the beast is no more."

"Daddy, you said this was a happy story, but the prince is still dead. The princess has to live alone now," complained his daughter, her mother's pout upon her face.

"I was just getting there, my dear. Now, there is a magic that is so unique that not many know of. It's called the Soul's Twin. And that's exactly what the prince and princess were, Soul Twins. Without even knowing they were doing it, the two of them were completing an ancient ritual of the Soul's Twin. For when the princess killed the beast in revenge of her dead love, there was a blinding flash of light. And once she could see, the princess only saw one thing: her prince, alive and whole, reaching for her. Crying out in delight, she reached for him and they embraced. 'I thought I killed you,' she cries to him.

"'I know,' he says. 'And I know you didn't mean to. I love you,' the prince declares.

"With tears in her eyes at the truthfulness of his words, the princess responds in kind, 'I love you, too.' And they live happily ever after." The children both clapped as he concluded his performance. Now finished his story, Pan went to his daughter first to kiss her goodnight.

"Daddy, is Mommy OK?" she asked him as he leaned down to kiss her.

"She's fine, sweetheart. She hasn't been sleeping much and that's making her act a little silly. Give her a few days and she'll be back to normal, I promise." He hoped this was a promise he could keep. He kissed her forehead and went to Shade's bed.

"Tell Mommy that the best way to fall asleep is to have

a lullaby sung to her, like she does for me," Shade said as Panken sat down on his bed.

"I will. Now get some sleep," he said as he kissed his son's forehead. "Goodnight you two, I love you."

"Goodnight Daddy, we love you," they chimed in unison. Panken walked to the door, and with a wave of his hand, extinguished the light. With an internal sigh, he went to find his wife.

Chapter 25:

A Lesson on Toxai

When Panken returned to their chambers, Iselda was pacing the length of the room. "They're still worried about you. I told them that you hadn't been sleeping well. Shade suggested a lullaby," Pan told her, stopping her pacing.

Iselda felt tears come to her eyes at the mention of her son's attempt at comfort. "They know we lie to them and yet they still try to help; we have the sweetest children in the world." Now the tears flowed freely.

Pan went to her and held her tight in his strong arms. "It's OK, we lie to spare them pain. Innocence shouldn't be torn away in one grand swoop, but in many tiny ones over time. Now what's this business of 'personal war'? I don't think I've ever heard that term before."

In a desperate attempt to lighten the mood Iselda quipped, "After ten years of reading yourself to sleep every night, you still have no knowledge of the world." Pan gave a half smile but wordlessly urged her to get serious. "Personal war is a philosophy the Toxans believe in. Before Annabelle first became Empress, Toxai was a land ruled by lords constantly trying to outwit each other. It got to the point that civil war was a constant possibility, but no definitive factions could be drawn as each lord no longer trusted his equals. So instead of having the country kill itself, the idea came that only those with grievances would fight.

"After about a year of back and forth fighting and killing, a new set of rules was introduced; rules that if broken meant loss of title and banishment from the country. The war was to be declared in writing before any attack could be issued. And perhaps the most important rule was that only the two parties involved could be killed - there were to be no bystander casualties. But anything else that made your opponent submit was allowed.

"This is what Annabelle has declared against me: my family and friends will not be killed, but you can guarantee they'll be harmed. That is why I'm having the men look for a girl: because she is the Empress of Toxai, not a girl. And I will not let anything destroy the innocence of my children before they are even five years old!"

Iselda could tell this was a lot for Pan to take in just by how long it took him to respond. "OK, makes sense when you think about it. But why has she waited all this time? You seemed a little surprised to have this happen now. And what does she have against you, anyway? The note said you tried to kill her and that you broke an oath..."

Remembering these parts of her past, Iselda bowed her head. "In one of my first lives, I found myself in Noigler, the capital of Toxai. Rumours of the newly reincarnated Empress had spread across the country. As this was her first death, most people were, naturally, wary of a thirteen-year-old girl claiming she was the reincarnated Empress that had died six months previous. I was drawn to the possibility of another immortal to spend eternity with. I waited to introduce myself until it was confirmed that by some miracle, the Empress had been reincarnated.

"We became very close; she was probably my first real friend - I could tell her anything. At the height of this friendship, we vowed to be friends for all eternity, to take care of each other always, and, what I'm sure was a bid to make me think I was acting like my mothers, reject the company of men so long as we lived.

"Also during this time was when I started to think that death might be better if it lasted longer than five minutes. We fought when I confided this in her; she claimed dying was the sign of a weak soul, and the wish to die the weakest of all. It was then I tested a theory I had about our immortality: only dying of natural causes allowed us to come back to life. After a week of acting like all was forgiven and we were once again friends, I crept into her room and tried to suffocate her, as my powers caused a natural death. She overpowered me and gave me the night to leave the country.

"When the sun rose the next day, she let the Crusaders know who I was. It only took them two weeks to find and kill me. Since then, I've used false names in the hopes of not being rediscovered and betrayed. It would appear that having me burned to death was not enough to satisfy her wrath." Iselda shivered at the prospect that Annabelle's wrath was to be visited upon all she loved. It was not often she wished to have her powers back, but this was certainly one time when she needed them back.

"She sent the Crusaders after you? You were friends with the Empress of Toxai?" Pan asked with what seemed to

Iselda like wonder, and not the horror she suspected he'd respond with. "Is there anything you haven't done, my love?" He was amazed at her life experiences?!

But she half indulged him, anyway. "It would appear I haven't protected my family like I swore I would." Tears had returned to her eyes, as she thought of her beautiful children down the hall. Pan pulled her back into his arms as he saw the tears and gently rocked her from side to side.

"No harm will come to us; we won't be used against you. I won't allow it. Shade and Nikki are safe, and I am more than able to take care of myself, if need be. Now, you need to rest; it's late and I doubt you're going to sleep much as it is. If you want, I'll put you under a sleeping spell; dreamless and you're sure to get enough rest."

"There's only one thing I need tonight," she said, shaking her head.

"What's that?" asked Pan, clearly curious.

To answer his question, she took his hand and led him over to their bed. Pulling him in close, she whispered, "You," into his ear and started to kiss him. Pan took to the hint quickly and soon had pushed her onto the bed where he slowly loved his wife for the rest of the night.

Chapter 26:

Annabelle's Conditions

The next morning, Iselda woke with the sun. Quietly pulling herself away from her husband, she quickly dressed and went to see how the search for Annabelle was going. She was just about to enter the throne room when she saw Shaw. He visibly paled as she approached him.

"Your highness, please forgive me. I had no idea the girl was a threat, she seemed so harmless I-"

"Enough, I know you aren't to blame for this, Shaw; you're just the messenger. So stop begging for forgiveness, it's been given. Just tell me, have you found the girl who gave you the letter?" Iselda said before she had to listen to more of his grovelling.

"No, my lady. But every available guard has been tasked with finding her. Lykane was able to draw an exceptional likeness, so we should have her soon." No sooner had Shaw said this, that General Vanto entered the throne room leading a small girl to Iselda's side. The girl was skinny, even by Toxan standards, and had light brown hair and eyes that were a brown somewhere between her husband's and his best friend's hues. She didn't look more than thirteen or fourteen. She understood why Shaw hadn't assumed she was a threat, Annabelle looked positively innocent.

"My Queen, we found the girl you requested. She's unarmed and appears to be alone," he said soberly, clearly uncertain about detaining a girl.

"Thank you, Vanto. Please, leave us." The two guards uneasily put fists to their hearts and had only taken a step away when Iselda continued, "And General, a verbal reprimand is all that is needed." Vanto nodded his head in understanding. Turning her attention back to Annabelle, Iselda lost all pleasantness. "What are you doing here, Annabelle? You've had centuries to do this; why are you insisting on starting a personal war with me now?"

"I insist on nothing, Iselda. We will engage in this and see it to its conclusion. As for why now, your continued existence only came to my attention five years ago. I only had to wait for that body to die before I could continue what the Crusaders clearly failed to do."

"You know better than most that you should never send a man to do a woman's job, Annabelle. But they did kill me, burned me to ashes; it was quite painful."

"That's good to hear, Iselda; but you still live - and you broke our vows! You've lain with a man, and bore his children-"

"Leave my children out of this! They are innocent! If you lay a finger on them-"

"Relax, Iselda. I'm not so heartless." For a moment, Iselda thought Annabelle was telling the truth, and she believed her. "You always wanted children, and I would not tear that from you. No, your children will not be harmed

- physically, anyway."

"What is it you want, Annabelle? We can't die, so why are you here, if not to hurt my family?" Iselda was now quite confused by the actions of her old friend.

"Your children are not the only people you would risk your life to save; you have friends and a husband who will sacrifice themselves before letting you be harmed. And you can die now; you gave up everything your mothers gave you - all to be with a man. We could have ruled together, but you betrayed all we stood for; you brought this upon yourself."

"And if I were to kill myself now, would you be sated?"

"No, I wouldn't be! Taking the coward's way out to be noble is not an option you have; for if you do, your debt falls to those of your bloodline! Either you die by my hand, or your children do. Or, if you wish for your children to live and no harm to come to your loved ones, come back to Toxai with me. I'm returning home now. If after a month after my return you are not in my palace, the real warfare will begin. Goodbye Iselda, hope to see you soon." Without looking back, Annabelle turned and left. Iselda followed her, making sure that she left without any detours.

Chapter 27:

Heartbreaking Goodbyes

When Iselda returned to the throne room, Pan was seated in his chair. He looked relieved to see her when she came in. "I was worried last night was goodbye. I heard they found her; what happened?" His voice was strained, and Iselda realized that this turn of events might bring back painful memories for him.

She went to him and pulled him out of his chair and into her arms. She was seeking as much comfort as she was giving, and he seemed to understand this. "She came to give her conditions. If I wish for her to not harm anyone, I'm to be at her palace within a month. If I choose war, she claims she will not harm the children; but should I kill myself to try and end this," here Iselda couldn't think about what she had been promised. But she pushed through the pain, "If I sacrifice myself, she will kill Shade and Nikki."

Iselda felt Panken stiffen at this revelation. "And how long will you be gone?" he asked, knowing her plan without her saying it.

"For as short a time as possible, but I believe she'll

have me stay until I die." Tears were in her eyes, flowing uncontrollably. "I don't want to go, but she's left me no other choice, Pan. Please say you know a way to stop this. I-I-I can't leave my babies; I won't leave you!" From here, her speech was unintelligible.

"Shh-shh. I know, I know. I'll look for something. To free you, all of Braria will help."

"We'll help too, Mommy," Shade and Nikki declared together as they entered the room hand-in-hand. Iselda's legs gave out as she heard her children prove they were aware something was troubling their parents. Tears anew crashed through her eyes. The two of them ran to her, worry etched identically on their faces. "Mommy...?"

Wiping her eyes, Iselda pulled her children in close. "I'm ok, you just scared me." The twins looked at her and then at each other, communicating in ways she couldn't fathom. But when they looked back at her, she knew they didn't believe her.

"Did Daddy sing you a lullaby last night, to help you sleep?" Shade asked.

"No," she answered truthfully. But upon seeing him glare at his father, she quickly added, "But he did help me relax and that helped me very much. He said you wanted him to sing to me; but you know how good a singer Daddy is." This brought a smile to Shade's face as he knew his father was not good at singing. Pan just rolled his eyes; this was a bit of a sore subject for him.

"Why are you crying, Mommy? Why are you sad?" Nikki asked. And by the look on her face, Iselda knew she could not lie, again, to her children.

"Mommy's sad because she has to go away for a while,

and she doesn't want to," Iselda said. "I want to stay here and plan for your birthday in a few months."

Not even the mention of their birthday celebration made the two of them stop thinking about what troubled her. She really did have the sweetest children in the world. "We'll go with you, Daddy too, and we'll have our birthday with you," Nikki said, thinking this would make her mother stop crying.

But Iselda just shook her head, more tears flowing. "I would love it if you could come with me. But this is something Mommy has to do on her own. You two have to stay here with Daddy and help him with the petitioners, answering just like Mommy would. You two are strong and smart, and Daddy's going to need your help while Mommy's gone. Can you be brave for Mommy and Daddy?" *Dear spirits, I don't want to leave them, but it's the only way to keep them safe. Help me, please, Mothers.*

They both nodded that they could be brave for their parents. "We'll be brave, Mommy," Shade said. "When do you leave?"

"Not today?" asked Nikki, clearly worried that she was leaving right now.

"No, no sweetheart! Mommy doesn't have to leave for a couple of days. But I want to spend every moment I can with you and your brother, is that alright?"

In response, the two of them gave her the biggest and tightest hug they'd ever given her. Iselda took this to mean yes, and that made her smile. "Of course, Mommy, whatever you want," they whispered to her as they hugged her.

Standing up, Iselda tried to put on a smile. "OK, Mommy's hungry and she knows you are too. So why don't we go into the kitchen and ask Chef Alix for something to eat?" she asked them in the most enthusiastic voice she could. They both nodded and were tugging her hands. "You two get a head start; I need to talk with Daddy for a quick minute and then I'll be right behind you." She gave them a smile, which was returned more sincerely and then they took off.

"How long do you plan on staying?" Pan asked when they could no longer hear the sound of their children.

"A week," Iselda said, her smile gone. "Can you promise me something?"

Pan stepped in front of her, seeming to realize that she couldn't face him on her own at the moment. "Anything," he said solemnly.

"Promise me you will never tell them the full truth of all this. Promise me you won't tell them where I am; I don't want them to grow up and try to come rescue me. Toxai is to be no more to them than a far off country. And above all else, don't send someone to find me, or come looking for me yourself." She couldn't look him in the eye as she asked these things of him. It hurt enough to ask.

"Iselda...?" The pain in his voice was all she could bear. Without waiting for his answer she fled the room in tears - tears that she would have to hide from her children in two minutes.

※

Pan didn't know how long he stayed standing there, staring at the spot where his wife had stood. It wasn't until he was slapped hard across the face that he came out of his trance. Before him stood his best friend and the namesake for his son, Shade; he had his arm poised to hit him again.

"Ah, so you are alive," Shade said with a smile, as Pan rubbed his face.

"Not for much longer," Pan responded in a dejected voice.

Clearly sensing something was wrong, Shade's smile disappeared and he became serious at once. "What's happened? You wouldn't stand still for hours on end and ignore me for twenty minutes if something wasn't happening."

"Last night Iselda got a threat from an old friend. This morning when the one that gave the threat was caught, the two chatted, and Iselda was given the choice between having her loved ones hurt or going to Toxai and restating the friendship she and its Empress once shared. She's leaving in a week, and I can't do anything to help her. She won't even let me tell Shade and Nikki what's happening or where she's going." Pan was close to tears as the events of the past day came to him. "I can't just let her walk into this and not do anything, Shade; what do I do?"

"I'm not sure there's really anything you can do. But knowing you, you'll find a way to set her free; you won't rest until you do. And I'll help in whatever way I can. Iselda's family and you do anything for family."

Pan was deeply touched by his pseudo-brother's words. "You always know what to say to make me feel better, brother. I don't know what I'd do if I lost you."

"You'd probably marry my wife," Shade said with a small smile.

Pan looked at Shade in shock. Not since Shade had started to see Marina, had Pan made any brazen comment about his best friend's wife. Many times over his decade long hiatus Pan had thought of Marina, but his love for Shade had always been foremost in his mind. "Shade, I'd never-"

"I know, Pan. I know you would never do anything to hurt me; whether I was dead or not. And I'm sorry I said it; it was just something to try and make you smile. It's behind us and we need to focus on Iselda. Tell me everything you know, so that I can help as much as possible," Shade said as he pulled Pan out of the throne room and to a more private area of the castle.

Chapter 28:

Letters

The last week Iselda was to spend in Braria went too quickly for her. She wanted to have been stricken ill, making her unable to leave; anything that gave her a reason to stay with those she held most dear. But nothing ever happened.

True to her word, she spent every moment with her son and daughter, trying desperately to memorize everything about them. They did anything and everything together for that last week. But she had not seen Pan since she ran from his side. She needed him now, more than ever.

After she had put the children to sleep for the last time, she started to pack. She only packed a few dresses and a couple of travelling outfits. She also packed one special dress, her blackblood wedding dress, as well as pictures Lykane had drawn of her family and closest friends. She was just about to write her goodbye letters when there was a knock on the door.

Composing herself before going to answer it, she wiped away the tears, but the sadness would not go away. She opened the door to find her children, her sadness mirrored upon their faces. Only sobs came as she beckoned them to her. They ran to her and all three released the tears that had been threatened since she told them she was leaving. "Oh my darlings, I'm sorry, Mommy is sorrier than you'll ever know. Forgive me, please."

"We know, Mommy; you have to go, to keep us safe," Nikki said. Iselda could not say anything to this; all she could do was nod. They had figured it out, despite her best efforts to conceal the truth. "Daddy will save you, Mommy; he promised he would."

"We want you to have something, so we know you're safe," Shade said, pulling a piece of cloth from his pocket. He handed it to her.

When she opened the cloth, she audibly sobbed. Wrapped in the cloth were a ring and a necklace, both bearing the intertwined K's that made up the Kanta family crest. Both were made from the purest Brarian silver, and clearly made for someone older than her children. Engraved in each was the phrase: *To love someone is to hold them in your heart forever*. She clutched the cloth in her hand and pulled it to her heart. "How long have you two had these?" she asked, when she felt her voice was steady enough.

Despite everything, they both blushed at this. "One day when we were playing, we decided to play dress up. So we went into yours and Daddy's closet and we found a box with our names on it. We looked inside and took these," Nikki said, head bowed in shame. When Shade saw what his sister was doing, he too, bowed his head.

"It's alright, sweetheart; these were made for you. The day you were born, after I had recovered some of my strength and you were asleep, I found the finest craftsman in the city and I asked him to make me these. Only the two of us knew they existed. I was going to give them to you for your sixteenth birthday. They were to become heirlooms, for you to give to your children, and they to theirs, and so on until the end of time." She expected the tears to flow as she told them this, but none came. Perhaps she could not cry anymore. "I can't take these, they're yours. They were meant to remind you of me, not me of you." She handed back the cloth to Shade.

Before he took the cloth, Shade looked at his sister, who nodded at him. He accepted the cloth, but took the necklace out and handed it back to Iselda. "Take the necklace, Mommy. We can share the ring. Now we can remember each other," he said. Her heart broke as her children refused to have her leave them without a memento.

Iselda put her arms around them and hugged them as tight as she could. "Thank you. I will never take it off," she said as she took the necklace and put it around her neck. Its weight only served to remind her that she was about to lose all she loved, everything she had wanted from life. Standing up, she looked into their eyes, Nikki's beautiful blues and Shade's deep browns that were twins to his father's, and did the bravest thing she'd ever done. "OK, you two need to get back to bed, Mommy needs to finish packing for her trip." She'd tried to smile, but the overwhelming pain she felt made it come across as a grimace.

They held up their hands to her and she knelt down to give them one last hug. She tried to put every bit of unconditional love for them into it, as she knew they were doing to hers. "We love you, Mommy," they said in unison. Love flooded her heart as she held her children to her.

Releasing them and kissing them both she said, "And Mommy loves you." The tears seemed to be back, but she held them at bay trying to be strong for her babies one last time. "Now, off to bed," she said as she led them to the door.

As she shut the door, Iselda's will to hold in the pain left her and she truly vocalized her suffering. For nearly an hour, she sat slumped against the door, crying out her heart. She finally pulled herself together enough to get up and walk over to the writing desk. She forced herself to write four letters, one to her family at large, and one to each of them individually, starting with Nikki's.

> *My Darling Daughter,*
>
> *You cannot know how it pains me to have to leave you like this, and I hope you never have to know what it is I'm feeling. You can't even imagine how long it was that I wished that I would be blessed with a daughter. And a more beautiful girl has never existed.*
>
> *I used to imagine watching my daughter grow up, and all the things that I'd teach her - all the knowledge I'd gained through the years, helping her find love, and the joys of motherhood. There was supposed to be no secrets between us, and nothing would ever be too much for you to ask of me. And the fact that I will never get to do these things with and for you destroys my heart like nothing else.*
>
> *I hope you understand what I mean when I say that I'm writing your letter first*

because it's easier. I've imagined saying these words to you for my whole life and not having to think right now helps. I love you Nikki, more than I can put words to. You are my firstborn, and I want nothing more than your happiness, no matter what that is.

Forgive me,

Your loving mother, Mommy
P.S. Remember, I will always love you.

Once she was finished the other three letters, Iselda sealed them all in one envelope and placed it on Pan's pillow, just like he'd done for her on their wedding day. And with a final look to the room that had been her home for the last five years, she picked up her bag and left.

For the past week, Pan had spent every moment combing the volumes of texts in the castle's Blackreich and libraries, not even eating or sleeping in his need to find some form of solution. But when he realized that the day Iselda had said she was leaving had arrived, he rushed to their chambers. Hoping to catch her before she was gone forever, he raced to say his final goodbye. But when he got there, all that was left was an envelope on his pillow. Realizing he'd never even told her he loved her again before she left caused Pan to drop to his knees. He'd wasted his last opportunity to spend time with her, completely out of her presence.

The next thing that Pan knew was that his children were holding him and crying. He held them to him as tightly as he could, as if his arms alone could keep the world at bay. It was then that he remembered the envelope. Lifting his children up and placing them on his bed, he picked up the envelope and showed it to them. "Mommy left us a goodbye," he said as he opened it. Pulling the letters out, he noticed only one was directed to all of them, and it was here he started.

"'To my loving family. First, let me say that I love all of you with all my heart, and that it shatters my heart to have to leave you like this. I never wanted this to happen and I cannot apologize enough. I wanted us to be a family forever.

"'Second, I've left you all an individual letter, saying all that I never got the chance to say. They are private and should not be shared with each other, as I wrote them specifically for each of you.

"'And finally, though we all wish for me to be in mine and Daddy's room right now with you, I plead that you do not attempt to find me and bring me home. Your lives are worth more to me than my own, and I do not want you risking yours for me.

"'With all my love, Mommy.'" Panken finished reading the letter, and then handed his children their respective letters. "Now, remember what Mommy said, these are private." They both nodded their understanding and began to silently read their letters in private. Panken got off the bed and went to the writing desk to read his letter.

My dearest husband,

As I know you will not rest until we are back in each other's arms, at least grant my request that you will not be restless in front of Shade and Nikki. They have to accept that I'm gone and you being private about your searching for answers will help. Be careful, though, they are more intuitive and resourceful than we could have ever imagined. They knew why I was leaving without me telling them. Protect them and teach them and let them make mistakes; they look up to you like no other person in the world - don't destroy that. Do everything we said we would do when we learned we were going to be parents.

I'm going to stop at Kailee's and Sabrina's and have them come and help you. I know you won't admit to needing the help, but just take it. And don't forget the people; you are still the king and cannot give up that duty just for me.

I'm writing your letter last because it is too painful to have to say goodbye to you forever. And I'm sorry that the other night did turn out to be goodbye. But I don't think I could have handled it if I saw you right now. Saying goodbye to those two angels we call son and daughter was more than I could take. The past five years of my life have been the most wonderful of the many

I've lived, and that's all because of you, my love. If there is one thing I regret, it is that we only had the five years, and not the fourteen we could have had, had I not been afraid of what you would do to me if I came to you the moment I stepped foot in Terang. I'm sorry for making you wait, and I'm sorry for putting you through all this. I can only wish for a permanent death now so that we may be united in the underworld.

Goodbye Panken, I will always love you.

Your Loving Wife, Iselda.
  P.S. Tell my babies that I love them, every day.

The page the letter was written on had numerous tear stains on it, from both his and Iselda's tears. He realized that his hands were shaking, so he put down the letter and put his face in his hands. How he hoped that his palms would force the tears to stay in his eyes. He hadn't felt like this since his mother died.

After a while, he realized that someone was rubbing his back. Not being able to have his children being the ones to comfort him, he reached out to stop the hand. But while the hand was small, it was too big to be either Shade's or Nikki's. Turning to see who was rubbing his back, he was surprised to see Marina.

"Marina, what are you doing here?" Pan asked, a little too harshly for his dead voice.

"All I can do," she said, as she took one of his hands in both of hers and gently squeezed it. "Shade told me what happened. I'm sorry, Pan. I wish I could help, but I know that I can only be a shoulder to cry on."

"I may need more than one."

"Then it's a good thing I have two, isn't it?" She tugged on his hands and Pan stood up. No sooner had she put her arms around him did Pan truly start to cry.

Chapter 29:

Helpful Friends and Family

Iselda took a calming breath before she knocked on the door. She knew that Sabrina had set herself up as a healer, working in closer to the centre of town. Kailee, she knew, would be at home, probably cleaning. How she envied the simplicity of the girl's life.

Iselda was reminded of the first time she'd come to her friends' home to tell them she was pregnant with twins. Like then, she had her hood up to conceal her identity, but this time it was the middle of the day. Finally steeled to what she knew must be done, Iselda knocked.

It took Kailee less than five seconds to open the door. Lifting her head so her friend knew who she was, she brought a finger to her lips to keep the girl from calling out. "May I come in?"

Kailee immediately recognized that something was wrong by the sound of Iselda's voice and stepped aside so that she could enter. Closing the door behind them, she asked, "What's wrong, Iselda?"

Iselda saw the worry in her eyes and couldn't stop herself

from letting out a cry and hugging the girl. "Everything," she sobbed into her friend's shoulder.

"Come and sit, and tell me what I can do to help," Kailee said in her calm voice, pulling her over to the couch. "Start from the beginning and take as long as you need."

"The beginning, right," Iselda said, taking a few breaths to help her calm down. "Well, I guess this begins in one of my first lives. I found myself in Toxai, where rumours were scandalizing the country of a girl who had walked into the capital and declared herself the reincarnation of the recently dead Empress. After a couple of weeks, the palace declared that the girl was in fact their dead ruler reborn.

"Naturally, this intrigued me, as I thought myself unique in regards to immortality. So I introduced myself to the girl, and found a kindred spirit. For the first time in my existence, I had a friend who I could tell anything to, without fear of betrayal. I had someone like you, Kailee." At this compliment, both women smiled.

"As we grew closer, we came to believe ourselves in love." Kailee was slightly shocked at this. "Now that I know love, I know what we had wasn't love; but that didn't stop us from pledging ourselves to each other, and only each other. We were to rule Toxai together, immortal queens.

"But I had lived for many years already, and eternal life was starting to lose its lustre. One night after making love, I confided this to her. She became enraged like never before, calling me weak for wanting to die, and threw me out of the room. I knew then that she didn't love me, and I was deeply saddened by this.

"It was then that I decided to test a theory I'd had. Every time I had died, and the one time she had, it was from natural causes. So I thought, maybe we had to die unnatural deaths. I acted as if all was forgiven for a week, and then when I thought she was sleeping one night, I took a pillow and tried to suffocate her with it." Kailee raised a hand to her mouth in horror at this, but Iselda continued anyway. "Naturally, she woke up and pushed me off her. She screamed at me to get out and to never show my face to her again.

"So I left that night. But the next morning she summoned a group of soldiers who hunted witches and others of magic, and told them who I was and sent them after me. Two weeks later, they found and captured me. They burnt me alive until I was no more than a pile of ashes. That was the most painful thing I have ever experienced."

Kailee was clearly mortified by Iselda's tale. But she knew the worst was yet to come.

"Ever since then, I knew immortality could not be escaped. I used different names to hide who I was, so that she never would know I'd survived. Until I married Pan.

"Somehow, word got to her that I was the new queen of Braria. Last week, she declared what the Toxans call personal war against me. It's a form of war they practice that only allows the warring parties to die, but that doesn't mean you can't hurt those they care about to make your enemy submit. She said that if I returned to Toxai, she would spare my loved ones." Now the truth seemed to dawn on Kailee, and she knew why Iselda was so distraught.

"I had to say goodbye to my husband and to my four-year-old children, tell them I will never see them again, so that they would be safe." Here is where the tears started to flow. Immediately Kailee stood up and moved closer so she could offer a comforting hug to her friend. "And now, Kailee, I must ask you to do me one more kindness."

Kailee looked as if her heart had broken, just hearing her friend's misery. "Oh Iselda, anything; anything at all." Her eyes had turned to steel, showing she meant what she said.

"My family's been torn apart; I need you to fill the hole my leaving has caused. I need you to be the mother to my children. Will you do this for me?" Iselda trusted many people to do many things; but for the most important thing, she trusted only the woman in front of her.

Kailee looked completely shocked. Her mouth moved, but no sound escaped it for a few minutes as she gathered herself. "Are...are you sure?" she finally asked.

"They are the most precious things I've ever laid eyes upon. You are one of the kindest and most beautiful people I know, Kailee; and it is only you that I trust with this duty. From the moment that I knew I had to leave, from the moment I knew I would never see my children again, I only thought of you as the guiding hand that would raise them."

Kailee was speechless. Iselda knew that she loved Shade and Nikki as her own children, and that they loved her as a beloved aunt. She also knew that this was a large burden to place on her friend. But Kailee nodded her head. "I thank you, for thinking of me as your surrogate. I love those two so much, and I know they love me. I will try my best to live up to your expectations and level of excellence."

Kailee gave Iselda a hug, knowing this was ripping her friend's heart to pieces. Iselda clung to her friend as tightly as she could, seeking much more solace than Kailee could offer. "Thank you," she whispered in Kailee's ear, never meaning the words more than right then.

They stayed locked in this embrace until Sabrina came home. When she saw that Iselda was lying on the couch and silently crying, she rushed to her side and began to hold her tight. She was also about to ask what had happened, when Kailee shook her head. Iselda was thankful for their silence; having to hear and explain her pain made it hurt more than it already did. She never thought she'd wish this, but she wished she could forget about her family so she would not feel so heartbroken at having lost them.

After a while, Sabrina got up to make some supper. Kailee helped Iselda move to the table when Sabrina said it was ready. Supper was to be soup. It was hot and the burn helped Iselda take her mind off everything for a while.

When everyone had finished their second bowl, Sabrina looked at Iselda, then at Kailee who gave a slight nod. "What's wrong, Iselda?" she asked in a tentative voice.

Unable to answer this same question again, Iselda simply said, "Pan needs your help to help me. If you'll excuse me, I need to rest and I can't hear this again. Kailee will explain all you need to know." And without looking back at her hosts, Iselda ran out of the room, fell onto a bed, and cried herself to sleep.

The next morning, Iselda got out of bed and started to get ready to leave. It was then that she realized she had taken Sabrina's and Kailee's room. As she walked down the hall, she noticed that both her friends were either still up or had risen before her. Sabrina went up to her with tears in her eyes and silently gave her a hug. Iselda returned it, trying to wordlessly let Sabrina know her sympathies were much appreciated. "I've told Pan that I'd send you to help. He's most likely not slept in days and may be a little hostile; if he is, please don't hold it against him. Let him know that in order to see every option clearly, he'll need to rest. Don't let him work himself to death." Kailee and Sabrina nodded they would see to this. "Sabrina, do you mind if I have a minute with Kailee?"

Nodding, Sabrina answered, "Whatever you need, Iselda." She left the room to give them privacy.

"Kailee, what I told you, yesterday, about how me and the Empress used to be lovers," Kailee nodded to show she remembered, "don't tell Pan; he knows that she was my first friend, but he doesn't know how close we truly were. As far as he knows, we pledged to be friends forever and swore off the company of men. If he knew the full extent of our relationship, his heart would be even more broken than it already is. Please, don't tell him Kailee."

Kailee nodded her head. "I didn't even tell Sabrina; I figured you wouldn't want others to know."

"Thank you; you really are one of the kindest people I've ever known." Kailee just smiled and bowed her head in gratitude. "I'm sorry for last night; I left you to explain everything and then took your bed, I should-"

"It's ok, we both understand completely. What you're going through, I couldn't imagine what it feels like. But I know that in your castle there are three people who are feeling exactly the way you are and who are trying their hardest to find ways to bring you home." Kailee gave a weak but encouraging smile. "This country loves you, and many of her peoples will not stop until you are returned to us."

"But I've asked them not to. I know Pan won't listen to that, and that's why I'm having Sabrina go with you. But my children, my sweet angels, must not entertain notions of my return. Don't let them spend their lives hoping that someday I'll return; false hope is the cruelest of fates."

"Iselda...? You can't seriously want that, for your children to give up on you."

"No, I don't want that, but it will save them pain in the long run and help them move on. For them to hope that I will one day be returned to them is what I hope they will dream of, even though it will be painful when they realize I won't be coming back." Iselda let out a sigh, as she knew what being told that she wasn't coming back would do to her babies. If it weren't broken into a million pieces already, her heart would have broken because of it. "There is one thing I ask you do. Every day, when you wake up and when you're putting them to bed, tell my little ones that Mommy loves them." Iselda's throat closed as she thought of her children, and she was unable to continue.

Kailee nodded her assent. "I will, every morning and every night." Realizing that the time for words had passed, Kailee stepped forward and hugged her friend. Iselda noticed Sabrina was just entering the room, so she motioned her over to them. Iselda was then stuck between them in their last three-way hug.

After a minute, Iselda released herself from them. She looked at her friends and yet more tears came to her eyes. "Thank you, you two. Better friends would be hard for me to find, and none could replace you. I've trusted you with the welfare of the three most important people to me; please take good care of them. Now, goodbye." Without waiting for a response, she turned and headed for the door. She turned back for the briefest of moments, and saw that both Sabrina and Kailee had tears in their eyes. She then stepped out into the morning, continuing on her march to prison.

Pan couldn't do anything. He couldn't eat or sleep, nor could he talk. The only thing he could do was hold his children to himself. Both Shade and Nikki begged him to get up and help bring Mommy back, and as much as he wanted to, his heart constricted whenever he tried. Shade had tried bringing him texts from the castle libraries for him to read that he thought might be helpful, but the words had disappeared before him. Marina seemed to be the only one to get him to move; she'd lie down on his bed and hold his hand, he could only squeeze hers in return.

On what he guessed to be the fourth day since Iselda had left, he felt the tingle of magic flow through him. The magic helped him regain control of his body; it relaxed his muscles and cleared his senses. Once his sight wasn't blurry anymore, he saw Sabrina sitting beside him. She was breathing hard, as if she'd run all over the castle. "Are you there?" she asked.

He tried to sit up, but she put a hand on his chest to keep him down. "Yes." His voice was weak and barely above a whisper. "It's been a long time since I felt another's magic flow through me."

"I'm surprised you felt anything; you paralysed yourself

with your own magic. I've been here for nearly three hours trying to get you to relax. I had no idea a person could paralyse himself with his own magic; what did you do?" Sabrina asked with cautious curiosity.

"To be honest, I don't know. Marina moved me onto the bed, I closed my eyes, and when I opened them, I could barely move. How long have you been here?" His throat was dry, making his voice rougher. Sabrina handed him a glass, and he swallowed its contents in a single gulp. Whatever it was, it tasted awful, but he could feel his throat getting wetter.

"About half a day. I spent an hour or two with my niece and nephew before Shade came and told me about you. Kailee's still with them." After a short pause she asked, "How are you, Pan?"

Seeing the genuine concern in her face, Pan lifted his hand. She took it in hers. "I'm in more pain than I thought possible. When we were in Vagala, she gave me a dose of pain. It was only for a second, but it felt as if my entire body was being poked with white hot, thin pieces of metal." Pan gave a small shiver at the memory.

Sabrina nodded, with a small smile, "I remember."

"This is worse. Compared to what I'm feeling now, the pain she gave me was a pulled muscle." Sabrina winced at the comparison. "It should not be possible to feel this way and still be alive." Sabrina squeezed his hand and he felt the familiar tingle of her magic spread through him, heating him as if he had crawled under a thick blanket. "Thank you, but that doesn't help."

"It's all I can do. I can't heal these kinds of wounds, no one can. The only way you can get better is if we bring her back.

And we need you at your best to do that. So get some rest and some food. I'll be in the Blackreich when you're ready." Dropping his hand, Sabrina got off the bed and turned to leave, but stopped at the door when Pan called her back.

"How is she?" Pan feared the answer, but needed to know it.

She just looked at him with a sad expression. She let out a sigh and said, "She feels all you feel; only magnified. She's lost everyone she cared about, and has probably never longed for death more."

Pan closed his eyes and let the tears flow as visions of his wife danced through his head.

Iselda knew she was in Toxai the moment she stepped foot in it. All vegetation was wilting, in a constant state of dying. Where she had once found curiosity, she now only saw her reflection. Like everything around her, she was slowly dying. The past day and a half of walking nearly directly west had seen her from OJA through Vanus to where she now stood, an hour past the Toxai-Vanus border.

She knew she was only a half day's walk from the palace beneath Noigler, but she could not force herself to continue at the moment. She fell to her knees and clutched the necklace her children had given her. She had lied to Kailee; being burnt to death was not as painful as this. From the pack she was carrying she removed a drawing, the newest of the three she'd brought. On the anniversary of her wedding this past year, Pan had asked Lykane to paint a large portrait of himself, Iselda, and their two children. It had taken a few hours, but the end result was so beautiful and life-like that Iselda had demanded a copy for herself, only smaller. This copy was just as beautiful and was now the only way she could ever see her family again.

As she cried over the picture, she felt a brushing on her back as if the wind was rubbing it. She turned and looked to see the pale outline of a woman. She wasn't dressed, though she didn't appear to be naked either. She seemed somehow familiar to Iselda; she just didn't know where she'd seen her. But then she saw her eyes, and she knew right away who this woman was.

"Your highness," Iselda said, addressing her predecessor.

"There is no need to be so formal, Iselda. We are family." Evelyn's voice had that eerie quality to it that Iselda now associated with the dead.

"Forgive me, Evelyn, but I feel we are not family anymore. I don't think I deserve to be called your family anymore." Iselda turned her head away in shame as she said this.

She felt the ghostly pull of fingers on her chin, urging her to look at her husband's mother. "You will always be part of my family," Evelyn said. This caused Iselda to finally turn her head and look at her. "You made my son the happiest I'd ever seen him," she said, indicating the picture Iselda had been crying over.

Iselda sobbed as she looked at the picture. "And now I've taken that happiness and thrown it away," she cried.

"No, child, that happiness has been stolen from both of you. You are not to blame for it. You are just as much a victim as the rest of your family."

This only made Iselda cry harder. "Please, go away,

Evelyn. I can't have you here, you remind me too much of them. Please go!" Iselda sobbed.

"They look just like you," Evelyn said, ignoring Iselda's wish. "Except for their eyes, those come from their father."

"That's the first thing he said, when he first held Nikki and she opened her eyes. He cried out at the fact that they were yours. It was then that I decided to give her your name, instead of my mother's," Iselda said, confiding the truth of the situation.

"Your mothers don't hold it against you, you know. They understood why you did what you did, as they do now. That is why I am here, to extend all of our sympathies and to offer you as much help as we can provide." Evelyn's voice was so calming that Iselda couldn't help but think that it was Pan talking to her.

"You talk like him, or he talks like you."

Evelyn just nodded. "Not many realized how much of me is present in him. People only see his father when they look at him. And while he is the spitting image of his father, his heart is mine. That is why he misses me so, as I miss him." If Iselda didn't know spirits couldn't cry, she would have sworn she saw a tear roll down the woman's cheek. "I cannot stay for much longer, my dear. The time for parting words is now."

Iselda felt a jolt of panic; despite her earlier plea, she didn't want Evelyn to go. "No, you can't go! I need you here with me." At this, Evelyn smiled. "Is there a way?" she asked desperately.

Seeming to know what was being asked of her, Evelyn answered, "I don't know; your mothers have gone to Hados to ask that very question. When they have an answer, I will come to you. Until then, stay strong my dear, and know that all those who love you are trying their hardest to help you." As soon as she was done talking, Evelyn became more transparent until she was gone.

New tears stung Iselda's eyes. But unlike before, these were tears of gratitude; gratitude that those who had never met her were even trying to help her. This gave her a new resolve. And while she knew that she was to be held hostage, she would fight her way through to the time when she would be freed.

Chapter 30:

The Secrets of the Twins

Kailee looked in the direction Shade and Nikki had suddenly, and simultaneously, turned their heads. The doorway they looked at was empty, which confused her. They suddenly turned to each other and a grin formed itself on both their faces. "Daddy!" they cried and ran out the door.

"Wait!" Kailee called after them, but it was too late. Getting up to chase after them, Kailee went out the door. Turning to her left, she heard them again call for their father, just as he rounded a corner further down the hall. Hand-in-hand, the children raced for Panken, who'd dropped to a knee to welcome them. Kailee ran down the hall to meet them and noticed that all three were smiling.

She couldn't explain what had just happened. Somehow, Shade and Nikki had both realized that their father was coming and had rushed to him, knowing exactly where he'd be.

"You're OK!" Nikki shouted as she continued to hug her father's neck.

"Yes sweetheart, I'm OK," he told them.

"Look Daddy, Auntie Kailee and Auntie Sabrina are here!" Shade said, with such enthusiasm that Kailee's heart swelled.

"Yes, I know; Auntie Sabrina's the one who made me better. It's good to see you, Kailee," Pan said, standing up and giving her a hug.

When after a minute he released her, both their hands were being tugged. "Come on, Daddy, come on Auntie Kailee," the twins said in unison. "We have work to do!"

"We do?" both Pan and Kailee asked together.

"How you do that?" Shade asked as both he and Nikki stopped pulling them and turned around, nearly getting run over in the process.

"Do what?" Kailee and Pan again asked together. Kailee was a little curious about the abrupt change in subject.

"Talk like us? Together," Nikki questioned.

As Kailee heard the answer to her question, all she could do was laugh. When Shade and Nikki looked at her like she hurt their feelings, she stopped laughing. Clearly, this was quite a serious matter for them. So she explained, "Oh, you guys, lots of people say things together like you do. Except when we do it, it's an accident - we don't mean to say the same thing at the same time, it just happens. Your Daddy and I aren't like you two; our minds aren't connected, we just happened to think the same things just now, that's all."

Shade and Nikki considered this for a second, looked at each other, and shrugged their shoulders. Then they turned around and started pulling Pan and Kailee again, back to their room. As they were being dragged, Kailee gave Pan a look asking if he thought that interaction was weird. He nodded, but shrugged his shoulders. He clearly thought nothing of it other than his twins being twins.

When they were all in the room, Shade and Nikki let go of Pan's and Kailee's hands. Shade went to close the door as Nikki went to her bed. Lifting her pillow, Nikki grabbed a ring that Kailee had never seen before, though it looked like it matched the necklace Iselda had been wearing. As soon as she grabbed it, she let out a shriek and dropped the ring back on the bed. Before either Pan or she could ask what was wrong, Shade ran to his sister's side and held the ring for himself. He got a puzzled look on his face for a few seconds and then broke into a smile, which was quickly mirrored by his sister. Kailee looked to Pan for an explanation but he seemed to be as confused as her.

Seeming to sense the confusion in their father and aunt, Shade and Nikki turned to them. "It's Mommy," Shade said, "she's not sad anymore!"

"Well, she's sad, just not like before. Something's happened to make her stronger, in here," Nikki explained with a tap to her chest, her heart.

Kailee was still confused and looked to Pan in hope of some clarification. But he only had eyes for his children, and the ring Shade held. "You can communicate with Mommy, with that ring?" he asked, pointing to it.

"Not like we do, Daddy," Nikki said, indicating her brother and herself. "More like..." she trailed off as she tried to find a comparison her father would understand.

"Like when Mommy had us in her tummy," Shade said. "She would know if everything was ok or not when we told her. Here," he said, as he took his father's hand and put the ring on his small finger. "Do you feel her? Do you feel the new strength in her? Her pain has been eating her heart, but something's happened to make it not hurt so much." Shade now reached for his sister's hand, which she gave. She then placed her other on top of her brother's, over the ring. "Now think of her, Daddy, and she will feel your love for her, and how much you miss her. Mommy will know how you will fight until she is back in your arms." Pan had closed his eyes as soon as Shade told him to think of Iselda. And as Kailee watched, Pan's face became serene and almost peaceful.

After a minute, the children removed their hands and the ring. Pan dropped to a knee and started to cry silently. But Kailee could tell that a great weight had been removed from his shoulders. As Shade went to return the ring to its place beneath Nikki's pillow, Nikki put a hand on her father's cheek. "That was beautiful, Daddy. Mommy is very blessed to have you love her as much as she loves you. What you just felt for her will give her lots of strength." She had tears in her eyes as well. If Kailee hadn't seen it with her own eyes, she wouldn't have believed that the words Shade and Nikki had just said to their father were from two four year olds talking; the words seemed more like something an adult would say.

Kailee took a step towards Pan but was stopped by Shade tugging on her hand. He shook his head at her and whispered, "Come with me, Aunt Kailee." Hoping to have something explained, she followed. But she was even more confused when he went to the floor-length mirror. Taking her hand in his, Shade mumbled something she couldn't understand. Suddenly, the mirror vanished, and in its place was a hallway. Shade led her through the hallway to what Kailee could only describe as a study. The room wasn't all that big and the small desk and bookshelves took up most of the room. In the back left corner, Kailee could see a staircase going down.

"Where are we?" she asked.

"Nikki and I call it the quiet room. We come here to rest and collect our thoughts." He seemed so grown up that Kailee was constantly reminding herself that he was only four.

"Why have you brought me here, Shade?"

"To talk to you about Mommy. You know things about her, even Daddy doesn't know. You are the one she asked to be our new Mommy. You have a bond with her that Daddy doesn't understand. Why are you so important to Mommy?" he asked.

"You don't understand either, do you?" Kailee asked him. He turned away from her, clearly upset by this. Kneeling down so she was at his eye level, she rubbed his back gently. "Sweetheart, your Mommy finds me so important because I'm the first person who showed her true kindness. After living her whole life fearing what people would do to her if she was open about herself with them, having someone know who she was and be kind to her felt really nice. I'm your Mommy's best friend because when she wanted a friend, I alone stepped up. And she's always remembered and cherished that moment."

Shade turned back so he was facing her again. He looked her up and down for a quick second and then was hugging her. "Thank you, Aunt Kailee," he whispered in her ear.

"You're welcome, sweetheart," she said, hugging him back. "Now, can I ask you a question?" she asked as she pulled away from the hug. When he nodded, his dark hair bounced carelessly and he had the biggest smile on his face she'd seen since she arrived. "You and Nikki have magic, don't you?

But it's a different kind of magic from your Daddy's, or even Aunt Sabrina's, isn't it?"

Shade turned his gaze down the hallway they'd come from. Kailee waited a few moments until he turned his head back to her. Grabbing her hand, he started to drag her back towards his room. When they had returned, she looked back to see the mirror had returned.

Nikki was smiling at Shade as she noticed, (more like sensed, Kailee thought) his return. Pan was sitting on Shade's bed, looking a little confused as Shade placed Kailee at his side. He then went to join his sister at the door, holding her hand. They just stared at the door for a minute, their smiles growing. Finally, after who knew what kind of clue, they opened the door to find Sabrina, hand poised as if ready to knock. They giggled as if they had planned this and it had all gone exactly how they hoped.

"Auntie Sabrina!" they chimed in unison as they grabbed her hands and led her to Kailee's free side. They then climbed Nikki's bed and faced them. "We want to tell you all something," Nikki said.

"Something that you've all noticed, but dismissed," continued Shade.

"We have magic!" they both declared. A declaration that was met with gasps from both Kailee's right and left.

"That's impossible!" Pan said. "I tested you for magic myself, the day you were born."

They were shaking their heads as soon as he said 'impossible'. "No, Daddy, it is possible. We have magic; it's just different from yours and Auntie Sabrina's," Nikki said.

"Your magic affects the body, our magic affects the soul," Shade clarified. "We can feel everyone's emotions; the more love between us, the better we can tell how you feel. That's why we knew why Mommy left or that you needed to let her know you loved her."

"We also don't need words to communicate with each other; since we are Soul Twins, our thoughts are never just in our head alone." This was met by more gasps from Kailee's sides, but she was lost as to why this news shocked them. Surely they'd noticed how they looked at each other and somehow seemed to be communicating.

"You're Soul Twins...?" Sabrina asked in wonder. Perhaps that was what the gasps were about. Whatever these 'Soul Twins' were, they must be something of magic, because Kailee had no idea what they were talking about.

Then the twins looked at each other in a way Kailee instantly recognized. She had seen Pan look that way at Iselda just as much as Iselda looked at Pan; she'd seen that look on Sabrina's face more times than she could count. It was the look only the deepest of lovers shared. Seeing it on the faces of these two four year olds was a little unsettling.

"Yes," they said in unison. "We are Soul Twins." Kailee looked to her left and right, hoping for someone to have an explanation for why this was such a big deal. When she looked at Pan, she noticed he'd gotten incredibly pale. All of a sudden, he just fell back; he'd fainted.

Kailee immediately got up and went to the other bed to shield the children from seeing this and allow Sabrina a chance to revive him. But then she noticed that both Shade and Nikki had a small, amused smile on their lips.

Behind her, Kailee heard the sound of Pan coming to and she returned to her seat. When Pan was seated properly, he gave his head a small shake. Nikki gave a little laugh and said, "Sorry, Daddy, but what we told you is the truth, and not a dream." She gave another small laugh but stopped immediately when he looked at her. Her smile changed from one of mischief to one of sympathy.

"Is… Is there anything else we should know about you two?" Pan asked, caution heavy in his voice.

Shade and Nikki gave a quick glance at each other and then nodded. "Not about us, no," Shade said.

"But about Auntie Marina, yes," Nikki continued. "She has the same magic we do." Kailee gasped along with the others this time. "She's not as strong as we are and she doesn't know it's magic, but it's true."

Sliding as one off the bed, Shade said, "We know this is a lot to take in, but you had to know. We'll let you work this out," Taking his sister's hand, they left the room, shutting the door behind them. Kailee, confused as ever, looked to Sabrina for some type of explanation.

Pan put his face in his hands; with everything going on this was exactly what he needed: another problem. First, his wife was kidnapped by an immortal enemy; now his children declare themselves Soul Twins. These last couple of weeks were quickly becoming his least favourite.

"Will one of you two please explain what that was all about?" Kailee asked. Pan looked at Sabrina, hoping she would explain.

When he realized that she wouldn't, he gave a sigh and stood up. "What don't you understand, Kailee?" he asked.

"The Soul Twins part; why is it so important and what does it all mean?"

"Ok, um, Soul Twins are basically magical soul mates. It's much more complicated but that's what it boils down to: two people who are so perfect for one another, that they share everything. And I mean everything: thoughts, emotions, desires. It's as if they were one person in two bodies; hence the term, two identical souls in two different people." That was the best Pan could do, for being put on the spot.

"So… that's why…?" Kailee started.

"The look?" interjected Sabrina, to which Kailee nodded. "Yes, they need no one else than the one whose hands they hold; they will never look for another. Soul Twins are so rare that people instinctually do not question it."

"But…they're four!" Kailee iterated. She seemed to be thinking of this differently than she should, Pan thought.

"It's not like you think it is, Kailee. The moment Soul Twins first meet each other, they know that this is the person they will spend the rest of their lives with. It's not necessarily romantic, even though most eventually end that way. They may grow to be chaste partners, though they will love no other. Perhaps, with them being so young, it gives us a chance to watch them, make sure they do nothing to ruin themselves or others." Pan sincerely hoped he was right.

"And you're OK with this?" Kailee shrieked at him.

"No, but I do accept it. And that is all I really can do. Think about it, Kailee, they are my children; I want nothing more than their happiness. And each other is what makes them happy. You love them, don't you? Don't you want them to be happy?" he asked her, forcing her to understand.

"Yes, I love them and yes I want them to be happy."

"Then you must accept this. You may not like it, but you have to accept it. For denying it, is a denial of them. And if you deny them, they will pull away from you. Remember, they can see our emotions," Pan said, hoping this would convince her.

Kailee looked to be confused, but she nodded her head. Pan was greatly relieved that she could accept this new challenge. "Is there anything else that flew over my head in that tell-all?"

Pan would let Sabrina answer this one; he needed to think of ways to get his wife back. Now that he knew her resolve had changed to that of a fighter's, he knew he had to renew his efforts. "If there was, I think it might have gone over all of our heads," Sabrina said. Pan stood and the door opened, revealing Shade and Nikki.

"We knew you'd understand!" they squealed as they ran to him. He dropped down and gave them a hug. "Go, Daddy," they said as he released them from the hug. "Go help Mommy!"

Standing up, Pan looked to Sabrina. "Come on," he said, "I need your help." Sabrina got up as well, and went to him. She crouched down and, smiling at Shade and Nikki, held out her hand. The twins took it in theirs after a fleeting, curious look. It occurred to Pan, that they were sharing emotions, Sabrina was getting a feel for their power and how it worked.

When it seemed she was done, she let go of their hands and gave each of them a kiss. "Thank you, that was very interesting," she said to them. Turning back to Pan and standing up she said, "OK, let's go; we've wasted enough time already." And the two of them left for the Blackreich.

Chapter 31:

Immortal Revelations

It had been nearly seven hundred and fifty years since Iselda had been in Noigler, but it still looked the same. The streets were still dirt, the few standing buildings were barely more than limestone huts, and in the very centre of this pathetic excuse for a city was a tower of marble; the only piece of the palace that was her destination that stood above ground. Once the tallest tower of the palace, the marble tower was now its only entrance.

Iselda was about to enter the palace, when she felt, she didn't know what she felt. It was a feeling she'd had before when she was pregnant: unconditional love. But there was something else to it that she couldn't discern. She thought about it for a minute and it hit her: it was Pan's love for her. She didn't know how she knew that, but she knew it was true. Somehow, Pan was telling her how he felt and how he would never give up on her. And she thought of her feelings for him, hoping that wherever he was, he was feeling her love for him. Slowly the feelings changed and for the briefest of moments, she knew that her baby boy was the one whose feelings she felt. Four words came into her head that made her fall to the ground and cry out. As clear as if he was right in front of her, she heard him say *I love you, Mommy*.

Iselda clutched at the necklace around her neck, the necklace her son had given her, and whispered, "And Mommy loves you." And as suddenly as they came, the feelings were gone. Tears came to her eyes, as the leaving of the feelings was like leaving her family all over again. For a half an hour she cried, unable to stop. She somehow knew the feelings her husband and son had sent her were meant to help her, to give her strength.

Pulling herself together, Iselda indeed, felt her resolve strengthen. Getting off the ground, she continued up the stairs to what was in reality a window, but served as the entrance to the palace. Once inside, she climbed down the five hundred and seventy-nine stairs that led to the throne room of the palace, where she knew Annabelle would be waiting.

Along the way, she met no one; but Annabelle had never been one to have a full castle. She didn't fear assassination attempts or thieves, for who would steal from the immortal Empress of Toxai. Iselda didn't get lost, despite the vastness of the underground palace, as buried memories guided her feet to the plain double doors that lead into the throne room. Pushing the double doors open, she marched into the room. Everyone turned to look at who would enter the room in so bold a fashion as their conversations died. Iselda looked to the high vaulted ceiling of the room that was shrouded in shadows, watching for movement. "Annabelle," she said in a soft voice that carried well in the silence. "Come and say hi,

Annabelle; come and play." Iselda knew these words would confuse her friend; they were the words Iselda had said to her the night she tried to kill her, before they'd made love.

Suddenly, Iselda was forced to her knees with a push from behind. Turning her head to her right to see who had pushed her ended with her being slapped. "You will address the Empress by her title, do you understand?" a female voice demanded. Iselda knew this woman would be in skin-tight leather dyed an acid green: a Mordian. Iselda didn't respond, which she knew would only incite the Mordian.

She braced herself for the blow she knew would come. She heard the leather creak to her side. "No, Tatiana," came a voice from above. "The only one who gets to lay a hand on her, is me," Annabelle said before jumping from her hidden perch. She landed not ten feet from Iselda.

Walking up to her, Annabelle was just barely taller than Iselda on her knees. "Leave us," Annabelle said. Everyone took to the doors that Iselda had left open in their haste to obey their leader. "You too, Tatiana. She cannot harm me here." Iselda turned to see the Mordian leave. She closed the doors behind her, and they were alone.

"You're earlier than I expected, Iselda. What's the matter, couldn't wait to leave your man?" There was a smile on Annabelle's face as she asked this.

Standing up so she did not have to look up at her captor, Iselda said, "Do not mistake my wish to make sure my family is safe as an eagerness to be with you. Pan will find a way to free me, and when he does, I shall truly enjoy killing you."

"Well, I hope you use something better than a pillow," she said with a laugh.

Seizing her by the throat and slamming her against a

nearby column, Iselda squeezed and lifted. And when the girl's eyes were level with hers, she said, "How about my bare hands?" She squeezed a little more to emphasize her point.

Annabelle only smiled. "You haven't changed, Iselda. Still so rash," she said with a laugh. "That's why I love you."

Upon hearing these words, Iselda squeezed as hard as she could. "You never loved me! And I stopped loving you a long time ago!" she yelled at the girl as she choked her.

Still, all Annabelle could do was smile. She brought her hand up and tapped Iselda's around her throat. Iselda released some of the pressure so she could talk. "Like I said: so rash. And I did love you - I still do! Even though I know you broke your vows to me, I still love you, Iselda."

"No, what you have for me isn't love, Annabelle. It's anger and regret and lust, you only think it's love because you've never felt the real thing." Iselda wanted her to see the truth of this.

"And I'm supposed to believe that you, Iselda Ness-"

"It's Kanta, Iselda Kanta," she interjected with a squeeze.

"Fine, Iselda Kanta, the daughter of Isabelle Megta and Zelda Kanvice, knows real love? That you're in it, with this Pan?"

"Yes," Iselda said, tears brimming in her eyes. "Yes, I love him. There are only two people I love more: my children. The three of them have brought me more joy and happiness in the short five years we've had together than anything else in the many lives I've lived. It was Pan that led me to finally meet my mothers; mothers who have accepted him and have grown to love him. As we speak, they are all looking for ways to free me from you. If you truly loved me, as you say you do, you'd let me go so I could return to my loved ones." As she finished, Iselda lowered the girl to her feet and released her throat.

"Your tears don't fool me, Iselda, nor do your words. You claim that your mothers have accepted and grown to love him. Your mothers, the two most prolific haters of men in all of history, whose sole purpose for creating you was so that you could lure men into your bed and kill them, for all eternity; you think people will believe you when you say they're OK with you loving a man. These claims are pathetic, and quite frankly an insult to your mothers. What would they say if they heard you?" Annabelle demanded as she glared at her.

Iselda lashed out again, grabbing the girl's throat and lifting her back up. "Do not presume to know more about my family than I do, Annabelle. My mothers hold great sway in the underworld, and trust me, they are very eager to get their hands on you. You had me killed once, and now you rip me from my happiness, from all I've ever wanted from life. The next time you visit the underworld, you will be stuck there." Iselda could not hide her malice and hatred for this girl. "I should kill you right here, right now."

At this, Annabelle just smiled that irritating smile of hers. "And what makes you think I'll go to the underworld if I die? Hados has never held much sway over me, and I've never been to the underworld. No, my immortality came from an infinitely more powerful source: the same one as you, I believe." Iselda wanted to beat that grin off her face.

"The Goddess gave you your immortality? Now who's being pathetic?"

"It's not nice to presume to know someone else's family, Iselda," she said cryptically.

"Throwing my own words back at me, cute. But you're no more related to the Goddess than I am," Iselda sneered.

Shaking her head as best she could, Annabelle said, "No, Iselda, that's where you're wrong. For you see, Lilith is my grandmother."

Iselda dropped the girl and backed away from her. It couldn't be true; no legend ever spoke of Nina having a child. "If you're Nina's daughter, why does no one know of you; why is there no legend of you?"

"Because the men who killed my mother, also killed me. She'd hid me from the world, in a hope to keep me safe. The night she died, I ran to hide under her bed." Annabelle's eyes began to get misty. Iselda could not think of a time she'd ever seen Annabelle cry. "But the brutes took her to her bed and defiled her, again and again and again until every last one of them had had their fill, many times over. She only cried out once and never used her powers; so great was her love of humans that she forgave them, even as they defiled her.

"And when they were done with her, they chained her down to the bed, using gold shackles. Do you know what gold does to divine beings? It's like acid to us! I had to sit and wait as I listened to her whimpering, knowing how much pain she was in, but unable to do anything to help her. While she was chained down, the men talked of ways to kill her.

"After much debate, they decided they wanted to carve her heart out. They used a gold dagger to carve out her heart. At this she finally screamed the most painful scream I've ever heard. And the men, they cheered, celebrating the fact that they made her cry out. They were surprised that she didn't die once her heart was removed and still beat in the hands of the man who had removed it.

"My mother was panting, proof that she still lived. But the man who held her heart stabbed it with the gold dagger. Her breath caught and there was a burst of light, and I knew my mother was dead; killed by the things she'd loved into being.

"I screamed and jumped out from under the bed and attacked the man, using every ounce of divine power I possessed. But his reflexes were quicker than I suspected and he slashed my throat open.

"They then left and set the house on fire. I couldn't move as I felt the wood starting to burn beneath me. Suddenly there was a figure above; she removed the dagger from my throat, but it was too late, I was dying.

"The figure removed her hood, and I recognized Lilith, my grandmother. She pulled me out of the house and started to cry. She brought her hands to my throat and blessed me with eternal reincarnation. I became a spirit then and searched for a child of the men who'd killed me and my mother so that I may return the favour." The hatred in her eyes scared Iselda, who, despite herself, was feeling sorry for Annabelle. "After I killed the men, Lilith came to me and told me I was not allowed to kill anymore. My revenge had been fulfilled and I was to return to my normal life. As a final tribute, I built the Temple of the Goddess in honour of my mother and made it so no man would ever be able to desecrate it." Tears flowed from both their eyes.

"I hate men!" she declared. "And none of them deserve happiness." The hatred behind these two claims would have made anyone blanch. Iselda was horrified at the tale she'd just been told.

"And what of women? Do we deserve happiness?" she

asked tentatively, but firmly.

"Not if that happiness is a man. You broke your vow to forsake all men, Iselda. And for that, you must pay." Annabelle's voice had lost the anger it had contained when retelling her first death, as if she was truly remorseful about having to punish Iselda.

Kneeling so that she had to look up at Annabelle, Iselda asked, "And what punishment do you see fit to give me? I don't regret breaking the vows we made to each other, Annabelle; I just regret that you think you punish me alone." Iselda bowed her head, ready for whatever came.

But nothing did. Looking up she noticed that Annabelle had a shocked look on her face. "You are giving yourself to me? You accept your punishment?" she asked, confused.

"What I accept is that you are so blinded by your hate that you will do anything to sate it. I understand why it is you hate; I've been in that dark place myself. I also understand now why you were so angry with me for wishing to die. Perhaps if we had been more open with each other, we would not be here like this. I know this world can be cruel, but I also know it holds many wonders. And if you let me show you those wonders, your hatred might not be so blinding."

Now it was Iselda's turn to have a hand around her throat applying slight pressure. "You think I need help?! You think that I lack something and that I need your help to find it?" Annabelle asked angrily.

"Yes, Annabelle, I think you need help. Help remembering who you were before your mother died. I do not think you were this consumed by hate and vengeance when your mother was alive. And I think you need help to regain that part of yourself. I will give you all the help that I can to achieve this, but you must be committed to it," Iselda said, looking into her eyes and trying to reveal the truth of what she said.

Loosening her grip but still maintaining a chokehold around Iselda's throat, Annabelle's expression softened. "You've changed, Iselda. You used to look down upon those who wanted to change people like you're suggesting I change."

"I fell in love, Annabelle, and became a mother; nothing changes you more. You may still find that way of thinking to your liking, but I've become ashamed of the person I once was. So many years ruining the lives of strangers and those I called friends; I wish I could take it all back." A few tears fell from Iselda's eyes as she repented.

The hand around Iselda's throat slowly fell away. Turning away from her, Annabelle quietly said, "Come with me." Standing up, Iselda walked behind the girl as she led the way to her private chambers.

Or at least that's where she thought she was being taken. But Annabelle did not turn into her chambers as Iselda thought she would. Instead, she walked deeper into the palace, far deeper than Iselda had ever been. When they reached an apparent dead end, Annabelle walked up to the wall and pushed in a brick that was just a little over her head.

The wall opened to reveal a shrine, a shrine that Iselda could only assume was meant for Nina. It was barely more than a few candles surrounding a small wooden statue, but when Annabelle knelt down as if to pray, Iselda followed suit. Not knowing what to pray for, Iselda chose a prayer she guessed Nina might choose to listen to. *O, Goddess Nina, I know I do not pray often and that right now I am at odds with your daughter, but I pray you hear my prayer. I pray for my children, that they grow to be happy and good leaders to their people. From one mother to another, I pray for their happiness, whatever it may be. Nina, hear my prayer.*

When she was done praying, Iselda remained kneeling. She did not want to disturb and possibly anger Annabelle while she continued. Iselda waited for another twenty minutes until she heard Annabelle rise. The hard stone floor had not felt comfortable to Iselda's knees and she got up quickly. She looked at Annabelle as she set about concealing the shrine. When she was done, Annabelle turned towards Iselda, and reaching out, took her hand in hers. Gently tugging, Annabelle pulled Iselda back to the area of the palace that held the Empress' private chambers.

She stopped at a door Iselda knew well; it was her old room. Annabelle opened the door and led her inside, still leading with her hand. Iselda was shocked, she didn't quite remember every detail, but it seemed as if the room was exactly the way she'd left it.

"It's exactly the way you left it. No one's been in here since you left, except me. I wanted it ready, in case you survived and ever came back," she said, finally letting go of Iselda's hand. Walking over to the small desk in the corner, she picked up something. Returning to Iselda, she placed the object in her hand.

It was a ring bearing the Toxan Royal seal: a skull with a snake slithering through its eye sockets. The inner band was engraved with the words: *As Eternal as We Are*. It had been a long time since Iselda had thought of this ring, a longer time still since she'd had it in her hands. Looking down, she noticed Annabelle was wearing hers. "You still wear it?"

"I never take it off; at least, not until I'm about to die." Iselda didn't doubt these words; she could see the truth of them in her eyes. A silence fell between them for a moment that reminded Iselda of what it used to be like between them. "You were wrong before when you said that I never loved you. I did, and I still do," Annabelle said, with the slightest shake in her voice.

Iselda stepped forward and encircled her old lover in her arms. Cautiously, Annabelle raised her arms and returned the hug. "I know. It was me who never loved you, Annabelle. You were so good to me, but I was blind to it all. And now, you will forever hate me when I tell you that I cannot love you. My heart belongs to another, and I can no more love you than I can go back in time," Iselda said softly.

"I know. You love Pan. And I don't hate you, Iselda. I'm broken-hearted over you. And that has left me empty and numb to everything except the flames of hate that have always consumed me." Here, Annabelle dropped her arms and pushed away from Iselda. "Get some rest. I'm sure you're tired from your journey here. I'll leave you for the night." And she turned and left the room, closing the door behind her.

Chapter 32:
Pure Love

Kailee was confused. The recent revelation that Shade and Nikki were Soul Twins, and what that meant, had left her not knowing what to think. On the one hand, she loved them as if they were her own children and wanted them to be happy; but on the other hand, she found the fact that they were Soul Twins to be a bit perverse. But Pan had said that if she let these feelings become rooted in her, the children would see it and try to distance themselves from her.

So she buried her feelings and tried to think of them as she had before. She knew they could sense her unease. But rather than pull away, they seemed to try and make her feel better. They had stopped holding hands when they were with her and had started to vocalize their private conversations. She had never had a problem with these things, but she understood that it was Shade and Nikki's way of trying to help her adjust.

Pan and Sabrina had spent the entire night down in the Blackreich, which had left her with Shade and Nikki for the past day. They seemed to be constantly talking to one another, and Kailee wondered if this was the amount they always were communicating. As she pondered this and what it would feel like, she lost focus on them.

When she realized that they were quiet, she looked to them in alarm, making sure they were alright. They had been watching her, and once her focus returned to them, they giggled. Kailee smiled but asked, "What's so funny, you two?"

"We stopped talking a half hour ago," Nikki said with another giggle. Kailee felt a little embarrassed as her cheeks flushed at this. Shade got up, walked over to her, took her hand and dragged her back to where his sister was waiting.

A little confused, Kailee asked, "What's going on?"

"We're helping you," Nikki said. "We want you to understand how we feel."

Kailee was a little shocked by this. "You don't have to do that, sweetheart. I understand."

Shade shook his head. "No, Daddy was right, but he gave a bad description. He doesn't understand, either." He took her hand in his, as did his sister, then they took each other's. "We will show you, so you can understand."

"Before we show you our love, let us show you yours. Think of Auntie Sabrina," Nikki instructed. Kailee did, and could feel them amplify her feelings; emotional magic, indeed. "Now think of Mommy." Kailee thought of Iselda. "Now think of us." She thought of them. "Think of family." She thought of everyone she considered her family. "Think of home." She thought of her small house in OJA, and then Braria in general. Whenever she thought of something, she'd feel Shade and Nikki amplify her feelings, her love for that person or thing.

They let go of her hands and she opened her eyes and looked at them. "Did you feel all those loves? Feel how they were all different, but still love?" they asked her in unison. She nodded her head. Taking her hands again, they said, "Now this is the love we feel for each other." What Kailee felt next, she couldn't fathom. It was love, but unlike any form of it she'd ever felt before. But then, she realized that was because it wasn't a single form of love; every type of love she felt within herself, was within this maelstrom of love. And then it hit her, this was love; not the different categories man had built it into, but the thing itself. It was pure love.

Kailee wept as she realized this, and the children let go of her hands. She clutched her chest as the feeling went away, hoping to contain it within herself. And when it slipped through her fingers, the tears stung.

When she'd calmed down after five minutes, Kailee looked at Shade and Nikki to see them smiling. "That's what you feel for each other?" she asked and they nodded their heads. "And you didn't make it stronger so I could feel it, did you? That's the intensity of your love for each other, isn't it?" Again, they nodded their heads. "It's so beautiful," she whispered in astonishment. Opening her arms wide, Shade and Nikki came to her and gave her a hug. "Forgive me, little ones. I didn't understand, but I do now. And I'm sorry I didn't trust you."

"We forgive you," they said, hugging her tight. "It's not your fault; you didn't know."

Kailee cried as, once again, Shade and Nikki showed how uniquely mature they were for their young age. "Thank you for sharing that with me; it is the most beautiful thing I've ever felt." She meant it, too; for as long as she lived, Kailee would never forget that feeling.

Disengaging himself from the hug, Shade got up and walked over to his bed. Before she could even ask what he was doing, Nikki answered, "He's checking on Mommy, making sure she is OK." Kailee nodded her understanding to this.

As soon as she did, she felt Nikki tense, and they both whipped around to see what Shade had to say. Kailee noticed he held the ring from yesterday. "What's wrong, Shade?" she asked.

He didn't respond at first and Kailee realized he didn't know; he was trying to discern whatever it was that allowed him to verbalize the emotions he received from the ring. After half a minute, Nikki got up and ran to him, took one of his hands into hers, and held the ring with the other. Suddenly they were crying and Kailee jumped to go and comfort them, but then she saw they were smiling.

Kailee didn't know what had happened but she knew it was something good. She didn't think that she had ever seen the two of them with such big grins. "What is it? You guys are killing me here!" Kailee asked in frustration after they'd been jumping up and down for a minute. But instead of answering, they skipped to the door, waited for five seconds, and then opened it. And in walked Pan, Sabrina running to keep up.

"-tell me what's going on?" Sabrina was asking as she came in.

"It's Mommy," said Nikki.

"She's confident she's coming home!" Shade declared. This was a declaration that made the three of them drop their jaws in astonishment. None of them had dreamed that after being gone a week, Iselda would be coming home.

"Explain, now," Pan demanded, a little too aggressively Kailee thought.

"I don't know," Shade said with a small pout that Kailee knew he got from his mother. The fact that he didn't know clearly had upset him but he didn't care because of the end result. "Something changed overnight, mean lady's Mommy's friend again! And Mommy thinks, hopes, she can come home soon!" And for the second time in as many days, Pan fainted from something his children had told him.

Chapter 33:
Hope Versus Hate

For the first time in two weeks Iselda woke feeling confident. If the end of the previous night's events were to be believed, Annabelle seemed to be having a change of heart. Iselda wanted this to be true more than she wanted most things right then. She'd keep to what she had said the previous night: she would lead Annabelle back to the person she was before.

When she'd been up for an hour, there was a knock on the door. Curious as to who would knock and not just come in, she went and opened the door. She was shocked to see Annabelle standing there looking contrite. "May I come in?" she asked.

Iselda stepped aside to allow her to enter. "This is your home, Annabelle; you may do whatever you wish to do."

She just smiled a smaller version of the smile that had so infuriated Iselda the previous day. "But this is your room, and I wish for you to feel as welcome as you can."

"Well, not throwing me straight into a dungeon was a good start," Iselda said, trying to make light of the fact that she was still here under threat. "And this can't be my room; I haven't lived here in a long time."

"I know," Annabelle said hollowly. "I know better than you, I think, how long it's been." The conversation was very awkward and Iselda knew they both felt it.

There was a long silence as the awkwardness grew. Iselda wanted to break it, but what she wanted to say needed to be broached delicately and at the right time. Now, if she could only figure out when that was.

But luckily, she didn't have to, as after a minute of silence, Annabelle broke it for her perfectly. "I brought you something I think you'll enjoy," she said, holding up a piece of paper and a self-inking pen. "For your family - they need to know to stop looking for a way to break you out of here."

Iselda was stunned. Could it be true, was she to see her family again? Trying to hold in her excitement at this prospect, Iselda asked, "And why should they stop? Are you letting me go?" Annabelle just nodded, placing the paper and pen down on the desk. Iselda let out a shriek of joy and ran to make sure her pack had everything in it. She heard a noise behind her and the door slam.

Turning back to the room, Iselda noticed she was alone once again. She then realized what the sound was: Annabelle crying. Forgetting about her things, Iselda left the room in search of Annabelle. Having an idea of where her friend was, Iselda let her memories return and guide her feet.

When she was at the doors to Annabelle's private chambers, she knocked. She found it odd that despite Toxai being infamous for its lack of vegetation, the doors to this palace where all carved with scenes of forests and lush meadows; was Toxai once a land of greenery? When after a minute there was no answer, she knocked again. This time, the doors were thrown open as Annabelle screamed "What is so-" She stopped as she saw Iselda and was about to close the door when Iselda stopped her.

"Wait! Please, can we actually talk?"

"Don't you want to be getting back to your man?" Annabelle asked, anger once again in her voice. Iselda noticed her red and puffy eyes and the streaks from tears falling down her cheeks and couldn't help but feel saddened.

"Not like this, with you still mad at me. You're my friend, Annabelle, and I don't want to leave you when you're sad. Please, may I come in?" Iselda asked with a bowed head.

"Very well," Annabelle said after a short pause. Iselda could tell she was trying to act cold and detached to hide her pain. Iselda walked in and closed the doors behind her. Annabelle hadn't changed her decorum in the past seven and a half centuries, for the room still had the tapestries of wars long forgotten hanging on the walls, as well as one Iselda now recognized as the Temple of the Goddess positioned so that Annabelle would wake and see it every morning.

"I'm sorry," Iselda said. "I shouldn't have reacted like that in front of you, knowing how you felt. It was insensitive and a complete negation of my saying that I'd become a better person."

"Yes, it was," Annabelle responded, the hurt back in her voice. "But I understand why you jumped for joy when you found that life sentences here only last a day." The coldness of her voiced had returned. "I will not go back on my word; you are still free to go." The girl turned her back on Iselda and walked to the four poster bed, clinging to the nearest post.

"Not like this I can't. I promised that I would help you

find your old self, so you wouldn't be so consumed by hate. I-"

"Did you ever stop to think that maybe I like the hate?!" bellowed Annabelle, as she turned back to Iselda and seemed to grow bigger and more menacing with every step. "Did it ever occur in that young brain of yours, that hate is the emotion that gives strength to people, that it is hate, and not love, that binds all peoples? Did you ever think that I would HATE you?" She spat this last sentence in Iselda's face.

Iselda just nodded. "Yes, I thought you were capable of hating me; I thought you did all these years. But I feared the truth even more; I feared that I would have to face your love again. I knew that I would end up leaving you again if I did, and then you really would hate me. And I didn't want that," she answered meekly.

"Enough! Enough with your manipulations, Iselda," cried Annabelle, "I can't take them anymore. Say what you want to say, and then get out!"

"What I want? What I want Annabelle, is for when I leave here, for there to be an open invitation for my return. I want-"

"No! No that's not what you want!" There were tears in Annabelle's eyes as she denied Iselda.

Her own anger flaring, Iselda raised her voiced to match Annabelle's. "Well, then, what is it I want? If you think you know me so well, please tell me, what do I want?"

"You want him! Your Pan! So go to him!" Annabelle, to punctuate her point, opened a door for Iselda.

Having had enough of the fight, Iselda stepped out the door, but turned back to prove her point one more time. "When you calm down, I hope you realize that it was you and not me that made me leave. I came here to try and fix whatever was left between us, but your hatred blinded you to a genuine offer of friendship. Goodbye Annabelle, I hope that your hatred is all you need." And with that, Iselda turned to leave as the door was slammed. She returned to her room, collected her things, and made her way out of the palace.

Chapter 34:

Overdue Healings

When Pan came to, he found himself on Shade's bed. He noticed Sabrina sat at his side and that Kailee and his children were not in the room.

As if she could read his mind, Sabrina said, "They went to get something to eat. When they realized you just fainted because your mind overloaded they seemed to think it was funny; they said they liked your new hobby. I do too," she said with a smile.

"Thanks, but it seems it's not the only one you like," Pan said. To answer her confusion, he continued, "We can't keep meeting like this; someone might get the wrong idea."

She just faintly smiled. "The only one who's going to get the wrong idea is you, Panken," she said. Then, for no discernible reason, she gave his stomach a little tap. "Get up, there's been a development," she said.

This instantly got Pan's attention and he sat up. "What do you mean 'a development'?" he asked. He didn't want to think it, but was Iselda to be held captive for longer still?

"They're not sure," she said. "But they seem to still believe she's coming home," she added to quell his fears.

"Then, what's the development?" he asked, confused as to what was so important.

"They seem to think she's going back," she said, bracing herself for the explosion she seemed to think was coming. When it didn't, she looked at him. "Don't faint again." It was said seriously, but Pan caught the underlying joke.

"Why would she go back? Why wouldn't she come straight back here?" Pan couldn't believe what Sabrina was telling him.

"Calm down, Pan. Shade and Nikki aren't even sure she's going back. I know Iselda would never do anything that denied her all this," she said indicating first Pan, and then the room at large. "You need to remember that this girl was Iselda's first real friend, and friendship is something I know Iselda values above almost anything else. The only reason I can think of for her going back is if she's trying to salvage some form of that friendship. And that may take some time, especially with the hurt there." The look in her eyes made Pan realize she spoke from experience.

Taking her hand, he said, "Yes, but they're worth it." He saw the wetness in her green eyes and before she could start to cry, he pulled her into his arms. And a flood of memories came back to Pan, memories that he'd all but forgotten. A drunken night that he'd barely remembered the next morning, a private dinner at the Nosiop Inn, holding her at the caves as *The Mantras of Power* lay open behind him, the clumsy first time they'd spent the night together, and a hundred others that he'd tried to bury for fifteen years. And then tears started to fall from his eyes. "I'm sorry," he whispered.

Pulling back a tiny bit so she could look in his eyes, she asked, "For what?"

"Everything. I'm sorry for never letting you explain, I'm sorry for banishing the two of you, I'm sorry for not speaking to you for ten years and then demanding your help out of nowhere, but mostly I'm sorry for not letting you know how sorry I was all these years," he sobbed.

"Thank you, but I'm sorry too. I'm sorry you found out about me and Kailee the way you did, I'm sorry I never wrote and I'm sorry I've been on my guard these past five years." She seemed as sorry as Pan knew he was. He nodded his thanks and kissed her forehead. "Friends?" she asked with a hint of a smile.

Shaking his head, Pan said, "No, family." As he said this, they found themselves embracing again.

The door opened and Nikki and Shade came running in with smiles, followed closely by Kailee, who had a smaller smile brightening her face. Letting go of each other Pan asked his children, "And how long have you been waiting outside that door, waiting for us to make up?"

"Since you woke up," Nikki said as if she were discussing her dress and not admitting to spying on her father. "We wanted you to be friends again with Auntie Sabrina."

"Of course you did," he muttered under his breath. "So, what's happening with Mommy? What's this new development?" he asked, trying to contain his worry.

"It's OK, Daddy," Nikki said, clearly sensing said worry.

Shade went to his pillow and grabbed the ring. The moment he touched it, he gasped and his head bent a little. Pan didn't have to be able to understand emotions to know what his son was about to say. "Mommy's going back to help her friend." Pan tried to stay calm and not break down in front of his children, but he couldn't help the tear that fell down his cheek.

"If you can, will you tell her to be safe?" he asked his son. Nikki was hugging his leg and he could feel her trying to make him happy by shrinking his pain.

"I already did, Daddy," Shade said, as he put the ring under his pillow and hugged his father's other leg, adding his power to his sister's.

Iselda had walked most of the day and was now near the border between Toxai and Vanus. She stopped to rest under a tree for a moment to collect her thoughts. Since leaving the palace earlier that day, she'd gone back and forth between what she should do. On the one hand, she wanted to return home and let her family know she was alright and that she would never leave them again. But on the other, she wanted to return to Annabelle and try and fix their relationship. She had decided that once she crossed the border, there was no turning back; but the border was still a few miles away.

Just when she thought she couldn't make up her mind, a voice brought her back to her surroundings. "What's the problem today, child?" Evelyn asked, causing Iselda to jump. She hadn't noticed the former queen's appearance. In the shade of the tree, her form was more discernible than it had been the previous day.

"I can't make up my mind," she replied, glad to have someone to help her decide.

"About what? Isn't this what you wanted, to be free to return to your family?" she asked. "You're not going to keep my son waiting, are you?" Evelyn seemed to be angry with her.

"Of course it is; I want to see Pan as soon as possible!" she claimed.

"Then why haven't you gotten yourself a horse to cover more ground so as to be home sooner? Why have you lazily been walking all day?" Iselda didn't have an answer for this and so she stayed quiet. "It must be very important if it's holding you here, away from all you love," the queen said gently. "Tell me dear one, what troubles you?"

"I don't know," Iselda said. "Ever since I got that letter, I've prayed for this moment; but now that it's here, I can't seem to seize it. My heart's weighed down by what happened in the palace. I left Annabelle there bathing in her anger and hatred after promising I would help her escape them. But when I tried to help, she told me to leave."

"Ah," Evelyn said. "You're trying to decide whether or not to go and help your friend." Iselda nodded to confirm this. "Let me ask, the first time you tried to turn away from anger and hatred, how successful were you? Did you quickly find yourself returning to it until someone was able to help?" Again, Iselda nodded, keeping her head bowed in shame. "And the person who helped you, what's your relationship with them like?"

"She's closer to me than a sister; no favour is too big for her to ask," Iselda said, as a tear rolled down her cheek at the thought of Kailee.

"Did she ever give up on you? Or is she always there for you when you need her?"

"She's always there for me, no matter what," Iselda said, standing up.

"Where are you going? Have you made up your mind?" Evelyn asked, a small smile tugging at her lips.

"Yes, I have. Thank you, Evelyn, for all your help. But there's something I must do, before I can go home. Will you let him know that I'm sorry for prolonging our suffering, but this was something I had to do?"

With a tap to Iselda's necklace, she said, "He already knows." And as quick as she'd come, she was gone.

Swinging her pack back over her shoulder, Iselda was about to head back to Noigler when she felt the same feeling she'd gotten right before she'd felt Pan's love for her, that feeling of connectedness. But instead of feeling love, she felt her caution rise. And just like last time, she heard her son's voice as the feeling of raised caution faded. *Be careful, Mommy. We love you.*

※

When Iselda got back to the palace it was the middle of the night. She had to be careful not to get caught by any guards, or worse a Mordian, so that Annabelle would not be alerted to her presence. She used passages that she recalled were not heavily patrolled until she found herself outside 'her' room. She opened the door and quickly went inside. The room was about the same size as her and Pan's room in Terang, but less crowded. The bed was smaller than her own, as was the writing desk, but that was all there was in the room. No tapestries hung from the walls. They were actually quite bare; Iselda's taste for decoration had only manifested itself within the last hundred years or so.

Walking over to the bed, she dropped her pack and flopped onto the bed. Iselda was tired from the walk that had taken most of the day, and then the rushing back here. She would surprise Annabelle in the morning; she hoped that catching her off guard would make her more open to Iselda's insistence at trying to help her. But before she could plan further ahead than that, sleep took her.

When Iselda woke up, she hid her pack under the bed to continue the ruse of her not being here. Knowing that only Annabelle went into the room, however, made her fairly certain that she would not be discovered. Giving the room a quick glance to make sure it was the way she'd left it the day before, Iselda went to the small mirror hanging on the wall across from the bed.

Running her hands along the wall behind the mirror to find the switch, Iselda felt the raised part of the wall and pressed it. In the middle of the room a hole appeared just big enough for her to fit through into the secret passage below. There was a hiss as the centuries-old air trapped in the passage escaped. Iselda made her way over to the hole, jumped down into it, and replaced the tiles back into the floor above.

The tunnel wasn't very big and Iselda had to hunch over to be able to walk it. It was dark inside so she couldn't see, but she knew that if she kept her hand against the left side wall, she'd reach her destination. So she set out, hunched over and blind, her hand the only guide. She ignored the large amount of dust that running her hand along the wall puffed up into her face.

Thankfully the passage wasn't all that long and Iselda was soon at the entrance to Annabelle's room. Pressing her ear to the removable tiles, she tried to hear what was going on in the room. She didn't hear anything, so she felt around for the switch that would release the tiles. Bracing herself against the tiles, she hit the switch and slowly dropped the tiles.

The sudden light briefly blinded Iselda, but her eyes quickly adjusted. Now that the tiles were open, she could hear something: crying. She could hear the heart-wrenching sobs Annabelle was crying over her, and knew she had done the right thing in coming back. Poking her head out to see if she could see where Annabelle was, she figured she was on her bed as she could not see her from her vantage point of the floor.

As quietly as she could, Iselda lifted herself out of the tunnel, wiping off as much dust as she could. Facing the bed, she slowly stood up and found Annabelle facing the wall with her arms wrapped around her legs and face against her knees. Very slowly, and trying to make as little sound as possible, she went to the crying girl. Sitting at the edge of the bed, she tentatively reached out a hand and rubbed Annabelle's back.

The moment her hand made contact, the girl's body tensed. Turning to see who was at her side, Annabelle swatted her hand away when she saw it was Iselda. "Why are you here?" she demanded in a threatening voice as she pushed herself as far away as she could from Iselda.

"Trying to be a good friend," she said gently. "I want to help you, Annabelle."

"I already told you: I don't need your help; nor do I want it!" she said icily.

"Then why were you crying, if you don't need my help? If everything's OK like you say it is, why are you all alone in your room, crying?"

"You know why! You're the one who told me!"

"So, everything's not alright. You've realized that your anger and hatred have had negative effects on your life; that's why you cry?" Iselda asked, still trying to be as gentle as possible.

She saw the tears burning Annabelle's eyes as they tried to escape, but she held them back. "Yes," she said in a tense voice, "that is why I cry."

Nodding, Iselda continued, "Do you want these effects to stop? Do you want your life to be happier, more joyful?"

"Yes." Annabelle was starting to let go of the anger and let the pain shine through.

"Then let me help you," Iselda said, holding her arms open. In lieu of a response, Annabelle crawled over to her and into her open arms.

As Iselda hugged the girl to her and rubbed her back, Annabelle started to cry again. She cried for nearly twenty minutes before she was able to calm down. "Thank you," she whispered in a hoarse voice.

"Anytime, Annabelle; I'll always be there when you need me. All you have to do is ask." Iselda really wanted this point to get through to her. "We're friends, Annabelle, and friends do everything they can to make each other feel better."

Nodding her head as she pulled back and disengaged herself from the hug, Annabelle wiped the tears from her eyes. Iselda didn't move as she saw Annabelle lean in, and pressed their mouths together. She didn't try to stop the kiss by pushing Annabelle away, nor did she return it. Her lips were thin, but Iselda could still tell that Annabelle was very good at kissing. After a minute, Annabelle removed herself from Iselda's lips and said, "I'm sorry, I shouldn't have done that."

"It's ok, Annabelle. The love you've held for me all these years had to be released. But, it cannot happen again." As she said this, Annabelle looked like she was about to get mad and throw her out again. So she continued, "There is little I wouldn't do for you, Annabelle, but this," she said indicating the two of them, "is something I cannot do. While I can't force you to love another, I highly suggest you try. For finding someone who loves you and who you love in return, will be the way you change. It won't be easy, but you have to try," Iselda urged.

"And if I can't let you go?" Annabelle asked quietly.

"You don't have to let me go. You just have to let yourself love someone else, and over time the love you have for me will change and will not hurt you anymore. But you must be patient; love is not always easy and you can't give up on it the moment it gets tough. If I'd given up on Pan the first time it got tough, we would have only been together for a couple of weeks. And you know what? When I realized he was doing everything he did for me, I was so happy that I had to restrain myself from kissing him." Iselda hoped the mentioning of Pan and her love for him would not anger Annabelle.

Thankfully, she didn't appear to be angry. "That sounds wonderful," she said, new tears coming down her cheeks. "But how will I find love, Iselda? How will I know if it's real or not?"

"That I cannot answer; you have to discover love on your

own. But having been in love before, you will know it when you feel it. You will know if the love is real by all the little things your lover does. Do they smile when they see you, do they comfort you when you're upset, do they hold you tight at night? At least, that's how I knew. If you're honest and open with them, they'll grow to love you," Iselda confided.

"I'm the immortal Empress of Toxai, the world fears me; how could anyone love what they fear?" Annabelle asked in a small voice.

"The same way Pan did: they look past it. You don't intimidate them and instead, you show them you can be gentle and kind. And when your anger does rise, you apologize after it's cooled and trust they can see that you're not always angry, that you are only human."

"But I'm not only human. I'm the granddaughter of Lilith."

"Trapped in a human body for so long, you've become more like us than her. You may not like it, but it's true. And accepting your humanity will only help you become a better person."

Annabelle nodded her head at this. "It's something I've long feared, being human. I didn't want to be like the men who killed my mother and me. I didn't want to be a beast."

"And you're not a beast, Annabelle," Iselda said. "What those men did to your mother is unforgivable, and should shame every man that hears it. But not all males are the beasts you've thought them to be. My son, my darling Shade," she said while unconsciously touching the necklace around her throat, "is the sweetest boy I've ever known. I don't have to tell him something's bothering me, he just knows and tries to make me feel better anyway he can. He's never without his sister's hand in his. Do you think he'll grow to be a beast?" she asked.

"No, I don't think your son will grow to be a monster. Perhaps, I've let my vendetta cloud my vision for too long; I've had men in my court my entire reign, and none have ever given me reason to hate them." Annabelle had stopped crying and Iselda hoped that this admittance was her first step to becoming a better person. "You weren't wearing that when I was in Braria," Annabelle said with curiosity, pointing to Iselda's necklace. "But now, you keep reaching for it, especially when you mention your family. Why's it so important?" she asked.

"Because it was a gift from my children. The night I left, they came to me with this and a matching ring. I was going to give this and the ring to them when they turned sixteen as heirlooms. I told them that I couldn't take these; that they were theirs, but they gave me the necklace anyway. They said it was so that I could remember them and know they were alright." Turning the necklace over, she showed Annabelle the inscription.

"'*To love someone is to hold them in your heart forever.*' That's beautiful."

Iselda nodded her agreement. Thinking this was as good a place as any to have Annabelle think on everything she'd been told, she stood up. Seeing Annabelle's look of fear, she said, "You need to think on this, Annabelle. And while you are, I need to write a letter to my family and tell them what's happening; like you said yesterday, they need to stop looking for ways to break me out of here. But I'm not leaving until I feel you can handle the change without me. Reflection will help you better understand your feelings, and once you can do that, you can start to live happier." Giving her one last hug and a kiss to her cheek, Iselda dropped herself into the passageway and returned to her room.

Chapter 35:

Correspondence

The past few days for Pan had been hard. While he knew his wife was OK, thanks to bi-daily checkups on her by Shade and Nikki, the fact that he hadn't seen her in nearly two and a half weeks was starting to irritate him. Even knowing that she'd been freed, and was able to leave whenever she wanted, was not able to substitute for her presence anymore.

Since hearing that Iselda was free, Pan had started to continue his kingly duties of answering letters to different towns that asked for his advice on whatever, seeing to the petitioners, and other such activities. He knew that Iselda had been trying to lighten their spirits when she said it, but Pan had brought Shade and Nikki to the throne room to get their input on the different issues. While he found that they tended to think the same way as he did about most things, he did find that when their thoughts differed, he would discover a new way of looking at the situation.

The last of the day's petitioners had just been seen when Shaw entered the room leading a man who looked like he could use a good meal. Snapping a fist to his heart, Shaw said, "Sire, this man just arrived saying he had a letter for the king. Upon seeing the envelope it was in, I noticed the same colour of sealing wax from the Queen's letter," he bowed his head here in slight guilt at the mention of the Empress' threat, "and I thought you'd want to see him right away." Pan could clearly tell that the man was trying to redeem himself.

"Yes, thank you, Remus. I can take it from here," Pan said climbing down from the raised platform that held the thrones to the two men below. Shade and Nikki were right behind him. Handing him the letter and giving another fist to his heart, Shaw left. Opening the envelope, Pan immediately recognized Iselda's writing and heard his children gasp behind him as they realized this as well. "This letter is in the hand of my wife," he told the scrawny messenger. "The person that gave it to you, describe them, what they said, how they were dressed, everything. Now!"

The messenger jumped at being yelled at, but bowed slightly and said, "I don't know her name but she wore a form-revealing blackblood dress, her hair was long and dark as night, and her eyes were the colour of amethyst. She said that I was to come here and find a soldier at the castle named Remus Shaw and tell him I had a letter for the king, and then show him the letter. She said to suspect him to treat me a little roughly, and she apologized if he did. He didn't, by the way. She said that if I did what the king asked, I'd not be harmed." His voice was very raspy and timid.

"Iselda, her name is Iselda. And she is the queen of this country. Was that all she said?"

"She said that I was to wait for your reply and that I was to get here as fast as I could. And if the king didn't believe me, she said that I was to tell you that she hopes that you haven't been singing a lullaby to her son, as you are a horrible singer." He said this last sentence really quickly and then braced himself as if he expected Pan to attack him for insulting him.

But Pan, as well as Shade and Nikki, just laughed. "Indeed, you got this letter from my wife. What's your name, messenger?"

"Rex, sire, Viktor Rex."

"Well, Mr. Rex, I apologize for my rudeness, but the last time someone from your homeland came to deliver a message, it left us in a bit of an uproar. Allow me to offer you some food and a bed while you await our reply."

"Thank you, your highness; that's most kind." Pan could tell he was quite eager to both eat and sleep.

"Shaw!" Pan called to the hallway. And when the soldier returned with a fist to his heart, Pan continued, "Please escort Mr. Rex here to the kitchen and tell Alix to let him eat as much as he wants. And when he's finished please show him to the Nosiop Inn and arrange for him to stay the night. You can tell Jensen that he's here as my guest and that I'll pay for his room when I come to see him in the morning." Shaw gave one last fist to his heart and led Viktor to the kitchens.

Once Shaw and Viktor were gone, he felt a tugging on the envelope in his hand. Looking down, he saw Shade was trying to pull it free. "Come on, Daddy, what did Mommy write?" Nikki asked from his other side.

Leading them to the steps of the raised platform, Pan removed the letter from the envelope and unfolded it. "Let's see," he said taking a seat on the steps. When Shade and

Nikki were snuggled comfortably on either side of him, he read, "'My dearest family, I find it hard to believe that it was barely a week ago that I was crying over my last letters to you, for the wonderful has happened: I've been set free and can return to you. But that being said, there is something that I must do here first, I must help my friend. This may take some time, but don't worry, for I'll be home in time for Shade's and Nikki's birthday feast.

"'I also want to thank you all for somehow sending me your love and support; they came just when I needed them most. I don't know how you sent your feelings, but I'm thankful you did. I don't know if you felt my love for you when you sent me these feelings, but I tried to send it. I love and miss all of you so much and can't wait until we are reunited.

"'Since being here, I've had some interesting encounters. But perhaps the most interesting was meeting the spirit of Evelyn. You really do have her eyes, Nikki. She sends all her love and says she misses you Pan with all her heart.'" Here Pan had to stop. The mentioning of his mother had reminded him of how much he missed her. Understanding how he felt and why, his children hugged him tight.

After a brief pause and silence for his mother, Pan continued, "'Now, while I am safe and no longer a prisoner here, I still request that you not come to me. Where I am is very dangerous to people who don't know the land, and I don't want you to fall prey to it. If I'm not home sooner, I'll be home for the birthdays in a few months.

"'But until then, I love you.' That's it, that's all she wrote. Now we have to write her back," Pan said to the simultaneous nods of his children. "Ok, let's go get Auntie Kailee and

Auntie Sabrina so they can help us," he suggested. As he hadn't read a part of the letter that seemed to be addressed only to them, he figured they should get to respond as well. Shade and Nikki just nodded and started to pull him to the room where their aunts were staying.

A week had passed since Iselda had sent her letter. In that time, she and Annabelle had regained the closeness they had once shared, this time without the physical intimacy. Annabelle had come so far in this week alone that Iselda had high hopes for being able to return to Braria before Shade's and Nikki's birthday.

There was a knock on the door, which brought her out of her looking at her pictures. Getting off her bed, Iselda put the drawings away and went to answer the door. Standing there was the man she'd sent to deliver her letter and Annabelle.

"This just arrived for you," Annabelle said, indicating the man.

Stepping aside to allow them to enter, Iselda smiled at her friend's attempt at humour. "Do you have something for me, Mr. Rex?" she asked. He held up an envelope, but when she reached for it, he pulled back.

Giving a look of confusion to the man, he explained. "Before I'm to give this to you, its senders wanted me to test you to make sure it's being received by the right person." Iselda gave a nod to this, despite her confusion. "First, the king says that for nine years, you waited for him to come to you. Why didn't you ever go to him?"

"Because I thought it was better if we met on his terms, rather than mine, like we ended up doing, anyways."

"Correct. The prince asks about the source of his lullaby."

"The lullaby I sing my son is derived from old prophecies, like some of the bedtime stories his father tells him and his sister."

"Correct again. And finally, your friend recalls that during the boat ride, she told you of a man who she'd met when she was a child. What was the man's name, and why does she remember him to this day?"

This question gave Iselda pause. The journey to Vagala was a long time ago, and she could only remember talking about one man, Pan. Knowing she wouldn't get her letter if she didn't answer this question correctly, Iselda racked her memory for the answer. "His name was…Sodah, and she remembers him because he said that she would have a role to play in bringing love back to the dead and eternal one; after he told her this he smiled at her funny and kissed her forehead." As she finished her answer, Mr. Rex bowed and handed her the envelope. And with another bow to Annabelle, he left.

Quickly glancing at Annabelle before she opened the letter, Iselda noticed that Annabelle looked a little pale. "Are you OK?" she asked. She didn't respond, so Iselda asked again, and again Annabelle didn't answer. In fact, it seemed Annabelle was completely in her own head. Shaking the girl until she was back outside her head, Iselda again asked, "You OK? You've been staring into space for five minutes."

Shaking her head, Annabelle answered in a distracted voice, "It's nothing; I just remembered something my mother told me before she died." Bringing herself completely back, she nodded to the still unopened envelope in Iselda's hand. "Are you going to open that?"

Iselda let go of her concern; it was just an old memory. Turning back to the letter she said, "Yes, but do you mind if I read it in private; I need a moment alone with them."

"Sure, I have something to do privately myself, anyways. I'll see you at dinner," Annabelle responded with a quick hug and left the room. She left more quickly than usual.

Ignoring this, and returning to the envelope, Iselda opened it. Pulling out the two letters inside, Iselda saw that one was from Pan and the other from Kailee. She read Kailee's first.

> *My Dearest Friend,*
>
> *As I've been told not to tell you everything that has happened since my arrival, let me first tell you that your husband and children are doing fine. They miss you and want you to come home as soon as possible, but they are fine.*
>
> *I have done what you asked and started to plan for Shade's and Nikki's birthday celebration, but hiding things from them has become difficult. I probably shouldn't have said that, but from what I gather, you knew this already. I have tried my best to be as discreet as possible when snooping for gift ideas and other such activities.*
>
> *Sabrina sends her love and hopes you know what you've gotten yourself into. And while the entire castle and country are worried about you, Pan, Nikki, and Shade*

> *have reassured everyone that you're OK and that you'll be home in a few months. As for me, I'm just thankful you're trying to help someone try to become a better person. I know you think I helped you out of your darkness, but you did that all yourself; I just gave a nudge.*
>
> *Love and miss you lots,*
>   *Kailee*
> *P.S. If you want to get your children what they want for their birthday, all you need to do is come home and give them a big hug and kiss.*

Iselda could only smile at her friend's advice for a gift. She was glad she had Kailee as a friend; she always knew what to say to make her feel good. A tear rolled down her cheek as she enjoyed the bitter-sweetness of the letter.

Turning to Pan's letter, Iselda wondered if all that had happened would be explained in it.

> *To My Beautiful Wife,*
>
> *First, let me apologize for not being there your last week here. I was searching for ways to help you escape your fate, but I also couldn't bear to have to say goodbye to you. When I realized that the day had come when you said you were leaving, I ran to find you so that I could say goodbye. Alas, you had gone. It's OK; having to say goodbye would have been just as painful as finding our room empty. I hold nothing against you,*

for I wasn't there for you.

Second, come home quickly. Much has been revealed that I need to talk to you about in person so I know you understand. But the smallest of it is that Shade and Nikki have magic; I was shocked too. And it is through this magic that we have not fallen to pieces, for they can somehow sense your feelings and thoughts and interpret them for us to understand. That's how I sent my love for you, to you; and yes I felt yours for me. And they felt it, too. They miss you, and so do I.

Thank you for sending Kailee and Sabrina; the help they've given is immeasurable. And you'll be happy to know that Sabrina and I have finally made up and forgiven each other for all that has bothered us.

I know you were only trying to make them feel better when you said it, but I've started to have Nikki and Shade help with the petitioners; they're quite insightful. They really enjoy it, and I think this will be my gift to them. If one good thing has come from you leaving, it's how much it has matured Shade and Nikki - I think they're more mature than me.

I think I now understand how you felt when we returned from Vagala. The fact that we can be together, but you're not letting us to make it ten times stronger for when we finally are, is really, really *annoying. But I understand what you're doing and why you feel you must.*

I'm glad you met my mother, and thank you for sending her love. If you see her again, please return it and tell her I miss her and Father.

I long for your return,
 Panken
 P.S. Don't worry, I haven't been singing either of my children lullabies, as I'm a 'horrible singer.' You'll pay for that one.

Iselda was glad Pan had ended with humour. It meant that he was, indeed, fine. Perhaps *just fine*, she thought with a small smile at the memory. Clutching her necklace, she thought those two words as hard as she could; hoping they'd find their way to Pan. He'd laugh when he heard them.

Chapter 36:

Serious Giggles

As Iselda hadn't eaten much that day, she left her room to find something to eat. She knew dinner with Annabelle wasn't for another hour, so she went straight to the kitchen. As she walked the service routes, she was reminded of all the times she'd done this to go to her castle's kitchens and laugh at Alix yelling in his foreign tongue at everyone. As she thought this, it made her heart crack; her homesickness wasn't enough to break her heart, just enough to crack it.

Upon entering the oddly small kitchen despite the vastness of the palace, she saw the lone cook at a pot over a fire. He was a very thin man, although he wasn't very tall. His hair was grey, at least the few strands he had left. And when he spoke, it was always in rhymes. Turning away from what was in the pot, he saw her. "What can I do for you; weren't you planning on dining for two?"

"Yes, I was. But I haven't really had anything to eat today, and I need something to quell my hunger for the moment until dinner is served. Is there something small I could take?" she asked.

The cook started to shake his head, but then bent down to a cupboard and pulled out a small loaf of bread. "Viktor tells me, the food you eat has great beauty. Have some fresh bread, so you don't wind up dead," he said with a small smile as he handed her the bread.

Ripping it in half and returning one half to him, Iselda said, "Thank you, but I only need half. And Viktor's right, the food in Braria is very good."

Taking the half of bread she'd given him and replacing it in the cupboard, he said, "Now run along child, the soup is not yet mild."

Turning to leave, Iselda took a bite out of the bread. Discovering that it was indeed fresh caused her to give a moan of pleasure. The cook just chuckled behind her at this response. She'd never had bread so fresh in Toxai, even when she'd first started her friendship with Annabelle. She tried to take her time and savour the goodness of it, but her hunger had her stuffing it down her throat. It was gone before she was down the first hallway leading away from the kitchen.

Once she got back to her room, she pulled out the picture of her family. Smiling sadly at it, she felt a tear roll down her cheek. Wiping it away, she felt her hand return to her necklace. Annabelle had been right; she couldn't leave it alone, especially when thinking of her family.

Suddenly there was a feeling of connectedness in her chest, and she knew her children were checking up on her. *I love and miss you*, she thought, now knowing her children could understand her. And she felt that they loved and missed her also. And just as she had both times she felt them, as the feelings faded she heard Shade's voice in her head. *Daddy says he's 'just fine' and that the challenge is still on. We love you*. Even as the tears at feeling them leave again flowed, Iselda couldn't help but laugh. Pan had remembered and known what she meant by *just fine*. And if the challenge was still on, she had some work to do.

For the next hour, Iselda thought of the day she had told Pan she loved him for the first time… and the events that followed. When there was a knock on the door, Iselda sat up, stiff as a board. Wiping her hand on her dress, she rushed to the door before whoever was there knocked again. But she couldn't hide the flush of her skin or her heavy breathing.

Opening the door, she found Annabelle standing there. "I thought I'd walk you to dinner," she said. "Are you alright?" she asked when she saw Iselda's flush and heavy breathing.

"Wha-I'm fine, just reliving old memories is all. Come on, let's go get some dinner." She wanted to get Annabelle away from her room at the moment so it could air out. So she took her hand, using her non-sticky hand, and pulled her towards the dining room.

But despite these efforts, Annabelle still seemed to figure it out. "Missing Pan, were we?" she asked with that infuriating smile of hers. Iselda just nodded, which caused the girl to laugh. "Sorry, I didn't mean to disturb you," she said, clearly trying to be mature about it by suppressing her giggles.

"No you're not," Iselda said tensely. This just caused the girl to laugh more. And while she didn't appreciate being laughed at, Iselda was glad that Annabelle was laughing rather than sulking.

By the time they were seated at the table, Annabelle had stopped laughing, but that annoying smile was harder to get rid of. The table they sat at was rectangular and quite large, nearly taking up the entire room. They sat across from one another and began eating the soup the cook had made for them. Also on the table was the half loaf of bread that Iselda had returned; she quickly took a chunk and dipped it in the soup. When she put it in her mouth, she again couldn't hold in the moan of pleasure. "Please, not at the table, Iselda," Annabelle said with another fit of giggles.

"It's the bread!" Iselda defended. "Try it!" So Annabelle did, and she moaned as well. "You see, I told you." Annabelle stuck her tongue out at this, which Iselda returned in kind. Clearly her children had syphoned away her maturity.

"OK, enough with the silliness," Annabelle said, despite being the instigator. "I have something serious to discuss." This caught Iselda's attention, as she put her spoon down. "It has to deal with something you said earlier. The answer to your friend's question, can you elaborate?"

Catching the seriousness of her tone, as well as the fact that her smile had disappeared, Iselda racked her brain. "Not well, I was surprised I remembered as much as I did. She only brought it up once and we've never discussed it again since. Why, what's so important about it?"

"It's something my mother said to me the day she died. She called me the eternal one and said the dead was waiting for me, that the dead loved me. I didn't think much of it as she was always saying random things, like she couldn't put words together properly. But hearing you say that makes me wonder if there was something to what she said."

"I don't know, Annabelle. I only had a conversation about it; it was Kailee who met this man. I could send her a letter asking about it, but other than that, there's nothing I can do."

"I don't want you to send her a letter. I want you to bring me to her." This immediately froze Iselda in place as she looked at her friend in astonishment. "Yes, I'm serious about this, Iselda. Will you take me to this friend of yours?"

Trying to find her voice, Iselda chose her next words carefully; she remembered the last time they'd talked about her returning to Braria. "You realize that Kailee is in Terang, at my castle?"

"Yes, I realize that. But with you by my side, I think I'll be OK. Besides, you need to see your husband," she said with a small smile. "And then maybe I'll return alone and try to stay changed without your guiding hand."

Iselda couldn't speak. She wanted to run to her friend and tell her it was a deal, but she was mindful of Annabelle's sensitivity. So, she slowly got up, walked to Annabelle, and gave her a hug. "If you're sure this is what you want," she said in a shaky voice, "then I shall take you to meet my family."

"It's OK, Iselda. You can be happy about this. We'll leave tomorrow." As she heard this, Iselda gave an elated cry and returned to her seat. They finished the meal in silence and once they were done, Annabelle led her, arm-in-arm, back to her room. "I'll have the carriage ready for first light, so we can leave as soon as we wake," Annabelle said once they were at the door.

"Are you sure about this, Annabelle? While I can guarantee that you won't be killed, I can't guarantee Pan won't try to hurt you. Despite everything, he can be vindictive at times. And you've certainly provoked him enough."

"I'll take whatever he gives me; I've wronged and hurt him grievously. He deserves a vent for that."

Perhaps Annabelle would be alright on her own after all. Taking responsibility for her actions was one of the last steps Iselda had taken. And the fact that Annabelle was offering herself to what Pan would do to her, showed Iselda how much she'd truly changed. "I'll try to control him as much as possible," she promised as she walked into her room.

"Thank you. I'll see you in the morning. We'll use the tunnel to wake each other up; although I think you'll be awake before me." Giving Iselda one last hug and kiss to the cheek, Annabelle left. And all Iselda could do was cry tears of joy.

As she closed the door and turned to run to her bed, she noticed that someone was already sitting on it. Evelyn was waiting for her, more solid than she'd ever seen her. "Evelyn? What are you doing here? I didn't know you could appear in the castle," she said as she ran to her.

"We good spirits can appear anywhere in Toxai," she said. "I'm here to deliver you a message, well two actually. The first is from Leo, your mothers, and I: we wish you and your loved ones a blessed reunion. And we send our love to our grandchildren on their upcoming birthday.

"The second was delivered to me by Hados himself. He says he'll see you soon, but that you should not fear this meeting, for it is the culmination of your efforts. I don't know what he means, but he would not rise to me to deliver it himself if he didn't think it was important. I suggest caution in these next few days."

Iselda nodded blankly. She'd never heard of Hados delivering a message himself, and the fact that she was going to meet him soon didn't sound good to Iselda; even if she was told not to be fearful of this meeting. "Thanks," she said in a high voice. Swallowing to try and hide her fear, she continued, "Pan sends his love and says he misses you both so much. Is there anything you'd like to send him, any message you or Leo want him to have?"

"Just that we love him. But don't be afraid, child. I do not think you'll be dying soon. While I can claim no knowledge of him, Hados seemed ecstatic that your meeting was soon. Something beyond death is making him act." Iselda didn't know what could be more important to Hados than death, but whatever it was, it was important enough to have him delivering messages himself.

"OK, I'll pass along your love. And thank you, for helping me when I needed it."

"Anytime, child, anytime. Now go to sleep, you'll need the rest if you're going to win that challenge." Iselda wondered how she knew of that, but when she went to ask her, Evelyn had gone. Taking her advice, Iselda prepared herself for bed and tried to fall asleep.

Chapter 37:

Celebration Announcements

Pan knew that his children were looking for him. It was the same feeling he felt right before they told him that Iselda was coming home, or that they thought she was. It was like a cry in his head: he could hear Nikki yelling his name. The moment he felt her calling, he'd stood up from his throne, excused himself in the middle of a petitioner's request, and ran from the room towards his children's bedroom.

He expected that they'd be in their room waiting, like the last time, but he found them running towards him. They had the biggest smiles on their faces so he knew that whatever they had to tell him was good news. He saw both Kailee and Sabrina running behind them with confused expressions.

Pan stopped when he was a few steps away from Shade and Nikki. But they didn't; they grabbed his hands and pulled him in the direction he'd just come from. When they'd reached the throne room, they let go of his hand but ran to the steps. Everyone was now watching them as they ran up the steps and stood in front of the Royal thrones. Looking out at the room with those big smiles, as one they said, "Mommy's coming home!"

For a moment, everyone was quiet. And then, once the message sunk in, there was a huge cheer. All around him people were hugging each other, no matter who they were. Trying not to faint again as he'd never hear the end of it if he did, Pan walked to the bottom of the stairs. "Are you sure, this time?" he asked loud enough for all present to hear.

They nodded their heads. "Yes Daddy, we are," Nikki said.

"They left this morning, before the sun got up," Shade assured, but then covered his mouth at his father's reaction.

"They?" he asked calmly. The room had grown tense as Shade covered his mouth, and even more so with Pan's question.

Nodding slightly, Shade answered, "She's bringing her friend. They'll be here by dinnertime the day after tomorrow." Nikki shook her head at her brother, and Pan realized that he wasn't supposed to know this bit of information. It also proved that while their minds were one, they were capable of having their own thoughts.

Wanting to make Shade feel better, Pan turned to the room looking for someone. Spotting him in the back, he called, "General Vanto." The crowd cleared a path for the general as he made his way up to Pan. "General, would you please go down to the kitchen and tell Chef Alix that he needs to get busy? He is to prepare the grandest feast he can imagine for when Iselda returns in two days' time. Tell him that besides all of Terang being invited, he is cooking for a visiting dignitary, the Empress of Toxai herself."

Snapping a fist to his heart, Vanto said, "It will be done, my lord." And he left to complete his mission.

Walking up the steps so he was behind both his children,

Pan spoke to the remaining crowd. "You'll forgive me when I say I'm sorry that the recent weeks haven't been the greatest if you've come to me. But I must again ask that you wait. Until our queen returns, I cannot help you. Now please, go and spread the word of the feast I just ordered; I meant what I said about all of Terang being invited. And if a feast is not the compensation you wish, next month's taxes are on the House of Kanta!" This made the crowd cheer more than when they were told Iselda was coming home, but he let this go.

As Sabrina and the remaining guards tried to get everyone out, Pan sat on his throne and beckoned his son to him. Placing Shade on his knee, Pan whispered, "Thank you for telling me. I know you and your sister didn't want me to know, but it's better that I do. This way I don't do anything mean to Mommy's friend when she arrives. You did the right thing, Shade."

He gave Shade a hug, which was eagerly returned. "Thank you, Daddy," was whispered in his ear and he felt a flood of love for him come from his son. And when he let go, he saw Shade turn to his sister and stick his tongue out at her. Nikki returned in kind but then gave Shade a hug, which he returned. Pan guessed that all was forgiven and that had probably been the biggest problem in their relationship. He wished all his relationship problems could be solved that way.

"Come on you two, we have to get ready for when Mommy gets back. And I don't know about you two, but I want to look my best for her - I want the first kiss." He knew that turning it into a bit of a competition would draw them out.

Releasing each other from their hug, they looked at him, then at each other. With subdued smiles of mischief, which he could see plenty of in their eyes, they said, "Try all you want, Daddy. We'll be the ones she runs to for hugs and kisses." Sticking their tongues out at him, they turned and fled the room. Perhaps they weren't as mature as he'd made them out to be in his letter.

Chapter 38:

Returning to Terang

The past two days had seen Iselda and Annabelle all the way from Noigler to OJA. The horses had run non-stop and were very tired when the carriage pulled to a stop outside of Kailee's and Sabrina's house. Iselda figured that her friends wouldn't mind that she used their house as long as she cleaned it before she left.

But as she got out of the carriage, Iselda realized that they weren't the only ones at the house. Coming out of the house to see who had just arrived was Jayne, Kailee's older sister. Iselda had met her only twice, but she'd always gotten along with the woman. She was about as tall as her sister, but with blonde hair, green eyes, and wider hips. As Iselda looked upon her best friend's sister, she thought once again how Kailee looked nothing like anyone in her family.

When Jayne saw who it was that exited the carriage, she gave a small smile. "I should have known it was you, your highness. The country is completely abuzz with the rumour of your return and what your husband has declared be done for it. When you say no taxes next month, that is going to spread," she said with a smile.

"We just left yesterday morning," Iselda said, shocked. "Do you think we could spend the night here, Jayne?"

She just nodded. "For the queen, anything. I'm sure my sister wouldn't mind. I was just leaving anyways."

"Thank you," Annabelle said, stepping out of the carriage and stretching.

Jayne gave a curious look to Annabelle. "Who's this?" she asked simply.

"This is Annabelle; she's one of my oldest friends. She wants to meet Kailee and talk to her about the man she remembers from when she was younger." Iselda didn't want to go into details about everything.

Jayne nodded again. "Don't worry about cleaning up when you leave; I've got it covered." Seeing Iselda was about to protest this, she added, "You're her guest, Iselda, and I'd never hear the end of it if I let you clean up. You know how Kailee is." Realizing she wouldn't win this argument, Iselda just nodded. "And when you see my sister, tell her she owes me big for this."

"I will. Goodnight, Jayne." Iselda said as she and Annabelle went into the house. The surprisingly burly carriage driver was to sleep in the small carriage. Once inside, Iselda showed Annabelle to the spare room. "Try not to touch anything; Kailee's a bit obsessed when it comes to having things in their place. I'll let you sleep till late in the morning; the horses need the rest as well. We should be in Terang in a few hours after we leave." They said goodnight and went to bed.

The figure before her looked at her with eyes blacker than black. His hair was the same colour and came down to his half exposed chest. The toga he wore looked like something that hadn't been worn for millennia, outside of Rupublikos, and seemed to be made of smoke. His skin was pale and despite his decrepit look, Iselda instinctively knew he was quite powerful.

Looking away from those dark eyes, Iselda found herself to be in a circular throne room. The figure sat in one throne, while the other looked like it hadn't been sat in since the dawn of time. Seeing her looking around, the figure pointed to the floor. Looking down, Iselda saw that a mosaic covered the space between her and the figure. But this was unlike any mosaic she'd ever seen, for the two depicted figures moved.

Holding each other close, the two danced in circles within the mosaic. One was clearly meant to be the being before her, a smile on his face. Looking back to the figure, she saw only sadness. The other figure was harder to describe. Her eyes never stayed the same colour and her hair was every colour imaginable. She, too, was smiling as she danced. Iselda had the strangest sense that she knew this woman, but couldn't remember where she'd seen her before.

"Iselda," the figure across the mosaic called in a slow, deep voice. "Please, Iselda, please return her to me."

Iselda woke from the strangest dream she'd ever had to see the moon was still high in the sky. Confused, but still tired, Iselda tried to forget the dream as she let sleep reclaim her.

When Iselda woke the next morning, the sun had barely risen in the sky. Still confused by her dream, she kept her promise to Annabelle and let her sleep, as she went to the kitchen. Finding something to cook for breakfast, Iselda started a small fire in the cooking stove. She'd found some eggs and figured that they would do. As she cooked, she thought of what her dream could have meant. But all she could think of was it was her mind putting visuals to the pain she'd been feeling over having to leave her family. But even as she decided this was the cause, she still wanted to know who that woman had been, and why she felt she knew her.

The first batch of eggs she made, she took out to the driver. Waking him up by offering him breakfast and telling him where he could find some food for the horses put him in a good mood. Letting him know that the horses wouldn't have to go so hard today, and that the journey was to be short, he knew would make the horses very happy. After he'd had the eggs, he left to get the food for the horses.

Returning to the house, Iselda found Annabelle at the stove, cooking another batch of eggs. "I didn't know you could cook," she said as she watched Annabelle add some herb to the eggs.

"I wasn't always royalty. For the majority of the lives I've lived, I've been a simpleton. And as I'm sure you remember, you have to cook when you live alone. It may have been a while, but I think I still got it."

The way Annabelle moved around the kitchen was quite graceful and Iselda found a subtle beauty to it. And when she saw the layout of the plate, how the bread, meat, and eggs were arranged, she wondered why her friend had never become a chef. Taking a forkful of eggs, she gave a loud moan. "Dear spirits, Annabelle, this is delicious. Why have you never become a chef?"

Sitting down with her own plate, she shrugged her shoulders. "I don't know; I didn't want to be spending my life serving some king his meals. Meals he'd probably just wolf down and not appreciate the care put into them."

"Well, I've spent plenty of time watching our chef go about cooking and he doesn't move as gracefully as you did just now; you could certainly give him a few tips. And Alix is one of the best chefs I've known," she said to emphasize her point.

Annabelle just blushed at the praise, a rare occurrence even after she had changed. "Thank you. My mother taught me," she said quietly. Iselda just reached out a hand and took her friend's, giving it a small sympathetic squeeze. "When do you want to leave?" she asked after a minute's silence.

Pulling her hand back so she could eat, Iselda said, "After this delicious breakfast. Let the horses rest for a bit more; we'll be in Terang before nightfall." Annabelle just nodded and returned to her food as well.

After an hour, they were on the road again. The carriage wasn't very big, but Annabelle's size went a long way in keeping them from being uncomfortable. When they'd been on the road for a while, Annabelle broke the silence. "The other day you mentioned that the lullaby you sing your son is based on prophecy, as are some of Pan's bedtime stories. Why?" she asked.

"It was Pan's idea. He wanted to have them learning, without realizing it. And he thought that prophecy was by nature, a story. Because he can understand prophecy to a degree, he's able to discern the tale within and build a story around it. As for Shade's lullaby, it speaks of an old Gothtorian prince who was betrayed by the one person he thought would never turn against him: his sister. It's morbid, I know, but when Pan told me the story, the words came without my wanting them to and Shade loves it so much, that I've just not really thought of it."

"You tell him the story of Slac Hino?" Annabelle asked in astonishment. Iselda nodded her head which made Annabelle give a snort of laughter. "You know he was the one that formalized the Gothtorian language?"

"No, I didn't know that."

"Yes, he was a true champion of the people; a people that realized too late that several prophecies spoke of him. He didn't deserve the fate he received; even I was outraged when I first heard the truth. Gothtor has never been able to recover from seeing his blood on its hands." Iselda was taken aback by this revelation, and even more so when she saw a tear slide down the girl's cheek. "I hope you don't dishonour his memory in your son's lullaby."

"Annabelle...how did you know Slac Hino?" Iselda asked. What she really wanted to know was why Annabelle shed a tear for this man, but didn't want to appear insensitive to the fact that this man had earned her sympathies.

"I didn't know him. I had gone to Gothtor to learn Gothtorian. And one day he came to the village I was staying at to do the kingly thing. But there was this little girl who was very sick. Slac Hino went to see her and tried to make her feel better, but there was nothing he could've done.

"The next day, she died. And when he heard this, he fell to his knees in tears. After crying publicly over this six-year-old girl he'd just met for five minutes, he got up and went to the family to give his condolences. He attended and spoke at her funeral the next day and commissioned a statue to be built in her honour. And as I saw him do all this, I thought that it's for men like these that Lilith stopped me from killing every one of them.

"Slac Hino's death at the hands of his sister was the first thing that made me question my hatred. But I countered this thought with the thought that he was only one man, and that he was the exception to their brutality," she concluded as the tears really started to flow. Iselda held her arms open and Annabelle climbed into them willingly, seeking the comfort of her friend.

"It's OK, Annabelle, it's OK. You've changed; you properly mourn him now," Iselda reassured continuously. For twenty minutes, Annabelle cried at her former self. It was another twenty before she released herself from Iselda and moved back to her side of the carriage.

"Thanks," she said. "But I have another question. Why is it Shade's lullaby; do you have a separate one for your daughter?"

"No, Nikki doesn't have a lullaby. I'm sure she knows what I sing to her brother as well as myself, but she's never needed one. Before Pan had his prophecy idea, I'd sing to them in their crib. Five seconds in and Nikki would roll over and go to sleep; but Shade would watch me until I was finished singing before rolling over," Iselda explained. "And there's nothing in this world or the next that will stop me from singing to him tonight," she added fiercely.

"I'm sorry, Iselda, for pulling you away from your children. I should have thought my actions through and realized that what happened to me, I was inflicting on your children," Annabelle said with her head bowed contritely.

"It's OK, Annabelle, you're bringing me home to them now. It's been three weeks but, I've had contact with them and know they're OK," Iselda said, again clutching her necklace, and giving her friend a reassuring smile.

The rest of the journey was passed in silence. But after an hour and a half, Iselda began to see the outer rings of Terang. She saw the torches lining the street and leading to the castle and knew that Pan indeed knew she was coming. But she was concerned by the fact that the city seemed to be empty; not one soul was outside on the streets and the torches that led their way were the only source of light she could see.

But this fear was squashed when the carriage entered the castle courtyard. While the courtyard was a large empty space on any other day, tonight it was packed so tightly that the path for the carriage was just barely big enough for it to fit through. And everyone was cheering.

When the carriage came to a stop at the bottom of the stairway to the large double doors that led into the castle, the crowd cleared from the stairway until only seven people were on the stairs. But Iselda only had eyes for three of them. Pan stood in the middle of the stairs with Shade and Nikki on either side. He was dressed in the traditional Brarian ceremonial robes: black pants and shirt, a white jacket with gold embroidery along its neck down along the edges, and a black, floor-length cape with the blood red 'K's of the Royal seal, as was Shade. Nikki was wearing a blackblood dress, which along with her dark hair that was pulled back, brought out the colour of her beautiful eyes. Pan had clearly worked hard to impress upon her the importance of her return.

Iselda could barely wait for the driver of their carriage to open the door, and when he did and she stepped out, the crowd roared deafeningly. But she only had eyes for Pan, whose brown eyes brightened as he saw her. Stepping aside so Annabelle could step out as well immediately brought a hush to the crowd.

"Welcome, Empress Annabelle, to Terang. I am Panken Kanta, the king of Braria. Please, allow my wife and queen to escort you inside to the largest feast this country has ever had," Pan said in what Iselda had come to call his official voice. It was the voice he used at formal affairs and was meant to be grand.

Annabelle took Iselda's arm that was offered and the two of them slowly climbed the stairs. When they reached Pan, Shade, and Nikki, Iselda stopped. Kneeling, she held her arms open but did not have to wait long for them to be filled. Shade and Nikki ran to her and gave her the biggest hug she'd ever received. Holding them to her as tightly as she could, she gave both of them a kiss and whispered, "I missed you." They just nodded against her, as she felt unconditional love flood her heart and repair it.

Standing back up and turning to Annabelle, she saw her friend was pale. "Annabelle…?" she asked hesitantly. Iselda saw Annabelle's eyes flutter and Iselda stepped closer to catch her as she fainted.

Chapter 39:

Hados

The crowd gasped as the girl fainted. As everyone was watching Iselda give Shade and Nikki a hug, nobody saw how Annabelle had been staring right at Kailee when she fainted. To Kailee, it looked like the girl had seen a ghost, as she'd stopped dead once she saw her and seemed to be muttering something to herself until Iselda took notice of her.

"Ladies and gentlemen, please remain calm," Pan was saying to the gathered mass. "If you'll make your way inside please, your food is waiting. I will take care of our guest and will be down to join you all shortly. Please, go have your dinner, the situation is under control." Slowly, the crowd disappeared into the castle until only the Royal family, Shade, Marina, Kailee, and Sabrina remained in the courtyard. "Let's take her inside."

They entered the castle and headed for Pan's and Iselda's room. Once there, Iselda placed Annabelle on the bed and stepped aside so Pan and Sabrina could assess her. Kailee took this moment to go to Iselda and give her a hug. "Welcome home," she said.

"Thanks, Kailee. You have no idea how good this feels," Iselda said, returning the hug. "Is she going to be alright?" she asked Pan and Sabrina.

"She's fine; she just fainted is all. Although, I don't know why," Pan said, causing Kailee to blush.

That was all Iselda needed to hear; once she had, she ran to Pan and started to cry. Marina silently motioned everyone out of the room so they could have their privacy and shut the door once they were all out. Once in the hallway, Shade and Marina announced they were heading down to dinner to make sure everyone was behaving.

A minute after they left, Pan and Iselda opened the door to their room and let everyone back in. Shade and Nikki immediately ran to their mother as all three openly cried. "Oh, my darlings!" Iselda said as she embraced them. "Mommy missed you so much!"

"We missed you too, Mommy," Nikki said.

"But we knew we'd see you again," added Shade.

Before Iselda could reply to her children's optimism, there was a knock on the door. "Hello," said a slow, deep voice - a voice Kailee had heard once before, and had never forgotten since. "Please forgive my intrusion, but I believe I can help the girl you call Empress Annabelle," Sodah continued.

Kailee couldn't turn to look at the man she saw in her darkest nightmares. She'd become cold and numb all over, her body tensed to run at a moment's noticed. The only thing she could do was listen. "She's fine, she just fainted," Pan said cautiously. "Once her strength is recovered, she'll wake up."

"Forgive me, great king, but it's more complicated than her simply recovering her strength. She needs to remember.

Isn't that right, Kailee?"

The fact that he remembered her name was all that powered her to turn and look at him. He looked exactly the way she remembered him; he was at least as tall as Pan, if not taller, and despite looking like he'd just escaped the underworld, she got the sense that he was quite strong, powerful even. His eyes were black, the deepest black she'd ever seen; his hair was slicked back, tight to his skull, and matched his eyes perfectly. When Kailee realized that everyone was looking at her after this stranger had said her name, she knew she had to answer him. "All I know is…is that she looked at me like I was a ghost and then fainted," she said in a shaky voice.

"Yes, but not a ghost, child, a goddess. The one she calls mother: Nina." This claim was met by gasps from all the adults. "You really do look like her, Kailee."

"Kailee, who is this?" Iselda asked.

"Sodah," she whispered to further gasps by Sabrina and Iselda.

But he just chuckled. "While that is the name I gave you twenty-five years ago, it is not my name. You were so young; I didn't want to frighten you more than I already was. Especially since I needed your help, which you have given beautifully. I am Hados, Lord of the Underworld." Even the children gasped at this.

"This is the meeting you spoke of?" Iselda asked.

"Yes, Iselda, it is. Now, may I please help my wife?" Kailee couldn't believe the urgency in his voice. "I've waited for fifteen thousand years for this moment, and I do not wish to wait another."

"Wife?!" Iselda's voice was as disbelieving as Kailee felt.

"Annabelle isn't your wife! The closest she got to being married was when she was with me! If she were married, I'd know about it!"

"She doesn't remember," he said as a tear rolled down his cheek. He walked to the bed and sat down beside Annabelle. "But she will." Leaning down so his mouth was next to her ear, he whispered, "Korena, come back to me, my love." Pulling back so that he was looking at her face, he closed his eyes and kissed her. And when he removed his lips from hers, Kailee saw her eyes flutter open.

"Hados!" Annabelle said, and then she was embracing him. "My love, forgive me." Iselda heard Hados continually whisper the name he'd called her as they held each other, not unlike how her and Pan had held each other not five minutes before.

Standing up, Iselda called, "Annabelle...?"

Pulling away from Hados, Annabelle looked at her with a smile. "Iselda, my friend, thank you. Thank you so much!" she said as she got off the bed and embraced Iselda. "You have done more for me than I could have ever asked for. For the rest of eternity, should you ever want something, all you need to do is ask. All of you, all you need to do is ask."

"I think, Annabelle, I speak for everyone when I say an explanation would be nice."

"That will take some time, my dear. I will tell you our tale. But before I do, I believe there is a feast in your honour going on downstairs. Go to your guests, and reassure them that both their queen and her guest are alright."

"That would be easier done if you were there with me."

"I need a moment alone with my husband, Iselda. A plight I know you sympathize with. We will join you shortly and then we will tell you our tale."

Iselda only nodded her understanding and taking her children's hands in hers, led the rest of the group from the room. As they were descending the grand staircase that led to the main floor, they met Shade running up.

"I was just coming up to get you guys. Everything alright with our guest?" he asked.

"She's fine," Iselda said. "She just needed a moment alone to collect herself."

Nodding his understanding, Shade came up to her and gave her a hug, a hug which she returned. "Glad to have you back. My brother was getting a little worried before we found out you were coming home," he whispered in her ear.

"So was I," she whispered back as she released him from the hug. "Now lead the way; I want this over and done with as soon as possible." And so Shade turned and led them to the dining room.

"I know what you mean," Pan whispered in her ear at the bottom of the stairs. She just smiled at him.

Chapter 40:

The Full Story

As soon as someone saw them enter the room, they called, "Long Live the Queen!" This chant was quickly on every tongue in the room until she was seated at the head table.

But before she sat, she had to show her gratitude to the crowd. "Thank you everyone, this is quite overwhelming. When I left three weeks ago, I never thought I'd see anyone in Braria again; I thought I was leaving you all forever. And to be back home, and having you all hail me, it heals my heart. I've been told by someone who couldn't be here tonight that it has been decreed that next month's taxes are on us, and I wish to add to your reasons for celebrating. I'm declaring today a day of national celebration: every year on this day Braria shall celebrate by way of festivals. Forevermore, today shall be known as Reunion Day!" This declaration was met with more applause and cheering; but once the "Long Live the Queen" chant started up again, Iselda had to yell at them to go back to their meal.

As everyone was settling into their food, Annabelle and Hados came into the room and sat themselves between

Iselda and Kailee. Kailee didn't look like she enjoyed having the man who haunted her nightmares sitting beside her, but didn't say anything. Once their meals had been served, Iselda turned to Annabelle. "I believe you owe us a story, Annabelle. How is it that you came to be the wife of Hados?" The whole table leaned in imperceptibly at the mentioning of the story, Shade and Marina were confused as they had not been present when Annabelle had been awoken by Hados. Before they could interrupt, Pan shushed them and motioned them to listen.

"You're right, Iselda, I did promise you my tale. It begins before this world was formed. Lilith, Hados, and I willed ourselves into being and created order to the chaos that was these lands; beauty above and below the earth.

"But Lilith grew jealous of the connection between Hados and myself. One day she tricked Hados into thinking she was me. This union brought about life to this world, it gave Lilith Nina. When I learned of this I went to Lilith, enraged that she would betray me in such a way. We fought and she came out on top, cursing me to barrenness for all of eternity.

"Nina knew the truth of what had happened to create her, and she'd spend as much time with us in the underworld as with Lilith in the world above. I tried to convince myself that I should hate this child, that she was the culmination of what had gone wrong in my life. But despite myself, I grew to love her as my own daughter. When Lilith discovered this, she declared that Nina was only to visit the underworld once every twenty-five years; this was a double edged sword as we discovered that we could not go to the surface but once every twenty-five years - thankfully we were able to arrange it so we only went twelve and a half years without seeing each other."

"This was when Nina created humanity," Hados continued, picking up where Annabelle left off. "Forged from the elements of this world and having love breathed into them, my daughter created a race of companions for herself. But Korena and I were to remain alone. Seeing how my wife longed for a child to lighten our hearth, I went to the surface and demanded that Nina give me a human to take back to the underworld so that Korena would smile again. She told me that it was impossible, as the humans were made of the world above and they couldn't leave it.

"It was then that I introduced death into the world. In a rage at the fact that she would not create for me and Korena a companion, I ripped the soul out of the human she loved most and brought his soul to the underworld. This created a bridge between the worlds, a bridge every soul has since crossed, with the exception of one: yours, Iselda.

"But I came to regret this action. And when Korena realized what I'd done, she was furious with me. She went to Nina and tried to apologize for my behaviour, as well as offer herself as a replacement for the life I'd taken. She offered to have her memories blocked and be reborn as Nina's child."

"You know what happened next, Iselda. The humans attacked and killed Nina, who I now believed to be my mother, as well as nearly killing myself. But Lilith rescued me and blessed me with the gift of immortality. And after killing the men who'd killed my 'mother' I built the Temple of the Goddess, as a final tribute to her.

"Since then, I've wandered the earth, not knowing who I truly was and hating all those who reminded me of those that killed Nina. It was not until Hados whispered my true name that I remembered who I really was."

"I've had to wait fifteen thousand years until I knew she would be receptive of my company. But some things needed my guiding hand." Here Hados turned directly to Kailee. "My dear girl, I hope you can forgive me. That day twenty-five years ago, when I kissed your forehead, I gave you two things: a blessing, and a curse. I blessed you with the looks of my daughter, the goddess Nina. But to ensure you'd always remember the words I told you, I cursed you with nightmares of my face until you saw me again. Never again will you dream of my face," he said with another kiss to her forehead. Iselda thought Kailee looked scared, but at the same time relieved, relieved to be free of the burdens she'd unknowingly received as a child.

"I don't understand," Sabrina said. "How did you know that Kailee would play a part in this? How did you know any of this would come to pass as it has?"

"Not all magic in this world comes from Lilith," Hados said with a knowing smile. "The gift of prophecy is a gift I gave humanity after I realized what my actions had done. But the prophecies you have written down are not the only ones there are; I'm flooded with visions of humanity every moment of every day. It was through one of these visions that I found that Kailee would be vital to bringing Korena back to me."

"And how will you return to the underworld?" Pan asked. "By the sounds of it, the life Lilith gave you removed from you the ability to return home."

At this, both Hados and Korena looked sad. "I cannot. For when my body dies, my essence escapes to another body and takes it over. As Iselda said to me, I have lived in this world so much that it has become a part of me; and if I were to leave it, I would cease to exist," Korena said as tears started to fall off her cheeks. "We are to see each other once every twenty-five years for the rest of time."

As Korena started to cry more noticeably, Iselda saw Shade and Nikki get out of their chairs and walk around to her friend and her husband. Stepping into the space between their chairs, her children bowed to them. "Give me your hand," they said in unison to Hados and Korena. Tentatively, they gave their hands. Iselda didn't like the fact that her children were so close to the Lord of the Dead, but she knew they were only trying to help.

But when Korena gasped and pulled her hand away, Iselda knew something was wrong. "No! We can't do that!" she said to them.

"What?! What's going on?" Iselda demanded.

"Your children have offered to help," Hados said. "But what they suggest we do is too cruel, and that fate should not be visited upon anyone, least of all them."

"What is it? What did they suggest?" Iselda demanded. She didn't like the sounds of this.

Looking around, Hados said, "We should not have this conversation here; it will draw too much attention." Looking to Pan he asked, "Is there a place where we can continue in private?"

"Upstairs," he said tensely.

"Then let us go there." And with that, the entire table stood.

But as they were the head table, this didn't go unnoticed. A hush fell over the room as the king and queen rose. "Our conversation has turned to politics, and we do not wish to worry you with our shouting, as it's bound to become heated," Pan lied. "Please continue with the feast, we will be back shortly." And with that, they left the room and returned upstairs.

Chapter 41:

The Future of the Twins

Once they were up the last step, Iselda rounded on Korena and Hados. "What did my children suggest to help you?"

"They suggested that we take their love for each other," Korena said softly. This drew gasps from everyone except Iselda. Kailee even had tears come to her eyes at this.

"While I realize that this is a bad idea, why did you all gasp at it?" Iselda asked her friends and husband.

They all looked to Pan. "You remember how I mentioned in my letter that some things had come to light that I needed to tell you in person?" Iselda just nodded, now knowing that she wouldn't like what he was about to tell her. "Well, one of those things was that our children are Soul Twins."

Hearing this made Iselda's mind go blank. She just stood there, unable to contemplate what she'd just heard. And then it clicked. "WHAT?!"

She expected Pan to explain, but it was Kailee who came to her. "Calm down, Iselda." Calm? How could she be calm after hearing that? "I had much the same reaction as you when I first found out. But whatever you think it's like, I guarantee you, it's not. Using their magic, they showed me how they felt for each other; and it was the most beautiful thing I've ever felt. What they feel for each other is pure love. Not romantic love, not familial love, not maternal love: it's all those and so much more, combined and amplified to form pure love. And with their emotional magic they know that no one can love them as the other does. Look at them, Iselda," and she did. She saw them clutching each other in the middle of the circle that the adults had formed. "From the moment you knew you were pregnant with them, you loved them more than anything in this world or the next, did you not?" Iselda nodded that she did. "And all you want is for them to be happy; since you found out you were with child, that's all you've cared about, your child's happiness." Again Iselda nodded. "Then be joyous, for they have found what makes them happy."

Iselda just looked at her friend, a little shocked by the fierceness of her defence of Shade and Nikki. She looked to them again; they showed no fear, no anger; if anything, it looked to Iselda that they were pleading with her. Walking to them and then kneeling, she said, "Show me. Show me what you showed Aunt Kailee." They took each other's hands and then took each of hers. And she felt it; it was exactly as Kailee had described it, a maelstrom of every form of love she could think of, as well as some she couldn't, to form the most beautiful of all feelings: pure love.

Iselda felt tears sting her eyes. How could she ever have denied this? She'd suspected that the connection between them was stronger than she was willing to concede, but this was too much for her. She couldn't allow them to give this up, she wouldn't allow it.

When they let go of her hands, they gave her a hug. "It's the only way Mommy," Shade whispered in her ear. She felt Nikki nod her agreement against her.

Walking over to them and crouching as well, Hados said, "That may be, little one, but the fact remains, we cannot take that away from you. You and your sister still need your love for each other. And despite what this world thinks of me, I am not heartless; and to take this love away from the two of you would be a very bad thing."

Iselda thought she heard something in Hados' voice as he said this. "Do you mean that our love is important for the future?" Nikki asked, voicing the question Iselda had had at Hados' words, but had feared the answer. Her children were much braver than her for being able to ask it.

"I knew you two were special the moment I felt the creation of your soul," Hados said to her with a smile. "But you two already know the answer to that; you know what you are to do. But I will tell you something," he said as both Shade and Nikki looked to him. "The full extent of your impact on life is not yet foreseen. You two are major forces in the coming years, years that are full of forked prophecies. Not all of these prophecies have been passed to human minds, but all hinge on your decisions. I will guarantee that you will hear these prophecies before the time comes to make your decision. The rest, I leave to you," Hados said solemnly. To acknowledge what they were just told, Shade and Nikki again bowed to him.

He stood and turned to return to the outer circle, but Iselda called him back. "Was that necessary? To place such a heavy burden on two children, my children who aren't even five years old?" she asked with a not so subtle amount of malice.

Hados motioned for her to get up, and she reluctantly did. Taking one of her hands in both of his, he spoke in a tongue only she and Korena would know. "*Yes, child, it is necessary. I don't like it any more than you do, but it must be done. I do not reveal the future lightly, as I've learned that it often ends badly for those I wished to have warned. But your children are strong, the soul they share is one of the most powerful ever created, and I only wish for their well-being. However, there is one more thing I must do with them before I leave, and it must be done alone.*"

"*No, not alone! If you wish to speak with them to place more burdens on them, then I shall be there as well,*" Iselda said fiercely.

At this, Hados shook his head, a grave look on his face. "*No, Iselda, you cannot be. I must tell them something in the language of Soul Twins; a tongue that must remain hidden from everyone, save those who are Soul Twins. But if you feel you must know what I tell them, it is this: when the time comes for them to take up the sword, they will be betrayed. And this betrayal will be very painful, for it will cause the death of the one they love the most and give birth to the Beast. This Beast is to be their opponent and is not to be taken lightly for it is very powerful and remorseless. It will take everything they have, and then some, to defeat it. I will give them more details that I can't give you, but that is what I have to tell them.*" Iselda didn't want her babies to learn of this. She didn't want them to have to take up the sword, as Hados had put it. But she knew that they couldn't escape that fate.

Turning her back on Hados and every motherly instinct she had, she knelt to her children. "Take Hados to your room; he wishes to tell you more about your future," she told them, trying to hold back the tears.

But she knew they could see this, as they held their arms open to her. With a fleeting smile at their kindness, Iselda pulled them to her and hugged them tight. "It's OK, Mommy," they said in unison. And then they released her and took Hados' hands in theirs, pulling him to their chambers.

As she stood up to watch them go, she realized Pan was at her side. "What is it he's telling them?" he asked her softly.

Shaking her head, she said, "You don't want to know. I don't want them to know, but I know he wouldn't tell them if he didn't have to." Iselda flung herself against his chest as she cried at the fact that she had knowingly allowed her children to be hurt. What kind of mother willingly let her children be harmed when they could prevent it?

Seeming to know what she was thinking, Pan brought his arms around her and cooed in her ear. "It's better they be prepared for whatever he's telling them, rather than having to face it for the first time when it happens; the foreknowledge will allow for a sense of detachment. You're still a wonderful mother, and they will not think any less of you for giving them a moment alone with Hados; they know that you would willingly do anything to keep them from harm." Pan's words only strengthened her tears, as he vocalized her every doubt at that moment.

After a minute where the only sound was Iselda's quiet sobs, Marina said, "I think we'll go back to dinner and make sure everyone's still having a good time." By 'we' Iselda thought she meant her and Shade, but then she saw that Kailee and Sabrina were going with them, leaving only Pan and herself along with Korena.

After a few minutes of it just being the three of them, Hados returned, alone. "They wanted me to tell you that they wish to see the two of you. The two of you should be very proud, for what I told them was not easy to hear, and they took it very well. They're upset by it, naturally, but despite being only four and a half, they were quite mature about it." With this compliment, Iselda thought he was trying to compensate for what he'd just done to their children.

"We'll head back to the feast and tell everyone you needed a moment with Shade and Nikki," Korena said, reaching for Iselda's hand and giving it a squeeze. "Remember, today is a day of celebration; it's Reunion Day."

This made Iselda smile. "Thank you." Korena just nodded and took Hados' hand as they turned and walked down the stairs. As Pan put his arm around her waist, she turned to him and kissed him. Once they were finished, they turned themselves to their children's room, and set off to it.

When they entered the room, Iselda saw Shade and Nikki in the space between their beds that was Pan's stage for when he acted out their bedtime stories. They were clinging to each other and clearly crying. But when they saw their parents, they let go of each other and wiped the tears from their faces.

Pan and Iselda made to go and comfort them, but they held up their hands to keep them away. "No, do not try to make us feel better," they said in unison. "We need to feel this pain. But we need you to join us," they said as they sat.

Tentatively, Pan and Iselda made their way to their children and sat down. It was when she was seated that Iselda saw the quillum. "Where did you two get that?" she asked pointing to the crystal obelisk.

"From the Blackreich," Shade said, as if it were obvious. Neither Pan nor Iselda could get past the shock this simple answer brought.

"Daddy," Nikki said, as if she was afraid he would be angry with her. "We need you to give Mommy her powers back."

Now their children really had their attention: Iselda had never mentioned the fact she once possessed magic to her children and made everyone who knew that fact keep it to themselves. The fact that Shade and Nikki knew unsettled Iselda slightly. If they knew this, what else did they know about her?

"How-how did you learn of that?" she asked in a whisper.

At this, Shade bowed his head. "I'm sorry Mommy," he said. "I recognized your aura around this when we first found our way into the Blackreich. When we found the picture of the stone in one of the books, we figured it out. We don't know what they can do, but we know that it's unlike any other form of magic we've seen. Then we saw Mr. Hados and saw a reflection of the darkness of your powers. What's the part that's bright?"

Iselda turned to look at Pan, seeking his council on this. His face was unreadable and she took this to mean 'do what you think you should'. "Before I met Daddy, I had a very special type of magic - magic that I inherited from my mommies. I could hurt people, or make them feel really good and I could make them so they wouldn't die, or make them die. When I was younger, I used this power to hurt and kill people. But when I realized that what I was doing was wrong, I stopped. When I met Daddy, I asked him to remove them so that I could live normally." It wasn't the complete truth, but enough of it so they wouldn't be horrified by her.

The two of them nodded their understanding and turned back to their father. "Daddy, Mommy needs her powers back," Nikki said again, her brother nodded along.

"I don't know how to give her powers back, sweetheart. I've never used quillum like that." The look on Pan's face made Iselda believe it.

But apparently Shade and Nikki didn't. "Really?" they asked together. "You just destroy the crystal," they said plainly.

"And just how do I do that?" Pan asked in a tone of voice that made Iselda think that he thought his children were too smart if they knew things he didn't. Nikki laughed at this and Shade smiled slightly.

"Silly Daddy," Nikki giggled, "you ignite nightfire in the crystal; it will break and Mommy gets her powers back!"

"One of these days we are going to need to talk. The two of you know things that even I don't know," Pan said seriously. "But for now, why does Mommy need her powers back?"

Iselda had wondered this as well. Remembering what Hados had told her and Shade and Nikki made her even more uneasy about taking back her powers. As Pan finished his question, both he and Iselda looked to their children. For a long moment their faces wore identical masks that hid what they were thinking, but then, they simultaneously let out a sigh.

"To protect herself," Shade said with a small smile to his mother. Nikki just nodded her agreement.

"To protect me from what? What did Hados tell you, that he didn't tell me?" Iselda asked, gently trying to get to the real reason why they wanted her to have her powers back.

At this, both Shade and Nikki got tears in their eyes, but shook their heads. "Please, just do what we ask," they said with bowed heads.

Iselda and Pan looked at each other and wordlessly agreed to this. "Very well," Pan said. "You said I had to ignite nightfire within the crystal. How do I do that?" Iselda could tell that he found the whole notion of asking his children how to do something completely crazy, just by the way he asked.

Apparently, Nikki found this funny as she giggled at her father's dilemma. "How do you normally ignite nightfire, Daddy?" Rather than explain, Pan held up his hand and ignited a ball of nightfire in his hand. "Now, do the same thing with the flame in the crystal," Nikki said as if it was easy as putting on a shoe.

"For someone who can mentally tell me to come to her and read my emotions, you don't seem able to understand that I can't ignite nightfire outside the confines of my hand. I can send it out from me, but it must start in my hand."

"Then just hold the crystal in your hand." Seeing Pan shake his head at this, Nikki giggled again. "Well, what can you do Daddy? We can grab it, why can't you?"

This brought a look of shock to both Pan and Iselda. "You can touch the quillum, without it burning you?" Iselda asked.

Nodding, both Shade and Nikki reached out a hand and grabbed the obelisk. When they let go, they showed their hands and Iselda noticed nothing had happened to them. Tentatively, Iselda reached out a hand to the quillum and found that she could touch it.

The moment that Iselda felt the cool crystal beneath her hand, it began to glow a blood red. As the glow got stronger, so too did the heat of the crystal, culminating in the room being bathed in a blood red and her feeling as if her hand was being fused to the obelisk. A jolt ran up her arm and throughout her entire body, but rather than hurt her, it seemed to be strengthening her. And then the glowing stopped and her hand was able to release the quillum.

Looking to Pan for an explanation of what had just happened, Iselda saw his eyes explode open and he fell back, convulsing on the ground. Not understanding what was happening, Iselda crawled as fast as she could to him. But this only seemed to cause him more pain. Suddenly, Nikki was pulling her away and covering her eyes with something. "Don't struggle, Mommy, I'm helping Daddy. You need to go outside for a minute," she said in Iselda's ear as she tugged her out of the room and back to the hallway.

Chapter 42:
How We Were Before

Once in the hallway, Nikki removed the blindfold and Iselda saw that she was scared. "Sweetheart, what's wrong?" she asked, switching instinctively to being a mother.

"That shouldn't have happened. You shouldn't have got your powers back from simply grabbing the crystal for a second." Was Iselda the only one who'd realized that she'd held onto the quillum for more than a second?

"I have my powers back?" she asked slowly. While she didn't believe it, it made sense. But she'd always had control of them, so why had Pan just started to convulse?

"I don't understand," Nikki said. "Your powers were trapped; only breaking the quillum should have released them." The fact that her children were smarter than her husband with regards to magic was indeed off-putting.

"What happened to Daddy; what did I do to him?" Iselda asked, fearing the worst.

"He's OK, Mommy; the pain stopped once I covered your eyes. Your magic must have unleashed itself after being pent up in the quillum for so long. Give me your hand, Mommy."

Iselda gave her hand to her daughter and felt the glow of love and reassurance flow into her. Holding up a strip of cloth, the blindfold, Nikki said, "Put this on, and let's go inside. We need to make sure you can control yourself."

Nodding her understanding as she took the blindfold and tied it around her eyes, Iselda let her daughter lead her back into the bedroom.

Once back inside, Iselda could hear her husband's panting as he recovered from the dose of pain she'd inadvertently given him. "Are you alright?" she asked Pan in a small voice.

"I'm fine," he said in voice that was a little shakier than his own. "That was nothing. Are you OK?"

"No," Iselda replied honestly. "I seem to have broken the laws of magic and gotten my powers back, but without the control I used to have over them. I want to be able to see my husband without hurting him."

"I'd like that as well. But what happened when you grabbed the quillum? Something must have happened in that second you grabbed it."

Iselda wanted so much to go to him and be in his arms, but she knew that could risk him being hurt again. So she stayed standing where she was and answered his question. "It glowed blood red and heated up as the glow grew stronger. It got to the point where the whole room was blood red and it felt like my skin had melted and fused itself to the surface of the quillum. Then a jolt ran up my arm and throughout my body, leaving me feeling stronger. And suddenly, the glowing and heat disappeared; that's when I turned to you to ask what that was." As she explained, she felt her palm, making sure that it wasn't damaged.

She could hear the three of them mulling this over as they

tried to figure out what happened. She had Nikki take her to a bed so she wasn't just standing there. After about five minutes of silence as they tried to think of answers, she felt a weight on the bed beside her. She knew it was Pan; and as much as she wanted him close, she shuffled away. But he grabbed her hand gently, and she stilled. "Easy, love," he whispered. Then she felt his hands on the blindfold.

"NO!" she cried as she pulled away from his hands.

"It's OK, Iselda. You can control yourself, I know you can," he said. Taking a deep breath, Iselda nodded her head and once again felt his hands removing the blindfold. She kept her eyes closed even after the cloth was removed. "Iselda," Pan called gently. Tentatively, she opened her eyes to see him sitting there. He wasn't in pain; he was just looking deep into her eyes. And then he was kissing her.

As Pan pulled away, she clung to him. She wanted to feel his reassuring presence at her side as she took everything in. It wasn't until she felt Shade and Nikki climb onto the bed and hug her that she was able to release Pan and return to the matters at hand. Bringing her children to her front she looked them both deep in the eyes. "Tomorrow the four of us are going to have a very long talk where you're going to tell me everything you can about everything. Understand?" The two of them nodded that they did. "But for today, let's forget everything and pretend to celebrate," she added with a small smile.

They smiled widely and gave her another hug, which she took to mean they agreed to her plan. Releasing her from their hug, Shade and Nikki took one of her hands into theirs and started to pull her out the door. Looking back, she saw Pan smile as he followed them out.

Once they returned back to the feast, Pan immediately noticed that half the crowd had left; this still left the room quite full, just not as packed. He was secretly grateful for this, but would never have admitted it to anyone, because he knew it would be misconstrued horribly if the wrong people heard it. Like the last time that she'd entered the room, everyone cheered Iselda's return insistently. And like last time, she had to shout at them to get them to stop chanting 'Long Live the Queen.'

Looking to his brother, Pan saw Shade tilt his head to the side; he wanted to talk to him privately. So Pan went over to his chair. "Everything OK? You look a little pale." Leave it to Shade to be the one to see the slightest changes in him.

With a glance to the others at their table, Pan gave a small nod. "I'll tell you about it later. When were alone." Shade nodded his understanding.

The rest of the feast passed without much else happening. And after another hour and a half, the room was empty save for the ten of them. Once the table was cleared of all dishes and silverware and the guards had left, an uneasy silence fell over the table. Not every issue had been solved from when they were upstairs, and everyone's eyes were on Iselda.

"I want to help you, Korena," she said, looking to the girl. "You deserve to be with the one you love."

Korena smiled, but it was Hados that spoke. "Thank you child, but it cannot be done without the greatest of sacrifices. A love must be destroyed for us to be together in the underworld; I will not let you sacrifice any love for my happiness. Now that Korena knows who she is, we can be together. And that's what matters." Pan could tell that to say this caused Hados great pain, but it gave Pan an idea.

"When you say 'a love,' what do you mean?"

"A strong love, mutually felt between two people. Their bond must be strong, like brothers or lovers. Giving up your love of chocolate won't do," he said, somewhat guessing Pan's plan.

"Couldn't you just take one person's love?" Iselda asked.

Hados shook his head. "You don't understand; the love has to be destroyed. The two people who give it up will never be able to feel anything but respect for each other. They'll know how they once felt, but the place where that love once was will be empty. They would be changed, to the point of non-recognition. I will not inflict that type of misery on the world; I've done enough to it already." Hados' head fell as he said this last part; even after all this time, the god felt the pain of regret over the death he'd caused.

"Will nothing else suffice?" asked Iselda.

"No," Korena said, shaking her head sadly. "Sadly, it is the only way. You have all done so much for us; we couldn't ask you to do any more than what you've already done."

Pan knew he had to do something, he just didn't know what. Looking around the table, he saw seven faces screwed up as they thought of a way to help. Then his eyes met Sabrina's. They shared a moment and he saw her nod. Simultaneously, the two of them stood. "Take our love," Pan said to Hados and Korena.

"Daddy, no!" Nikki screamed, tugging on his hand.

Crossing to him, but crouching down to Nikki, Sabrina said, "It's OK, sweetheart, we know what we're doing. I know you wanted us to be back to how we used to be, but we can't go back there. We made up, but it still hurts. I've loved your father since we first met, but some things are just not meant to be." Sabrina stood up and Pan could see the tears in her eyes as she turned to face Korena. "Take our love; be together like we never could be."

"Are you sure?" Iselda asked.

Pan didn't know which of them she was asking, so he just nodded. He turned to Sabrina to see her crying. He pulled her into his arms and held her like he had all those years ago. He wished he still had the powers of the Time Wind; his power to bring her back to a happier time would have been well received right then, but then he realized that they needed to feel this pain.

When he opened his eyes, he saw Hados and Korena had silently surrounded them. While still holding her close, Pan angled Sabrina and himself so that they faced the deities. "Are you sure about this? For it cannot be undone. The place you hold in each other's hearts will be forever empty," Hados cautioned.

"Yes we're sure. Take it," Pan said resolutely. He felt Sabrina nod against him.

"Very well," Hados said. "Hold her tight."

Pan did as instructed and braced for whatever was to come. He felt Sabrina tense in his arms as she did the same. He closed his eyes, not wanting to know what Hados was about to do.

But before anything could happen, Korena called for Hados to wait. Pan opened his eyes and turned to the girl who he was trying to help. "Before you take their love, Hados, give them a minute to get everything off their chest," she said. Then she turned to the rest of the table. "This is to be their last moments of feeling anything for each other; they deserve some privacy." Everyone got up and walked to the far side of the room. Kailee and Iselda hesitated a moment before joining the others.

Pan looked to Sabrina, into her beautiful green eyes. "You don't have to do this, they'll understand."

"I'm a healer, Pan, this is what I do."

"You're supposed to heal yourself before healing others." She smiled at this piece of practice that she'd taught him when they first met. But then her face fell as she seemed to remember this. "I'm sorry we're doing this after we just made up," he said.

"Me too."

For a moment they were quiet as the situation made itself felt. "You were my first love, Sabrina, and I'm sorry for everything I did that hurt you."

"And you were the first and only man I ever loved, and I'm sorry for all the hurt I've caused you."

Pan pulled her into his embrace and they hugged each other tight. As they let each other go, their eyes met. Pan was helpless to stop what came next, even though he initiated it. They kissed, sensuously but chastely. After thirty seconds, they pulled away from each other. "Sorry, I shouldn't have done that. I don't know what came over me," Pan rushed to get out, but stopped when Sabrina placed a finger to his lips.

"It's OK, Panken, you were only a second quicker than me." Sabrina had a slight smile, a smile that made Pan think she was referring to more than this moment of quickness. The wink she gave a second later confirmed it.

Pan blushed slightly, but didn't say anything as he waved

the others to return to them. "No matter what happens, I love you," Pan whispered in her ear. In response, he felt the swell of heat that she'd always used to comfort him and he knew that she loved him too.

"Will it hurt?" Sabrina asked Hados in a small voice.

Hados, for his part, didn't shy away from the question. "Yes; but it'll be easier if you don't resist. Now, as you were." Pan and Sabrina pulled each other in tight, as Hados began to chant a harsh, guttural series of sounds. While Pan couldn't make out the individual words, he thought he understood the general meaning: Hados was calling on the forces of the universe to aid him in his task.

And then he felt it, the god's hand shoving itself into their chests and squeezing. Of the forms of pain Pan had felt, nothing would have prepared him for this. It felt as if his body was being torn open and his insides were being ripped into millions of pieces, one agonizing piece by agonizing piece. He tried not to fight it, but the way it made him feel made that impossible. And then the pain was gone.

Pan found himself on the ground, on his knees. Looking up, he saw Hados' hand curled in a fist, an orange glow coming from between his fingers. "Korena, come and drink of their love," he said softly. The girl walked to him and opened her mouth, tilting her head up slightly. Hados then squeezed his hand tighter, suffocating the light within, over Korena's mouth. Even as Pan felt his heart contract painfully, he couldn't look away as the orange liquid fell from hand to mouth.

As the drops fell, one by one, Pan could see the changes it brought. Korena started to glow, and there was a hunger in her eyes as if the love juice she was swallowing was the most intoxicating fluid in the world above or below. Pan wouldn't have been surprised if she took Hados' hand and started to lick it clean; she didn't.

After the last drop fell, the girl collapsed. Iselda moved to see if she was OK, but Hados held up a hand to hold her back. The glow soon faded and the girl's body jerked so that it was lying flat on its back. Then her back arched as if she was in pain and her mouth opened to scream, but no sound came out. Instead, it was the orange glow. And then Pan saw it: the hand that shot out of her mouth, then another, extending until what could only be described as Korena's true form, had climbed out of the girl's mouth.

As the girl's body slumped back to the ground, Pan looked upon Korena. She was as tall as Iselda, but darker skinned. Her hair was a jumble of every colour of hair Pan could think of, from white to black. Her eyes seemed to shift colours, unable to decide which colour they wanted to be. She had a full figure and when she spoke, it was with an ethereal voice. "So good to be me." She then bent down to the body she'd just climbed out of and took off the ring on the right hand, replacing it on her new right hand.

Stepping over the unmoving body of the girl, Korena walked over to where Pan and Sabrina had fallen to the floor after having their love removed. "Thank you," she said as she crouched down to them. "You have no idea how much this means to me, to be back in my own body and able to go home with my love. I'm sorry it came at such a price to the two of you. And if either of you two ever needs anything, just call my name, and it shall be done." She stood up and offered each of them a hand, pulling them back up.

The moment Korena let go of Pan's hand after he stood

up, Iselda and Nikki were holding him tight. And he could see Kailee was clutching at Sabrina the same way Iselda was clutching him. And then Nikki was hugging her aunt as well, as the rest of the group closed in to make sure they were alright.

Chapter 43:

Goodbyes and Goodnights

Iselda couldn't believe what her husband and friend had just done, and for a stranger they'd just met. The fact that Pan had given up something so precious to help an enemy, however former, only proved that he was the greatest of men, and made her love him even more. She held him tight as she asked if he was OK.

"I'm fine; I've never felt pain like that, but I'll be alright." His voice was a little tense, but she guessed that was to be expected. Even still, she unleashed a flash of pleasure to his heart; maybe having her powers back wasn't as bad as she thought it was. Feeling the gift she'd just given him, Pan whispered his thanks in her ear.

Looking to Sabrina and Kailee, Iselda was about to ask how Sabrina was feeling, but then decided that she probably felt the same as Pan and unleashed the same pleasure she'd just given Pan on Sabrina. Sabrina turned to her with a confused smile, but nodded her thanks. Then there was a tap on Iselda's shoulder.

Turning, she saw the new form of Korena, who was

smiling at her. "So, this is what you look like, is it?" And then she remembered the dream she'd had the previous night. The woman in the mosaic with the strange hair and eyes was the goddess before her.

Korena gave a small laugh, the most pleasant laugh Iselda had ever heard. "Yes, Iselda, this is what I really look like. Am I still beautiful?"

"You always were," Hados said in her ear, as he came and encircled her in his arms. Iselda saw Korena sigh in pleasure as she was finally able to feel her lover on her own flesh.

"He's right," Iselda whispered. "I always knew you were beautiful; I can now see the full extent of your beauty." Korena stepped out of her husband's arms and into Iselda's, as the two embraced. That's when Iselda noticed Shade was kneeling next to the girl who had been Korena. He was looking at her with a worried expression, as she still hadn't moved.

Releasing Korena from their embrace, she turned her to face her former host. "Is she going to be alright?" Iselda asked quietly.

Korena nodded. "She should be coming around anytime now." As if on cue, the girl's body stirred, which made Shade jerk slightly. Both Iselda and Korena gave a small smile as they saw this. "You were right," she said. When Iselda looked at her in confusion, Korena elaborated, "You told me he was the sweetest boy you ever knew the first time you actually mentioned him. Most every child would run to make sure their family members are OK, before seeing to others. Your son has barely taken his eyes off her since I got out, never even looking to his father or aunt. Even though I know he and his sister are more connected than anyone here, it's nice to know that they can still be different from each other."

By now, the others had seemed to remember the unconscious girl on the floor, who'd just had a goddess climb out of her mouth. Her eyes were starting to flutter, and as one, the group lurched to her. But Shade held up a hand, waving everyone away as the girl finally opened her eyes fully.

She looked to Shade, pushing herself up and away slightly from him. "Wh-where am I?" she asked in a shaky voice. "Who are you?"

Iselda saw Shade smile warmly to the girl, as he stood up and offered her his hand. "My name is Shade Leo Kanta," he said formally, with a slight bow of his head. "This is my home: Terang castle in Braria. What's your name?" Iselda's heart swelled with pride as she saw her son be a perfect gentleman to this perfect stranger.

The girl took his hand and stood up. Shade came up to the halfway point of her thigh. "Jazabel, my name is Jazabel," she said, looking around the room, not seeming to notice the group gathered not ten feet from her. "How did I get here? I live in Toxai; I don't even know where Braria is."

The girl was clearly scared at her situation. Iselda didn't blame her, she probably didn't remember much from the past month. And that's when Korena stepped forward and lowered herself down to the girl's eye level. "Hello, Jazabel," she said quietly.

Despite the gentleness of Korena's voice, Jazabel jumped. "You! I know you! What have you done to me?!" screamed the girl, pointing an accusatory finger at Korena.

Korena just smiled. "Believe it or not, I've done you a favour. I've released you from my servitude, after only a month. And once you've gotten some rest, you will be brought home, and never have to see me again."

"Why? Why are you releasing me? Is something wrong with me?!"

"Just the opposite. The fault was mine. For a very long time, I've needed a body so that I could live. Five minutes ago, I was made able to live without needing to take over another's body. You are safe here, and will be until you're returned home, when my friends won't be able to protect you anymore." The girl nodded slightly, and turned back to Shade. He gave her a warm smile and nodded slightly to her. Korena turned herself to Shade, crouching down lower so she was at his eye level. "Shade, can you take Jazabel to a room and make sure she's comfortable for the night?"

Shade nodded, giving a fist to his heart. Taking Jazabel's hand, he started to lead her away, but Iselda called him back. "When you're done, go straight to your room; it's way past yours and your sister's bedtime."

"Yes, Mommy," he said enthusiastically. And then he gently pulled Jazabel to the upper levels of the castle, where the guest rooms were.

Iselda walked to Korena and put a hand on her shoulder. The goddess turned around and stood back up. Iselda saw the tears in her eyes. "What's wrong, Korena?"

Wiping away the tears, she smiled weakly at Iselda. "It's nothing, just an old memory." She reached a hand out, and in an instant, Hados was at her side. "Let's go home," she said softly as she snuggled into the space under his arm, a perfect fit.

"I'd thought you'd never ask." Turning to the others, he said, "Thank you, all of you. And please, if you ever need anything, just ask. And Nikki," he added, waving her forward, "take care of yourself and your brother; help will always be there for the two of you."

Nikki nodded. "Thank you, Lord Hados. Say hi to my grandparents for me and Shade."

Chuckling softly, he said, "Always, little one, always."

"Iselda," Korena whispered. Iselda turned her attention to her friend. "Thank you, for everything. I'll miss you more than I can say."

Iselda nodded her understanding. "Me, too. You're always welcome here; don't be afraid of visiting." Korena just nodded.

For a brief moment, the room was completely dark. And when the light returned, they were gone. Iselda could feel a tear falling down her cheek, but she didn't wipe it away. Pan put his arm around her shoulder and gave her a one-armed hug. The others walked around so they formed a semi-circle looking to where the underworld deities had just stood. "Well," Marina said, "that just about blows every dinner party I've thrown out; how do you get these people to appear at your parties, Pan?"

Everyone either chuckled or smiled at her humour. And even though the question was a joke, Pan still answered. "The double edged sword of being king; I don't know how I'm going to outdo myself next year." More snickers followed his response.

Once everyone had settled down, Shade and Marina stepped from Pan's right to in front of Iselda. "I just realized, I haven't welcomed you home yet," Marina said giving Iselda a hug.

"No welcome's necessary, you helped Pan while I was gone," Iselda replied. "That's more than enough."

"Well, even still, I'm glad you're home." Iselda smiled and nodded her thanks. "But it's getting past Shade's and my bedtime. We'll see you later," she said as she and Shade gave everyone a hug and kiss goodbye.

Once they were out the door, the five who remained made their way to the upper level of the castle, to their rooms. At Kailee's and Sabrina's room, the goodbyes were a little more awkward. Pan and Sabrina tried to hide it, but Iselda saw it in their eyes. That would take some time.

When they got to Shade's and Nikki's room, Shade was already in his bed, waiting for them. He got out and ran to her and she bent down and scooped him into her arms, holding him tight. "Oh, sweetheart! That was very nice, what you did for our guest. When did you start acting like your father to the ladies?" He blushed at her praise and she replaced him into his bed. "And so handsome in those robes." His cheeks only got redder. She turned to her daughter, who was being helped out of her dress by her father, and said, "And you, Nikki, you looked beautiful in that dress. Blackblood really suits you, honey." She blushed like her brother and smiled with pride.

"It's because she looks just like you," Pan and Shade said at the same time.

Now it was her turn to blush. "Thank you," she said with a wide smile. Now ready for bed, Nikki gave Iselda a hug before going to her bed and crawling in. Turning to look at Pan, he seemed to know what she was asking before she even opened her mouth.

"I'll give you however long you need; just don't be all night. I'm still *just fine*," he said to her with a wink as he kissed his children goodnight. And with a teasing peck on the cheek, he was out the door before she could grab him for an actual kiss.

Once he was out the door, Iselda muttered just what she thought of that little stunt under her breath. "Tease." Standing in the centre of the space between their beds, Iselda made sure she had her children's full attention before she spoke. "Before I say goodnight, I want to tell the two of you how proud I am of you. You stayed strong when the unthinkable happened and helped your father make it through it all. And all the feelings you sent me came right when I needed them the most, and helped me more than I can say. You two are the most important things in the world to me, and I'd do anything to make sure you're safe. I love you with all my heart and I want you to know that I'll never leave you like that again." She'd had to push past the tears halfway through, but let them flow as she finished.

"We love you, too, Mommy," they said in their signature unison.

Smiling, Iselda went to Nikki's bed and sat down on it. Bringing her hands up, she removed the necklace that Shade had given her the night she left, and handed it to her daughter. "I don't need this anymore. And I know it's early, but it is yours." Nikki took the necklace and placed it under her pillow.

She then threw her hands around Iselda's neck, hugging her tight. And the moment her hands were around Iselda, she felt her daughter's love for her. She also felt just how much Nikki had missed her. Iselda just held her as tight as she could. "I love you, my darling daughter," she whispered, using the name she'd used in her letter to Nikki. After a minute of holding each other tight, mother and daughter let each other go and Iselda kissed Nikki's forehead. "Goodnight sweetheart, I'll see you in the morning."

"'Night, Mommy." And like every night, Nikki rolled over and went to sleep.

Iselda gently pushed herself off the bed and crossed to Shade's bed, where her son was waiting patiently. "Where did you put Jazabel?" she asked quietly.

"She's in the room with the red curtains upstairs. It has the softest bed in the entire castle."

Iselda couldn't help but smile at her son's generosity. "You know, it's things like that that make me say you're the sweetest boy I've ever met. Korena agrees; she was brought to tears seeing you be so nice and polite to Jazabel. Never lose that part of yourself, sweetheart. OK?"

"Don't worry, Mommy, I won't," he said with a slight blush. "Are you going to sing to me?"

"Every night, whenever you need or want me to. You're my baby boy; I'd do anything for you." Iselda slid herself closer to Shade as she prepared to sing his lullaby.

Ages ago, when our world
Was a little older than new,
There rose a king whose greatness
Was rivalled by very few.

He vowed to protect all,
To right all that was wrong.
And so he did,
Till the day his life was gone.

The Kanta Chronicles

The lands cried out
The day he died;
Saying 'He was our leader,
He should be glorified.'

But the doers
Of this dirty deed,
Denied their cries.
Citing warnings, he didn't heed.

So great was the king's greatness,
So strong his love of all,
The warnings he couldn't believe
Who was to bring his downfall.

So while you sleep, consider this:
'Tis good to be kind to all in your eyes.
But throwing caution to the wind,
Would be very unwise.

Shade had joined her on the last verse, as he always did. As they finished, Iselda thought Shade would roll over and go to sleep like his sister, but he stayed looking at her.

"Mommy, is that true, what you sing of the king?"

Iselda was shocked; if he knew that she drew most of the lullaby from prophecy, shouldn't he know it was true? "As far as I know. The king's name was Slac Hino, and he was one of the first kings of Gothtor. He was a very kind man and a great king. Sadly, he was killed by the one person he thought would never betray him: his sister. When he died, the people found the truth of his death in prophecies, and revolted against her. After a long war that tore Gothtor apart, she was finally captured and killed. The country has never been able to recover from this piece of tragedy and is now mostly deserted. It's very sad."

"Yeah, it is. Maybe I'll restore it to its former glory," he said, smiling at the prospect.

"Don't bite off more than you can chew, Shade. Your future is already going to be difficult enough." At the mention of this recently revealed truth, his smile disappeared. "One day at a time, sweetheart. If anyone can fight off the cloud of darkness over Gothtor, it's you and your sister. As long as you follow what your heart tells you is right, no one can say you're wrong." He nodded and she kissed his forehead for a long moment. "Now, enough philosophy; it's time for sleep. I need you up early so you can help Jazabel until she leaves."

"OK, Mommy," he said with a yawn. "Goodnight."

Iselda sat on his bed until his eyes closed and his breathing indicated he was asleep. "Goodnight, sweetheart," she whispered. With one last gentle kiss to both her children's foreheads, Iselda left to say one last goodnight.

When Iselda walked into her bedroom, Pan was already on the bed. But before either of them could be better than *just fine*, she needed to make sure he was alright. So, she pulled him off the bed and asked him to help her get ready for bed. "Are you OK, darling?" she asked gently.

He didn't stop unlacing her dress, but Iselda heard his breath catch slightly. After a moment's silence, he released a long breath. "I don't know; I feel fine, but like Hados said, there's an emptiness inside me that doesn't feel…right. You should ask me again in a while and make sure it's not too unbecoming." His voice was a little tense, but the light kisses he was placing up and down her neck made her forget that.

From there, she turned up the pleasure and pushed him back to the bed. "How do you feel?" she purred, still standing at the foot of the bed.

Smiling crookedly, he plainly said, "You're going to have to do better than that if you want me to be better than *just fine*. You sure you have all your powers back?"

"Is that a challenge?" she asked in a husky voice as she paced the width of the bed.

Standing up suddenly, Pan grabbed her and shoved her onto the bed, face down, and held her down. Leaning on top of her, he growled in her ear, "You bet it is." It was very rare that Pan was rough with her, but when he was, Iselda knew she was in for a good night.

As an excited shiver went down her spine, she tried to turn over onto her back, but Pan held her in place. "Tell me, my king, what must I do?" she asked, trying unsuccessfully to control her breathing. "What must I do to make you feel better than just fine, master?"

In the corner of her eye, she saw Pan smile. And to answer her question, he flipped her over and sent her back five years into the past. How she'd missed her powers from the boat ride.

Chapter 44:

Tears of Pain and Joy

Despite getting very little sleep the previous night, Iselda woke feeling quite relaxed and well rested. Waking in Pan's arms and having his smiling face the first thing she saw tended to have that effect. "Did I win the challenge?"

"I've forgotten how fun your powers could be," he said. "I haven't felt like this since the boat ride."

Snuggling up to him, Iselda placed her head on his chest, listening to his racing heart. "I'll take that as a yes." Looking up at him, she saw Pan nod. Placing her hand over his heart, she could feel its beating. "I overdid it, didn't I?" she asked with a smile.

"Yes," Pan answered with a smile. "Luckily for you, pleasure seems to be a very good form of medicine. After what I went through yesterday, I wasn't sure if I would make it. Maybe our new friends were helping."

"Maybe," she sighed, once again resting her head on his chest. They laid like that for a quarter of an hour, enjoying the intimate moment. But once the sun was in their eyes, they knew they had to get out of bed. Dressing in comfortable clothing, the king and queen walked to their children's room.

When they got to the door, it opened to reveal Shade holding Nikki, stroking her hair. Iselda wanted to run and comfort her daughter, but knew why she was crying. It was heartbreaking to see them in pain when she knew she'd allowed it to happen. They looked up when they saw her and Pan enter, and Nikki wiped her tears away.

Smiling, they chimed in unison, "Mommy! Daddy!" Iselda could tell Nikki's smile was forced, and she swore to herself she'd help her daughter get through this sadness. The twins ran to their parents and the four encircled each other in a group hug.

Turning to Shade, Iselda smiled. "Honey, why don't you and Daddy go and make sure Jazabel is OK. Nikki and I will meet you in the kitchen for breakfast."

Shade looked at her for a moment, then to his sister. "OK, Mommy." Grabbing his father's hand and pulling him out of the room, he said, "Come on, Daddy!"

After they could no longer hear their footsteps, Iselda picked Nikki up and brought her to her bed. "What's wrong, sweetheart?" she asked gently.

Nikki just clung to her waist. Iselda could hear her sniffling as she tried to not to cry. "I can't tell you."

"Sweetheart," she said, tilting Nikki's chin up so they were looking at each other. "I'm you mother, and you can tell me anything. No matter what anyone says, no matter the nature of what you have to say. I'm here for you, no matter what. Nothing could make me betray your trust." Iselda wanted Nikki to open up to her, to trust her.

"It's what Hados told us, about who would hurt us," she

said quietly.

Iselda had to hold back a cry as her fears were realized. But the tears couldn't be hidden. "Did-did he tell you who it would be?" She feared the answer but needed to know. She'd protect her children for as long as she could.

Nikki nodded, and then buried her face in Iselda's side as she started to cry again. Perhaps Iselda didn't need to know who would betray her children. As she cried silently, Iselda tried to comfort Nikki, tried to get her to open up to her. Holding each other tight, they sat for nearly twenty minutes silently crying their fears.

"He said it was to be someone very close to us, someone we trusted beyond everything. Someone we once called family. He said he didn't know who he was, but he said we had to love him, for his darkness would be hidden to all." Nikki was very quiet after she said this. Iselda couldn't stop her heart from breaking as she found out the path her children would have to take. But then she saw Nikki smile slightly. Sliding off the bed and grabbing her hand, Nikki said, "Come on, Mommy. Shade and Daddy are waiting!"

And the moment was over. Nikki was smiling as she pulled Iselda from her room and down to the kitchen for their family breakfast.

In the kitchen, Iselda saw Pan and Shade getting a cooking lesson from Alix. Pan and Alix were yelling at each other, while Shade sat on a counter laughing at the two of them. Iselda and Nikki silently joined Shade to watch the king and head chef bickering.

"Zat iz not 'ow you do zit!" Alix said, taking the wooden spatula from Pan and pushing him out of the way.

"How many ways can there be to flip an egg?!" Pan asked in exasperation. Iselda had to hold a hand to her mouth to keep herself from laughing.

While Alix listed off the numerous ways to flip an egg, each having its own rules of when to use it, Iselda turned to Shade. "How long as this been going on?" she asked in a whisper.

Smiling, Shade responded, "Since we walked in twenty minutes ago." Both he and his sister couldn't hide their giggles; Iselda was barely able to. "Daddy wanted to cook you breakfast himself." Iselda gave a knowing nod; this wasn't the first time he'd tried to usurp the kitchen from Alix.

"-so you see, zer are many vays to flip an egg, my king," concluded Alix. The two of them just stared at each other intensely for a minute. It probably would have been longer if Iselda was able to hold back her laughter. But as she burst out laughing, both king and chef turned to her in horror.

Seeing their faces only renewed her hysterics. Both rushed to explain, but she held up a hand. Forcing herself to calm down, Iselda stood up straight. "I don't know how many times I'm going to have to pull you two apart," she said with a serious tone and face. "The two of you are the king and head chef of all of Braria. For the love of the spirits, think of the example you're setting for Shade and Nikki! Pan, you hired Alix yourself; you know how he is with his kitchen! And you, Alix, while you may be the best chef in the country, can't you let him pretend to cook something once and a while?"

The two of them looked at each other and then turned back to Iselda with bowed heads. "I, guess, we could get along. Sorry sweetheart," Pan said contritely.

As Alix nodded his agreement, Iselda burst out laughing again and was joined by her children. "Oh, you two are too easy!" Iselda laughed. "But you're also entertaining when you fight." She gave the two of them a hug to show she was just messing with them, and then took the spatula from Alix. "Now, out of my way; *I'm* cooking breakfast."

Pan and Alix didn't argue with her and left her alone. She saw Pan take Shade and Nikki into his arms and walk to the small table at the other end of the room. "Not a word from you two," he muttered, but this only sent them over the edge of laughter.

Ten minutes later, Iselda set down four plates of eggs, sausages, and biscuits in front of them. They ate in silence, save the quiet snickers of Shade and Nikki, until Pan bowed his head. "OK, get it out of your system, you three." And the table erupted into howls of laughter. "I don't see what's so funny," he said quietly.

"That's because we're laughing at you, darling."

But before Pan could say anything, Jazabel walked up to the table, escorted by Alan. "I'm sorry to interrupt, but I was hoping to get something to eat," she said this to the table, but her eyes kept returning to Shade. Iselda also noticed that Shade couldn't keep his eyes off her, either.

"Of course, Jazabel," Iselda said, shifting out of her seat and onto Pan's lap. Shade in the meantime pushed some of his food onto the plate Iselda had finished with. Iselda also caught a shadow pass over Nikki's face, so quick she thought she'd imagined it. But she knew she hadn't when she saw Shade sit back down and draw her closer to him and kiss her cheek.

"Thank you, your majesties," the girl meekly said, as she started to eat. "This is quite good," she stated as she became more ferocious with her eating. Clearly, she was quite hungry.

"Did you have a good sleep?" Pan asked.

"Yes, thank you," she said as she took a moment to swallow her mouthful.

"And when do you want to return home?" Nikki asked. Despite her daughter's subtle rudeness, Iselda had to smirk. Is that what she looked like when she was jealous? Shade just held her tighter to him, giving her another kiss on the cheek.

Apparently, Jazabel didn't catch Nikki's slight and took it for her trying to help. "If it's not too much trouble, I'd like to leave shortly." She looked to Iselda and Pan with big hopeful eyes.

"Of course, my dear. We'll have the Toxan carriage that brought you here ready for immediate departure," Iselda said. "And we'll have our most loyal and experienced guard accompany you until you're safe at home."

"Oh no, your majesty; you don't have to do that! The carriage is plenty!"

"I know it is, Jazabel. But I don't send him for you; I send him for my friend, the one who brought you here, and for him. I promised my friend that I would make sure you got home safely, and my guard has spent too much time at the castle doing very little. Vanto needs the field time. Do you understand?"

"I think so, your highness. Thank you," she said, bowing her head.

"You're welcome. Now, do you want anything else for breakfast?"

"No, thank you."

"Well then, why don't you go back to your room and collect anything you need while I have the carriage brought to the front door," Iselda suggested. Jazabel smiled, and left to do just that; but not without one last look to Shade.

Chapter 45:

Goodbye to the Queens

Half an hour later, Iselda was waiting for Jazabel to be led to the main entrance of the castle. Both Shade and Nikki were seeing to that; leaving the king and queen a moment alone.

"How's Nikki?" Pan asked.

"Scared. She was just told that she has an important future for the world and that someone very close to her will betray her. And she's four! Add into the equation that she feels threatened by Jazabel and it's a miracle she isn't still crying."

"Why is Jazabel a threat?" She loved Pan, but sometimes he picked up on the worst things.

"I don't know. She should know that her brother loves her more than anything, but for whatever reason, she doesn't like Jazabel."

"We really need to have a talk with them, don't we?" Pan asked with a sigh.

"Yes."

And before they could discuss it further, the three children walked through the door. Shade was walking, head down, on Nikki's right, holding her hand, while Jazabel was on her left.

The carriage and Vanto were already ready to go.

Opening the door for the girl, Iselda offered her hand as Jazabel climbed in. "Once you're in Toxai, you should know the way. Just tell the driver where your home is. It should take you three to five days, depending on how fast you go. Vanto has some things for you when you stop for the night. Take care, Jazabel."

"Thank you, your majesties. You're too kind," she said to Iselda and Pan. Then she turned to Shade. "I'm glad to have met you, Shade. You're the kindest person I know." Shade blushed at the praise, but didn't say anything. Iselda saw him discreetly look to Nikki, but she seemed to be ignoring him.

Taking his sister's hand into his own, Shade said a quiet thank you, as Iselda closed the door. Turning to Vanto, she said, "Protect that girl and make sure she's alright before you come back. And if she asks, you're not only there to protect her; you're there to re-familiarize yourself with the field."

From his mount, the general snapped a fist to his heart. "Yes, your highness."

"Safe journey, my friend."

"Thank you, sire," Vanto replied to Pan.

And with that, the carriage driver snapped the reins and the carriage took off. Vanto was only a few feet behind them. The Royal family watched as the carriage disappeared into the distance, before returning to the castle.

※

Iselda was leading Pan, Shade, and Nikki back up to the twins' bedroom when she saw Sabrina and Kailee walking down the staircase. Stopping where she was, her group waited as Sabrina and Kailee descended the stairs.

"We've been looking all over for you," Kailee said once she and Sabrina had reached Iselda and company halfway down the stairs.

"We were just sending Jazabel home," Pan stated. Iselda saw that he and Sabrina were both looking anywhere but each other. Her heart gave a little wrench as she knew that this was going to continue for a while.

"Ah," Kailee said, noticing the non-looking as well. "Well, speaking of home, I think we should be getting home as well; our task here is finished. Plus, I need to tell Jayne what a horrible job she's done housekeeping for me." She said this last point with a smile, clearly enjoying the thought of teasing her sister.

But the mention of Jayne reminded Iselda of something. "Oh! If you get a second in your berating, let her know I say thank you for the other day and sorry I left her a mess to clean up." Kailee just nodded as she stepped in for a hug, which Iselda returned wholeheartedly. "Thank you, Kailee. You've no idea how much everything you and Sabrina have done over the past few weeks has meant to me. You're the greatest friends I could have ever asked for." Iselda meant every word that she'd whispered into her friend's ear.

"It's never a chore to come here and live like queens," she whispered back with a small giggle. At the comment, Iselda gave a small giggle as well.

Pulling out of their embrace, Iselda looked directly into Kailee's blue eyes. "You two are queens." Looking over to Sabrina, Iselda extended a hand and motioned her into the hug she was about to re-engage. "Thank you, sisters; I don't know what I'd do without you."

"Anytime," the two said in unison. The three sisters hugged each other tightly for another moment or two before releasing each other. Then Kailee and Sabrina said their goodbyes; Sabrina's and Pan's goodbye being painfully awkward. And then they made their way down the rest of the stairs.

Turning to Pan, she gave him a look that he knew instantly. It was her 'I want to help them' look. He just nodded and she turned down the stairs. "Sabrina! Wait!" she called as she ran to catch them at the bottom of the stairs. When she got there, she looked at Kailee with the same look she'd given Pan. And just like Pan, Kailee knew that this was to be a private conversation and left to make sure they had enough supplies for the day's walk.

Before Iselda could even ask the question, Sabrina shook her head. "No, Iselda, I'm not OK. But I knew what I was doing, and would do it again. I think we just need some time before we can push past the awkwardness. Give us a year, and then ask how we are. We spent ten years longing to feel each other again, and then another five to forgive those ten years. We'll be OK, just not for a while." Sabrina offered a sad smile to Iselda as reassurance.

"Don't force it for our sake," Iselda said, giving one last consoling hug.

Sabrina just nodded. "We'll see you in a few months for Shade's and Nikki's birthday. And thank you for your concern."

"What are sisters for?" And with one last hug, the two said goodbye as Sabrina went to join Kailee at the castle gate and Iselda went to find her family so they could have their long overdue talk.

Chapter 46:

A Family Talk

As Iselda walked into the room, she noticed that her husband and children were sitting on the floor, waiting for her. She sat with them, but couldn't think of what to say. How did she have this kind of talk with four year olds? Looking to Pan for help, Iselda found that he had none. Letting out a sigh, she began, "OK, yesterday I told you two that we needed to talk when I found out you had magic, among other things. And while you've shown me what you can do, I'm still a little confused. Can you explain to your father and me what exactly you can do?" She thought this would be a very good place to start.

Shade and Nikki looked at each other and nodded. "Our form of magic is like any other form of magic, we just happen to control emotions," they said in unison. "The stronger our connection to a person, the better we can read and control how they feel."

"So you can read our emotions like they were written on our foreheads, but you can't read the emotions of strangers, like petitioners?" Pan tried to clarify.

They just nodded. Nikki continued, "But we can't read everybody equally. I can more easily understand people closer to Daddy; whereas Shade has an easier time with those closer to Mommy. And we have to be touching someone, or something similar to what they're touching, to control their emotions."

"That's why I only heard you talking to me, while I was away," Iselda said to Shade, fitting a piece into the puzzle. Shade nodded. "That's why you gave me the necklace."

"I wanted you to have a connection to us, in case something went wrong. Your feelings towards the necklace and ring added to my ability to know how you were feeling even over the great distance." Iselda wanted so much to hug him and smother him with her love right there, but knew she had to hold back. Shade, clearly knowing this, smiled, "I love you too, Mommy!"

Iselda smiled at his enthusiasm. In a way, their powers weren't all that different from their father's Time Wind powers; they both could manipulate how others were feeling; they just went about it differently. "Alright, I think I understand. But what about the two of you being Soul Twins; how did you know?"

At hearing this, her children looked to one another with a loving look. "Most everyone can't remember things before they were born," Shade said. "But we do; I remember feeling this terrible ache in my heart, as if it was torn in two and I only had half. I don't know how long I felt this way, but I touched something and the purest feeling overcame me. It was Nikki, and she'd been having the same experiences as me. We then realized that we each had the missing half of a heart that had caused us such pain. We had no concept of words, but we knew the feelings we made each other feel were unlike anything we'd ever feel again, except with each other. We loved each other, and would do any and everything to please each other."

"We know every little thought the other thinks; sometimes we don't even know who's thinking it," Nikki continued with a smile. But then the smile went away. "And it hurts to be out of sight from one another," she said quietly as she took her brother's hand into hers. Or was it he that took hers?

"Hurt? Hurt how?" Pan asked with concern.

"Like how you felt when Mommy left," they said. "Only worse."

Pan went pale at this response. "If it hurts that much, why do you ever leave each other's side?" he asked in a hollow voice.

"Because we must," they whispered. Iselda saw the tears in their eyes, but also knew they couldn't take her comfort. "It's easier here, because we know we're safe at home."

"But when Shade goes on his Reckoning," Nikki rushed to get out, as if the very thought of it was painful, "I must stay behind, as he travels to far off lands. That will be nearly unbearable." Shade put his arm around her as she started to cry, holding her tight.

This time, Iselda did get up, as did Pan, and went to comfort them. Encircling her daughter into her arms, Iselda quietly cooed into Nikki's ear. Pan was doing the same for Shade. "If it's too much, you can go with him," she whispered.

Nikki just shook her head. "We already discussed it; we won't have traditions break for us. Our pain is to be another part of the challenge." The way in which she spoke of it made it clear to Iselda that she didn't like this decision, but she was going to live by it.

For a long moment, the four clung to each other tightly. Iselda found herself wishing she didn't know this fact about her children. Maybe some things were best left for the two of them alone to know. She knew the power of secrets. But apparently, her husband did not.

Letting go of Shade and prying his wife away from Nikki, Pan reformed the circle. "There's one more thing I'd like to discuss," he said. "What is it that Hados told you about the future last night?" His wording made Iselda believe he was asking her this as well.

And when he turned and looked directly at her, she knew. "All I know is… is that they have a war in their future. It will start by someone they love betraying them; the one they love most will die and the Beast will be born. I don't know if they'll win, but if they do, it'll take everything they got." Iselda pulled Shade and Nikki close as she finished.

Looking down to them, Pan asked, "And what did he tell you? Or can you not say?"

Looking to each other, either for guidance or strength, Shade spoke up. "He told us one of the prophecies. He said it dealt with the start of the war. '*Beware the fiend, once called friend; a betrayer in deed, feeding only his greed. Between loyalties, a lover will be torn and their life is the first you shall mourn. Thus begins the war of all time, all over the squabble of yours and mine.*' He didn't tell us what it means; he just gave us those words."

Pan just nodded at his son's words. "Perhaps you aren't yet meant to know the meaning of the words," he said thoughtfully. "I'd write them down, somewhere you can continue to add new prophecies over time. A book you tell no one of, where you can ponder their meanings. I'll have a blank book made up for you. Hide it in a place only the two of you know it is, that way you're the only ones who can read it. Prophecies are dangerous, and not to be taken lightly."

"Hados told us those very words, Daddy," the two of them said together. "And he gave us a book that would add the new prophecies as he released them. Don't worry; we've hidden it somewhere safe." Pan simply nodded to this information.

With these matters settled, silence grew. But none of them moved to leave. Then Iselda realized why. "This was meant to be a family discussion, not an interrogation of you two. Is there anything you want us to tell you, something you want clarified?" she asked her children.

Looking to each other, Iselda realized that they were engaging in their silent communication. After a moment, they looked to her. "Why didn't you want us knowing you had magic?"

The question caught Iselda off guard; she didn't think they'd want to know this, she didn't even know. "I don't know. For a long time, I was a bad person, someone everyone thought should be dead. I guess I didn't want you to know that part of my life - the days of the Dark Union." She hadn't used those words to describe herself in a long time.

And the look her children gave as they heard her old nickname was reason enough. They were shocked, shocked because they recognized the name. "You're the Dark Union?" they asked with a hint of fear. "But-she's dead!"

"Yes, she is." This only confused them more. "She died

when your father kissed me for the first time. She led a miserable life. I live a very happy and fulfilling one. And I've never regretted giving up that life, for in return I got everything I ever wanted," she said with a smile down at her lovely children.

Shade and Nikki got up and gave her a big hug. Iselda took this to mean they understood and that nothing had changed between them. "Is there anything else you two wish for us to tell you, or does your ability to read our emotions tell you all you need to know?" Pan asked. Releasing her from their hug, Shade and Nikki turned to their father and shook their heads. "Then come on," Pan said, standing up and walking to the door. "It's time to begin your training. If the two of you are going to fight a war, you need to be as prepared as your soldiers."

Snapping fists to their hearts, Shade and Nikki followed their father out the door. Iselda's heart caught for the slightest moment, for she realized that her children were leaving childhood behind as they walked out that door. Standing to follow them, Iselda vowed to herself that she would make sure that they still had fun, that they had time to be children.

Part Three: Shade and Nikki

Chapter 47:

Reckoning Rituals and Secrets

Taking a deep breath, Shade Leo Kanta pushed open the doors that led into the castle's throne room. Dressed in the loose white robes that his ancestors had donned for generations, Shade walked to his parents' thrones. The past eighteen years hadn't exactly been meant to prepare Shade for this moment, but he'd been preparing for it anyway. Tonight was his *Nuitnoire*, the night before his Reckoning where he chose his task. A Reckoning was the task every prince of Braria undertook during their twenty-second year to prove themselves worthy of the crown; failure was not an option. Left alone on the throne room steps that held the raised dais, he cleared his mind of everything, even Nikki. This was his task and his task alone.

As he knelt upon the stairs that led to his parents' thrones, he let his empty mind wander. His father had told him that the trick to choosing his task was to clear his head of all thought, save for the thought to clear his head. As often happened when he tried to clear his head, images of Nikki wove in and out of focus. Shade let them last for a few moments before shaking them off; he couldn't think of his Soul's Twin this night.

Next, his mind brought the many memories of his mother singing his lullaby; but he only heard her voice as he gazed upon his reflection in a mirror. As he had not thought of these images himself, he assumed it was part of the ancient magic of the *Nuitnoire* that gave him clues as to what his Reckoning would be. As he looked into his reflection, he saw that his face was no longer his; it was half his and half Nikki, then his mother, his father, his Aunt Kailee, Aunt Sabrina, Uncle Shade, and Aunt Marina. Each face was only there for a second, but with each one, the colour of the mirror changed as if it were trying to visually represent the relationship between them.

Finally, the faces stopped changing, resting on a face Shade only saw in his deepest dreams: Jazabel. The colour of the mirror was that of a mirror. And then there was only one word in his head, a name: Rheta.

Shade opened his eyes to the growing light of dawn. The night was over; it was as if it had passed in a mere twenty minutes. As he stood, he heard the door behind him open. Turning, he saw his father entering the room arm-in-arm with his mother. Barely a step behind them was Nikki, the spitting image of their mother. But where his mother's eyes were amethyst, Nikki's were the purest blue Shade had ever seen. Smiling at the love of his life, he opened his mind to her. *Good morning,* they thought simultaneously.

As his biological family approached, Shade straightened himself; this was still a formal event. "My son," his father said in what his mother often called his official voice. "The time has come; have you found yourself a quest for your Reckoning?"

"Yes, Father, I believe I have," he said with a bow of his head. Raising himself back up straight, he continued, "Ever since I was a child, I've been fascinated by the crumbling nation of Gothtor. And it is there that I must go to find the Mirror of Rheta." Shade looked to his mother as he said this, judging her reaction. It was her that had first told him of Gothtor, she knew just how much he was excited by this quest. Not much was written about the mythical mirror, but what few sources there were always hypothesised of a hidden magic that the Mirror of Rheta possessed.

You couldn't pick something a little closer? Nikki asked in a teasing tone. But despite her tone, Shade knew she was quite serious. Gothtor was one of the northernmost countries in the world; the journey alone would take a few days each way. The furthest they'd ever been from each other was the length of the castle. This was not going to be easy for either of them.

With a look back to Nikki, his father said, "Very well. You have until midday to gather supplies before you leave." Then the official quality to his voice disappeared and he became Shade's father rather than the king. "It's also the time you have before you decide if Nikki will accompany you. You know better than I do the toll this will take."

Shade could feel the longing rolling off Nikki as she wanted so much to accompany him, or was it he who wanted her to come with him. *It's both of us* she thought to him, *but I'm willing to go through with this the way we always said we would. As much as it will kill us, I'll stay behind, if that's what you want.*

You know that's not what I want Shade thought back.

"But it is what I'll do. I will do this on my own. I just ask one allowance."

"And what is that," his mother asked, speaking for the first time since entering the room.

"Let Nikki walk me out of the city, alone."

"Of course," his parents said in unison. His mother continued, "Now, go pack. Be sure you have enough."

Shade looked to Nikki as he took a step towards the door. *Go, I can't help you; this is for you to do alone.* Shade felt the effort it took her to say that calmly; he felt the tears she was trying to hold back. But he did what she said and left for their room.

Up in his room, Shade wrapped the four loaves of bread he'd taken from the kitchen in a cloth and placed it on his bed, beside all the other things he planned on bringing with him. There wasn't much, a few changes of clothes, a couple of water canteens, the loaves of bread, a portrait of Nikki that she'd given him this past year as a birthday present, the letter his mother had written him all those years ago, and of course his sword *Peacemaker*. As he looked at the items laid out on his bed, Shade couldn't help but feel something was missing. Unable to figure out what was missing, and knowing he had a limited amount of time, Shade set about packing everything.

When Shade was halfway through packing, there was a knock on his door. Wondering who it was, he opened it to reveal his Uncle, and namesake, Shade. "Hey junior, mind if I come in for a minute?"

"I'm not really supposed to have anyone in here; Nikki's not even in here."

"Relax, your father won't say a word - I came into his room as he was packing for his Reckoning. And besides, I have something I've wanted to give you for a while now," he said, indicating the blanket under his arm.

"Really, a blanket? It's so thoughtful, senior," Shade said jokingly. But he stepped aside to let the other Shade in.

"It's what's in the blanket. And Marina would kill me if I ever gave this blanket away." A look he'd never seen from his uncle before now passed across his uncle's face - heartache. But despite his words, he handed Shade the blanket. He continued as Shade opened the blanket: "If you want to take it with you, you can, but you don't have to."

In the blanket was a wooden carving. It was small but the detail was incredible. It was Shade's favourite animal, a wolf. It was sitting with its head thrown back in a howl. Shade was awed by the beauty of the trinket. "Wow! Thanks, Uncle Shade, this is amazing!" This is exactly what he was missing.

"I'm glad you like it. I originally carved it for your twentieth birthday, but Marina hid it on me and only just told me where she put it last month."

"You carved this?!" Shade asked in disbelief. "I didn't know you could do that."

"It's just a hobby. Before I could be any good, your dad took the throne and has had me as his most trusted adviser ever since. His asking for my opinion on everything leaves me with little time to myself." They both chuckled at this, making fun of the man they both loved to death. "I carved him howling because there's so much in a howl. I'll let you decide why he is."

Giving his namesake a hug, Shade said, "Thanks, Uncle Shade."

"No problem, junior. Now, I'll leave you to your packing."

"Wait, Uncle Shade. Can I ask you something, since you're not here?" Seeing his uncle nod his head, Shade asked a question that had troubled him over the years. "Not that it's any of my business, but why did you and Aunt Marina never have children?"

Shade regretted asking the moment he saw his uncle's grimace and felt the waves of guilt and sadness that flowed off him. But the next moment, he was smiling a small smile. "For the same reason I do most things: your father." Shade looked away in guilt as this was revealed, which caused his uncle to grab his shoulder. "It's not what you think, Shade. Marina and I always wanted a child of our own, but we decided that marriage was as far as we'd go. Your father had just banished Sabrina and Kailee not too long before we were married, and I didn't want to appear that I was rubbing it in his face that I had what he'd given up.

"As the years passed, we again discussed having a child. And we succeeded. But before we could tell anyone the good news, your grandmother died and the depression Pan felt only intensified. Those few days between her death and funeral were the lowest I've ever seen your father. I wanted to tell him that Marina was pregnant, for I thought it would help lift the pall that loomed over him, but your aunt thought differently. She thought that the news that she was pregnant would only worsen his depression. And though I to this day have never told her this, I feared that as well.

"And then we made the hardest decision of our lives,

one we have come to greatly regret. We decided to abort the pregnancy. We told your father that we wanted to get away to escape the depression that had settled over Terang, but we were actually heading to Ichmensch to see a cut wife. Marina cried the entire journey there." Here his uncle looked away from Shade as he relived the painful memories.

Shade wanted to say something to his namesake but no words came. He was about to give his uncle a hug when he continued, "There was a complication during the procedure, and Marina was left unable to bear children ever again. When the cut wife told us this, I nearly killed her in a sorrowful rage. But after smashing a table and a couple of chairs, I saw the utter sadness in my wife's eyes and the rage left me; leaving only the same sadness she felt.

"As we returned here, we barely spoke to one another and I feared she had come to hate me and the fact that I loved your father more than I loved her. But as we walked back into our home, she flung herself into my arms and apologized for making me agree to that course of action. We avoided your father for the next month, as we both subconsciously blamed him. It was the first time since we'd met that I hated your father. But when he confronted us about this, we lied and told him we were giving him his space in the wake of his mother's death.

"All this was all but forgotten by the time we found out about your mother being pregnant with you and your sister. And for the briefest of moments after I heard that news, I remembered all that I'd sacrificed for your father that he had no idea about, and the hatred I once felt towards him rose within me. But I immediately buried it in the joy that he was finally happy." Wiping his eyes from the tears that had flowed at his tale, the elder smiled at the younger. "I'd appreciate it if you kept this to yourself, even from your sister if that's possible. Your Aunt Marina and I have moved past the pain and have had more than our fill of parenting in helping you and your sister grow to be the people you are today. We've treated you as if you were our own children and couldn't be prouder of you two."

Being pulled into a hug, Shade let all the love he felt for his aunt and uncle flow from him into his namesake. He also sent his feelings of empathy and sadness over the tale his uncle had told him. Releasing him from the hug, his uncle gave Shade a thankful smile. And with that, the older Shade left the room and closed the door. Turning back to his bed and pile of things to bring with him on his Reckoning, Shade returned to his packing, a new burden on his shoulders.

Chapter 48:

Soul Twins Goodbyes

Shade stood at the gate that divided the castle from the rest of Terang with his black mustang Isabelle, the weight of his uncle's revelation heavy on his heart. He'd named his horse after his mother's mother. When his mother had first heard this, she'd laughed until she had tears in her eyes, saying that while Isabelle would appreciate the honour, she'd probably never thought that her name would be given to a horse. Shade hadn't minded; he liked the name and he thought that Isabelle would enjoy the colour-coding.

When he and Nikki were six, their parents had taken them to a horse farm about an hour to the north of Terang. There, they were given first pick of the thirteen newborn foals to raise as their own mounts. Every day for sixteen years, Shade and Nikki had spent at least an hour with the horses they'd chosen, training them to follow their commands and allowing them to grow accustomed to the presence of the Soul Twins. In many ways, the horses were closer to Shade and Nikki than most people in their lives, for Shade and Nikki feared no judgement from them and were able to be themselves.

He was about to leave to go find his sister, but turned back to see his parents one more time. His mother was trying to hold back the tears with a smile, but it didn't fool Shade. She would miss him more than she would ever admit. And then there was his father, a proud smile on his face, but anxiety about his and Nikki's first separation on his mind. Leaving Isabelle, he walked back over to them forcing a smile on his face.

He gave his mother as big a hug as he'd ever given her while trying to have her relax. Despite these feelings he sent her, she whispered, "Be safe, sweetheart."

"I will, Mom. I've got the best Nercomerc in this world or the next with me." She laughed at this.

But then her expression got serious again. "Watch your back, honey. Gothtor may be crumbling, but there are plenty of dangers on the way there."

"I know, Mom," Shade said. "That's why I'm bringing this," he said with a tap to *Peacemaker* on his right hip.

His mother just nodded her head. Shade knew his mother didn't like to see him with the sword in hand; she preferred to think of him as the carefree four-year-old she thought he was before they'd learned of his and Nikki's destiny. But being able to sense when his mother was worried from the time he could walk rarely left him carefree.

Next, Shade turned to his father who pulled him into a brief, tight hug. "Remember what you've been taught: diplomacy before death." His father's voice was a little tight.

"Will you two relax?" he asked, unable to take their worry and sadness. "I'm going to look for a mirror, not sign up for some far off war. I've already done that!" They smiled slightly at this, but this only brought out more worry in his mother. "I'll be safe, Mom, relax. You've got enough to worry about with Nikki; she'll need you now more than ever."

Hey! I heard that! And I'm not the one taking off for some mirror and leaving the person that means the world to me behind Nikki thought at him in a mock angry tone from somewhere in the castle.

Did I say anything untrue?

Did I? This time her tone revealed her heartache. Shade was about to ask where she was when he heard the *clop-clop* of a horse's hooves behind him and saw his parents' expressions of shock as their focus shifted behind and above him.

Turning, Shade saw why his parents were shocked. Atop her own horse - a chestnut mustang named Chinook - was Nikki. Shade had always found her beautiful, but in the hours since he last saw her she had transformed herself into a more beautiful goddess than Korena. Her usually straight hair was curled in loose tendrils that framed her beautiful face. The lost length of her hair brought out the gorgeous rise of her lovely neck. And her dress; it was his favourite colour on her: an exact match to the purple of their mother's eyes. It looked like the dress was modelled after his mother's wedding dress, but where the original had white floral stitching, Nikki's had blackblood stitching.

"Surprise," she said to him in her soft voice.

"…Wow!" was all Shade could say.

"You look beautiful, darling," his father said from behind Shade, who was blinking repeatedly trying to be able to have his mind comprehend the vision before him.

Forget beautiful, there's no words that even come close to describing how you look Shade thought.

Nikki just blushed, which just added to the perfection for Shade, and said, "Thank you. I'm glad you like it."

Like it? I don't think I'll be able to leave you behind with you looking like that. I literally can't take my eyes off you, Nikki.

I noticed. Now come on, I want this over and done with as soon as possible. As she thought this, Nikki guided Chinook over to Isabelle, forcing Shade to follow her.

As he climbed atop his mount, Shade couldn't remove his focus from his sister. He could hear his parents protest his leaving without saying goodbye, but he didn't care; all that mattered at that moment to him was memorizing everything about the way Nikki looked. And as she urged Chinook into a faster trot, he was mesmerized by the way her hair bounced into the air before falling down upon her back. Shade had Isabelle stay behind them so he could watch this alone.

Nikki led them through the less crowded areas of the city, twisting and turning her way to the northeast corner. Once they were out of the city proper and starting to enter the outer rings, she stopped and dismounted. Shade followed her lead, and took her free hand into his. Her hand was so soft, and Shade loved the feeling of her fingers interlaced with his.

As they walked, they were silent while enjoying the intimacy of the moment. When they past the last farm, they continued until they were in the seclusion of the forest trail. Stopping, Nikki pressed herself against him, as he wrapped her in his arms. She started to silently cry, as he held her.

I want to go with you.
I know.
But I know I can't.

I know.

Why did we agree to have it this way?

That I don't know. But it's too late now to change our mind.

I know. There was long silence as they clung to each other, unable to let go. *I know you have to go, but I don't want you to.*

I know. I don't think I could let you go.

Don't you ever.

Never. But as I promise that, I have to break it. But I'll promise something in return.

What?

That I'll be back as quick as I can; and when I am, we'll tell the kingdom. And then we'll be together forever.

Really? You'll marry me?

I've been married to you since before we were born. But I'll say 'I Do' to you in front of anyone you want. We'll make it 'official'. As Shade thought this, Nikki looked up at him. Tears streaking down her lovely face, but unable to mar her indescribable beauty, Shade saw the hope and longing in her eyes. And then he did something that he'd never done before, but had wanted to do since they were seven years old.

He kissed her.

Not the little pecks on the cheek they'd given each other when they'd been unable to contain their feelings, or when seeking forgiveness; he actually kissed her as he'd seen his parents kiss each other when they thought they were alone. Her lips were soft and wet from her tears.

Nikki was only shocked for the briefest of seconds, before moaning into his mouth and returning the kiss as passionately as she was receiving it. But they couldn't kiss forever, and they soon ran out of breath. Pulling away to breathe, the twins panted as they looked into each other's eyes, stunned at what they'd just done.

Why haven't we done that before?

Because everyone would go crazy if we did.

I want you to stay even more now. I won't be able to forget that and it will make me miss you more.

And I won't miss you?

I know you will. But you know you have it easier than I do; you know I'm safe at home and when you'll be home. I have to wait indefinitely, worrying if you're safe, until you walk back into the castle. You know Mom and Dad won't let me stand here waiting for you.

I never thought of that, I'm sorry.

It's OK; you've been focused on other aspects, like facing the dangers out there. Speaking of which, it's getting late; you should get going. Mom and Dad are probably wondering where I am.

I don't want to leave you; especially right now.

I know, but you must. The sooner you leave, the sooner you'll be back, and we can continue from where we leave off today. As she thought this, Nikki pried her hands from around Shade's neck and tried to loosen his grip on her waist. Shade didn't want to let her go, but she was finally able to free herself from his grip.

Turning away before he lost the will to do this, he reached up to pull himself onto Isabelle. But before he got his foot in the stirrup, Nikki grabbed his hand again. "Wait," she said softly. Shade didn't turn around until she called his name.

And then she was in his arms, her mouth on his. Not knowing when he'd be able to feel her again, Shade tried to commit this moment to memory for the long journey ahead. But then she pushed herself away. "I'm sorry. I needed that," she said as new tears came to her eyes. "I love you."

Shade climbed himself up onto Isabelle before turning to face his sister. "And I love you." And before his courage fled, he kicked his heels and Isabelle sped away. As she did, Shade felt his heart break as he left his love behind.

Chapter 49:

Reckoning Pains

Nikki watched as her brother disappeared into the darkness of the forest trail. It took everything she had to keep herself rooted to where she stood and not go after him. Now that she had tasted his lips, she needed them with her always. She'd wanted to kiss him as she just had since she was seven. How she'd been able to restrain herself for the past fifteen years, she'd never know.

But as Shade disappeared, she felt a hollowness in her heart she'd never felt before. Pulling herself upon Chinook, Nikki could barely hold herself upright. "Let's go home, boy. Quick as you can." She put a hand to Chinook's neck and let some of her pain into the horse. He seemed to understand as he took off at once back towards the castle.

As she entered the castle courtyard, the sun had nearly set and she saw her mother sitting on the grand steps. She stood up when she saw Nikki enter and started to walk to meet her at the stables. As Nikki dismounted, she found herself in her mother's arms. She felt pleasure rise within herself as her mother tried to silently comfort her, but it didn't work. Nikki started to shake as she let the pain take her. Leaving the stables, her mother all but carried Nikki to her room.

Once inside, Nikki walked as best she could to her bed. The imprint of her brother on her bed called to her as she crawled into it. Out of the corner of her eye, she saw her mother about to leave. "No Mommy!" It had been a long time since Nikki had called her mother that.

"What do you need, sweetheart?" her mother asked as she walked to the bed.

It took Nikki a moment before she knew what it was that she wanted. "Sing Shade's lullaby."

Her mother got an odd look on her face at this request. Not once in her life had Nikki asked for her mother to sing to her. But then Nikki saw her flash of understanding, as she started to sing the lullaby.

When she was done, her mother reached out and took Nikki's hand, giving it a light kiss. The small gesture reminded Nikki of Shade and she felt herself relax slightly at it. "How did you do it, Mom? How did you leave us when you felt this way?"

"It wasn't easy; it was the most painful thing I've ever experienced. But I had faith in your father; that he'd find a way to get me away. And then Korena showed me how miserable she'd been, and I knew I had to stay; despite everything, I owed her."

"You miss her, don't you?" Nikki asked trying to forget about her own pain for a moment.

As she waited for an answer, Nikki felt the guilt and longing that the question had released in her mother. "More than I should. I only ever told Kailee this, but Korena and I used to be lovers. And while I love your father with all my heart, I still find myself thinking of her in that way." Nikki was shocked to hear this. She knew her parents loved each other, she just never thought of them loving another. "That stays between us, OK?"

"Of course, Mom," she said as she locked this information in the part of her mind that even Shade had no access to.

Her mother stood to leave as she said, "You should get some sleep and let dreams of him comfort you. And before you know it, Shade will be back. He'll be back in that spot you're lying on, holding you in his arms."

"Don't go, Mom. I need you here. Please," Nikki whispered. Her mother walked to the other side of the bed, laid down, and slid her arms around Nikki.

"Of course, sweetheart. I'm here whenever you need me. I'll always be here." Nikki snuggled herself into her mother's arms, imagining they were her brother's; they certainly held her like Shade's did. And then she drifted to sleep.

※

Three days after leaving Terang, Shade found himself somewhere close to the border between Creavitia, Mouria, and Gothtor. Being so far north meant that the heat was oppressive, and his canteens were almost out of water. He'd stopped at a small lake to refill them the day before, but the heat was so strong that the water he didn't drink evaporated within the canteens. The heat, combined with the physical pain in his heart, had made the journey very slow.

Pausing to look at one of the maps that he always kept in

Isabelle's saddlebag, Shade blinked away the sweat and the pain. Finding the area he figured he was in, Shade realized he was about to find a respite from the heat that would last for the majority of the rest of his journey: the Valle Ragaz. The Valle Ragaz was a canyon that ran from the Creavitia-Mouria border up into the majority of Gothtor, as it branched out into what mapmakers had dubbed the Candelabra. Unfortunately for Shade, the closest 'candle' to Victorinox had him returning to the scorching heat for at least a day.

Spirits renewed with the prospect of not being so sweaty, Shade urged Isabelle into a light gallop. "Don't worry, girl," he encouraged after the horse gave a whine. "We'll be out of this insufferable heat by nightfall, if you keep this pace up." And upon hearing these words, Isabelle gave a surge of speed that nearly unseated Shade. Quickly tightening his grip on the reins, he gave a small chuckle at Isabelle's enthusiasm to escape the heat.

After five hours of the constant pace maintained by Isabelle, Shade found that the Valle Ragaz was well named. The high canyon walls provided shadows deep enough to keep one cool, as well as allow for small shrubs and even slender trees to grow. It was at one of these rare trees that he dismounted Isabelle, with a gentle rub to his bottom. The long day of riding had not been comfortable, but he hoped tonight's rest in the coolness of the Valle Ragaz would ease the knots that had formed up and down his body since he'd left home. After tying her to the tree, Shade set about removing Isabelle's saddle and making sure she was comfortable for the night.

He'd just started the fire he was going to use to cook the

rabbit he'd caught the night before when he sensed that he wasn't alone in the canyon. Ignoring the heat, Shade grabbed a branch from the fire, and with its light, circled his campsite to ensure that he was alone. Replacing the branch, Shade glanced out into the darkness. Looking to Isabelle, Shade noticed that his horse was already asleep. Sitting back down, Shade pulled the knife from his belt and started to skin the rabbit.

Tossing the fur and organs he'd removed onto the fire, Shade skewered the rabbit and placed it over the fire to cook. As he heard a rustling of leaves that suddenly stopped, he drew *Peacemaker* from its scabbard and stood up. The gentle curve of the sword caught the light from the fire and reflected it out into the darkness around him. That's when Shade heard the sound of a twig snapping behind him.

Jumping to the other side of the fire, he saw a man step out from the bushes and into the firelight. His clothes were all black, seamlessly covering everything from the top of his head to the soles of his feet, and making him a shadow in the darkness. Only the grey eyes of the stranger were visible; Shade was dismayed at the resolve he saw in those eyes. He had a small sword in his left hand; its blade splotched with dried blood stains.

That's when he noticed the two others behind him.

Lowering his sword slightly, Shade said, "I don't want any trouble. I do not have any gold and the supplies that I do have are nearly gone. That rabbit is the last of my food," he said with a point to the fire. Turning it over so that it wasn't burning on one side, Shade returned to his plea. "The rest of the things I have are only valuable to me."

"That sword and horse have value to us," the man with

the grey eyes said with the slight accent of the nomadic tribes that roamed the deserts of the north. "And trouble is exactly what you're going to get." And with a nod to his partners at Shade's back, the attack began.

Turning around in a flash, Shade noticed that the two who ran at him were smaller than their leader. The larger of the two carried a double-headed axe; its blade covered in runic symbols that Shade knew detailed its bloody history. The smaller one carried a wooden-handled trident; each point jagged at uneven angles to give its victims unpleasant rips upon removal. Shade also realized that the smaller one was a girl.

But before Shade could be dismayed by this turn of events, the two nomads were upon him. Upon deflecting the downward swing of the axe, Shade let go of his mind and let his instincts take over. Having been trained to use any and every weapon every day since he was ten gave him the confidence that he could hold his own. His muscles knew this dance well: defend, defend, attack, attack, attack, defend, attack, defend, attack, attack. As Shade fought with the two strangers, he kept a wary eye on the one who seemed to be their leader, but he seemed content to let the others fight Shade.

Finally, Shade was given an opening. Without a second thought, Shade plunged *Peacemaker* into the chest of the nomad with the axe. The jolt of the unexpected impact forced the cloth covering his face to come loose and Shade saw that he was simply a boy, no older than seventeen. Removing his sword, Shade repositioned himself so that he faced both the leader and the girl with the trident. Taking a breath to recompose himself, Shade awaited the coming attack.

But as the boy's body slumped to the ground, both remaining attackers ran to him. The leader cradled the body in his arms, holding the head to his chest. Removing the cloth covering his face, Shade saw that the man had to be the boy's father. And then it hit him: he'd killed someone, a boy. The weight of that knowledge nearly brought Shade to his knees at his victim's body. Seeing the father whisper something to the corpse of his son in his native tongue, Shade wished he could take it back. The pain of loss rolling off the two of them was nearly too much for him to bear.

Taking a step towards them, Shade recoiled as the girl raised her head and looked at him with such hate in her eyes - blue eyes that for a second he thought were Nikki's. She picked up the axe the boy had dropped and charged at Shade with a cry of fury. Stunned by what he'd done and the hatred in the girl's eyes, Shade did nothing until it was almost too late. "*Khalida, duwabifo!*" the father shouted.

Shade caught the axe as she swung it down. Ripping it from her fingers, Shade dropped the axe and looked into the girl's eyes. "I'm sorry. I didn't want to hurt him, but you left me no choice." He felt tears fall from his eyes, and these tears seemed to make the girl's rage falter. Looking behind the girl to the man still holding his son's body, Shade continued, "Please, leave before more people are hurt. I do not wish to have any more blood on my hands."

Sheathing *Peacemaker*, Shade stepped to the fire and picked up the rabbit. Handing it to the woman, she took it with indifference. There was a dead look in her eyes. "He was to be my husband," she said hollowly. Dropping the spit with the rabbit on it, she lunged for the axe, picked it up, and swung it towards Shade again. "HE WAS TO BE MY HUSBAND!" she shouted as she swung.

This time, Shade didn't defend. Pulling the knife from his belt, he stepped into the space created by her swing and lodged the knife between her breasts. The axe fell to the ground with a dull thud as the girl fell back, a dark stain growing on her black clothes. Turning to the father, Shade fell to his knees as tears anew stung his eyes. "Please, I do not wish to kill you too. Leave and take your son and his beloved's bodies. Bury them in the ways of your people. And if it is any solace to you and those who loved them, I'm sorry, sorrier than I have been about anything."

The father looked at Shade with such sadness that he could barely hold his gaze. He stood, leaving his son's body, and walked over to Shade. He gave a series of whistles, and three horses appeared in the firelight. The father looked down upon Shade, his grey eyes judging him at his word. Then he returned to his son's body, picked it up, and laid it over the back of a horse. Then he did the same for the girl.

Just as he was going to leave, Shade stood and turned to him. "I wish to pray for their souls, but I cannot without their names."

The father looked at him without taking his heavy grey eyes off Shade's brown ones. "My son's name was Ishmael and his betrothed's was Khalida. The day after tomorrow was to be their wedding day." Shade turned his face away in shame at hearing this. "And while you pray, add this to your prayers: pray that I never see you again, for if I do, it will be your father and beloved who are in mourning."

Shade watched as the man left on his horse, holding the reins of the other two that held the bodies of his son and his son's beloved. Once he could no longer hear or see any sign of them, Shade walked over to Isabelle. Throwing his arms around the horse, Shade let his tears flow as his body shook with the weight his soul felt. How had he been so ruthless, so quick to kill? He hadn't hesitated, but rather plunged both the blade of his sword and knife into those two nomads, not even as old as himself.

In the dying light of the fire, Shade found the rabbit he'd given to Khalida. Looking it over, he found that, surprisingly, it was evenly cooked. Wiping the dirt from it, Shade ripped the rabbit in half, throwing one half into the fire. Looking to the stars, he whispered, "Hados, Lord of the Underworld, and Korena his bride, hear my prayer. I wish for the souls of Ishmael and Khalida to be happy in death; bring their souls to the Gates. I have never asked for anything, and have spent my life in preparation for the battle that you said I needed to be at the forefront of. I sent them to you, unwillingly, and plead that they are granted favour. If you grant me nothing else in life, grant me this."

His appetite gone, Shade wrapped the half of rabbit he still held in his hands. Putting it in a pouch on his saddle, Shade saw the worn piece of paper that was the goodbye letter his mother had written him eighteen years ago. Needing something to comfort him, Shade pulled out the letter and sat himself at the fire. Throwing his last stick onto the fire, he read the words that he'd read countless times before.

> *To my Baby Boy,*
>   *I do not even know where I can start. In truth, it wasn't until I met your father that I wanted a son. But, for all my years wishing*

for a lover like Daddy, and a daughter like your sister, I think it is you who I will miss the most. While you all hold possession of my heart, I've always felt that your hold was the strongest. This doesn't mean that I love Daddy or Nikki any less than you; it just means that the love I have for you has affected me more than I thought possible.

I wish I could watch you grow up into the great and wonderful man I know you will be. Your kindness is unmatched by anyone I've ever met, and I don't want you to lose that part of yourself. Trust your instincts, my beloved son, and they will not lead you wrong. Remember what I've taught you and your sister: honesty will open more doors than any riches, crowns, or swords ever could.

I love you, Shade. Mommy loves you more than she can put words to and it breaks my heart to leave you like I am. Forgive me, my Baby Boy, for ripping off the happy smile that has always been on your face.

The love I have for you shall only be surpassed by how much I'll miss you,
Mommy

As he read the words his mother had written in sadness, Shade felt himself smile. Seeing the written proof that his mother knew that their relationship was slightly different than those she had with her closest loved ones, even Nikki and his father, always lifted his spirits. Looking down to the ring on his finger that his mother had had made for him when he was born, Shade felt all the love she'd felt from her first learning she was pregnant to her teary goodbye three days ago. Besides Nikki, there was no one Shade loved more than his mother; and it was that love that he used to help him through the night.

※

Nikki sat at the table in the small dining room that was in the private quarters of the Royal family with her mother and father, as a simple vegetable stew was being served. She knew her parents were talking, possibly even to her, but she ignored them as she'd been ignoring the world for the past three days. The ghost of Shade's lips on hers, and the way they had made her feel, was all she could think of. But every time she tried to remember the perfection that were these memories, the further that they became; until moments like now when she feared that the brief kisses hadn't actually happened.

Looking away from her food and up at her parents, she saw the worried expressions that were on both of their faces. Forcing herself to smile, Nikki took a spoonful of stew that was their dinner. The smile she gave at the taste was more natural as she said, "This stew is quite good. Alix never ceases to amaze me with the wonders he creates. Don't you agree?"

Her parents smiled, but she saw the concern still in their eyes. "He certainly has a talent for making the simple delicious. I've never regretted hiring him," her father said with a small, but forced, smile.

"Not even when you try to usurp the kitchen from him to make Mom breakfast?" Nikki asked with a mischievous giggle.

Both her parents smiled genuinely at this, as the concern slowly left their eyes. "Well, maybe then," her father said with a small laugh.

"Oh, but I do so enjoy watching you two argue pointlessly," her mother said as she took her father's hand and laughed at him. Nikki, who also enjoyed watching her father and Alix argue over the most benign things, laughed as well at this. Her father just made a face at the two of them, which caused them to renew their laughing.

It felt good to laugh, Nikki realized. With her body and mind tense with worry for her Soul's Twin, she knew that she needed to relax. But being able to force herself not to, when it came to worrying about Shade's safety, was something that she knew she would never be able to do. As she thought of her brother and how she wished he would return to her soon, Nikki didn't realize that she was gripping the knife before her on the table. Her knuckles were white as she held the knife in a grip and her heartbeat and breathing increased.

Seeing this and the fear in her eyes, Nikki's mother looked at her with concern. "Sweetheart, are you alright?" she asked in the voice she used when she was more worried than she wanted others to know she was.

But before Nikki could answer, a pain the likes of which she'd never felt crashed over her. It wasn't a physical pain, but rather an emotional one that Nikki knew he brother was feeling. With a cry of anguish, Nikki doubled over as her right hand went to the necklace around her neck. Her left hand, still gripping the knife as tightly as it could, would not move from the table.

In a flash her parents were at her side. Her father was trying to remove the knife from her death grip, while her mother was simultaneously shooting her with pleasure and trying to draw the pain out of her. Both of their efforts were useless as Nikki started to convulse.

And then the pain doubled.

Nikki couldn't even cry out; the pain was so intense. Her parents had pulled her away from the table and were laying her on her back so she wasn't in danger of hurting herself. The looks on their faces were heartbreaking, as they could not help her. But then the pain increased again, and Nikki lost consciousness.

Nikki's eyes snapped open. She didn't know what had happened, but it was extremely difficult for her to move. Turning her head to take in her surroundings used most of the energy she had. Seeing that she was in her room, and that she was alone, slightly confused her. The last thing she remembered was unbearable, emotional pain. Surely her parents wouldn't leave her side until she awoke. But then she saw the figure who stood at the doorway. "Dad…" Her voice was so weak she wasn't sure he heard her.

But then he turned towards her. It wasn't her father as she thought it was, nor was it her mother. With the aid of the candelabra that was on her bedside table, Nikki was able to see the muscular frame of her friend Romulus Shaw. When he saw that she was awake, Romulus ran to her bedside and knelt down. "Princess Nikki," he said, visibly relieved that she was awake. "Are you alright?"

"I…I thi-" Nikki's voice was so weak and her throat so dry that she couldn't even talk anymore. Realizing this, Romulus reached for a cup on her bedside table and held it to her lips. Sipping at the awful tasting liquid until her taste buds could no longer take the flavour, Nikki felt her throat become wet. Taking a minute to allow her mouth to adjust to the aftertaste of the liquid, Nikki nodded her thanks. "Thank you," she said in a voice barely above a whisper. "And I think I'm alright; a little stiff, but otherwise alright. But Romulus, where are my parents and why aren't they here?"

"You've been unconscious for a few days, Princess. Your parents have been at your bedside since you collapsed. Your Aunt Marina finally convinced them that they needed to rest. I told them that I'd spend the night watching you and wake them if anything changed in your condition." His hazel eyes looked upon her with a devotion that had made her brother both jealous and amused on more than one occasion. "I should go wake your parents; they'll want to know you're awake."

"Romulus, wait." She waited until he was once again kneeling at her side. "Let them sleep; they need it and I don't know how long I'll be awake for." He gave her a look of concern to which she gave a reassuring smile. "I'll be alright, Romulus, I promise."

Seeing her smile made Romulus smile as well. "I know you will…Nikki." It was the first time he'd not called her by her title since they were old enough to understand its purpose. The look in his eyes made Nikki's breath catch as she saw the love he held for her, as well as feeling that love roll off him and nearly smother her. Misunderstanding the catch of her breath, Romulus immediately set about apologizing.

But before he could get the words out, Nikki said, "You don't need to apologize to me, Romulus. We've been friends all of our lives, and I know you love me." This caused him to look at her with the slightest trace of fear. "I'm not mad about this, Romulus; I'm actually quite flattered. But, I can't return these feelings, unfortunately. My heart belongs to someone else."

Romulus looked down as she said she loved someone else. Looking at her after a minute of silence, he had a small, sad smile on his lips. "It's Shade." It wasn't a question, but Nikki still nodded her head. "He's the only person who has spent more time with you than me. He loves you too, you know."

"I know," Nikki said with a content smile. "I've known how he's felt about me since before we were born, as he's known about my feelings. We're what's called Soul Twins; we could no more not love each other than you could live forever. Please don't tell anyone this, at least not until he gets back from his Reckoning."

Romulus nodded his assent, as he took her hand in his. Leaning in, he kissed her fingers lightly before he stood up. "You should get some sleep; I can see that you're still in some pain. I'll tell your parents that you woke up in the middle of the night, but that you asked me to let them sleep."

"Thank you, Romulus. Goodnight." And with that, Nikki returned to a sleep numbed by pain and haunted by nightmares of her brother just out of her reach.

Chapter 50:
The Secrets of Victorinox

Shade had once asked his father if his mother had ever shot him with pain. He had looked at Shade funny for a moment and then chuckled. He said that before she had realized that she loved him that she had. He said it was only for a second, but he could still feel the sting if he thought about it. He'd also said that that was not the most painful thing he'd ever felt, for physical pain can only hurt so much.

Shade knew what he'd been talking about, and knew that his father had indeed once led a painful life. But Shade doubted if his father's pain had ever felt like this, this aching in his chest that made it hurt with every inch he moved. The pain at being so far away from Nikki was the worst of it, but his guilt over the lives he'd taken only made him feel worse. Since leaving Terang a week ago, Shade had experienced more pain than he thought was possible to ever live with; every night he dreamt of Nikki, but she was just out of his reach, and when he woke, and the nightmare faded, his emptiness returned. He was incredibly glad for Isabelle's presence, for without her, he'd never have been able to take one step.

But now, he had finally reached his destination. He was finally at Victorinox, or what was left of it. The palace was divided into two sections: the palace proper and the cathedral. The cathedral was definitely the worse off, its roof nearly completely collapsed and vegetation had overgrown most surfaces. The palace seemed to be in much better shape, at least from the exterior. Victorinox, in its entirety, was massive with spires from both the palace and cathedral reaching high into the sky. The whole thing was built upon a plateau in the middle of a nearly barren field and made of solid white marble that Shade knew had taken nearly a decade to complete.

In the light of the full moon, Shade couldn't make out every detail of the palace's and cathedral's intricate designs, but he could tell that Victorinox was once a place of great beauty. Even in its current state, Shade still thought the entire palace beautiful. He tried to imagine it in the sunlight when it was first completed, nearly thirteen thousand years ago. He didn't think his imagination did it any justice.

Dismounting Isabelle and leaving her tied to a nearby tree, Shade started up the nearly overgrown staircase that led up to the palace. Three thousand three hundred and sixty-nine steps up at a near forty-five-degree angle had kept the palace safe for thousands of years. He thought that with every step up, his pain would be compounded, but oddly, Shade found that each step he took made it more bearable. Once at the top, he found himself in reverent awe as he stood in the shadow of Victorinox. He heard the flutter of wings and looked up to see a large group of bats fly overhead.

Suddenly, he felt a blade at his throat and another on his

back. "If you wish to live, you won't turn around," a female voice whispered into his ear. "Who are you and what are you doing here in this sacred place?"

Shade thought the voice sounded familiar, but he couldn't place it. Not wanting to antagonize the woman into attacking him, Shade answered her question. "My name is Shade Kanta, and I mean no harm to this place; I know just how sacred it is."

"I highly doubt that, Prince of Braria," the woman said, "but I trust you." Shade felt the blades at his back and throat drop, as he turned to face the woman. But in the shadows of the palace, he couldn't see her. "It's been a long time, Shade Leo," she said, taking a step back so her face was in the moonlight.

"Jazabel?" Shade asked in disbelief. But even as he asked, he knew it was true; he could feel that feeling he'd had when he'd first met her: the feeling of connection. She just nodded. "What are you doing here? I thought you were in Toxai." Not that he was disappointed to see her.

"I live here now." Shade felt the sadness that rolled off her as she revealed this. "Ever since I last saw you, I've been unable to stay in one place for very long. My parents died before I got home, and ever since I've been wandering the world. That is until I came here; it was like I was drawn here by some unknown force." She didn't look at him as she told him all this, but Shade could tell she was confused as to why she'd been drawn to Victorinox of all places.

"I'm sorry, Jazabel. But why did you never return to Braria? You would have been welcome there." He took a step towards her wanting to offer comfort, but she shook her head.

"No, Shade, don't come any closer," she said in a tight voice. "And I know I would have been welcome in Braria, I just chose not to return. Many things have changed in the past eighteen years, but one thing that hasn't is my memories of Braria. And my memories of you and your kindness." She turned away from him as she said this. "You never answered my question, Shade. What are you doing here?" Her voice seemed more restrained as she asked this.

"I'm on my Reckoning; I search for the Mirror of Rheta. I don't suppose you know where that is?" Shade did not like the prospect of having to search the entire palace for the object of his quest; that would only add time he could not afford to waste.

"I've never heard of this Mirror of Rheta, so no, I don't know where it is. The palace is full of mirrors, so I guess I can let you take one. Is there anything else you seek?" She still wouldn't turn to look at him.

"A grave, the grave of Slac Hino." Shade could sense the unease and longing in her; she was conflicted over something. He wondered what it was.

"Ahh, that, I do know. In the cathedral, walk down the stairs to the graveyard. In the back corner is a marble coffin upon a raised platform. That is Slac Hino's grave." Finally, she turned back to him, but she still didn't look at him.

"Thank you, Jazabel. It was good seeing you again," Shade said as he walked over to the cathedral. When she didn't respond, he looked back to where she had stood, but she was gone. Again he heard the flutter of wings overhead as bats flew by.

In the side wall of the cathedral was a hole where Shade thought a window must have once been, and it was here that he entered. Once inside, Shade descended the surprisingly still intact stairs until he reached the bottom floor. This floor was covered in overgrown grass as well as stone grave markers.

Trying not to step on any of the graves, or at least where he thought they were, Shade made his way to the back corner. With the help of the full moon, he was easily able to spot the grave. It was completely white and had the imprint of the great prince on the lid.

Stepping up onto the platform, Shade placed himself at Slac Hino's side as he looked to his stone face. And in the language the prince had formalized, Shade spoke, "*Great prince, it is a great honour to finally find myself before you. For my entire life, I've wanted to come to your home and restore it to its former glory. But as I stand here, I see that for me to do so just might destroy the beauty it now possesses. I want you to know that the example you provided all those years ago still carries weight to those of us who came after you. I still try to emulate your percepts of a leader of the people. And the fact that your life ended the way it did is a complete tragedy and that those who know your story never let it be forgotten.*"

"Well, you people don't know the full story," an ethereal voice said from behind Shade, startling him.

Shade turned to the sound of the voice to find the spirit of the man he'd just been talking to. His thick hair and scruffy beard were brown and in need of a good brushing; his eyes were hazel; and there was a scar that ran diagonally through his right eyebrow. "Slac Hino!" he said as he dropped to his knees. "*This is an honour beyond words.*"

"You do not need to speak Gothtorian, I understand

your tongue. And while you think this an honour, it is I who is honoured. Stand up, dear prince; there is much to discuss and that marble can become quite painful. You are in enough pain as it is, and I do not wish to add to your pain more than I must."

Standing up, Shade gazed upon his idol reservedly. "If you know I'm in pain and believe what you have to say to me will add to it, then I can only conclude one thing: Hados sent you."

The spirit smiled. "Very good. The Lord of the Underworld did indeed send me to you. I have watched those who honour my legend from the other side, but none have ever held me to the esteem you do, Shade Kanta; I have waited a long time for this meeting.

"But to my duties first; I have a new prophecy for you, that once again concerns the start of your conflict. '*Yours and mine, Mine and yours: Equal claims to what remains. Shameful secrets will lead to greater regrets, as your gain was once his pain; see tables turned at an out spurned.*' I'm told the 'greater regrets' is the death spoken of in the first prophecy you received. And this death will be especially hard on you, for you will be closer than your sister to the one who dies."

Shade closed his eyes at the mention of Nikki, the emptiness once again filling his chest. And as he felt a tear roll down his cheek at the thought of the death still to come in his life, he looked again upon Slac Hino. "You have indeed brought me more pain, but I do not blame you for it. I would have eventually had it anyway. You said you have looked forward to meeting me for a long time; just how long have you known about this meeting?"

"Since long before you were born. If you're in the right

place at the right time in the underworld, information is very easy to come by," he answered. "And before you ask, I'm here to tell you the truth of my life, and more importantly, my death. Let me start by saying that all the stories of me are true, but they do not give an accurate picture. For my many virtues, I had some crippling vices. The biggest two of these were arrogance and lust. My arrogance led me to believe that because I was so loved, I was invincible; despite what I read in prophecy. And my lust was the reason I was killed.

"Rheta, my sister, was who I was in lust with. But as I'm sure you know, people don't look kindly upon that sort of thing. And I was one of them; I thought myself disgusting and evil for the thoughts that ran through my head. For a long time, I was able to control my feelings, until the night she came to me. She told me she knew of my feelings and that she'd let me indulge them, as she'd thought of it as well.

"For nearly a year, I was in the most wonderful of dreams. But they all came crashing down when she met a man by the name of Cosmar, and stopped everything. She fell in love with him and I knew my appetites would never be sated again. So I devised a plot to kill Cosmar.

"With as much stealth and cunning as I possessed, I found myself an assassin who would not be able to be traced back to me. I brought him here, hid him in the room Cosmar had taken up residence in, and told him to wait until me, Rheta, and Cosmar returned from a hunt. He was to knock him around a little and make some noise to give me and Rheta an excuse to return to the room to see what was happening. We entered at the perfect moment: Cosmar was just going limp in the assassin's arms. And before either of them could react, I notched an arrow in my bow and killed the assassin; ensuring Rheta never found out the truth.

"I gave her six months to mourn the loss of her lover, and think of me as the man who had brought justice to his killer, before I tried to bed her again. She refused and told me to never touch her again; she was to never know the love of another now that her heart was dead. I waited another three months and then tried again, and this time she gave into me.

"But when we were finished she said she knew the truth; she said she knew I killed Cosmar. I, of course, protested, saying that I killed his killer. She said that was to protect myself, as now only I knew the full truth of the situation. And then she told me she hoped I'd enjoyed my last moments of life, before confessing she'd poisoned my drink. If I killed her lover so only I could be with her, she would kill me because she couldn't be with him."

Shade was disturbed by the story. His lifelong admiration for the man whose spirit had just confessed to being petty, spiteful, and murderously jealous had taken a devastating blow. "Why? Why would you do that? She was your sister! And you stole her happiness to recreate your own, setting off a chain of events that led to the desolation of your country!" Shade was furious at the hypocritical man before him.

"Like I said earlier, the honour people throw upon me isn't deserved. My death was earned, and it saddens me that I brought my country down with me. But I've spent the last thirteen thousand years trying to make up for that. I still believe in the percepts that I wrote for one to be a good leader. And I still practice them: honesty to all about all, having the courage to do the right thing, and above all, a love and respect for all living things, past, present and future.

"That's why I told you this, so the world can finally truly judge me. And if Gothtor is to be rebuilt, its true past must be known. People too often either see only the good or bad of things; they need to be able to look at both aspects before forming their opinions. Learn from both the rights and wrongs I've done. You said that you've followed my percepts all your life; you should continue to do so, even if your opinion of me has changed from learning the truth." Slac Hino didn't yell, despite the force in his voice. His hazel eyes implored Shade to understand what was being told to him.

Shade didn't want to admit it right then, but Slac Hino had a point. His words rang true in Shade's ears. Taking a moment to consider what he'd just been told, Shade looked down upon the stone face on Slac Hino's grave. "There is wisdom in your words, great prince. Sometimes the truth hurts, but after the pain goes away, you become stronger. I'll carry your full story forth, and let the masses judge you accordingly. I shall lead my life continuing to try and reach my all, as you said one should. And even though I think less of you now, I would like you to know that I still look up to you and consider this encounter a great honour." As Shade turned back to the spirit, he saw the small prideful smile on Slac Hino's lips.

"My time here is almost up, but there are a few more things I wish to tell you. The first is that, despite the odds and the thousands of years it took, Rheta has forgiven me. The second is that what you came here seeking is in the room at the top of the turret in the southernmost part of the palace. Your prayers about the spirits of Ishmael and Khalida have been answered; I saw to that myself. They forgive you, Shade, and thank you for reuniting them; so let go of that guilt, even they admit you had no choice but to kill them. And finally, the woman who told you where to find me is a very unique person. Bring her back to your homeland and see just how unique she is."

Shade had tears come to his eyes at the mention of Ishmael and Khalida. He was a little confused by this last point, but nodded his head. "Thank you, Slac Hino; I'm glad to have met you."

"It was my honour, Prince Shade. Do not forget all that I've told you, and good luck with whatever the future brings you, after your war."

"Thank you, but how do you know I'll live through it?"

"I don't." And with that, he was gone. Turning back to the marble coffin, Shade placed a hand on the stone shoulder. And with a whispered word of parting, Shade left to find the turret with the room that held the Mirror of Rheta.

The turret Shade believed to be the one Slac Hino had talked about seemed to be the most well preserved of all of Victorinox. And as he climbed the spiral staircase up to the room, Shade realized that he had no idea what the mirror looked like. Every reference to it only said that it was small. He had no idea how he would recognize it. Perhaps it would be the only mirror in the room.

When he got to the top of the stairs, Shade saw that the door had been kicked off its hinges; most likely when the country revolted against Rheta, he surmised. But upon entry, he knew it to be true. The room was once someone's bedroom. And Shade had a good idea of whose room it was.

Judging by the size of the room, the ornateness of the furniture, and the fact that dresses and other feminine garments lined the room's dust-covered floor, Shade figured this was once Rheta's bedroom. Everything looked like it was out of place. When the revolution happened, looters had ransacked the room, leaving what they thought worthless behind. Looking around, Shade found a portrait that had fallen behind a wardrobe and brought it over to the large broken stained glass window to look at it. In the little light he knew the painting was of a woman, who he assumed was Rheta, and he wanted to know what she looked like.

But when he blew the dust away and was in the light of the window, Shade nearly dropped the portrait. He couldn't believe what he was looking at; the resemblance was uncanny. Staring back at him was Jazabel, but he knew it wasn't actually her, it was Rheta. Unique indeed; perhaps there was a reason Jazabel felt drawn here.

Putting the painting back where he found it, Shade continued to search the room. As he pulled out dresser drawers and shoved his hand into them, he felt a little disgusted with himself. Stopping what he was doing, he again pulled out the picture of Rheta. And in her native tongue he said, "*Forgive me, princess. It is not right for me to be doing this and I do not wish to disrespect your memory. What happened to you is unjust and I'm sorry for it.*" Drawing his hand down the painting while pretending Rheta could feel his touch, Shade felt a raised surface.

Smiling to himself at the cunning of the woman, he again walked over to the window. Looking upon the back, he found the frame opened from there. Opening the back,

Shade found himself looking at the silver of a small circular mirror. He picked it up and immediately knew this was what he was looking for. He didn't know what the mirror could do, but he could feel a reflection of his own magic within.

Replacing the back, Shade once again spoke to the portrait. "*Thank you, Rheta. History remembers you for killing your brother, but I shall remember you for your cleverness. And don't despair; your mirror will once again be in your hands.*" He put the Mirror of Rheta into his pocket, as he returned the painting to where he'd found it once again. Shade then took the time to try and tidy the room up by putting away the clothes, straightening the furniture, and finally replacing the door as he left.

Standing on the steps that led up to Victorinox, Shade gave one last look at the place that had been in his dreams since he was a boy. Perhaps he would return one day with Nikki, and together they'd discover the marvels of this once great palace. Turning to leave, Shade heard the now familiar flutter of bat wings overhead.

"Leaving without saying goodbye?" Jazabel asked from the shadows. She once again had positioned herself so that only her face was visible.

Turning back towards her, he said, "No, just putting what I came for with my horse. Besides, I can't say goodbye to you just yet."

"And why is that, Shade? You have what you came for; were you planning on staying here with me?"

Shade thought he heard the conflict he'd felt in her as she asked this last question. "No, Jazabel, I cannot stay here with you. But I would like you to accompany me back to Braria. You do not have to stay if you do not wish to; but if it's alright with you, I would like the pleasure of your company for a while longer."

Jazabel got a sad look of joy on her face. "You are a rare man, Shade Leo Kanta. In a world where light can be hard to find, you shine brighter than anyone I've ever known. And it is that light that holds me back. I'm sorry but I cannot go with you," she said as she turned back to the shadows.

"Jazabel, wait!" Shade called. She stopped, but didn't turn to look at him. "What's wrong, Jazabel? I can sense the conflict within you, but I don't know what it's over. You know you can tell me; I'm not a judgemental person."

She turned back to him, her face half hidden in the shadow, and studied him. After a long pause, she let her breath out and looked him in the eyes. "I trust you, Shade. And you've never told me a lie before. But before you say anything, I request you let me explain." Without waiting for his reply, she stepped out into the light.

Shade got an eyeful as he gazed upon Jazabel. He could not call what she was wearing clothes for it was simply leather cords. Her breasts were barely covered by a thin piece of material shaped like a bat. The same sheer material covered her legs halfway up her thighs. The most covered part on her body were her forearms, which were covered in leather sleeves the undersides of which were criss-crossed. Everything was black, which made it stand out against her pale skin. Shade tried to keep his composure, but he knew his shock was written across his face.

Seeing this, Jazabel got tears in her eyes. "I'm sorry, I shouldn't have done this. I knew how you'd react," she said as she turned back to the shadows.

Before she disappeared again, Shade said, "Jazabel wait! I'm sorry; your outfit took me by surprise. I haven't seen that much of a woman since I was eight years old and still bathed with my sister. Please forgive me. I owe you a chance to explain, whatever it was you were going to explain; and I would very much like to hear it."

She didn't turn back to him until a few minutes after he stopped talking. With a deep breath, she turned and looked into his eyes. "I'm a Lady of the Night, Shade. Do you know what that means?"

"I'm a well-read man, Jazabel, but I've never heard of a Lady of the Night before," Shade said with a shake of his head.

"That's because we keep to ourselves. Ladies of the Night have a certain affinity for darkness; we're drawn to it like a moth to a flame. But it's not just the darkness of night that draws us; it's also the darkness of one's soul. Like you were able to see the conflict in me, I can see the darkness in others. And the more darkness I see, the more I'm drawn to a person.

"This leather around me," she said pointing to her attire, "is my life. If it were ever to be cut, I would die. And if others knew who I was, they'd try to kill me. This is the reason I've wandered the world; for every Lady of the Night knows that other women can tell what we are, and they either kill us or have us banished from their villages for it. That is why I like it here; it's safe, and I can feel the darkness that has settled over this place. It feels like…a memory of a dream of home. And that is why I cannot return with you to Braria."

Shade was certainly at a loss of words at this. But then some came to mind. "You've trusted me with your most guarded secret, Jazabel; now allow me to return the favour. Have you ever heard of Soul Twins?" Shade took the look of shock on her face to mean yes. "Well, I am one with my sister as the other. Throughout my entire life we have never been more than the size of our castle apart, until this week. I'm in more pain than I can put words to, and will be until I see her again. But our country does not know this about us, and will most likely shun us when we tell them. We very well may have to force ourselves to others to continue our family line.

"But if there's one thing I've learned in the past eighteen years, it's that nothing in my life is an accident. I was meant to come here even before I was born. And I believe our meeting again means something. I feel myself being drawn to you, Jazabel, in a way I've never felt before in any other person I've met. And when I learned that I was to come here, I saw your face. I don't know why or what it means, but I think the answers lie somewhere in Braria. I understand and empathize with why you're here, but I promise you, Braria will never drive you away."

Jazabel just looked at him as he came to her and took her hand into both of his at the end of his speech. "You speak pretty words, Shade, but you can't guarantee them. But I, too, have felt the draw to you; I felt it from the moment I met you." She then brought herself to Shade, hugging herself to him. Unsure of what exactly to do, Shade slowly brought his arms up and wrapped them around her back. "But I will go with you, to help you find the answers you seek, if you protect me as you've promised to do," she said, looking into his eyes.

"With my life," he said, as she rested her head upon his chest. And for a moment, his ache for Nikki was gone.

Chapter 51:

Reunions

Nikki felt hollow and like she was withering away. It had been nearly two weeks since she'd felt any trace of her brother and she didn't know how much more of this pain she could take. Every night she'd dreamt of him, but every night he got further and further away. She'd barely eaten or moved since she'd told Romulus about her and Shade, and she knew her family was worried about her.

She noticed that her father was sitting beside her, but she didn't know how long he'd been there. She used all her energy to look into his eyes, Shade's eyes. Seeing those eyes that she had adored her whole life gave her the strength to focus on what he was saying. "...eat something. If you don't start to eat something soon you're going to end up starving yourself to death. And think of what that would do to your brother; he'd kill himself just to be with you, and losing the two people she cares the most about would destroy your mother. So, sweetheart, please eat something, anything."

When she didn't say anything right away, he got up to leave, tears falling from his eyes. Nikki hated seeing tears in

Shade's - no, these were her father's - eyes, and she needed them looking into hers. "Wait," she said in a hoarse whisper. Her throat was so dry she was only sure she spoke from the pain of moving her mouth. And she saw her father turn to look at her, hope evident in every wrinkle on his face. "Water." He held a glass to her lips, gently pouring it into her mouth. "Look...eyes," she croaked. Despite the water, her throat was still very dry.

Even with her vague instruction, he was able to figure out what Nikki had meant. Levelling his eyes into hers sent a small chill through Nikki. "He loves you and will be home to you soon," her father reassured. "Do you think you can eat something?"

Nikki nodded, and found that her neck hurt. "Small and soft." Her father just nodded as he started to rip a loaf of bread into tiny pieces and held them up in front of her, asking if that was OK. Nikki nodded that they were.

"It's fresh; Alix just gave it to me just before I came in. Everyone wants you to get better. But I understand if you feel like you can't do anything; just eat this bread and you'll be fine," he said to her as he fed her the bread.

Nikki continued to eat until half the loaf was gone, taking breaks to wet her throat and wash the bread down. The bread was doing what her father hoped it would; it was giving her some strength. But her body was so sore that that strength wasn't really useful to her. "Dad, my body's sore. Can you take the pain away?" she asked after she felt her stomach couldn't take much more bread.

But before her father could answer, her heart contracted painfully causing Nikki to curl herself into a ball in pain. Then the pain was gone and she felt that her heartbeat was stronger now.

Her father looked at her in concern as she pulled herself out of the ball she'd folded into. "Nikki, are you alright?" he asked, his worry clear on his face. He took her hand and Nikki felt the tingle of magic as her father tried to take the pain away.

Feeling her muscles relax as her father continued to try and heal her, Nikki let out a breath. With a hand on her heart, she looked to her father. "I'm fine, Dad. It's OK. I think that was Shade; he's close. He's almost home," she said in between large, panting breaths.

Nikki saw the relief in her father's eyes as she said this. Whether he was relieved she was alright, that she would be soon, or that Shade was safe and would be home soon, she wasn't sure of. But maybe it was all of that.

For the next two days Nikki felt her strength return and she was sure that her brother was coming home. It was now the second evening since she'd felt the heart contraction, and she was getting restless. She felt he'd be back in her arms before the night was out, and had dressed herself accordingly. Earlier that day she'd washed away the past week and a half of lying in bed and had lightly curled her hair again. She'd also worn the same amethyst dress that she'd worn on the day Shade had left.

She paced the length of her room, constantly looking out her window to try and see Shade returning home. But as the sun set and darkness covered the city, she was able to see less and less. The clouds covered the moon, making the only light the lanterns left in the windows of taverns and homes. No longer able to see, Nikki opened her window so as to hear when Shade approached.

For five minutes all she heard was the nightlife of Terang. And then, she heard it: the sound of a running horse. Excitement rose within her as the sound got closer and closer to the castle. And as the horse entered the castle courtyard and she saw a rider jump from its back and run towards the castle, Nikki rushed out of her room as fast as she could.

She heard the castle's main doors slam open all the way up in her room and then his voice, Shade's voice, calling to her. "NIKKI!? NIKKI!?" She heard the need in his voice as she ran as fast as she could to the staircase that led to the entrance lobby.

With the same need she heard in his voice, she called to him, "SHADE! SHADE!" As she turned the corner to the hallway that led to the main staircase, she saw him as he reached the top. And finally she saw the deep brown eyes she loved so much.

And then she heard him in her head as their connection was renewed. *Nikki* he thought and she felt the relief in his finding her. As she jumped into his arms, he swung her around once before he set her down. Then his lips were on hers, kissing as if only her lips could give him breath.

I missed you; I missed this.

You have no idea.

Don't you ever leave my side again, Shade! My heart can't take it.

Pulling away so he could breathe, Shade looked into her

eyes. "Never, love. Never again will we feel this pain." And then he was kissing her again.

"Pardon the interruption, but I believe there was more than one person who missed you while you were away, Shade," Nikki heard her mother say from behind her.

Ignore her; she can have you when I'm finished.

But Shade pulled away anyways. *If we see her now, we won't have this deadline looming over our heads.* Walking to his mother, Shade gave her a long hug. "I missed you, Mom. And it's good to be home."

"I'm just glad you're alright; you know how worried I was," their mother said.

"I know, Mom. I've got so much to tell you. But where is the king? I must speak with him at once."

"The king is here," her father said, standing at the top of the staircase. And when Nikki saw her father, she was struck by how similar his and his son's posture was. Despite their looks, father and son had many things in common.

Releasing his mother from her hug, Shade turned and walked to his father. And when they were only a foot apart, he bowed slightly, saying "Father."

"Do you have what you sought, Prince Shade; or was the task too high of a challenge?" Nikki noticed her father's voice had that official quality to it. And when Shade spoke, his voice had a hint of that same quality.

"I would not have returned if I was unsuccessful. If you would all please follow me." And with that, he led them down the stairs, out the door, and over to the stables. But before entering, he stopped and turned towards them. "Before we continue, I must ask that the three of you keep an open mind. Some things that are about to happen may be a bit surprising to you and I have made promises that I intend to keep." The three of them nodded they would, and Shade continued on his way to Isabelle. At his horse, Shade reached into a pouch and removed something wrapped in cloth. Opening up the cloth, Shade held it out to their father. "I present the Mirror of Rheta."

Their father picked up the mirror with a hand on the handle and another on the top of the mirror itself. "Very good, Shade; very good indeed. Now, let us see if it works."

"And how do we do that? What does it do?" Shade asked.

At this, the king chuckled. "You are our family's leader in everything Gothtorian, and you're telling me you don't know what this does." Shade shook his head that he didn't and Nikki could feel that he was slightly disappointed to have this revealed. "The Mirror of Rheta," their father continued, "is said to have the ability to show a person's relationship with another when the two of them hold it. I don't know how it does it, but I assume it has something to do with the magic you and your sister wield, for I can feel no magic in this mirror."

"I think you're right, for when I hold it I can feel a reflection of my own magic within." The four of them giggled at his pun.

"Now all that's left to do is have someone hold the mirror with you," their father said as he replaced the mirror in the cloth Shade had first presented it in.

"I think I know just who that person is, father. You can come out now." As Shade spoke this, Nikki noticed a figure behind Isabelle for the first time and watched as it walked around so that they were on the same side of the horse as the Royal family. The figure wore a hooded cloak that was drawn around them, hiding their body from view. Shade stepped between the figure and the rest of them as he said, "Father, Mother, Sister, allow me to reintroduce you to Jazabel." And as he said her name, he pulled down the hood, revealing the woman's face.

"Hello, your majesties. It's an honour to meet you again," she said with a small smile and bow of her head. It had been eighteen years since Nikki had seen Jazabel, but she looked exactly the same; her body had obviously matured, but she was still the same girl who had inflamed Nikki's jealousy.

Surprises indeed.

She's here as part of my Reckoning. And please be nice, it's been a while since she's had anyone to talk to.

Nikki was the first to speak. "Why Jazabel, how lovely it is to see you again. I hope my brother's been treating you properly." Nikki noticed her mother give her a subtly raised eyebrow.

"As I'm sure you know, Princess Nikki, your brother is always the perfect gentleman, especially in the presence of a Lady." Her head was once again bowed as she spoke, but Nikki thought she sensed a smile and a secret at these words.

"And Shade, how is it you came to find yourself once again in Jazabel's company?" her father asked the very question on Nikki's mind.

"She'd taken up solitude at Victorinox and helped me in navigating it. I believe that it is fate that we were to meet again, for even the spirit of Slac Hino said I should bring her back with me." This claim was met by gasps from everyone; apparently, he'd not even told Jazabel this. "And during the *Nuitnoire*, it was her face the visions rested upon. I believe that it is her and my relationship that is meant to be shown."

Upon hearing this, Nikki rounded on her brother with an angry look - a look that was not lost upon anyone. *You never mentioned that!*

I didn't want to upset you more than you already were. And you owe a great debt to her, for I would not have been able to last much longer had she not accompanied me home.

I owe her nothing except a slap across the face! I don't trust her and she always seems to be taking you from me!

You'd know I could never leave you. But if you don't trust her, trust me. I'm nearly certain that she won't stay long, but I've promised her that she will not be harmed while she is here.

Fine, I shall act like nothing's wrong. But she better leave soon.

You said you'd have an open mind, Nikki.

I said that before I knew what you meant.

Shade just heaved a sigh as Nikki's face tightened into one of suspicion. "Let's just get this over with," he said as he took the mirror in his hands. "Give me your hand, Jazabel."

But the simple request was answered by a look of panicky fear from the woman. "Shade..."

"You heard what my father said, Jazabel. We have to hold the mirror together."

"Not while they're here." Nikki wondered who she meant, specifically.

"Jazabel, I apologize, but I need them here; they may understand the mirror in a way I can't alone. And it's easier to have them see it for themselves rather than having to describe it to them afterwards."

"But Shade... you promised-"

"That no harm would befall you. And have I ever lied to you before, Jazabel?" Her only response was to shake her head. "Then why would I start now, with something that's so important to you?" Lifting her chin with his hand he whispered, "It'll be alright."

She nodded her head. "OK," she said as her arm reached out from within the cloak.

But as soon as Nikki saw the black leather sleeve, she drew the sword at her brother's hip and levelled it at Jazabel. She saw the droplets of blood near the hilt. Reining in her concern, she noticed her mother raising a threatening hand towards Jazabel with a small snarl, ready to unleash a dose of pain at a moment's notice. "What are the two of you doing?" her father asked in exasperation.

"She's a Lady of the Night!" Nikki snarled.

"A what?"

"A Lady of the Night," her mother said in a clear voice. "A purveyor of darkness; wherever a Lady of the Night goes, tragedy is never far behind."

"That's enough!" Shade said in an authoritative tone. "Like the last time she was in Braria, Jazabel is our guest. The two of you promised me that you would have an open mind; this is what I spoke of. She has done nothing that warrants your hostilities, and is only here to help me in this. While she is in Braria, she will be treated as any other citizen. No harm shall befall her; is that clear, Mother? Nikki?"

Nikki was completely shocked by the forcefulness of her brother's voice, not to mention the look he gave her, and she could tell by the look on her parents' faces that they were too. Never had Shade used that tone with anyone, least of all her and their mother. Lowering the sword, Nikki looked at her brother. "Shade...?" She was hurt from the way he'd spoken to her, and the look in his eyes told her he knew this.

"I'm sorry, but this is my wish and command."

Iselda lowered her arm as well. "Very well; if you feel so strongly about this, there's not much I can do. Nikki, give your brother's sword back; as Shade promised, we will not harm Jazabel." Her mother's voice was tense, but Nikki still handed over *Peacemaker*.

You knew, didn't you?
Yes, but it doesn't change anything; I still trust her.
Haven't you ever heard of the concept of caution?
Yes, why do you think I'm standing between the two of you?
Ha-ha; I still don't like this.
I know.

"Ok," their father said tensely, "now that that's settled, I think, shall we continue?" He looked over to Jazabel, as if it was her decision if they continued or not. Jazabel held out her hand and nodded as Shade placed the handle of the mirror in her hand. The group gathered around Shade and Jazabel, all eyes on the mirror.

Nikki didn't know what to expect, nor did she know what help she would be in understanding whatever happened. But then she saw the streaks of gold and blood red draw into the centre in a vortex. The multiple streaks of the two colours went swirling and swirling, even after they'd reached the centre.

"Huh," her father said.

"You understand it, Dad?" Shade asked.

"I think I do, but I want to check the library before I say anything."

"Ok, let's go to the library," Iselda said.

"I'd like to stay out here, if that's alright," Jazabel said.

"I think you should come in, Jazabel," her father said.

"This is your relationship to Shade we're going to be talking about; you deserve to know the full extent of it."

"If you say so, your majesty," Jazabel relented, clearly uneasy at the thought of entering the castle.

"Before we go in, I want a moment alone with Jazabel," Nikki said. When everyone looked like she was asking for them to part the clouds, she elaborated, "I won't hurt her; I just want to talk."

All eyes were on Shade, who looked to Jazabel. She gave a slight nod and Shade looked to Nikki. "Five minutes." And without looking back, he led their parents back to the castle.

When she figured they were out of earshot, Nikki rounded on Jazabel. "I trust you know how important my brother is to me, Jazabel." When she saw the woman nod Nikki continued, "So I don't need to tell you how I will react if you ever hurt him. I don't know what your relationship with him is and I don't care. He's mine: my brother, my lover, my world. You hurt him in any way, and I will kill you; do you understand?" Nikki could see the fear in the woman's eyes and knew that she'd made her point perfectly clear.

Turning to go inside, Nikki didn't even look to see if Jazabel was following her. "Princess Nikki," Jazabel called, making Nikki turn to look at her. "I do not intend to ever hurt Shade. He's the first one to talk to me with any form of respect in nearly sixteen years. And hurting him would pain me more than you know. Your brother is one of the purest people I've ever met, and despite what you may believe, I do not wish to destroy that. He's been on my mind for the last eighteen years and I never thought I'd see him again. And I know that after tomorrow I probably never will again. Is it so much to ask for, having a few moments with my only friend?"

With an internal sigh at what she was about to do, Nikki walked back to Jazabel and put a hand on her shoulder. She jumped at the contact but didn't pull away. "No, Jazabel, it's not too much to ask. He's thought of you a lot as well since we first met. I admit that I'm not fond of that fact, but I know that he couldn't control it. So come on; let's go find out why the two of you are drawn to each other so strongly." And with a small, forced smile, Nikki led Jazabel to the castle library.

Chapter 52:

Deaur Sange

Shade looked up as he felt Nikki return to see her leading Jazabel to him and his parents. He tried to find anything that spoke of the conversation she'd just had with his sister but couldn't see anything. Looking at Nikki searchingly, he was unsettled by her easy smile. *What did you talk about?*

We just discussed a common goal. You can ask her yourself; I was nice.

I believe you. Turning back to his father Shade asked, "So Dad, what do you think my relationship with Jazabel is?"

His father flipped a few more pages in the book he held before smiling and placing it down on the table they'd congregated around. Pointing to a definition on the page he said, "That: *deaur sange*. Golden blood is the literal translation, but it has a more tragic meaning when applied to relationships."

Shade looked down and read from the book. "'*Deaur sange* is a rare but unkind form of magical relationship. It consists of two people whose hearts are connected, but despite their efforts, they cannot be together. Life interferes cruelly; but despite this tragic aspect, the friendships shared by *deaur sange* are one of the most beautiful one can experience.'"

"Are we all satisfied?" his father asked. Shade was unsure who the question was meant for.

"When it says rare, how rare does it mean?" Jazabel asked.

Shade saw his father shrug his shoulders before answering. "I don't know; I've never met a pair of people who were *deaur sange* before. But knowing this text as I do, I'd say that there's only one set every couple hundred years or so. I don't know that much about the subject; but I think that the two of you are very unique as I'm nearly sure there's never been a pair like you two. Your age difference alone is unheard of, not to mention your other qualities."

"Our age difference? There's only nine years between us," Shade commented, confused as to why this was a big deal.

"Most people who have a magical relationship are closer in age, such as you and your sister. That's a bit of the other extreme, but it proves the point. There's usually no more than a year between you people," his father said with a wave of his hand in the direction of his children and Jazabel.

This was yet another thing that made Jazabel a very unique person, Shade thought - which reminded him: he had one more promise to fulfil. "You're right, Father, Jazabel is very unique. And that uniqueness is why I do this." Turning to Jazabel, he picked up the Mirror of Rheta from the table. "Jazabel, I want you to have this. I know it is not custom for me to be doing this, but this mirror is rightfully yours in ways I'm not sure you understand. Please take it and do whatever it is you wish with it."

A stunned silence fell over them as Shade finished.

Nikki was the first to recover as she asked him, *What are you doing?*

Fulfilling a promise.

"What do you mean, it's mine? Until today, I'd never seen it before," Jazabel admitted.

"But it looked familiar to you, didn't it? Like a memory of a dream?" Shade prodded. When he saw Jazabel nod slightly, he smiled. "I think I know why you were so drawn to Victorinox, Jazabel."

"I already told you why," she said.

But Shade shook his head. "I know you did, but what I have to say is something you'll want to hear. The reason you felt so at home at Victorinox is because it once was your home."

From the silence that followed, Shade knew he had everyone's attention. Like his father before him, Shade loved to tell things that most would tell simply in an overly dramatic fashion. And so he waited until she'd recovered from this statement before continuing.

"What?" Jazabel asked in a whisper.

"The last thing the spirit of Slac Hino said to me was that you were a very unique person, and that I should have you return to Braria with me to see how unique. Then, while I searched for the mirror, I found another thing that makes you probably one of the most unique people to ever walk this world. I found the mirror hidden in a portrait of Rheta herself. In Rheta's portrait the face staring back at me was one I recognized, for I had already seen it once that night. It was your face, Jazabel; you and Rheta look more alike than my mother and Nikki do.

"So again, I offer you your mirror, Rheta, Princess of

Gothtor. If you don't believe me, Jazabel, as I know this sounds crazy, I shall show you the painting. I made a promise over that painting to your former self that this mirror would be returned to your hands, and I always keep my promises." Shade knelt down on one knee and bowed his head as he held up the mirror to Jazabel. In the corner of his eye, he saw Nikki and his parents kneel as well.

Jazabel stood there looking scared and very awkward as the Royal family of Braria knelt at her feet. Reluctantly, she reached out her hands, causing her cloak to open for a brief moment as she took the mirror. "Um, thank you, Prince Shade, for keeping your promise," she said in what was clearly meant to be an official tone, despite her nerves. "Now will you please stand up? This is really awkward. I long ago gave up the chance to be royalty, and I have no wish to be a queen."

Shade stood up, as did his family. Smiling at Jazabel he said, "Thank you, Jazabel. Your help over this past week is immeasurable. I can see that you're tired. Allow me to escort you to a room so you may get some rest."

Before she could answer, Nikki spoke. "No, Shade, you will do no such thing." Everyone stared at her, clearly thinking she was pressing her luck, but Shade could see differently. "I shall take her to a room and make sure she has everything she requires. Besides, you said you needed to talk with Mom." She gave him a small smile as she asked him, *Do I not get to know her?*

"You're right, of course," he answered both her spoken and unspoken requests. Turning to his mother, he asked, "Mom, why don't we go to my room? I know you're just dying to hear of my trip and my conversation with Slac Hino."

His mother looked from him to his sister, trying to discern what had passed between them. But she nodded and said, "Of course, sweetheart." She offered him her arm, which he took as the two left. Looking back, Shade noticed how his father was only a few steps behind them, leaving Nikki and Jazabel alone in the library.

"Follow me," Nikki said to Jazabel as she started out of the library. But rather than take the main way to the bedroom that was her destination, Nikki took the service routes so as to keep Jazabel hidden from sight. They didn't say a word until they got to the room; it was the same room as the one that Jazabel had stayed in the last time she was in Terang.

Leading the way into the room, Nikki motioned Jazabel to the bed before closing the door. "I'm sorry for threatening you, Jazabel. It's not something that princesses do to each other and it was unwarranted. I just can't help myself; sometimes I get so possessive of him that he literally has to restrain me," Nikki confessed as she walked over to the bed and sat down.

"You can't possibly believe that I'm a princess! I'm a Lady of the Night, not some reincarnated Gothtorian princess," Jazabel said, but Nikki could sense some further discomfort.

"I've seen the painting he found in his memory. You do look exactly like the woman it depicts, even if you aren't dressed the same." The look of fear that Jazabel gave at this almost made Nikki laugh. "If you want, I'll let you have one of my dresses for when you're in public so you don't have to wear that ridiculous cloak."

"Oh no; I couldn't wear your dresses. And besides, I can't take this leather off," Jazabel protested.

"The little I know about your kind tells me that, but I meant as something to wear over top of the leather. And it's the least I could do to make up for my behaviour; don't you want to be able to go out in public and not have the entire town staring at you?"

"More than you can possibly know. But I'm quite reclusive and practically nocturnal; there's no reason for me to own a dress when I live alone." The resign in Jazabel's voice made Nikki feel pity for her for the first time.

"Well, what if you didn't; what if you lived in a populated part of the world? Would you take a dress or two then?"

Jazabel just looked at Nikki with a confused but scared face. "What are you saying?" she asked tentatively.

"I'm extending an invitation for you to live here in Braria, in Terang, so as to be able to be with your *deaur sange*. Shade will never force you to stay, and nor will I, but I know that the two of you have missed each other since you parted. And I know that you're very important to each other. You're a part of Shade, Jazabel, and that makes you a part of me; I don't want to see my favourite half sad as I know he will be if you return to Gothtor. I'm asking you to stay here in Terang." As Nikki asked this she felt her words were true, even if she hadn't known they were until after she said them.

"Nikki...you can't be serious," Jazabel said, not addressing Nikki by title for the first time. "You can't seriously want me here. Didn't you hear what your mother said? Tragedy isn't ever far behind a Lady of the Night. That's not untrue, I'm afraid. Not to mention that if anyone else ever found out, I'd be run out of the city at the very least. I appreciate the offer, but I can't stay no matter how much I want to." There were tears in Jazabel's eyes as she finished speaking.

Taking Jazabel's chin into her hand and lifting it Nikki said, "Jazabel, you can stay here; you can live here in the castle if you wish. And as long as you wish it, your identity will remain hidden, as my identity as my brother's Soul Twin has been since we first revealed it to our parents. Shade would never allow anyone to harm you in any capacity: while you are here you're under his protection. No one goes against Shade when he proclaims something. You don't have to decide what you'll do right now; I just wanted you to know that the option was there if you wished it."

Jazabel flung herself at Nikki, embracing her in a tight hug. Tearfully she said, "Thank you; thank you so much. I know that we aren't exactly close and that this may be a bit painful for you to do, but you have no idea how nice it is to have a woman be so nice to me, even if you have your own reasons for doing it."

Nikki slowly rubbed her back as she said, "Shade told me you'd been lonely these past few years. And believe it or not, I think we have some strong common ground between us, Jazabel. We both have to hide our true selves from the general population, and that can take a toll after so long.

"As I grew up, I had to control the closeness I had with Shade when others were present; I had to act sisterly to him, unable to indulge in my true feelings for him. For the first time in our lives we kissed, right before he left on his Reckoning. And as I stood there watching him ride away, I felt that my heart grew hollower with every step he took away from me.

"The past two weeks have been extremely hard for the both of us as we'd never before been more than a few hundred feet away from each other and have always spent every available second together. He said that the only way he got through it was because of you. So you're right in saying that I have my own reasons for wanting you to stay: I owe you a great debt, Jazabel, and I wish to pay it by the way it was paid to me. Your presence kept Shade's heart from falling apart, so his shall keep your heart together."

"You're too kind, Nikki."

"It's something I've picked up from spending so much time with the kindest man in the world."

Both women smiled at the truth of the comment as they held and comforted each other. After some time, Nikki left to have a proper reunion with her brother.

As Shade led his mother into his room, he felt a twinge of sadness for what he was about to reveal to her. She'd built Slac Hino up to be this mighty champion of the people, and he was about to destroy that. To put off the inevitable he decided to order the conversation as Slac Hino had. Sitting her down on his bed, he said, "Before I tell you what I want to, there's something I have to say. I was given another prophecy."

His mother just looked shocked for a moment before recovering with a look of empathy. "And what did it say?" she asked in a resigned voice. His mother knew that these prophecies were meant to help her children, but she hated the fact that they never brought any good news.

"*Yours and mine, Mine and yours: Equal claims to what remains. Shameful secrets will lead to greater regrets, as your gain was once his pain; see tables turned at an out spurned.* Those are the words. I don't know what it all means, but the 'greater regrets' are the death that is said to start the war. And the one who is to die is to be someone who is closer to me than they are to Nikki."

His mother closed her eyes as she stood to give him a hug, a hug which Shade returned more earnestly than it was given. "Your father said that having the foreknowledge of all this would help you deal with it when it came to pass, but I disagree. Knowing you're unable to do anything from stopping it is much worse, even if it does give you some form of detachment from it all. I've never liked you having to do this; no one should ever have to do this. Your sister and you were so young when we found this out. You've had this weight on your shoulders your whole lives and it's not fair!" She started to cry as she vocalized her frustration at what her children had had to deal with since before they were five years old.

Rubbing her back, Shade tried to calm his mother down. "It's ok, Mom. Compared to not being able to tell the world of how much we love each other, this is nothing. I know you dream of how our lives would be if we had a normal life, but in all honesty, the training we've received these past eighteen years has helped us more than you think. We know you tried to give us time to have fun and be children and we thank you for that. Despite the pain we know to come, Nikki and I are glad it is us leading the fight and not someone without the proper resources."

Kissing his forehead affectionately, Shade's mother looked deep into his eyes. "I'm so proud of the two of you. You're too mature for your age, you always have been, and you try to find the beauty in everything no matter how ugly. There's never been a day that I've felt you never gave your all to whatever you were doing and I've never had to discipline you two. As wonderful as that is, I feel as if I've missed out on a part of motherhood. But if that's the price to pay for having the most wonderful children of all time, I'll continue paying it gladly."

"I'm sorry you feel that way, Mom. If you feel you need to yell at me to have the complete mothering experience, I certainly deserve it tonight after yelling at you like I did back in the stables," Shade said as he bowed his head contritely.

"I can't yell at you for that. While I don't think you've ever been that forceful with anyone, what you said was right. It was not right for us to attack Jazabel the way we did, and I'm sorry for reacting that way. And I can't yell at you for doing what was right and being who you are: the kindest person in the world." She gave him a small smile as she gave him the praise she'd been giving him since he came up to her knee. Pulling him over to the bed and sitting the two of them down, she asked, "Now, I thought you were going to tell me of your meeting with the spirit of the great Slac Hino?"

"You may want to reserve on the calling him 'great' until I tell you what he told me." His mother gave a confused look at this as Shade had always worshipped the prince. "I want to start off by saying that everything you've heard of him is true; it just doesn't give the complete picture, for we must remember that he was a man and had vices like the rest of us. His were lust and arrogance and they are what brought about his downfall.

"Like many men, he wanted the one thing he couldn't have: his sister, Rheta. And so he hid his feelings and tried to move past them. But when Rheta confronted him about his feelings and offered him the chance to indulge them, he couldn't resist. And so for a year they enjoyed each other's company in ways society tends to frown upon.

"But then Rheta met someone else and put an end to their affair. This greatly angered Slac Hino and he devised a plan to have his sister's new lover killed. To appear the hero, he then killed the man he'd hired to kill his rival.

"Slac Hino gave Rheta six months to mourn her loss before he tried to bed her again, but she rejected him and declared that she'd be chaste for the rest of time. After another three months, when he again pressed her, she relented. But it turned out that she had poisoned him already and this was her way of saying goodbye to her brother. When they were finished, and right before the poison killed him, she confessed to knowing what Slac Hino had done. He protested, but was unable to convince her and he died shortly after that."

The look of shocked disgust on his mother's face was probably a mirror to his own when he first heard the tale. "Well," she said in a measured tone, "that certainly adds to the morbidity of the whole thing. But I can't say that I blame his sister now; if someone ever killed your father I wouldn't be able to control myself. Knowing the truth makes me feel wrong for encouraging your adoration for him."

"I felt the same way when I was first told; I even yelled at him in anger for telling me the truth and making me feel that I was the better man. Then he reminded me that just because I now knew the truth didn't mean that I had to only focus on the negative. Instead, I could now judge him properly.

"He said that none before me had ever honoured him the way I had. He told me his story so that I could tell the world the truth and start Gothtor on a road to recovery. I'll admit that my opinion of him has lessened, but I still hold him in high esteem."

His mother just smiled warmly at him. "Like I said, you find the beautiful in the ugliest of things, and that is what makes you the kindest man in the world. It's what makes me proudest of you: the fact that you have never lost that part of yourself. And I hope you never do," she said, standing up just as there was a knock on the door. "Looks like I'm just in time. We're finished, Nikki, you can come in," she called to the door, knowing who it was.

Nikki came in and went to her brother's side. *Have you told her about what you promised me yet?*

No, not yet. I was going to wait until tomorrow but I don't see why we can't tell her now. It being as late as it is, she might be more receptive of it. Turning back to his mother before she could leave, Shade called her back into the room. "We have something to discuss with you."

"What is it, sweetheart?" she asked.

Taking Nikki's hand into his own, Shade said, "We want Braria to know about us. We're tired of having to hide our love. It's not fair to us or the people; we should be honest with them about everything. We know that there may be complete disgust at this, but they deserve to know, just as we deserve to be allowed to be ourselves."

Their mother was shocked as Shade finished and he worried that he'd gone too far. But after a moment, she smiled at them. "You're right; you and the people deserve that. But before you do tell the country, I think we should discuss this with your father. Many a night we have discussed the act of revealing you to the country; it's time we included you in those discussions. Tomorrow after breakfast we shall talk, ok?"

"Ok, Mom," Shade and Nikki said in unison. "Goodnight!"

"Goodnight, you two." Giving each of them a kiss on the cheek, their mother turned and left.

As soon as the door closed, Nikki pulled Shade in close and started to kiss him. Shocked at first, he soon was returning her kiss passionately. *I thought she'd never leave.*

Ha-ha, what did you expect? I just got back.

I expected that you would just hand over that bloody mirror and then take me up here so we could finally do what we've wanted since we were twelve. Stopping the kiss and pulling away so she could speak, Nikki said, "Instead, you take your dear sweet time, and show off your scantily clad Lady of the Night friend, who turns out to be your *deaur sange*. You've been home for an hour and a half, and I'm just getting to be alone with you now!"

Her brother heaved a sigh. "It sounds worse when you say it like that. But I'd like to point out that you added to some of that time as well, with your wanting to spend some alone time with Jazabel. If you'd let me take her to her room, we'd be past kissing by now."

"Yes, but I wouldn't have been able to invite her to stay in Terang if you had."

This statement surprised Shade and it took him a moment before he could respond. "You invited her to stay?" he asked with a pause between each word. "In Terang?" When she nodded, he asked his most burning question: "Why?"

"Because I knew you wouldn't even mention it. You'd let her leave and resign yourself to hardly ever seeing her again, if at all. The two of you would be miserable at never seeing each other and I don't want you to ever be miserable. And she's had enough pain to last her a lifetime. Don't you want her to stay?"

"You already know the answer to that, love. But I also know she's scared of being here. And I don't want her to live in fear for my sake."

"I know. I told Jazabel that we wouldn't force her to stay, but if she chose to, she would have your unyielding protection. I gave her the night to decide," she said as she leaned back in to kiss him. But before he could lose himself in the kiss, Nikki pulled away. Shade looked into her eyes and mind to see why she had stopped. In response, all she did was partially pull his sword out of its scabbard.

Looking away in shame, Shade could feel her probe his mind for details, but they were locked away in the part of his mind that he kept hidden from her. "Please do not ask me about that; it is a painful memory that I alone must bear. I do not wish to wound your heart at the telling of it." He still couldn't look at her.

"Shade Leo Kanta," she said in such a stern voice that he turned to her in surprise. When she continued, it was in a much softer tone, "You bear too much for any man. I am the person who knows you the best and who loves you the most; let me help you bear the burden that so weighs your heart." Her blue eyes implored him to trust her with this secret.

"I was attacked, and I defended myself," he said evasively.

"You're a horrible lair; even if I didn't know and love you like no one else, I would be able to tell there's more to the story than that."

"Lethally. I defended myself with lethal results."

"Shade! Just tell me the truth, the full truth," she said as she stroked her hand through his dark as nightfire shoulder-length hair.

Sighing, Shade finally looked back into her eyes - eyes so full of love for him that he almost found himself losing himself in them. "Three nomads attacked me the third night after I left Terang. I tried to reason with them, but they would have none of it. The oldest, who was their leader, made the other two attack me; my training is the only reason I'm alive. And then I saw an opening and exploited it without hesitation. That's when I saw that this nomad was just a boy, and the leader's son.

"When I realized what I'd done, I could barely breathe; I had killed this boy, without hesitation. How could I have done such a thing? I begged the other two to stop and leave me in peace. I also said how sorry I was, even offered them the little food I had left.

"But the girl, the fiancée of the boy I'd just killed, would not be sated so easily. She attacked me and I disarmed her. Then she attacked me again, having regained her weapon, and I killed her without the slightest hint of reluctance to the deed. Once again I found myself on my knees, begging the father to leave me in peace. With the death of his son and would-be daughter-in-law, he finally relented. Taking their bodies, he left me in peace." The tears flowed out of his eyes as he relived the moment in his life he wished he'd never lived.

Nikki's hand gave his a gentle squeeze. "I'm so sorry you had to do that," she said gently. "But know that you weren't alone in feeling the pain of killing." When he looked to her with confusion, Nikki elaborated, "The third night after you had left, I felt an emotional pain so terrible that I was knocked unconscious for a few days and remained bedridden until two days ago." Taking a hold of her necklace in one hand and her brother's hand he wore the matching ring on in her other, she held them for him to see. "You sent me your pain when your body couldn't bear it, and I sent you the strength I didn't need to carry on until you were home and we were together again."

Shade felt his heart lighten at hearing her say this, despite the fact that he'd subconsciously given her unbearable pain. Smiling he said, "Slac Hino told me that they forgave me for killing them, and even thanked me for reuniting them in death. He told me to let go of this guilt I still feel."

Kissing the fingers she still held in her hand, Nikki nodded slightly. "Yes, you should. It's not healthy; and just because you don't feel guilty doesn't mean you have to forget. You did all you could, Shade; they gave you no choice." When she saw him smile, she gave him a gentle kiss. "Now, enough of pain; time for pleasure." And then she was kissing him passionately. It took him all of half a second before he was returning the kiss just as passionately. *Let's move past kissing, shall we?* his sister thought after a few minutes.

I couldn't agree more. Not too long after Shade thought this he was on top of her, letting her adjust to the new sensations they would experience for the rest of the night. And just before they fell asleep, there were only three words on their minds: *I love you.*

Three years later

Chapter 53:

Duties and Gifts

The sound of clashing steel was barely audible over the cheering of the crowd full of soldiers, servants, and townspeople that surrounded the duelling swordsmen. The crowd shifted as the two men in its centre moved around the castle courtyard. Sparks flew when particularly hard blows were made, causing the crowd to cheer even louder. Where the Brarian princess had once found reluctance in watching, she was now drawn in as much as the crowd that came daily to watch her brother spar with their good friend. "He's getting stronger," Jazabel said, indicating Shade. "Brudas will be pushing him harder than ever now."

Nikki turned to her best friend with a smile as they watched from the throne room balcony. "That will only spur him on to try and defeat your fiancé even more. You know as well as I how seriously Shade takes these training sessions." Jazabel just shook her head at Nikki's theory about why their fiancés did this. Ignoring this, Nikki took Jazabel's hand in her own. "What should we wager today?"

Smiling, Jazabel thought for a moment. "A secret," she

said with a mischievous look in her soft brown eyes. "One we have never told anyone. Even Shade."

Nikki thought Jazabel had some nerve assuming that Brudas would win, but she didn't say anything. "I try not to have secrets from him. But I do have some. You have yourself a bet." Shaking hands to show the terms of the wager were agreed upon, Nikki and Jazabel turned back to the duel, leaning on the balcony's stone ledge to see better. It took her a half an hour before she realized that Brudas was indeed going to win.

Brudas was taller and stronger than any man she knew, and this made him feared by many. But Nikki knew him to be gentle and kind and not as intimidating as his appearance led many to believe him to be. He had come to Terang not long after her and Shade had told Braria the true nature of their relationship. To everyone's great surprise, the country accepted this news with open arms. Brudas said he came to play his part in the upcoming battle that Shade and Nikki had been planning for, claiming he knew it would soon be upon them and that they needed all the help they could get. His strength alone was well received, but when Shade and her father saw him with a sword, they were quite enamoured. The subtle grace and chilling deadliness with which he wielded his blade was apparent to all who saw him.

Nikki was quite happy for Jazabel; she'd chosen a good man for her fiancé. These sparring matches were something he and Shade had done since Brudas had proposed to Jazabel six months previous; they claimed it was all in good fun, but Nikki secretly thought it was to see which of them was better for her friend. And while Brudas won most days, Shade was able to defeat him at least once a week. The daily duels had grown in popularity and duration in those last six months to the point where her mother had jokingly suggested they start charging people to see the two-hour event.

As Nikki watched her brother, she got the sense that she'd seen this duel before. *You know he's backing you into a corner. This is going to end just like it did two days ago.* She often wondered if these private conversations between her and her brother ever distracted him from the duel, and so tried to keep them to a minimum. But whenever she could, she tried to help him pick up on the patterns in Brudas' technique.

That's what you think; I have him right where I want him.

You always say that right before he beats you. Can't you ever concede defeat? We're getting married tomorrow and I don't want you looking like less than your best for our birthday. Can't you accept that Jazabel loves him?

I already told you that's not what this is about. We just want to better ourselves; I'm happy for Jazabel and I know Brudas will take good care of her. And I will look fine tomorrow; it's you who's going to look more beautiful than ever. All eyes are going to be on your beauty to the point where they won't even realize I'm there.

I'll be looking at you. As Nikki thought this last thought to her beloved, she saw that he'd been backed into a corner just like she'd said he would be. But when Brudas was about to deliver the final attack, Shade dove between his legs, stood up as fast as lightning, and swung his sword at Brudas' neck. He'd won.

The crowd had gone completely silent as Brudas turned around slowly, *Peacemaker* still at his throat. Even from her angle, Nikki could tell that he wore an odd expression. Then a smile broke out on his face. "Well fought, my prince. I think it is time for us to up our competition level," Braria's top swordsmen and commander of its guerrilla forces said in his distinctly Babomoran accent.

Lowering and sheathing his sword, Shade smiled in kind. "I think it's time you started using all your skills and giving your all, Brudas." The crowd laughed as cheers went up at Shade's unexpected victory. Turning his attention up to the balcony where she and Jazabel stood, he shouted, "I told you: I had him right where I wanted him. And I'll still be able to look my best for you tomorrow."

"You told him he was going to lose again, didn't you?" Jazabel asked in a quiet voice so that only Nikki would hear. "Or was it your 'they do it to prove themselves worthy of me' theory?"

Nikki looked over to see her friend smile teasingly at her. After sticking her tongue out at Jazabel, she replied, "Go to your fiancé and send mine up to me. We don't want their egos to be too altered by Shade winning twice in a row."

Jazabel just laughed at Nikki's unspoken 'both', but before she could leave, Nikki's mother walked out. "Actually, Jazabel, you're to send Shade to his father, who awaits him at their secret place. The king requires a private moment with the prince before the events of tomorrow, as does the queen with the princess."

Realizing the serious tone of her queen, Jazabel stopped laughing before giving a bow. "Yes, your highness," she said as she left. But before she went inside, she gave one last look at Nikki. "You can come to my office later and collect your reward." Her head gave a quick shake in disbelief at having lost two days in a row.

"Come with me," her mother said a few moments after Jazabel had left. Turning back to the castle, Nikki's mother led her to her parents' bedroom without a word. The silence unnerved Nikki who tried to read the emotions her mother was feeling, but she was only able to sense the pride and love her mother had always felt towards her and her brother. Even after twenty-five years, she was still not able to read her mother like Shade was.

Once they were in her mother's bedroom, Iselda closed the door and locked it. A private moment indeed, Nikki thought. Motioning her to the bed, Nikki sat while her mother stood over her. Nikki took notice of the grey streaks in her mother's hair, and hoped to look as beautiful as her when she was older. "I'm very proud of you, Nikki. You've grown into such a beautiful young woman I can hardly believe that I gave birth to you twenty-five years ago. I've looked forward to tomorrow since before you were born. I never thought that you would be getting married and becoming queen on the same day, but now I wouldn't have it any other way."

Standing up, Nikki gave her mother a hug. "Mom, all I am is what you've raised me to be. I owe everything to you."

"No Nikki," her mother said with a shake of her head, "it is I who owe you everything. You and your brother. The two of you have made me the happiest person in the world these past twenty-five years. I've lived many lives, but throughout them all I wanted to have a daughter of my own to show her the ways of the world. Being blessed with a son as well was a new dream I had once I married your father. And to see the people the two of you have become brings me such joy. I truly hope you find yourself feeling the way I do right now.

"But, enough of feelings," she said as she wiped the tears from her eyes, "I have more pressing things to discuss. I know that tomorrow is not only your birthday; it is also your wedding day. And don't forget that it's also the day you become queen. And being queen, let me tell you, is not as easy as I make it look." They both laughed at this for a moment before growing serious once again. "Being queen isn't something you can stop being when it gets too hard. And trust me, there will be hard days. Your actions will affect the entire country, so you must weigh them accordingly. Nothing is ever going to be black and white again."

"I know, Mom. I grew up watching you try to have everyone be happy even when you knew that they didn't like what you did. And if you could, you would always try to make it up to those who were unhappy with what you'd done. But how many times were the people upset with something you did? Maybe only ten times in twenty-six years as queen, and you made it up to them all in some way. You're a good queen, Mom, and you've been an excellent role model for me; I just wish you didn't have to step down for me to be queen. Braria will miss you greatly."

"And I shall always be there for it. Just because I will no longer wear the crown doesn't mean I will no longer try to better this country. I will still be here for you to call upon, should you ever want my help or opinion on something. But I know both your heart and your brother's and I have the utmost confidence that you will lead Braria to prosperity."

Giving her mother a hug, Nikki said, "Thanks, Mom. Your and Dad's support means a lot to Shade and me. We don't know what we'd do without you if you hadn't helped us through everything. I know we don't say it enough, but we're truly grateful for all you and Dad have done for us, and we love you with all of our hearts."

"And we love you with all of ours, sweetheart. And you don't need to thank us; parents are supposed to provide for their children." Mother and daughter held each other tight as their love for the other consumed them. Pulling away, the queen once again wiped her face of tears before speaking seriously. "There's one more thing I want to talk to you about. While Shade is forced to perform his first act as king before everyone tomorrow, your first act as queen is allowed to be done more privately. And like your brother's first act, it sets a standard for your reign.

"My first act was one of forgiveness, to your Aunt Kailee and Aunt Sabrina. And though it was your father who had been the one hurt by them, Kailee asked me for forgiveness. To this day I do not know why she asked me, but I did what I thought to be right. Pan let me make the decision of their fate, and I've tried to produce the same result in everything I've done since: doing what I thought right, no matter what.

"I'm not saying you need to do something like that once you're crowned tomorrow; I'm just saying to be aware of that first act. Little things matter. But as I said before, I know that by following your heart you will be a greater queen than I was."

"Thanks Mom, but you're a tough act to follow. And you had to learn everything right away; I've had my whole life. So, you-" Nikki stopped as her mother raised a hand to stop her.

"Enough, but thank you. I have a gift for you. It's something that I've had for a long time and I want you to have it," she said as she stood up and went into her closet. She returned with a small wooden box which Nikki recognized from her days playing in there; she had always thought it a simple jewellery box. "This is a memoire. Have you ever heard of one?"

"No, what is it?"

"It's a box where you can store all your memories. This box comes from Metalia, a country far to the west at the edge of the North Divide. The people there have an affinity for metal work. And though this box looks wooden, it's actually metal. Not long after the Crusaders killed me, I went there to see if they could make anything that would aid me in my quest for the location of my mothers' graves. I went to every metal worker in the country and found nothing of value, except this." she said as she handed the box to Nikki. Indeed, it was heavier than it looked.

"How does it work?" Nikki asked.

"You think of the memory you want stored and you let a few drops of blood fall into the box. The blood must be fresh, as by thinking of the memory, you have it running through your blood. And if you ever want to see it again or remember, all you do is inhale. The memory will still be in your head, but as I'm sure you're aware, memories fade over time. The memory in the memoire will retain the sharpness with which it entered, and will remain inside until the blood is wiped away."

"This is perfect, Mom. Thanks so much. Am I the only one who can see the memories within, or can I show them to others?"

"Don't you and Shade share everything already? What would you need to show him that he can't just enter your mind and see for himself?"

"I never said Shade. What you said is true; we do share everything. But what if I want to share my memories with another, could I?"

Placing her hand on Nikki's belly, Iselda asked, "Are you trying to tell me something, my darling daughter?"

Smiling but pushing the hand away, Nikki said, "No, not yet. We haven't been together in a few months. But that's what I'm asking."

"Yes, honey, others can see the memories in the memoire. I've cleaned it of my blood, so only your memories will be in there." And then Nikki was hugging her mother.

Chapter 54:

Shameful Secrets

As Shade made his way to his father, he found himself thinking of the next day - a day that would be filled with three times the amount of celebration it usually held. Truth be told, he wasn't as excited about tomorrow as everyone thought he was. He was fearful of his first act as king.

Finding himself at the caves that had drawn him in ever since he'd started down the path to manhood, he saw his father leaning against the entrance to the main cave. "What took you? I've been here for half an hour."

"Sorry, Dad; I'd just finished with Brudas, so I went for a quick swim to freshen up. What's so important that we need to meet here?" Shade asked.

Standing up straight, his father answered, "I wanted to make sure you were ready for tomorrow. I know I wasn't ready for my first act. I'd just banished your Aunt Sabrina and Aunt Kailee and my father was on his deathbed. I was utterly heartbroken and I ordered a feast to be held in memory of not only my father, but of all the past kings of Braria. Not many saw the pain in my eyes as I masqueraded in a smile that night. I don't want you to do what I did: just declare something to have it over and done with."

"Dad, I know that your ascension to the throne was under more sombre circumstances than mine, and no one holds that against you. The amount of pain you felt at it all, I understand. But I'm just as lost at what to do tomorrow as you were. I don't want to just do something to have it over and done with; I want my first act as king to be memorable and meaningful. Of the many things that have been placed on my shoulders, this is the one that has most weighed me down and the one I wish I could give to someone else."

"I was hoping you wouldn't say that. But perhaps you'll find inspiration from some unlikely source. Follow what you think is right and nobody can fault you. I have faith in you Shade, I always have. But enough of the future; it's time you learned of the past," the king said as he turned towards the caves.

"What do you mean?" Shade asked, causing his father to stop.

"You'll see; I have something to show you. Follow me," he said without looking to his son. He lit a ball of flame in his hand, which he used to light his way. Shade followed hesitantly, sensing the anticipation and dread rolling off his father, as Pan led him deeper and deeper into the caves. After ten minutes they came to a dead end, but Shade knew this was where they'd been heading to. For in the light of the flame his father cast to light their way, Shade saw an old lantern nailed into the stone. Suddenly, the lantern lit as the light in the palm of his father's hand extinguished. "What I'm about to tell and show you can be told to no one, not even Nikki. The only person you are to tell is your son, when you have one, and only when he is old enough. Do you understand?" the king asked in the most serious voice Shade had ever heard his father use.

"Yes, I understand. But I'm not going to like this, am I?"

"No, you especially will not like this. But you must know the truth. There is a reason why the males of our bloodline have been drawn to these caves since our family first came to Braria."

"I thought the Kanta line had always lived in Braria."

"Kanta yes, but we were not always called so. Six thousand years ago our ancestors lived in Nefas, rulers of the capital city of Babomorah. Back then our family name was Vigmece."

Shade let out a gasp at this. The Vigmece clan was ruthless in its rule. They had experimented with the limits of magic in the cruelest fashions imaginable. "We aren't related to those monsters! We can't be!" he shouted.

His father got a sad look on his face. "Unfortunately, my son, not only can we be, but we are." As if to prove his point, his father reached into a small fissure in the wall and pulled out something wrapped in a very old cloth. Despite the age, Shade could see the black 'V' that was the Vigmece family seal. "Within this cloth lies the greatest shame of our family," he said as he opened the cloth to reveal a simple wooden mask with curled tendrils at its top to look like hair, and a blank expression.

But Shade knew what it was. What appeared to be wood was actually bone, bones ripped from the body of a woman while she was still alive. "The Mask of Babomorah. I thought it was destroyed when the Vigmece clan was driven from Nefas. Apparently everyone's wrong."

"You of all people should know that history hides the truth of things by forgetting to mention them altogether. Or was *The Fictitious True Story of Slac Hino* something you invented?" The mention of Shade's tell-all dramatization of what Slac Hino had told him caught him off guard. "This Mask must be kept hidden at all times; if anyone ever found out we had it, they'd lose all faith in us. And people need to believe in their leaders.

"I don't want to have to tell you this, but you deserve to know. The woman whose life was taken to create the Mask was like you; she was a Soul Twin. Our ancestors were cruel people, for she'd only just met her Twin a few weeks before the Mask was created. They raped her and ripped her bones out right in front of him. All-"

"Stop! I don't want to hear it! Having that thing in my presence is enough. I know the stories of the Mask: a drop of virginal blood and you can see through the eyes of he whose heart is most turned against yours. Why have we kept it all these years? We've had six thousand years to destroy it, why haven't we? Why haven't you?" Shade demanded.

"For the same reason it was created: so we could know of an attack if we ever were to place our rule at risk. Let me assure you, I have never used this Mask. I've been tempted, but I've never known it to be used since it was brought here. I've tried to forget about it, but with this impending war perhaps you will need to use it."

"I will never use that thing! To do so would be wrong on so many levels! I never want to see that thing again!"

"That is your choice to make. I just hope you know the kind of restraint you will need." It was then that Shade saw the look of dazed lust in his father's eyes as he held the

Mask. "You have a real reason to use it, and fate has ways of getting us to do things that we never thought we would. I truly hope you never use this and that you destroy it, erasing this ugliness from our history. I couldn't because I was afraid that the moment I did, I would need it. It's better to not need something and have it than not have it and need it. Though it was created by evil, the Mask itself isn't evil; it's simply a tool for us to use." And with that, his father recovered the Mask and put it back in the fissure where he'd taken it from. He then put his arm on Shade's back and escorted him out of the caves and back to the castle.

Nikki went to find Jazabel. Her talk with her mother had left her in a state where she finally had the courage to do what her heart had told her to do for the past three years. She was going to talk to Jazabel and explain herself. As Jazabel now worked in the castle library as an archivist who catalogued and organized all the information within, that's where Nikki looked first.

Nikki found Jazabel working alone in her study at the back of the library. The room was quite spacious, offering enough room for a couch, desk, and a few bookshelves. The walls were black as night, painted so at Jazabel's request, and almost made the room seem more like a cave. Of the three bookshelves in the study, one held items Nikki knew that Jazabel valued above all others: the Mirror of Rheta, a small shadothyst statue in the fashion of totems found in Dougo, and the newest addition: a leather bound volume twice as thick as any Nikki had ever seen and with strange writing unlike any she knew of. Jazabel sat at her desk with a book in one hand, a feather quill in the other, and her ledger and notebook on the desk. Noticing her, Jazabel closed all three books, put down the quill, and said, "Hey, Nikki. What did your mom want?"

"To talk about tomorrow. But we need to talk, Jazabel."

Sensing that Nikki was being serious, Jazabel stood and took Nikki's hands into her own. Ushering the two of them over to the couch in the corner, Jazabel asked, "This isn't about the secret I owe you, is it? What's wrong, Nikki? Is everything alright?"

"Everything is fine, Jazabel. I just need to tell you something, something I should have told you a long time ago. A secret I've kept guarded against everybody." Nikki was looking everywhere in the room as she avoiding making eye contact with her friend. "It's about us."

Taking Nikki's chin into her hand and forcing her to look at Jazabel, she said, "What is it, Nikki? You know you can tell me anything."

"You know I love you, right Jazabel? We're like sisters, aren't we?" Nikki asked in a rushed voice.

"Of course we are. You're my best friend, Nikki. Now what's bothering you? You're not making any sense," Jazabel asked in a worried voice.

Taking a deep breath before releasing it audibly, Nikki whispered, "I don't trust you, Jazabel. And I don't know why. I don't know what it is, but something inside me feels… wrong when we're together. I've tried to figure it out, but every time I come up with an idea, I realize that that's not what's causing this.

"First I thought it was your relationship with Shade; but I was over that a month after we found out about it. Then I thought it might be because you're a Lady of the Night. But after half a year, I didn't care about that. I'm sorry, Jazabel, I really am; I don't want to have these uneasy feelings. But I do, and I feel that I need to address them with you." Nikki was in tears by the time she had finished and she clung to Jazabel in search of solace.

"Nikki...I don't know what to say. You're the closest thing I have to family; why haven't you ever told me about this?" she asked as she stroked Nikki's back gently.

"I don't know. At first it was for Shade; I didn't want him to think that I wasn't trying to be your friend. But as time went by, I tried to bury these feelings as we grew closer. I'm so ashamed of them, of myself, that I thought that if I could forget about them, they'd go away. But they haven't, despite my trying everything, and I can't take it anymore. I had to tell you. You deserve to know I feel this way." Nikki pushed herself away from Jazabel when she realized that her words forced her to stay away, and not seek her comfort.

"I can't say I'm not hurt, Nikki. For the last three years you've hidden these feelings from me and masqueraded in a false love for me-"

"No! I do love you, Jazabel! That's why I tried to hide and forget them, so nothing stopped me from loving you."

Standing up from the couch, Jazabel looked upon Nikki with a saddened but angry expression. "But you're only telling me this now. I thought you were different than everybody else, Nikki; I thought that you were someone who could look past the things that turned you against me."

Reaching for Jazabel's hands, Nikki pleaded, "Don't

you see, that's what I've been trying to do. You're my sister, Jazabel, and it pains me that I, for some unknown reason, can't trust you. I don't want to feel this way." Now on her knees, Nikki looked up to Jazabel with tears in her eyes. "Please, sister, forgive me; forgive me for something that I have no control over."

Jazabel just looked at Nikki with a pitying look. Then the anger disappeared and she smiled at Nikki. Pulling her up, Jazabel said, "I forgive you, Nikki. I can see that you're greatly saddened by your having these feelings and that for whatever reason you have them, you don't want them. I understand the need to keep these sorts of things hidden. I just hope that now you'll feel you can trust me with anything and tell me anything."

"Whatever you want sister!" Nikki said as she gave Jazabel a hug. "Anything at all." For a long moment the two of them stood there, before taking a seat back on the couch. "Can I ask you something?"

"Sure, I still owe you a secret after all. What do you want to know?" Jazabel asked with a smile.

"This isn't the secret I want to claim; I have something else in mind for that. What I'm asking now is something that I've wondered about ever since my mother told me of the Ladies of the Night. How did you become a Lady of the Night? Were you chosen, or forced into it?" Nikki asked. And then in a quiet voice she added, "Or did you choose to be one?"

The shock of the question was clear on Jazabel's face, but after a moment she was able to control it. "The answers you seek, Nikki, are secrets of the Dark, and shouldn't be divulged lightly." Nikki was about to plead with Jazabel, but

Jazabel sensed this and simply raised her hand to command silence. "To be quite honest, I think it's all three. When I was fifteen, I started to realize that I was different from other girls. I was going through all the other changes we go through at that age, but I was also finding myself interested in the night. I didn't sleep for a month as I just stayed up and watched the moon grow and shrink.

"I asked a friend if she ever stayed up to watch the moon all night. She just laughed at me and said that she never looked at the moon for more than thirty seconds. I knew then that I was going through something that didn't happen to every girl. It got to the point that my aunt and uncle had to bring a healer to see me as I'd lost all interest in everything but the night; I'd shrouded myself in darkness.

"But when he walked through my bedroom door, I saw it, his darkness. To this day, I've only seen one person with a darker soul. But I wasn't afraid; I was attracted to him. And when he asked my aunt and uncle to leave and he stepped up to me, I felt a shiver run down my back in anticipation. I grabbed him and pulled him on top of me, telling him to do everything he wanted to do to me. I told him that I could see the darkness within him and demanded that he unleash it upon me. Naturally, he tried to deny this and me, and he left running.

"Well, naturally my family ran back in to see what had happened. And that's when it happened. I pushed past my aunt and uncle and ran into the night, trying to follow the healer. And as I ran, my dress shredded off me, leaving me naked. But I didn't notice until the bats surrounded me and I felt the leather and mesh sear my flesh. And then I was one with the bats, being whisked away."

It was at this point in her story that Jazabel's eyes flashed from blissful to maniacal and then back to their normal reserved state. "The next thing I knew, I found myself in front of the healer, trapping him in an alley corner. Frightened by my sudden appearance, he asked me what I wanted from him and what I was wearing. But I was blinded; his darkness was gone and in its place was a light that had not been there a half hour before. I was so enraged at being duped that I turned to leave but turned back as he screamed. Turning to see what was happening, I saw him being attacked by the bats that had brought me to him.

"I just stood there as he begged me to help him. I knew I should've helped him, but instead, I relished in his agony and the knowledge that it was being done to please me. And as they finished ripping his flesh off his corpse, the bats showered me in his blood before taking me back to my home." Again, Nikki noticed the look of pure pleasure upon Jazabel's face as she revealed this. She was slightly disturbed by the lust that rose within her at hearing all this.

"I awoke the next night, remembered what had happened, and was completely horrified with myself. I ran from my room to find a mirror, but was stopped by my aunt as she saw me covered in dried blood and in the leather of my profession. It was then that I learned of the Ladies of the Night, of what I had become. She told me that the town was looking for the killer of the healer, and upon learning of what I had done, she smuggled me out of town. It is since then that I've wandered the world, until I found myself in Gothtor.

"I once met a fellow Lady of the Night in Arretenia. As she was older than me, she taught me much of what I know. She told me that I was the first Lady of the Night in nearly a decade, as well as where there were safe havens for us. For four months, she taught me everything about our culture and history; including our founder, Cadel Thymab: the queen of Cawdor who gave up her womanly nature to be remorseless when she tried to kill a more powerful king. The evil spirits indeed made her what she wanted, but it drove her insane. But before the fullness of the insanity took her, she took to her bed the son of the king she had killed. Their union gave her a child, a girl. But as her mother had given up all womanly nature, she had no milk to give. But the child rejected all milk and only when she drew blood from her mother's breast was she sated.

"Fifteen years later, the girl had nearly drained her mother of blood. Cadel Thymab was now dead to the world; her insanity and daughter's draining of her blood had made it impossible for her to do anything. But when she had drunk the last drop of her mother's blood, Cadel Thymab opened her eyes, which were now black as night, and told her daughter she had done well; not only had she slowly killed her mother over fifteen years, but she'd also unleashed a new magic into the world, a dark magic that affected all of her blood and bound them to the darkness of the world.

"All Ladies of the Night know that they chose the darkness they're born with, at the right moment. We bear many burdens that even the most knowledgeable of our culture - that's not a part of it - knows. People say that a moment in life will define you, and for us, that's more true than you know."

Nikki just sat there, completely stunned. She'd heard whispers that dealt with the two subjects Jazabel had talked about, but none ever made her feel horror like the truth had. But what scared her most was how she lusted to hear more. She'd come here to move past her distrusting of Jazabel, not give it another excuse to exist. She didn't want to have her friendship end by what she said next, so she took a moment to figure out what she should say. But as she tried to find something, Jazabel's face fell more and more to the point where it looked like she was near tears. Not wanting Jazabel to get upset in her trusting her right after she'd said she didn't trust Jazabel, Nikki said, "Don't cry. I was just trying to think of how to respond to that; it's a lot to take in all at once. I will be honest with you though: I'm a little scared by those stories, especially your story. You're such a gentle person, I couldn't believe you'd do something like that, were it not for the… pain of it in your eyes. That's all behind you, my sister; we all have shames in our pasts we want forgotten. But our shames are a part of who we are, and I wouldn't have you any other way, Jazabel. Like I said, you're my sister and I love you."

Jazabel smiled as she leaned in and gave Nikki a hug. They held each other tight for a few minutes, before Nikki got up to go find her brother. Before she could take two steps, Jazabel grabbed her wrist gently. "I still owe you a secret, and you said you had something in mind. Not to mention that you have yet to swear never to reveal what I just told you to anyone, even Shade."

Sitting back down, Nikki nodded her agreement. "Not a soul, I swear on Shade's life." Jazabel raised a surprised eyebrow, for Nikki had never made such a powerful vow to anyone before. She hoped that doing so would show Jazabel how much their friendship meant to her. "And the secret

I wanted from you was the truth behind your reaction to Shade calling you Rheta. You weren't as surprised by that revelation as you made us believe, were you?" Nikki asked.

Jazabel smiled faintly at the memory. "This is also something that you can't tell Shade." When Nikki again nodded, Jazabel continued, "You're right, of course. One of the things that I learned in the four months I spent with that other Lady of the Night is that some of us are the physical reincarnations of women of the past -women that history believes to be evil. I was surprised it was Rheta; she didn't seem to be the type of evil that would be reincarnated. That is until I read Shade's book, and then it made too much sense." Jazabel had closed her eyes at this last statement in what Nikki thought was pain. She was about to give her a hug when Jazabel stood and turned her back to Nikki. "Forgive me, Nikki, but I need a few moments to myself. I do not mean to be rude, but please leave."

Shocked by the sudden dismissal, Nikki stood to leave. Putting a hand on Jazabel's back, she felt her sister tense at the contact. Rubbing gently for a moment, Nikki said, "Feel better, Jazabel." It had been nearly two years since Jazabel had had this kind of sudden change in temperament, but the cure was always the same. "I'll send Brudas to you as soon as I see him." Jazabel only nodded as Nikki left her alone in her study.

After leaving his father as soon as they had returned to the castle, Shade found himself climbing the stairs that led to the ledge above the courtyard from the throne room. He couldn't believe what his father had told him; he couldn't be related to the Vigmece clan. He couldn't be the one in possession of the Mask of Babomorah. But even as he paced the balcony, he could feel the Mask calling to him, begging him to use it.

"Hard, isn't it, resisting the temptation that boils in your blood?" an ethereal voice asked from behind him, startling Shade from his contemplation.

Turning to see who it was, Shade saw the rainbow of colours that made up the strangely beautiful hair of the goddess before him. Her eyes shifted colour as well, never resting for more than a few seconds on one colour. "Korena," he said reverently, as he bowed to a knee. "My mother will be glad to see you; she's missed you a lot. And yes, it is hard, but my disgust helps me more than enough." *Mother,* he thought, *can you meet me on the balcony? I have a surprise for you.* Shade had never tried to contact either of his parents mentally before, but he figured that the love he and his mother shared would help his message find its way to her.

Korena just smiled. "Thank you; it's very kind of you to do that. But I guess you wouldn't be the nicest man in either world if you didn't do that. I'm afraid I can't repay your kindness, for I bring bad tidings." Her head hung as she said this.

Standing, Shade lifted her chin so that their eyes were level. "You can pay me back by spending as much time as possible with my mother today. But what news of the war do you bring, m' Lady?"

"Only that it comes. By this day next year, it will have begun," she said sombrely.

"Not tomorrow; please tell me it's not tomorrow!"

"No, Shade," she said with a faint smile, "it's not tomorrow. Your wedding day will go without a hitch, I promise."

"Thank you, Korena. We appreciate the warning."

Before Korena could say anything to that, Iselda's voice was heard from within the castle. "What are you doing, Shade? What's this surprise? And how were you able to talk to me like that?"

"A visit from an old friend," Korena said as Iselda came into view. And then the two women ran to each other. Holding each other tight, Shade saw them whisper into the other's ears but he wasn't able to hear what they said.

"I'll leave you two to catch up. I have some things to do anyways. It was good to see you, Korena, and thanks again," he said as he walked past them.

Finally releasing each other, his mother turned to him for the first time since she came to the balcony. "Ok, sweetheart. I'll see you later, and thank you again for this." Shade just nodded as he descended the steps back inside.

Iselda looked upon the goddess who had once been her lover with a fractured sense of longing. "I know you're not just here to see me, Korena; so why are you here?" she asked as she walked to the stone railing at the edge of the balcony.

Following Iselda, Korena answered in a similar fashion: "I came to warn your children. As I just told your son, the start comes; their war will have begun by this day next year. But do not worry, tomorrow will go as planned and shall be a day of much joy."

Taking Korena's hand into her own, Iselda kissed it. "Thank you. But isn't there a way you can make it so this conflict doesn't have to happen? Why must they fight?"

"Because they are the ones the Beast wants. I wish for everyone's sake that they didn't have to do this, but it must happen. Why, I cannot say, but I know it must. I do know that all will be revealed by the time it is finished. Your children are strong, Iselda. You must have faith in them."

"I do have faith in them. And I know they're strong; I've watched them grow for the past twenty-one years in the knowledge that this was coming. Not since the day you and your husband told them of their future have I seen them show any emotion to it, besides anticipation. They've trained hard and are ready to face the dangers ahead. I'm just worried that something will happen to them and I'll be left childless. And although I'm immortal again, I couldn't bring myself to find someone to father my children in the future. I love my husband." Iselda turned herself away from Korena as she said this last bit; hiding the truth that she knew to be in her eyes.

But as she felt a hand on her shoulder, she turned back to see Korena's eyes burning a fierce reddish pink. "And I love mine; but that doesn't mean that my feelings for you have died, my love," Korena said as she leaned in and gave Iselda a brief kiss. "But do not despair, for you are not immortal."

Iselda was completely shocked by this. "What do you mean?"

"I mean exactly what I said: you're not immortal. I was the one who gave you your powers back, Iselda. I would've thought you would have come to that conclusion yourself, but I guess you were content thinking it an accident. However, I must warn you that your powers will be useless against the Beast that comes for your children. I don't know how or why; I just know that to be true. And one more thing, though I know you and Pan wish to help your children in this, I ask that you do not enter directly into the conflict. I do not wish to have you come to the underworld before it is your time." Now it was Korena's turn to turn away.

"Are you saying what I think you are, Korena? That if me or Pan take up arms to help our children we will die?" Gently pulling her around so they were face to face, Iselda demanded, "Answer me, Korena!"

"It's not certain, but there's a high likelihood of that outcome, yes. And I want you to live to experience all that this life has to offer you. Even if it's not for another thirty years before I get to see you again, I'll gladly wait if it means you've lived fully."

Iselda drew Korena into a hug as she knew exactly how she felt. "Thank you, Korena. I know you've always looked out for me and my family and we're very grateful. I just wish we could see each other more often."

"And in time we will. In the meantime, I can always hear when you pray or talk to me in private. I won't be able to answer you, but I'll always be there for you. For now, you need to get ready for tomorrow and I must return to the underworld. Your parents send their love; shall I return it?" Korena asked as she stepped out of the hug.

"Always. And thank you, Korena, you're a good friend and I love you. *As Eternal as We Are*, right?"

At the mention to their old vow, both women looked to the ring on Korena's right hand. Iselda saw Korena smile and that a tear had fallen from her eye. "Right. Goodbye, Iselda, and good luck in the coming year." And before Iselda could say goodbye, Korena melted into the shadows and disappeared.

⁂

As Shade made his way to the library to find Jazabel, he saw Nikki leave. Taking a moment to just watch his beautiful sister, he felt his heart expand at the amount of love he felt for her. *Is Jazabel in the library?*

Turning to him as if he'd spoken aloud, he saw Nikki's bright smile, as well as the book she held in her hand. She answered as she walked over to him: *Yes, she's in her study in the back. But she's in one of her old moods. What did Dad want?*

To tell me of the past and give me an heirloom I didn't even know we had.

What? Don't I get to know what it is?

No, I wish I didn't know of it. And besides, Dad doesn't want you to know of it. Mom doesn't even know. That's how strong this secret is to us.

Ok, I'll try to forget it if it's that important. Do you know where Mom is?

Thank you. And I just left her out on the balcony with Korena. Apparently, our war is to begin within a year.

Korena's here? And Mom's alone with her?

Yes, but did you not hear what I just said? By this day next year, the war will have begun!

Yes, I heard you. But can't we deal with that after

tomorrow? I don't want anything to ruin it. And besides, knowing Mom's alone with Korena is more troubling at the moment.

Why? Because they love each other?

How do you know that? You're not supposed to know that!

Think about who I am. I've known for a long time. But it's good to see that it's one less secret I have to keep from you.

What other secrets are you keeping from me? And how many are there?

Not many. And I only keep them because I've been asked to. Don't you have secrets from me?

Yes.

That's what I thought. Now, why don't you go make sure Mom and Korena aren't doing something that could get them in trouble; I've got to talk with Jazabel.

Nikki just shook her head. "No; she'll only see Brudas when she's like this. She just kicked me out. She doesn't want to see us right now."

"I can calm her down just as well as Brudas. And I need her help with something." He could see that Nikki was about to argue, but he just gave her a pleading look, urging her to understand. "Speaking of help, why do you have my book? Don't you know the story already?"

Immediately, Nikki completely shut her mind from him, as her eyes evaded his. Shade knew, just by the fact that she'd never done this before, that he wasn't supposed to know anything about why she had his book. "It's to do with mine and Jazabel's daily wager; that's all I can tell you," Nikki said, giving him a quick kiss before making her way in the direction Shade had come from. Turning back for a second, she added, "And be nice to my sister." Shade just nodded as they turned away from each other and towards their separate destinations.

When Shade was just outside Jazabel's study, he heard the muffled sound of crying. Opening the door that separated the study from the library proper, he saw Jazabel crying on the couch in the corner of the room. He ran to her and pulled her into his arms. "Jazabel! What's wrong?"

Looking to him, she tried to push him away, which only made him hold her tighter. "Shade no! You can't be here! Please; I need Brudas. This isn't for you to help me with, White Knight." She used her nickname for him, like she always did when she was serious.

Shade let her go, a little hurt at her words. "I'm not leaving you until you tell me why you're in such a mood as to throw Nikki out and refuse my company and comfort."

She smiled weakly and wiped away the tears. "Shade, it's nothing. Just some old memories is all." Standing the two of them up and giving a slightly more convincing smile, she asked, "Now, what can I do for my *deaur sange* today?"

Taking her hands into his and looking into her eyes, Shade asked, "Are you sure you're alright, Jazabel?" When she nodded slightly, he continued, "I need your help. I don't know what I should do for my first act as king."

"Your first act as king? Isn't that a question to be put to your father? What help could I possibly provide?" Jazabel asked in a shocked tone. Her tone was so genuine that Shade forgot he was worried about her.

"You're so modest, Jazabel; you know me better than anyone besides Nikki. I've been scared of this for my whole life, and I'm asking you to help me overcome that fear by giving me some idea as to what I should do."

Jazabel smiled at his praise, but blushed all the same. "Well, you're in luck, Shade. Not two days ago I finished research on the past twenty first acts of the past twenty kings." Walking them over to her desk, she flipped through some pages in her ledger until she found the one she was looking for from the small, worn book. "Here's the list," she said as she handed it to him. "But I don't think you'll need it all that much."

Upon seeing the thin smile that curled at her lips, Shade asked, "What do you mean? This list is just the sort of thing I need."

"No it's not, Shade. All you need is right here," she said as she tapped the centre of his chest. "Following your heart has never failed you before, and it's certainly not about to start now. You're the purest person I've ever known - a true white knight. Braria loves you, and no matter what you do tomorrow, it still will. If you follow your heart, I know you'll be praised like never before." She gave him a slight smile meant to encourage him as she finished.

"Thanks, Jazabel; I knew I could count on you. Do you mind if I borrow this list for the night?"

Leaning up and giving him a kiss on the cheek, Jazabel nodded. "Of course not; anything to help the future king. Consider it my birthday gift to you. Is there anything else you need?"

"No, I've got everything I want or need. Thank you, Jazabel, I don't know what I'd do without you," Shade said as he turned to leave after a brief hug.

If he'd thought to look back, he would have noticed that his *deaur sange* had returned to her couch and resumed crying. But it wasn't old memories that brought tears to her eyes like she had said; she wept for what she knew was to come. "Forgive me, my love. I could not help myself from helping the Beast that comes for you and your sister-bride, the one I now call sister."

Chapter 55:
Two Weddings and a Coronation

When Nikki woke the next morning, she could hardly contain her excitement. Today was the day she would finally be wed to the man she loved the most, her brother Shade. As she stretched herself out of bed, she noticed her father was sitting at her desk. "What are you doing in here, Dad? You shouldn't see me like this; I'm barely dressed," she accused as she tried to cover herself up.

Her father just smiled, outlining the wrinkles that had lined his face for the past few years. "I'm here to make sure you're all ready for today. And I've seen you in less states of dress than this, sweetheart; so there's no need to be modest."

"But Daddy, that was years ago; I've grown up since then. And besides, I can get myself ready for today. I know how my groom likes me to look."

"I know, sweetheart. But Shade actually came and woke me up so that I could give you something from him - something he told me that would make everyone here today see you for the goddess you are."

Nikki could barely contain her smile and tears. Only in

their most intimate moments did Shade call her a goddess. "And what is that?" she asked in a shaking voice as she took a step towards her father, her modesty all but forgotten.

Standing up, he had his hands behind his back as he closed the gap between them. "This," he said as he brought his hands in front of him. In them he held a black velvet case, inside of which was a necklace. The chain was very thin, but intricately woven together, and the pendant that hung from it was a crowned heart, wrapped in feathered wings. She recognized it instantly from one of her favourite books. "The chain is pure crystal and the pendant is shadothyst, mined from the volcanic shores of Clowia. Shadothyst is the strongest substance that I know of, and it's expensive. I don't know how your brother was able to pay for this, but it surely cost him its weight in gold."

"It's so beautiful," Nikki said reverently. "And I can't believe he actually had them carve this."

"What is it? He said it was something you held dear, but I don't recognize it." Her father's confusion was clear on his face.

"That," Nikki said, indicating the pendant, "is Nameless. In Clowia, there's a legend that if Nameless ever comes to a girl, hope will always be with her. I read about it all in *Magic's Legends*; it's one of my favourite books."

"Where did you get a copy of that, Nikki?" her father asked with a slightly bewildered expression on his face. "I thought that all the copies had been destroyed or were held in countries that weren't on friendly terms with us. What have you and your brother been doing in your spare time?"

Nikki could tell by the look in her father's eyes that she had to tell the truth. Heaving a sigh, she looked into his eyes and said, "We've been trying to forge alliances so we could have more resources for when the Beast attacks. The copy I have comes from Ichmensch; we had Brudas retrieve it a year and a half ago in exchange for his teaching them some of his sword techniques, as well as safe passage for their troops should they ever need it, so long as they don't harm Brarian citizens. But we got more than just a book, Father; we got their loyalty in the upcoming battle. By next month we'll have a flowing trade ring expansion. You're not mad at us, are you?" Nikki was worried her father would get upset, and that would surely darken the mood of the day.

But he just shook his head. "No, honey, I'm not mad. I'm glad that you and your brother have been preparing yourselves for this coming battle. And the fact that you're doing it in ways that your mother and I never thought of just shows how thorough you two are being. You don't have to keep these kinds of secrets from us, but I understand if you felt you had to."

Nikki just gave him a big hug. "Thanks, Dad. This means a lot to us. Now, get out and send Mom in to help me. I have to be ready and look my best for my brother in an hour."

"Of course. Your Mom will come in a few minutes." And with a quick kiss to her forehead, Nikki's father left the room.

As she and her father reached the makeshift altar where her brother, Aunt Kailee, and Uncle Shade waited, Pan gave her a kiss on her forehead and placed her hand in his son's. Nikki couldn't stop smiling as she looked upon her Shade;

he looked so handsome in his robes that her heart could barely contain the love that was swelling within it.

That's a beautiful necklace.

Yes, it is. Thank you so much, but you really shouldn't have.

I know, but I wanted to. You look so beautiful.

And so do you. As one, the bride and groom turned to their aunt and uncle as the gathered crowd took its seats. "The sacred covenants of marriage are not to be entered into lightly," declared their Uncle Shade.

"They are an eternally binding agreement between two willing parties. Love must be present in their hearts, yet sacrifices are required to prosper. Shade and Nikki understand the requirements of this world and of the spirits in the next, and they are ready to pay the debts required," Kailee told the gathered masses.

"Nikki, as Shade's wife, you will become the queen of Braria. That title brings heavy burdens; none as heavy as the clause to the people stating you will do all in your power to protect and lead them to prosperity. Can you lead and protect us in such ways, giving your life if necessary?" her uncle demanded.

"Yes, I will give all I can give to further progress in Braria. If my life is the cost, I'd gladly pay it," Nikki said in a strong, clear voice for all to hear.

"Good. Now do you forever promise to love Shade; to make him happy and peaceful to the highest degree?" asked her uncle.

"That's all I've ever wanted to do." Nikki then gave her hand closest to her uncle to him as he sliced open her palm and let some blood flow into the goblet of pure Brarian silver that rested between the four on the marble pedestal.

Now her Aunt Kailee spoke to her brother. "Shade, as Nikki's husband, you will become the king of Braria. As king though, you must put your people above yourself or even your queen. Can you live with the terms as set down by the first king?" demanded Kailee.

"The majority of my life has been in planning of ways for me to help Braria; it's time I stop planning and start doing. Yes, I can live with the first king's terms," Shade said in a confident voice.

"Good. Now do you forever promise to love Nikki; to make her happy and peaceful to the highest degree?" asked their aunt.

"It's what I live for," her brother whispered. Then he gave his hand to his Aunt Kailee, who took it, sliced it open, and let the blood flow into the goblet.

"Nikki," Shade said, "by your oath, your love, and now your blood, you are forever bound to Shade Kanta."

"Shade," Kailee said, "by your oath, your love, and now your blood, you are forever bound to Nikki Kanta."

Now they spoke in unison. "Take the goblet with your blood and feed it to your spouse." The bride and groom did as instructed, drinking their fill. "Now, by our power, and in the presence of these witnesses, we declare you wed!" Everyone cheered as Shade leaned into Nikki and gently brushed his lips against hers in the lightest kiss he'd ever given her.

Now nobody can claim you as theirs; you're mine and mine alone.

I never was anyone else's. Unlike you, my husband. How Nikki relished those words: 'my husband'. As Shade pulled his lips off of hers, Nikki saw the semi-repentant smile on his lips. She smiled back to let him know that she was only teasing him. He gave her a slight nod that he understood.

Turning to the still cheering crowd, Nikki raised her hand to quiet them all down. "Thank you everyone. But today's festivities aren't over just yet. In just a few minutes our court chef will be bringing in a light lunch for everyone to nibble on while we prepare for the coronation. But we do ask that you wait until later to offer us your congratulations; we'd like a few private moments to ourselves. Thank you, and please enjoy!"

As if on cue, Alix walked into the room with some of the kitchen staff carrying platters of light finger food for everyone's enjoyment. Setting the platters down on the tables set up at the sides of the room, everyone went to the food as Nikki led Shade out to the balcony just up the steps from the back of the throne room.

Out on the balcony, Shade pulled Nikki into himself and kissed her passionately. After a minute of kissing he pulled back and looked at her with only love in his eyes. "I love you," he said.

Nikki could only smile as tears welled in her eyes. As each one fell, Shade wiped them away with a gentle swipe of his fingers, using a different finger for each tear. "And you are my everything; as I am yours." As Nikki spoke this strongest truth, she pulled her brother into another kiss.

But it was interrupted by a soft cough from the doorway. Giving an internal sigh, Nikki turned a glare to the intruder only to find her parents standing there. "Wasn't I clear when I said we wanted a few private moments to ourselves?" she asked, her teeth clenched in irritation.

The smiles on her parents' faces only served to irritate her further. Turning to her groom, she found the same annoying smile on his lips. *You told them to come, didn't you?*

No, but they are our parents. Besides they know to be quick or face your wrath. And look, they brought us some lunch.

Nikki just glared at him in response, but his smile was too infectious for her to stay mad at him. She turned back to her parents with a mostly genuine smile. "Mom, Dad, please join us!"

"We hope we're not interrupting anything important," their mother said with a teasing smile. "We can come back later if you want."

"Nonsense, Mom. You and Dad are always welcome in our company," Shade said as he walked with Nikki over to their parents. "What can we do for you?"

"We just wanted to make sure that you two were pleased with the ceremony that your aunt and uncle performed for you. You know it mirrored our marriage rites," their father said.

"It was wonderful; we loved it," Nikki said sincerely. "And we specifically asked Uncle Shade and Aunt Kailee to do it like yours. We know that Aunt Marina performed your wedding, but we wanted both sides of the family to be a part of this. We also wanted to give you the opportunity to relive old memories; memories we thought would be quite enjoyable to remember."

Both her mother and father got shocked looks on their faces as this was revealed. With tears in her own eyes now, her mother whispered, "They were. Thank you, but you didn't have to do that."

"We wanted to, Mom," Shade said. "Now, why don't you guys go make sure that everything is ready for the coronation and that everyone is enjoying themselves. As my bride so delicately said, we need a few moments to ourselves. You can come and get us when everything's ready."

Realizing that they were being told to leave, their parents said a quick goodbye and left them. And as soon as they were gone, Nikki pulled Shade into herself and placed her lips on his.

But before long, he pulled away. "What's wrong?" Nikki asked. Shade never pulled away unless he was out of breath or someone made him.

"Did Dad seem different to you? I thought I sensed something off in him?"

Trying to hide her guilt, she shook her head. "No, I only saw love and pride."

"You know you can't lie to me. What I sensed was pride, but not about today. This is something new that wasn't there yesterday when I talked to him. What did you tell him this morning?"

Heaving a sigh, Nikki said, "I told him about our dealings with other nations behind his and Mom's back. He was asking about my necklace and I let slip where it was from. He wasn't mad at us; he was actually quite proud that we took this initiative. You're not mad that I told him, are you?" she asked fearfully.

"No, I'm not mad. I was actually going to tell him and Mom later tonight." Smiling at her, he asked, "Now, where were we before we were so rudely interrupted?" Nikki just smiled as he brought his lips to hers.

An hour later Shade was kneeling at the foot of the steps that led to the raised dais in the throne room, with Nikki at his side. His parents were standing in front of them holding their crowns above their children's heads. "Do you, Shade Leo Kanta, promise to uphold the laws and practices of the nation of Braria; to never wilfully engage in courses of action that will result in turmoil; and above all, to give your life if necessary before any innocent is harmed unjustly? Do you vow to rule as the first king ruled?" his father asked in his official voice.

"With every breath I breathe, I will try to ensure Braria's prosperity, even if it should take my last. I, Shade Leo Kanta, forever vow to rule as the first king ruled," he answered in kind.

Now his mother spoke to him. "As Braria's newest crowned monarch, I, Iselda Kanta, accept your vow, Prince Shade. And in doing so, recognize you as our new king." As she finished, his father lowered the crown onto his head. "Arise, my son. Arise King Shade!"

And so Shade did, leaving all doubts and insecurities on the floor.

Now it was Nikki's turn. "Do you, Nikki Evelyn Kanta, promise to uphold the laws and practices of the nation of Braria; to never wilfully engage in courses of action that will result in turmoil; and above all, to give your life if necessary before any innocent is harmed unjustly? Do you vow to rule as the last queen ruled?" his father asked his sister, in that same tone he'd asked Shade.

And in the voice Shade had only heard when the two of them were dealing with foreign dignitaries - her own version of the official voice - his new wife answered. "Until my dying day will I try to better my homeland. So vow I, Nikki Evelyn Kanta, to lead Braria as my predecessor has these past twenty-six years."

"And as your predecessor, I, Iselda Kanta, accept your vow, Princess Nikki. And by doing so, I relinquish to you my title." As his mother said these words, she lowered her crown onto Nikki's head. "Arise, my daughter. Arise Queen Nikki!"

And so she did. As Shade took her hand and led her to the thrones waiting atop of the dais, their parents went to the front of the masses gathered. And as the new king and queen sat in their thrones, everyone else in the room knelt down on one knee. "Hail Shade and Nikki: the new king and queen!" their parents said in unison, and this cry was soon on every tongue in the room.

Only once Shade stood did the chant stop and everyone stood up straight. "Thank you, everyone. My queen and I are quite grateful for all of your support over the years, and we hope you continue to support us in the years to come.

"Before we can celebrate, there is one more thing that must be done: my first act as king. Before I perform this act, I want to tell you all of what this moment has meant to me. The truth is that I've been scared of this moment all my life. Like everything I've done, I wanted this to be meaningful for more than just myself. It wasn't until this morning that I had an idea of what I was going to do. But now that I have this idea, I can't think of any better.

"So, without further interruption, I invite my dear friends Jazabel and Brudas to join my sister and self up here on the dais."

Everyone was quiet as Jazabel and Brudas made their way to the dais and joined Shade and Nikki. *What are you doing?*

Can't you guess?

She doesn't want it to happen like this! You know that!

As close as you think you are to her, Jazabel and I are closer.

"The sacred covenants of marriage are not to be entered into lightly," declared Shade. The crowd gasped and Jazabel got tears in her eyes as they realized what Shade was doing.

"They are an eternally binding agreement between two willing parties. Love must be present in their hearts, yet sacrifices are required to prosper. Brudas and Jazabel understand the requirements of this world and of the spirits in the next, and they are ready to pay the debts required," Nikki told the gathered masses.

"Do you forever promise to love Brudas; to make him happy and peaceful to the highest degree?" Shade asked Jazabel.

In a shaking but clear voice, Jazabel answered, "Yes I do."

"Brudas, do you forever promise to love Jazabel; to make her happy and peaceful to the highest degree?" Nikki asked.

"Yes I do."

From his pocket, Shade pulled out two rings. On each was the symbol that Jazabel had requested be on her wedding rings: a sword with bat wings. He'd had them made when she first told him her and Brudas were getting married. Handing one to each of them, he turned to Jazabel. "Repeat after me: I, Jazabel Nyx, so vow to love you; and with this ring, so bind my soul to yours."

"I, Jazabel Nyx, so vow to love you; and with this ring, so bind my soul to yours," Jazabel said in a clear voice, even as the tears still flowed down her cheeks.

Next, Nikki turned to Brudas. "Repeat after me: I, Brudas Smiledoilt, so vow to love you; and with this ring, so bind my soul to yours."

Before Brudas repeated what Nikki had said, Shade thought he saw a brief look of pain cross his face. But before he could think of it, Brudas smiled and in a clear voice declared, "I, Brudas Smiledoilt, so vow to love you; and with this ring, so bind my soul to yours."

And now as one, the king and queen spoke. "By our authority and in the presence of these witnesses, we declare you wed! May you forever rejoice in your love for each other." And as the crowd applauded the unexpected union, Brudas pulled Jazabel to himself and kissed her fiercely.

That was very sweet, but I think that was cheating.

If it is, don't say anything; it's all I got.

Fine. So does this mean you and Brudas are going to stop duelling every day?

You know we only do it to keep sharp and always ready, right? It was never about Jazabel.

Keep telling that to yourself, husband. "And now," Nikki said to the gathered crowd. "My husband and I would like to invite you all to join us in celebrating this day of days. Let the music play!" And no sooner had Nikki said the word 'music', some was heard coming from the hallway outside the throne room. The doors opened and musicians came in playing every instrument imaginable: drums, flutes, guitars, and harps to name a few.

Taking his bride's hand, Shade led Nikki down off the dais

and into the clearing in the centre of the room. Everyone watched the king and queen begin to dance a slow, close dance as the music accompanied their movements. It was a song that they had heard as children and fallen in love with immediately. It had no lyrics that they knew of, but it spoke to them of a dancer in the moonlight, dancing his primal dance in the last untouched forest. And soon, Jazabel and Brudas were at their sides, along with their parents. Soon the whole room was turning in slow circles as lovers and close friends pulled each other close.

And then the music picked up the tempo and the formed couples dispersed to find new partners. Shade went straight for Jazabel, who was making her way over to him as well. "I'm sorry," he said as he bowed to her.

"For what? For marrying me?" she asked confused.

"Yes. I know it wasn't the way you wanted it done, and I promise to do it your way the next opportunity I get."

"Shade, you don't have to apologize. What you just did for me was beautiful in its own way. Without even meaning to, you've actually helped me; now everyone knows when I got married. And thank you for the rings; they're just the way I imagined them."

Smiling, Shade bowed his head. "I'm glad you like them, and I'm glad you liked the ceremony. Would you mind telling Nikki that?"

Laughing at his last comment, Jazabel just nodded her head as they continued to dance.

By the time dinner was served a few hours later, Shade thought he'd danced with every female in the large room at least once. He'd danced with his mother and aunts at least three times each, Jazabel another four times, and Nikki another ten - not to mention the maids, cooks, and townspeople who were all there. Dinner was to be duck and pheasant, another homage he and Nikki had thought to make to their parents' wedding.

As everyone seated themselves and began to eat, moans of pleasure filled the dining room. Even Shade had to give a moan as he took his first bite. Alix had outdone himself for this feast. This pheasant was even better than the one he'd had on the night he'd learned of his and Nikki's destiny, and he'd always thought that was the best food he'd ever had.

At his table were his parents, aunts and uncle, Jazabel and Brudas, along with himself and Nikki. Everyone was seeming to have a good time, at least if what they said as they came up to congratulate the newly wedded couples was to be believed. Everything seemed to be going the way he and Nikki had hoped.

Suddenly there was a blinding light and a howl of unearthly horror that shook the room. When the light faded and the wail ceased, there were four faded silhouettes of three women and one man who weren't naked, but not clothed either in the centre of the room. Not understanding what was happening, Shade stood and drew *Peacemaker*. But when he saw the spirits in front of him, he sheathed it immediately and ran to them. Nikki was right behind him.

Can it really be them?

Let's find out. "You four wouldn't happen to be our grandparents, would you?" Shade asked the four spirits in front of him.

"What kind of question is that?" demanded the lone male. "Has my son taken down all the pictures of me and his mother that once crowded this castle?"

"Actually, I have, Father," their father said, startling Shade with his sudden appearance at his side. "I had to make room for all the ones of me and my bride, as I'm sure my son will one day do." Shade noticed that his father's eyes were a little wet as he stared at his parents for the first time since they had died.

"Speaking of your bride, where is my darling daughter?" one of the women asked. The fact that her eyes weren't blue led Shade to believe this was Isabelle.

Appearing beside her husband came his mother. "I'm here, Mother. It's good to see you. It's been too long."

"That it has, Iselda; perhaps you should take a trip to the Temple and teach your beautiful daughter how to use it," said the woman to Isabelle's right.

"Do we not get introductions?" Nikki asked.

"Of course, sweetheart," Iselda said. "These are your grandparents: Evelyn, Leo, Zelda, and Isabelle."

As one, Shade and Nikki dropped to one knee and said, "It's a great honour to finally meet you four; we've grown up hearing many stories of you. We only wish we could've known you in life."

"Rise, fruit of my fruit," Evelyn said. "We are your grandparents, not Slac Hino. And we, too, wish to have known you in life. But we do not have much time, for the veil has once again been breached to allow well wishes to the newly wedded monarchs of Braria."

"We wanted to come and tell you both that we're so

proud of you. You've handled all of the challenges life has thrown at you with a grace and elegance that others your age would not have been able to show, myself included," their grandfather said.

"We also wanted to come and say we love you both very much. And, don't take this the wrong way, but we can't wait until the time we can talk for more than five minutes comes and not have to breach the veil to do so," Zelda said with a smile.

"We look forward to that day as well, Grandmother," Nikki said, smiling as well.

"We also bring the best wishes from both Hados and Korena," Isabelle said.

"And speaking of Hados and Korena," Evelyn said, "where is Sabrina?" Seeing Sabrina rise from her chair, Evelyn waved her over. "Come here, my dear." When she reached them, Evelyn continued, "I bring a message for you and my son; a message from the entire underworld as well as its rulers."

"What?!" asked Pan and Sabrina simultaneously.

"Not a soul doesn't know what the two of you did. Korena's return to her rightful throne has made the underworld a better place: a place worth spending eternity in. And all of us spirits are grateful for the sacrifice you made to bring her home to us. I just wish it didn't cost you what it did, as does your mother, Sabrina. She forgives you as well."

Somewhere behind them, Shade heard a glass break and the distinct shriek of his Aunt Kailee. But before he could turn to look at her, the snarl of his Aunt Sabrina's voice kept his attention forward. "My mother? You spoke to my mother? *She* forgives *Me*?!" Even Evelyn was shocked by the anger in Sabrina's voice and face at the mention of her mother. "But seeing as she's feeling motherly, you can send her my regards." The venom in his aunt's voice made Shade recoil away from her. Clearly there were some unresolved issues between his aunt and her mother. He made a mental note to ask her what those were and whose forgiveness needed giving.

But before anyone could react to what Sabrina had said, an unearthly howl was heard; Shade now knew the howling to be Zotz calling his grandparents back behind the veil. The four spirits turned to one another as they knew what they had to do. "We must be going. We love you all," Leo said.

"As we love all of you," Iselda replied. And as she said this the four faded into nothingness. Only Isabelle remained.

Turning to Shade, she winked at him. "I do enjoy the colour-coding," she told him with a smile, before vanishing herself.

With the spirits gone, the room seemed very quiet. Looking around, Shade noticed that everyone was staring at those in the middle of the room - or more accurately, at the place where the spirits of his grandparents had been. Giving a small smile of embarrassment, he said, "It's OK, everyone. That was just a wedding present to my bride and me from some old family friends. Go back to your dinners and continue your celebrating." Taking Nikki's hand, he led his parents and aunt back to their table where they enjoyed the rest of their meal.

As they finished their third helping of pheasant, Shade and Nikki looked to one another. Shade was now very anxious to get back to his room for his wedding night. *Please tell me we can go now.*

I think we've spent enough time here. Besides, the sun set hours ago. Let's go! And as one the king and queen rose, causing the room to fall silent. "My husband and I wish to retire for the night. But that doesn't mean that you all have to leave. There's another wedded couple that deserves to be honoured on their wedding day, not to mention that the former king and queen still eat. We will see you all tomorrow. Goodnight!" Nikki said.

But as her and Shade made to leave, their parents motioned for them to wait. "We have one more gift for you. And we don't want any arguments from the two of you. Understand?" their mother asked. When they nodded, she continued, "We're giving you our room. As king and queen, it's rightfully yours. We'll be taking Jazabel's room and her and Brudas will be taking yours. She asked it be that way, and everything has already been moved. So go and enjoy yourselves."

Shade thought he knew why Jazabel had asked to have his old room, but didn't say anything. He just smiled and gave his parents a hug, as did Nikki. *Are you sure it was never about Jazabel, because she seems to think so, despite never agreeing with me.*

Drop it, and let's go to our new room and acquaint ourselves with our new bed.

You had me at drop. And so the new king and queen left the dining room for their new chambers. As they entered, they took no notice of their things having been moved into the room, and proceeded to the bed as they discarded their clothes haphazardly in their hurry. Within minutes, Nikki was sitting atop her brother as she threw her hips into a recklessly abandoned rhythm to both their pleasure. And their pace didn't slow until the sun was well into the sky, when they finally collapsed onto each other.

※

A couple of hours after his children had left the feast in their honour, Panken Kanta found himself sitting alone at the table watching his wife dance with his best friend. Old age had taken its toll on Pan as he could no longer do everything he once could. It was when he saw Sabrina returning to the table alone that he decided to get up. Walking over to her, he took in her ever graceful form and her ever whitening hair - something that his own head was sprouting.

"I suppose that you want to know why my mother forgives me," Sabrina said to him as she took his offered arm.

"As well as why you think she doesn't deserve forgiveness," he replied as he led them to a corner of the room. Privacy wasn't an issue, as most everyone had left the feast, but they did this so as to inform their spouses and friends not to disturb them until their conversation was over and they'd returned.

"Did I never tell you why I left Vagala in the first place?" Sabrina asked with surprise.

"Perhaps; but it's been too many years for me to remember that conversation. Will you tell me again?" Pan asked.

"It's something only you can hear, Pan; for you cannot judge me." Taking a breath, Sabrina looked him in the eye as she let it out. "When I was a girl, it was just me and my mother. She'd moved to Vagala before she knew she was pregnant, so I never knew who my father was. I still don't know. I don't think she knew either, and that's one of the reasons I think she left.

"But she raised me well enough, until my powers manifested when I was thirteen. When she saw how powerful I was, it went to her head. She forced me to threaten anyone and everyone if they had something she wanted, no matter how small. And no matter how much I begged her not to make me do those things, she always made me do it.

"I didn't realize that she didn't have any power over me until I was twenty-two, when I finally challenged her to do her own dirty work and told her that she didn't scare me anymore. She told me to kill the woman she'd had a problem with, but I refused. For the first time in my life I used my powers against her as I threw her against a wall. It was then that I realized that she was scared of me, that I was the one with all the power.

"I fled Vagala not long after that, running towards a spot I knew she would never come to, for it's where she fled from before I was born."

If Pan could, he would have felt sorry for his friend, but their sacrifice twenty-one years ago had removed that ability from him. However, it hadn't removed his knowledge of Sabrina. "There's more to it than that, isn't there? She forgave you for more than just asserting yourself, didn't she?" Pan asked.

"Yes," Sabrina said, finally turning away from him. "When your mother said that my mother forgave me, she meant that I'd done more to my mother than just remove myself from her control." When she turned back to Pan and didn't say anything, he nodded that she should continue. With an annoyed sigh, she said, "What my mother forgives me for is killing her."

At hearing this, Pan was truly shocked. The Sabrina he knew would never have hurt anyone, unless given no choice. The Sabrina he'd loved abhorred violence, especially that caused by vengeance. "Killing your mother doesn't sound like something the Sabrina I know would do."

"My mother is the one person who I would kill," she said with a shake of her head. "When Kailee and I took you to Vagala all those years ago, we bumped into my mother. She waited until we were asleep before she took a knife to both our throats, and, with her identity hidden, threatened me with Kailee's life for taking everything from her.

"I pleaded with her to let Kailee go, that she was innocent and was not responsible for causing her pain. That's when she revealed herself and said that yes, Kailee had caused her pain, for she'd stolen her daughter away from her. That was when she dared me to see what was faster: her hand or my magic. My magic was faster. We fled Vagala the next morning."

Pan, despite himself, smiled. But then he thought of Kailee, who he still thought of as that mismatched girl and not the beautiful woman he knew and loved. He thought of the horror that being a part of all that would have caused. "Well, I know that my wife and children are grateful you were quicker, as am I, even if they don't know they are grateful for that fact. Does Kailee know it was your mother, or does she think it was a case of mistaken identity?"

"I don't know, but I think she knows. We never talk about it and I don't intend on doing so again." And with that, Sabrina left to go to her wife. Pan did the same, finding that she was sitting down and intently watching him.

Standing up as he approached, Iselda wrapped her arms around him as she kissed him hello. "Is everything alright? Is

Sabrina alright?" she asked as she released him from the kiss.

Staring into her amethyst eyes that he'd loved since he'd first laid eyes on them in the memories of others, Pan nodded. "We all have things in our past we want to forget. She, unlike the rest of us, had a bad relationship with her mother. She'll be fine as long as we don't bring it up again."

As he said all this, Iselda got a strange look on her face. "You know, when you and Sabrina sacrificed your love so that Korena could return home, I thought that I'd have to constantly be the one running between you two so that you could talk to one another. But after you got over the initial awkwardness, you surprised me: you became each other's confidant in ways that baffle all who know and love you. How is it that you two have somehow become closer since having it be impossible for you to love each other?" his wife asked with intense curiosity.

"Right before Hados took our love, Sabrina and I swore to each other that no matter what, we'd always love one another. And now that the only thing we can feel for each other is respect, it makes it…easier to trust one another with our shames. We know that we'll never be betrayed, unless circumstances dictate we be, and that it is the only way we can remain friends. We've done what we had to do to ensure that our emotional holes are filled, as well as keep this family together," Pan said as he looked at his still beautiful wife.

"You never cease to amaze me, Panken Kanta. And I do love your surprises," she said with a smile before pulling him into another kiss.

Chapter 56:

Jazabel's Real Wedding

Three weeks after her wedding, Nikki still felt the bliss of being a newlywed and was relishing in that feeling. Though she hardly got any sleep, she was well rested and always upbeat.

At least, on the outside.

Yet there was always the knowledge that the war she'd been preparing for since she was four years old was soon to commence. And although she was not scared, she was worried about the toll it would take on everyone she cared about. She was especially worried about Shade, for if Slac Hino's warning was to be believed, the death that signalled the start would be someone closer to him.

She could barely acknowledge it, but Nikki thought she knew who was going to die.

Nikki didn't want to think of that, not tonight; for tonight was to be Jazabel and Brudas' real wedding. This would be a wedding of the Ladies of the Night, the first in nearly three centuries, Jazabel had said.

When Jazabel had first announced her engagement to

Brudas, she'd left Terang to go to Cawdor, for in Cawdor was the tomb of Cadel Thymab's daughter, the location of the archives of the Ladies of the Night and their oldest stronghold. Nikki had wanted to accompany her, but had understood when Jazabel had said that only a Lady of the Night could enter the tomb. Two weeks later, Jazabel had returned with the thick book that now stood in her office and had been teaching Shade how to perform the ceremony.

Nikki didn't even know how she was to dress, let alone perform the rites. Jazabel and Shade had been very secretive about the whole thing; this had made Nikki very anxious about it, more so than she was already.

But the night had finally come when the wedding was to take place beneath the waning half-moon. She hadn't seen Brudas nor Jazabel all day, and only saw Shade because she refused to leave his side. As the sun set, Shade pulled her from the throne room to their chambers, the last of the day's problems having been dealt with an hour before.

There he got very serious as he closed the door. "Before we get ready for tonight, I want to impress upon you the importance of what we are about to do. First, we are about to become the only witnesses to the first wedding of a Lady of the Night in nearly three hundred years. Second, we are outsiders to this society, and as such shouldn't be allowed to watch, let alone perform, this wedding. Jazabel had to pull many strings just to bring home the book she brought - never mind that she was going to use it to teach me, and by extension you, their most sacred of rites. All of this was only made possible because we are *deaur sange* and I gave a blood oath that we would never speak of this night to anyone, not even Mom and Dad. Do you understand the honours and responsibilities that have been placed upon us by doing this?" Nikki knew just by the seriousness of Shade's voice that this was of the utmost importance. She'd never seen him this serious about anything, not even their destiny or relationship.

She took a moment as she thought this over before finally nodding. "I do understand. Jazabel may be your *deaur sange*, but she's my sister, and I'd give my life for her just as quickly as you would. It is on your soul that I swear that I will never speak of this night, outside of the four of us." Nikki looked deep into Shade's brown eyes as she spoke this solemn oath of her own.

After a long moment in which they judged the other's seriousness, Nikki smiled and gave Shade a quick kiss. "So, what am I to wear to this event? Does Jazabel have anything in mind, or do I get to choose?"

In response to her question, Shade gave her a twisted smile, something that she'd never seen on his face before. "As we are not Ladies of the Night, Jazabel has decreed what we should wear is up to us. She only asks that it be something that you feel brings out your inner darkness and that you allow that darkness to come forth. Ladies of the Night are drawn to darkness, so their weddings are meant to draw it out. Do you think you have such an outfit?" he asked her, that twisted smile still on his face.

Giving a mocking curtsy, Nikki imitated her brother's twisted smile. "I think I have just the thing. I'm sure Jazabel will love it," Nikki said, hiding her thoughts from Shade so as to surprise him as well. "Now, leave me to change. I'll see you at the caves." Not waiting for his answer, Nikki turned to her closet and shut the doors. She didn't even pull down her dress until she heard Shade leave ten minutes later.

As Nikki undressed, she thought of all she'd learned about the Ladies of the Night in the weeks since her coronation. She'd learned that the book Jazabel had brought from Cawdor was called the *Codex Nocturna*, and that it was written in the language of the Night. She learnt that Cadel Thymab's daughter, Pandora, had discovered the language upon killing her mother and unleashing the magic of the Ladies of the Night. Jazabel had also told Nikki that there were five types of Ladies of the Night: raven, snake, bat, wolf, and owl, but the only Lady who'd been of the raven type had been Pandora herself. She'd also told Nikki that every Lady of the Night could communicate with the animal whose type she fell under, for they were a part of her. Like her brother's attraction to Gothtor, Nikki had become obsessed with the secret society her sister belonged to with every new piece of information Jazabel had told her.

Shade stood in his black leather armour as he waited for Nikki, Jazabel, and Brudas to arrive. He also wore a black fur cape made of the fur from three large black wolves that he had hunted when he was fifteen. He'd hunted them solely for their fur to make this cape. It was the vilest he'd ever felt and only Nikki knew of the cape's existence. He'd never known why he had felt compelled to make it; maybe tonight's ceremony was why.

Suddenly he heard a noise behind him. Turning and silently drawing his sword, Shade melted himself into the shadows of the trees surrounding the clearing that held the entrance to the caves. But he saw only Brudas as he came into the clearing. Sheathing *Peacemaker* just as quietly as he'd drawn it, Shade stepped out into the moonlight.

Brudas was dressed in a similar fashion to Shade - black leather armour - but where Shade wore a cape, Brudas wore a helmet that only showed his eyes. In the shadows it seemed as if his eyes were only black holes against the moon's dull gleam on his helmet. Shade had forgotten how intimidating Brudas looked in his armour. His large size alone was enough to frighten all, but in his black armour in the shadows and the way his eyes looked like bottomless holes to the underworld even gave Shade a shiver of fear. "You could put the fear of death into Hados the way you look right now, my friend. Black in the darkness suits you well."

"Darkness is something that I've grown into," Brudas said in his deep voice. "And black suits you well also, White Knight," he added using Jazabel's nickname for Shade. Something was off with the way Brudas said 'White Knight'; it seemed like he was cursing Shade rather than praising him. "Where is our queen; is she not here as well?"

Before Shade could respond, there was another rustle in the bushes. "Yes, Commander, your queen is here," Nikki said in a menacing voice as she stepped into the moonlight. She wore a black dress that held the dress out away from her legs a small amount. In the front, the dress was cut away, allowing for her to take longer strides. This also revealed that she was wearing skin-tight, black leather pants. The tight jacket she wore was also black, as well as only half buttoned up, revealing her black corset. The shoulders and sleeves of the jacket were pointed. And her hair had been extended, gathered together into a single strand atop the back of her head and thrown over her left shoulder. And as always, around her throat was the necklace their mother had given her all those years ago. Then Shade noticed the cape that seemed to be the back of the jacket. It was made up of fake black feathers with red feather accents. The skin around her eyes and had been darkened, making the blue stand out even more. Her usually pink lips were now as black as her outfit. In short, she looked like the dark version of herself, and Shade loved it.

"The question, though, isn't where I am, but where your bride is," she continued in that menacing voice. The coldness of her voice sent a shiver down Shade's back and even made Brudas back up a step. Nikki was clearly letting her dark side out in full force.

But it wasn't Brudas who answered her question. "We still have much to do before Lady Nyx arrives," Shade said in his official voice. Drawing the dagger Jazabel had given him the day before from behind his back and handing it to his sister, he said, "Draw a Star of Death big enough so the four of us can stand in the centre of the star." Nikki took the dagger from him and immediately set about to complete her task. Turning to Brudas, Shade said, "You are to wait outside the Star of Death until I call you back in. Do not breach the seal until I say, understand?" The only response he got was the fist Brudas snapped to his heart before returning to the shadows of the trees.

"Into the Darkness, a call I send. I call forth those Dark Spirits that blocked remorse; I call ye forth to bless this dark union, as you blessed the dark mother's union to victim's unknowing son. Come forth, Dark Spirits, Ladies of the Night

past, and see darkness rule once again!" Shade called out into the night in the language of the Ladies of the Night. And as loud as he could, Shade shouted, *"Come forth, Lady Nyx; your darkest hour approaches."*

Not a minute later, Shade heard the flutter of wings. He saw Nikki look up just as she finished drawing the Star of Death with Jazabel's dagger. When the swarm of bats circled in the centre of the star at Shade's side and Jazabel seemed to appear out of thin air, Shade heard Nikki's gasp of astonishment. But he had no time for that right now.

Kneeling before Jazabel in only the leather and mesh of her true profession, Shade spoke, "Darkest Lady Nyx, all is as it should be. The Star of Death is drawn and the spirits have been called. Also, the queen has given her solemnest vow that the events of tonight will never be heard by anyone not present, ever."

Although his head was bent, he knew Jazabel was smiling. "Very good, King Shade. Please proceed." Standing, Shade motioned Nikki to his side as he readied himself for all that must be done.

Just follow my lead. When the time comes for you to speak, I'll think the words for you.

Ok.

Shade knew that despite her outward appearance, Nikki was very nervous about what she was about to do. But before he could try to reassure her, Jazabel gave him the nod to begin. With Shade situated in the point of the star pointing north, Nikki in the east point, and Jazabel in the west, Shade began. *"On this night, we four gather. We gather to perform rituals not performed in nearly three hundred years. But now, the time has come for the Night to bring another into Her fold."*

"*Beneath the sacred moon, Lady Nyx takes her mate. On this night of nights, the forces of darkness will gain the rights to three more lives as they save them inside the Star of Death.*

"*Lady Nyx, for nearly two decades you have served the Night faithfully. And now you claim to have found one whose darkness you say you can't live without. Describe his darkness to us all, to allow him entry into the protection of the Star of Death.*" Shade could tell by the look on Nikki's face that she didn't understand a word she had just said. But he didn't either; Jazabel had only taught him what to say, not what it meant.

"*Brudas Smiledoilt is the darkest soul I've ever met. For the past six thousand years he has lived waiting for the two people before me to be born: a pair of Soul Twins to avenge his murdered Twin. He masquerades as their friend, waiting for the right time to slowly kill my* deaur sange. *Though I love the two his wrath is aimed at, I haven't told them any of this, even though I've known since I first met him.*" Jazabel spoke in a clear voice, but whenever Shade tried to make eye contact, she avoided his gaze. He thought he saw her eyes glisten, she was so happy.

Turning to the trees as Jazabel finished, Shade sought out Brudas. "Brudas position yourself directly across from me and then walk in a straight line until I tell you to stop," he instructed, as Brudas followed them. "Stop!"

Once Brudas was in place, the Star of Death ignited in what looked to Shade like nightfire. He saw Nikki flinch, but when she saw him so calm, she relaxed as well. *It's ok, we're almost finished. No matter what happens next, don't move; if you do, you'll die.*

That's encouraging.

Shade just smiled at his sister's sarcastic fear. Next, he walked over to Jazabel and knelt down. Drawing his sword, he offered it up to her, "*The time has come Lady Nyx. Take this sword and put it in the fire. Once it is consumed by the flames, strike down the three of us. If both Brudas' darkness as well as your own is as you say, then we shall not be harmed.*"

"*I understand, King Shade,*" she said as she took the sword and plunged the blade into the flames. Shade stood and returned to his place as he watched his sword go from glowing orange, to glowing the same purple-black as the flames, and finally as if it seemed to be sucking all light from their small clearing into it. That's when Jazabel removed the sword from the flames. "Remember, you can't move," was all she said right before she turned to Brudas and plunged the blade into his chest.

Shade was completely stunned as she removed the blade and Brudas slumped to the ground, dead. And with quickness he didn't know she had, Shade watched in horror as she rounded on Nikki and stabbed her just like she'd stabbed Brudas. As Shade saw the life leave Nikki's eyes, Shade felt pain and rage like he had never felt before. But above everything else, Shade felt as if his heart would never beat again.

As he saw Jazabel pull his sword from Nikki's limp corpse, he saw the look in her eyes - a look he'd seen there many times, a look he hated to see there - pain. Shade saw the pain in her eyes and forgave her. Even though she had just killed his reason for being, Shade couldn't even bring himself to say one word to her as she took three steps towards him. And even though he knew he was leaving behind a world of pain for those he loved, Shade could only think to thank Jazabel as she raised the sword and plunged it into his chest.

Nikki woke with a start, but what she saw before her eyes made no sense. Brudas was standing once again, not even a hole in his armour from where Jazabel had stabbed him. Shade hadn't moved one inch to come and hold her one last time, and to her horror he was SMILING at Jazabel. She didn't know who to attack first.

Standing up, Nikki was about to run at Jazabel, but Shade held up a hand. *What are you doing?!*

I'll explain it all later. Before you ask, believe me, I'm very mad. But we came here tonight to marry Jazabel and Brudas, and that is not yet complete. We must finish if we are to get our moment at Jazabel, do you understand?

You're still doing this?! I know that you are the nicest man anywhere, but even this is just insane. She just stabbed me! And Brudas!

And me. And I still want to strangle her for all that, but we at least owe it to Brudas.

Fine; what must we do?

Just wait and I'll let you know. "*Lady Nyx, your words have been deemed true. The dark spirits have given their blessing to this union; Brudas is as dark as you say. I now command you to take his hand into yours. Call those who serve you and have them taste of his flesh, for theirs is the final blessing.*"

Jazabel walked over to Brudas and took his hand into her own. She then removed his glove and placed it in his belt before taking her husband's large hand into her small ones. Next she looked to the sky and in that secret language of hers called to the heavens. "*Pandora, Bruce, and Adriana, my dark generals, come to me and do as you once did. Taste the flesh of darkness and give your blessing to our union!"*

As she finished, Nikki saw the three bats descend to their master and stroke her cheeks with their wings. Jazabel cooed while still holding Brudas' hand as the bats landed on their arms and crawled towards his hand. One bat, the one on Brudas' arm, was black and grey and as big as Brudas' bicep with the muscles in its own body. The one on Jazabel's right arm was pure black and no bigger than her hand, while the one on her left arm was silvery-grey and the middle sized of the three. Nikki was utterly surprised when the bats, as one, bit Brudas' hand and took to the skies once again. Unable to tear her eyes from the winged fiends in the sky, Nikki couldn't believe it when they landed again on the arms of Jazabel and Brudas. And when they started to lick the wounds they'd given Brudas, all the anger in Nikki was replaced by confusion.

And then the bats were in the sky again, nuzzling the face of their mistress. Nikki couldn't believe how carefree and relaxed Jazabel looked as the bats stroked her cheeks like lovers with their wings and nuzzled their noses against hers. And then they were gone as Jazabel nodded to Shade to continue.

But it was Nikki who spoke next. "*Lady Nyx, the bats that serve you have given you their blessing. Brudas Smiledoilt has passed the three tests and his heart has been deemed black. And as your representative Lady of the Night, I declare you wed! Fair warning to all: the Dark has a new purveyor.*" As Nikki finished, Jazabel pulled Brudas to her, removed his helmet and kissed him passionately. As she did, the flames that had appeared when Brudas first entered the Star of

Death faded into the ground, returning them to the Pits of the underworld.

Are we done?

I believe so. She said that when the flames went out it was over.

Then can we kill her now?

Kill her, no; but we are going to talk to her now.

As one, the king and queen walked to their friends, coughing to break them apart. "Brudas, I owe these two an explanation; why don't you go back to our room and wait for me there. It should only take a few minutes." Brudas simply nodded and took off back towards the castle.

Nikki waited until he was back in the trees until she lunged at Jazabel, wanting so much to slap her, or worse. But Shade held her just far enough away that she couldn't touch Jazabel. "No, Nikki, we'll let her explain before we attack her. But it better be a good explanation, Jazabel." The way Shade was looking at Jazabel as he said that last sentence was the harshest look Nikki had ever seen him give. And for the briefest of moments, she felt pity for the older woman.

"I understand why you're angry with me. I didn't tell you what was to happen and then I stabbed you both in the heart, risking your lives in the process. I knew that you would be ok; I told the Dark spirits the truth and they saved your lives because of it. I didn't tell you because I thought you wouldn't go through with this; that you would have someone else do it, someone who doesn't love me like the two of you do. I didn't want to do it! Please, if you believe nothing else, believe that." As she finished, Nikki could see the tears in her eyes as well as the truth of her last statement, no matter how much she wished she didn't.

"We know you didn't want to hurt us, Jazabel, but you did. When you stabbed Nikki, do you know how I felt? Do you know the pain you put me through in those thirty seconds as I saw her lying on the ground dead?" Shade asked in a strained voice that tried to hide the pain he clearly still felt.

"Yes, I know how you felt and no words can accurately describe it," she said as her head fell in shame and sadness. "You wanted to hurt me and make me feel the same amount of pain as you were feeling. But above all the hatred was the emptiness at having lost your everything. And that emptiness still haunts you, even though you can feel her in your arms and see she lives. But I also know that as I stabbed you, you forgave me and were thankful I was killing you for I was reuniting you with Nikki. And I did, didn't I?" As she asked this last question, she looked up into their eyes, hope clear in her own.

Before Shade could fall for those eyes and make her forget the whole thing, Nikki broke away from his grip on her arms and stepped right in front of Jazabel so their faces were only inches apart. And then she slapped her hard across the face. When neither Shade nor Jazabel said anything, Nikki gave her one on the other cheek. "That's not how sisters are supposed to act with one another, Jazabel. And while I'm very angry with you right now, I can safely say I still love you. We wouldn't have made you find someone else if you had told us everything from the start. We would have trusted you enough to let it continue. But for right now, I can't look at you I'm so mad. Don't talk to me tomorrow, goodnight." Nikki used all her self-control to just turn and face Shade and not do anything more to Jazabel. "If you are not in our bedroom ten minutes after I get there, she will spend her wedding night in the castle dungeons. Understand?" she said to Shade with her most angry and serious of faces. Shade just nodded as she stormed off into the forest back to the castle.

"I guess I deserve that."

"Yes, Jazabel, you do. But I'll try to make sure it doesn't come to that, all the same, for I know you have longed for this night for a long time. You still haven't been with him yet, have you?" Shade felt disgusted with himself for asking such a question, but being this close to the Mask and the mention of Jazabel's wedding night overloaded his resistance.

"No I haven't; I've never felt a lover's touch before."

Now Shade really couldn't help himself as he pulled out a small cloth from his pocket. "I really can't believe I'm doing this, but I need you to do something for me."

"After what I just did, no favour is too big."

Handing her the piece of cloth, he said, "This stays between us, and I mean that. You can't tell Brudas or Nikki. Not a soul, do you understand?" When she nodded, he continued, "With this cloth, I want you to collect your virginal blood and bring it to me, here, tomorrow morning. And then never speak of this."

"My...virginal blood? What do you want with that?" The look on her face nearly made Shade tell her to forget it, but the Mask was demanding he use it now that he'd gone this far.

"That's my business. And I shouldn't have to explain to you why I need a favour done after tonight," he said to her harshly, too harshly. "I'm sorry; tonight's been very trying. I should get going; we don't want you to spend your wedding night in a dungeon, do we?" And without waiting for her reply, he turned back to the castle.

Just as he got to the tree line, she called him back. Turning, he saw her smiling at him, "Thank you, to you and Nikki. Without the two of you, none of this would have been possible. You two are the greatest thing that has happened to me, and I appreciate all you did for me tonight. I'll be here two hours after sunrise. One secret deed for another and then we go back to normal, deal?" Shade only nodded as he rushed off.

When Shade got back to his room, Nikki nearly ran him over trying to leave. She was about to yell at him for being in her way, but stopped immediately when she saw it was him. "You're lucky; I was just about to go get Romulus and tell him to start looking for Jazabel. I guess I'll let her have tonight."

She was still dressed in her dark outfit which made Shade smile. "You can't stay mad at her any more than I can; we love her too much. Besides, the ceremony's over. You can stop being the evil you; even if you're adorable when you're mad."

"What's gotten into you? You're too relaxed for what just happened. Don't tell me you've forgiven her already! She stabbed us; no *killed* us! How can you have forgiven her just like that?!" The way Nikki was looking at him made it clearer than any words could that he had to tell her the truth.

"We came to an understanding. She has agreed to pay me back in her own way. I'm still upset about it, but I don't want this to create a rift in our friendship that we can't cross. Haven't you forgiven her as well? She hurt us, yes, but we are still here, aren't we? Do you really want to stay mad at her forever?"

Nikki's expression softened as he asked her this and she cast her eyes downward in shame. "No, I don't want to be mad at her forever. But this certainly warrants some anger, Shade! She was willing to risk our lives without even telling us what she was doing! Doesn't that concern you in the slightest?"

"I trust Jazabel with my life, Nikki. And if anything, tonight has proven that trustworthy. I know that she would never do anything to hurt me, or you, without the greatest of reasons. And if she ever did, she would never willingly do it; she'd try to find a way to avoid it. Did you not look at her as she came at you? Was she not greatly pained by it all?"

"Yes, she was. And yes I have forgiven her for that very reason. You don't understand; I've been having trust issues with Jazabel and I don't want to go back to not trusting her. But after tonight, I don't know how to trust her again," Nikki said, embracing him tightly as she started to cry.

"It's OK; you don't have to start not trusting Jazabel again. You just have to change the way you're looking at this situation. Our lives were put in her hands and she saved us; that's all that matters," Shade said as he stroked her back, feeling the fuzz of the feathers. "We should get some rest.

We've had a trying night, and the longer we talk about it the harder it is going to be to get some sleep. You never know what the morning might bring."

Nikki allowed him to lead her over to the bed, but stopped just before they got there. When he turned back to see why she'd stopped, she had a playful smile on her face. *You never told me what you thought of my outfit.*

I thought it was obvious; I thought it brought out a beauty in you that I'd never seen before, but would definitely like to see again.

Good answer. As Nikki thought this, she undid the buttons that held the jacket closed. As it fell to the floor, Shade noticed that her corset had a section cut away as well which revealed her toned stomach. Kneeling down to give his wife's beauty praises, Shade kissed every inch of exposed skin. Within minutes, he'd exposed more and had her lying under him on their bed as his uncontrollable love for her took them to a world all their own.

Chapter 57:

Worries and Fears

Despite not getting more than an hour of sleep, Shade was up with the dawn. Knowing that Jazabel wouldn't be at the caves for another couple of hours, he decided to watch Nikki sleep for a while. She looked so peaceful when she was asleep, he almost hated to see her stir and wake up. But every time she did, she would look right at him and smile the most naturally beautiful smile he could conceive of. Even though they'd known they were Soul Twins since before they were born, Shade still couldn't believe how lucky he was to have such a wonderful woman as his wife.

After a half an hour of silently thanking whatever force chose to give him the greatest of eternal loves, Shade made to get up and get dressed. But as he shifted away from Nikki, she lightly stirred and began to seek him out. As she looked at him, she gave him that smile he loved so much. "What time is it?"

"Just after dawn. Go back to sleep; you've barely gotten any since we got married. And you don't have to do anything today, so you can catch up on your sleep."

"And what about you? You've gotten less sleep than I have. Don't you need a break? Come back to bed." The look in her eyes nearly persuaded him, but he knew he couldn't.

"I'm fine. I have a meeting in about an hour that I need to prepare for. I might be gone for a couple of hours, depending on how quick the meeting goes. I'll be back as soon as I have everything in hand, ok?"

"OK, be back soon. I want to wake up in your arms later." As Nikki laid her head down on her pillow, Shade nodded his understanding and kissed her lightly on the lips. He then got up and went about getting everything for his meeting with Jazabel.

※

Shade hadn't been waiting more than five minutes when he heard the rustle of leaves that signalled Jazabel's arrival. As she came into the clearing, she gave him a weak smile before looking to the ground in shame. Shade took a few steps to her awkwardly, as she did to him until they were able to reach out their hands and touch the hand of the other.

Still not looking up at him, Jazabel handed Shade the piece of cloth he'd given her the night before. Shade could see the bloodstains even as it was neatly folded. "That's as much as I could get without looking too suspicious. I hope it's enough for whatever you need it for," she said awkwardly.

Taking the cloth with delicate fingers, Shade pocketed it. "It seems to be lots, thank you," he said just as awkwardly. He thought that the awkwardness would stay that way for as long as they lived, the way it dragged on in this moment.

But when, after a minute of awkward silence, Jazabel turned to leave, Shade called her back. "Look, about last night, and this," he said with a tap to the pocket containing the bloody cloth, "I'm really sorry. Nikki and I forgive you; it's just that it took us by surprise to see you not only run Brudas through but also us. She's hurt that you didn't trust us with the truth, as am I, and that has made her angry. Hopefully later today she'll have calmed down enough for you to go and talk to her so as to air everything out."

"You and Nikki have every reason to be angry with me, Shade," Jazabel said from the edge of the clearing, finally looking him in the eye. "Not only did I not trust you with the most important part of the ceremony, all I told you to do was not react in any physical way. And then to do that to you... no Shade, it's I who am sorry. But I'm also thankful."

"For what?"

"That you finished the ceremony; that you did it in the first place in the manner which I requested. You both looked so hauntingly beautiful last night; thank you for dressing like that. It made everything all that much more special."

"We're glad you liked it, and we're honoured beyond words that you fought to have us perform it. We can't imagine what our lives would be like without you, Jazabel; you're closer to us than family. And we hope we never have to live without you in our lives."

Shade could see the tears in her eyes as he told her this, but the emotion behind her eyes he mistook for happiness and love. "I hope for that too," she said with a weak smile. "I'll let you get back to whatever it is you were planning on doing."

"Wait, Jazabel!" Shade called again. When she turned

back to him, he continued, "About last night, what did we say?" She'd only told him the overall tone of what was said and he wanted to know the specifics.

Jazabel simply looked off into the trees at the question before returning to him. "I really want to be able to tell you that, but I cannot. Only those who belong to the Night can understand the language of Darkness, for there's no way to truly translate it. And besides, you wouldn't be able to understand even if I taught you the language. Your heart is too pure," she said with a loving tap to his chest. And with a gentle kiss to the cheek, she turned and left.

Shade just watched as she walked away. In her simple grey dress and with her hair pulled back into a ponytail she looked so much more reserved than in her Lady of the Night attire. But in no way was she any less beautiful. She was so wise in his eyes, like his mother; perhaps her years spent in the dark and now the light had given Jazabel a unique outlook on life which made her wiser than others their age.

But as Shade thought of this, he felt his pocket grow heavy and the call in his blood beckon like never before. Without his telling them to, his feet carried him into the caves to where the pull felt the strongest. As he got to the dead end his father had taken him to just a few weeks previous, he noticed the lantern was lit. He didn't have time to ponder this, for he had to use the Mask. Every time he thought about it, the draw he felt only grew stronger.

Too pure a heart. If only Jazabel could see him now with the darkness in his blood taking over his every movement, every thought. Somehow he was on his knees and the Mask of Babomorah was lying on the floor before him, the piece of cloth with Jazabel's virginal blood at its centre. In his left hand was the water skin he'd brought, his right was on the stopper. With every ounce of will he possessed, Shade tried to stop from pouring the water. But even as the only thoughts in his head were how and why he shouldn't pour the water, that's what his eyes saw him do.

As the water loosened the blood from the cloth, he saw the Mask twitch. Its tendrils that were meant to look like hair curled in and flexed back out as if it were breathing; even the cloth floated up and down slightly as if breaths were being taken beneath it. And then, suddenly, the cloth was gone; the Mask had swallowed it! Now the Mask was in his hands, inching ever closer.

Shade fell back as the Mask of Babomorah snapped closed around his face.

※

Nikki woke to find that she wasn't in Shade's arms as she had hoped. The sun was high in the sky and he still hadn't returned. What kind of meeting was this? Usually his private meetings only took an hour or two at the most. Figuring he might have gone for something to eat, she pulled herself out of bed and got dressed before heading to the kitchens.

But when she got there, she couldn't see him at all. Glancing around, she saw Alix and made her way over to him. He was standing at a large cooking pot over a fire, stirring its contents. Giving him a tap on the shoulder, Nikki gave a small laugh as she saw him jump.

"Oh, your highness, it's just you," he said turning to her with a hand over his heart. "What can I do for you this fine afternoon, my queen?" The head chef's thin moustache and hair had turned from black to grey, and were now showing signs of its soon turning white. He'd also gotten stiff in his old age, no longer able to flutter around the kitchen at will. It was something that made everyone very sad, seeing this staple of the castle and friend slowly lose his ability to do the thing that made him the happiest.

"You can tell me if my brother has been down here recently."

"The king? No, I haven't seen him today. Is everything alright, your highness? Pardonnez-moi, but you seem stressed - more so than usual."

"I just had a long night is all; Jazabel and I had a fight. It's nothing to worry about, just a disagreement. And there's no forgiving needed, Alix; you can always speak your mind to me and Shade," Nikki said as she laid a hand on the chef's shoulder.

"If that is the case, then sit down, young lady, and have something to eat. Worrying is only worsened by an empty stomach," he said as he ushered her over to the small table that she'd had more meals at than she could count. Alix's lightheartedness made her smile and relax. Once she was seated, he returned to the cooking pot and filled a bowl with its contents. "It's chicken and vegetable soup," he said as he placed the bowl in front of her and produced a spoon from one of his apron's many pockets. "It's hot, so blow on it. And I don't want to see you worrying until you've finished the bowl," he added with a wink.

Nikki just smiled as she nodded and proceeded to eat the soup. Alix had been right: eating had made her less anxious about where Shade was, as well as other things. As she slowly ate, she thought of the upcoming war; this only served to renew her worry. Finding that her bowl was now empty, she got up to get herself another bowlful. This serving she ate more quickly as she wanted to go and talk with Jazabel and apologize for her behaviour the night before.

Five minutes later, Nikki was walking to the room she'd grown up in. She still found it hard to believe that it was now Jazabel's and Brudas' room. She knew she would never say it out loud, but Nikki secretly wanted them to leave the room when she and Shade started their family so that her children could grow in the same room as she had.

Nikki was just about to knock on their door when she heard moaning coming from the inside. Slightly embarrassed, Nikki backed away as quietly as she could so as not to disturb her friends. Running to her new room and scribbling a small note, she returned to her friend's door. She was about to slip the note under the door as it was opened to reveal a flushed and extremely content Jazabel - a look Nikki knew well.

But upon seeing Nikki kneeling on the floor, Jazabel paled. She was about to return to her room when Nikki stood and caught her hand. Turning back to her, Nikki saw the brave face Jazabel was putting on. Trying to give a sincere smile, Nikki asked, "Can we talk?"

Closing her door, Jazabel simply nodded. "Sure. Why don't we got to my office; I need to check a few things anyway." Nikki nodded to her friend's suggestion and they walked in an awkward silence to Jazabel's library office.

Once they were inside Jazabel's office, they both looked to each other and as one said, "I'm sorry-!" When they recovered from trying to talk at the same time, they pulled each other into a tight hug. When they let each other go, Jazabel led the way to the couch in the corner before saying, "You first."

"I'm sorry about last night. I shouldn't have acted like that. My shock at the whole thing greatly amplified my anger. That you not only stabbed me, but Shade as well, didn't help either. Add in the fact that I was trying to channel my inner darkness for nearly an hour before that, and you've got a recipe for an overreaction. I thought that I wouldn't be able to trust you ever again after last night, but Shade made me look at it in a different light. He made me see that last night was the ultimate test of trust, and that you passed it. I'm sorry I threatened to throw you in the dungeon on your wedding night. That was a little over the line." Nikki tried to send her sister the feelings of remorse and shame she was feeling about the previous night's events.

She guessed Jazabel felt her sincerity, as there were tears in her eyes. Nikki felt a wave of love and sadness roll off of Jazabel before she spoke. "I'm sorry for stabbing you and Shade; sorrier than you can know. And I'm sorry that I didn't trust you with the truth of everything that was to happen. But after what you just said about it only strengthening our bond, I'm glad I did it the way I did. As for threatening me, I would have spent the week in the stocks if it meant your anger was sated. And you had every reason to be angry with me. Sisters?" she asked hopefully.

"Always," Nikki said. They embraced again as they were able to move past this potentially damaging rift. And for the next hour the two talked of their husbands and how married life was treating them so far.

Nikki left Jazabel's office feeling a great weight had lifted from her shoulders. She wanted to find Shade so she could tell him how free she felt. She hadn't felt this free since the two of them had told Braria how they really felt about one another. But when she got to their chambers, he wasn't there.

Now Nikki was starting to get worried. He wouldn't just disappear without telling her about it. Every day since they were five years old - whenever they hadn't been training or doing some of their duties as royal heirs - Shade would spend in their room. She couldn't think of any place he'd be.

Writing a quick note to him just in case he came back while she was looking for him, she went to find her parents to see if they had seen him today. Arriving at her parents' new chambers, she knocked on the door. When after a second there was no answer, she knocked again, harder and longer this time.

This time, her mother answered the door, with a slightly annoyed expression. But when she saw it was her daughter, a smile lit up her face. "Sweetheart, what's wrong?" she asked upon seeing her daughter's shifting eyes.

"Have you or Dad seen Shade today? He left early this morning for some meeting but hasn't returned. He said it would only take a couple of hours at the most, but it's been nearly all day!" Nikki rushed to get everything out at once, as her fear grew and panic took hold of her mind.

"OK, OK, Nikki, it's alright. Your father and I have been in all day and he hasn't stopped by," her mother said just as her father came into view.

"What's going on?" he asked when he saw Nikki's worried expression.

"Shade's missing," she said before her mother could explain more calmly.

"How long since you last saw him?" her father asked.

"A little after dawn; he said he had a meeting in a bit and that he'd be back shortly. I can't even feel him and that only happened when he went on his Reckoning and...NO! He can't be, I'd know if he was, I'd feel it," she rambled to herself as she paced slightly.

"What is it, Nikki?" her mother asked. But before Nikki could answer, the image of her brother, her world, lying dead in some back street with a shadowy figure standing above him stopped her pulse and pacing. And before her parents knew what was happening, she fell forward as she fainted.

※

Shade sat alone in the dark with his arms wrapped around his knees as he rocked back and forth. How could he have used the Mask? How could he have committed such an immoral act willingly? And the things he saw; he'd never be able to forget them for as long as he lived.

Suddenly he heard a noise towards the entrance of the cave and then there was a blinding light. "Shade? What are you doing here?" It was his father. Shade couldn't look at him, he was so ashamed of himself. His father seemed to surmise what had happened, or he saw that the Mask was still out where Shade had thrown it after ripping it from his face. "You used the Mask. What did you see?" His father's tone wasn't judgemental; it was only curious.

"Things I never wanted to see," he said in a hollow voice. "I couldn't help it Dad, I swear I tried to stop myself a dozen times! It was like my body wouldn't listen to what I was telling it to do. I couldn't do anything but sit back and watch as I fed the Mask the virginal blood, and then as I drew it to my face." He still wouldn't look at his father as he confessed his weakness.

"It's ok, Shade; this is on me," his father said as he crouched down in front of his son. "I should have never told you of this accursed thing; I should have destroyed it like you said. You are not weak, Shade! And this doesn't take away any of your humanity." The way he said it almost made Shade believe him, but he knew differently. His father hadn't seen what he had.

Shaking his head, Shade looked his father in the eye. "No, you didn't see; so much chaos and pain, unbearable pain." His voice was still dead and hollow.

"Tell me, son. Let me help you understand." His voice was so gentle and compelling, Shade couldn't resist.

"First, he was with a woman, but she kept changing. I think he was thinking of another woman," Shade said after a few deep breaths to calm and steel himself. "But when they had finished, his thoughts were full of hatred so strong that it has consumed his every thought a thousand times over. And it's all directed at me and Nikki. He sees nothing but us lying on the ground dead as the other cries over the remains. For nearly two hours that Mask was on my face, and for three quarters of that time, that's all there was: my and Nikki's deaths. Not a single other thought entered his head, our deaths are everything to him. What did we do to incur such a wrath? We've never hurt anyone." For the first time in a long time, Shade was afraid for what was to come. "I'm scared, Dad; if he feels like that, how can I beat him?"

Taking Shade's hand into his own, his father waited until his son was looking him in the eye. "I don't know, but I know you'll find a way." Pulling Shade up with him, his father nodded back towards the cave's entrance. "Come on, Nikki's worried about you; so worried that she fainted after asking your mother and I if we'd seen you today. Don't you know that your wife hates it when you leave her side even for a minute?"

"Nikki fainted?! Is she alright?!" The emotion was back in Shade's voice as he asked about his sister.

His father nodded as he held Shade back for a minute. "She's fine, or she will be when she sees you're alright. Open yourself to her; let her know you're ok and that you'll see her in your room in fifteen minutes."

But Shade didn't do that. He just gave his father a quick hug and ran back to the castle in search of his world.

※

As Shade crashed through the door to his chambers, he saw Nikki turn to the loud sound. Her face was scared, but when she saw it was him there was only relief. With tears in her eyes, she ran to him and pulled him in tight, as he did to her. *Where have you been? I've been worried sick!*

I know, Dad told me. And I'm so sorry. I wasn't prepared for my meeting.

Don't lie to me! There was no meeting; what were

you doing?

Something I shouldn't have even considered doing. The fact that I did completely disgusts me.

What? Please Shade, tell me.

You don't want to kno-

YES. I. DO! I can handle it.

I never said you couldn't.

Shade! Please, just tell me.

Fine, but you're not going to like it. Do you remember the heirloom Dad gave me that I wasn't supposed to tell you or anyone about?

Yes...

It was the Mask of Babomorah; apparently we descend from the Vigmece clan.

"What?!" The shock on Nikki's face was nothing from the amount Shade felt in her. "You used the Mask of Babomorah?!" Her revulsion and horror was a complete mirror of his own.

"I swear on your love for me, I tried to stop myself. But I didn't have control of myself. It was like something or someone was controlling me. That's where I've been, trying to find a way to live with the knowledge that I had used that infernal thing. But the things I saw, they were so horrible. I saw into the mind of the Beast and all he thinks of is seeing us in pain as one of us lies dead in the other's arms. He's constantly thinking of ways to kill us that will cause the other the most pain. He hates us with a stronger passion than our love. He wants us to suffer the most agonizing of pains, to suffer as he has." Shade started to cry as he revealed this all to his sister. How could he burden her with this knowledge?

"Shade," she said in her gentlest voice, turning his face so their eyes were locked. "It's ok, my love. I'm scared too, but we can't let our fear haunt us. We need to find the courage to look this Beast in the eye and deny him what he craves most. We are strong, brother; and we have been preparing for this all our lives. We are each other's greatest strength and weakness; I need you to be strong for me so I can be strong for you. We now know something about him we didn't before. And we will use that." She kissed him as she finished and their love threatened to overcome them, but Nikki stopped to ensure that didn't happen. "It's late and we could both use some food. Let's go have some dinner, ok?"

Wiping his face clear of tears, Shade nodded and said, "That sounds like a wonderful idea. But when are your ideas not wonderful?" Nikki just smiled at this as she led the way down to the kitchens.

Chapter 58:

Lilith's Out Spurned

Nikki and Shade had just finished inviting both their parents, Jazabel, and Brudas for dinner when they walked into the throne room to wait for them. But when they got there, something wasn't right. Someone was sitting in Nikki's throne. And if there was one thing that really got under Nikki's skin, it was when people thought that they could just take her stuff for themselves. "Get off of my throne," she snarled at the woman.

Turning to see who was commanding her in such a fashion, the woman looked at them and smiled. Her skin was so pale that it was hard to tell her lips apart from her teeth. Her hair and eyes were the richest brown Nikki had ever seen. She wore a thin, white dress that blew lightly in a non-existent wind, with a light, baby blue cloak. The hood of the cloak was as white as her dress and pulled up loosely over her braided hair. But the smile she gave the twins wasn't as wispy as her appearance; on the contrary, it was quite unsettling.

Nikki knew who this was.

But Shade, apparently, didn't. "Who are you to think you can simply steal into this castle and sit in the queen's throne? And then you have the nerve to just smile that unsettling smile at us. You'll not be told again: get out of my sister's throne!"

The woman stood and turned to brush the seat of the throne as if she'd left dirt on it. And once her back was to them, she finally spoke. "Nikki, my dear, will you please tell your brother who I am to do such a thing." It wasn't a request, but an order. Her voice was very deep for her small frame.

Shade looked to her in search of an explanation. "We've met Hados and Korena; now Shade, I introduce you to Lilith, goddess of the land above," Nikki said in a meek voice.

The anger and confusion in Shade's eyes disappeared immediately upon hearing whom he was being so blunt with. Falling to a knee, Shade's voice also took on a meek quality. "Forgive me, great goddess; I didn't realize it was you I was speaking to."

Turning back to them, Nikki saw her smile the most satisfied smile she'd ever seen. "Yes, that much was clear, child. But there is no need to try and flatter me. I've already decided to help you." Both Nikki and Shade looked up at this. She motioned for Shade to rise as she walked from the dais to them at the bottom of the stairs to the platform. "Don't look so surprised. I've come to tell you that which you've always wanted to hear: you do not need to fight this war."

Nikki was too shocked to speak. She'd always had a small part of her that had wanted to hear those words. She knew her brother had fostered the same small sliver of hope also.

"If we don't have to fight, as you claim, why are you only telling us this now? You've had twenty-one years to tell us. Why should we take your word just like that when we know you are capable of great deception, and we've had numerous prophecies given to us that say we do?" Shade asked in a cautiously reserved but hostile voice that mirrored Nikki's own feelings.

"May I remind you that that 'great deception', as you call it, not to mention more recent things I've done, have led to the birth of you and your most beloved sister," Lilith responded in an angry tone, all traces of a smile gone. "There is nothing in this world that happens without my say; I am omnipresent. As for your questions, I've been busy the last hundred years making plans for the future and have only now had time to deal with pressing matters of the present."

Before Shade's comments got them into further trouble, Nikki spoke to Lilith in a less hostile tone. "Tell us, Lady Lilith, what is it you want?"

"Nothing the two of you could ever give. But that is beside the point of my visit. I'm here to try and tell you that if you stop preparing for this unknown war, it will not come. If you want your loved ones to live, you'll stop preparing for some unknown future war."

"We want to believe you, Lilith, but Hados and Kore-" Nikki started before Lilith cut her off.

"Hados and Korena have no right to interfere with this world! All they do is consume! They have their own world to keep control over. It's only a matter of time before Korena realizes that she is no longer cursed with her new body. And if Korena and Hados have a child, it will destroy this world. And that, I will not allow. She stole my daughter from me, twice, but she'll not take my world. You should have never sought to give Korena her body back. Your lack of thought to the consequences of your actions is why you are in the position you are in." Lilith had become livid at the mention of Hados and Korena; her eyes had darkened to the point that they were completely black and her voice had gotten even lower and more menacing.

As she watched their expressions, Lilith became more enraged. "I see that that whore and her bastard of a husband have gotten to you. Or maybe it's your humanity, that lust to show dominance by killing your presumed enemies. But whatever it is, know this to be true: your disregard for my gift of peace has been noted. Your war will come. The Beast, as you call him, has waited a very long time for this moment. Prepare yourselves, your highnesses, for my son comes now." And with a burst of light like the sun, she was gone.

As they recovered from the brightness, Nikki looked to her brother, as she tried to figure out what had just happened.

Shade couldn't comprehend what had just happened. Had he really just fulfilled the last part of the prophecy that Slac Hino had given him? *See tables turned at an out spurned*, that's what the prophecy had said. But he and Nikki hadn't said no to the apparent peace offering; they'd only questioned its sudden arrival. And the mention of Korena, a friend of their mother, had completely angered Lilith beyond reasoning. Not that she'd let them explain.

But before he or Nikki could say anything, their parents

walked into the throne room. Seeing the matching expressions of exasperation and worried confusion on their children's faces, they ran to them. "What's wrong?" their father asked.

"I think... we just invited our war to start," Shade said after a moment's pause.

"What?!" their parents asked in unison.

"Lilith, she was here," Nikki whispered. "She said she came to give us peace."

"Lilith? Lilith was here?" their mother asked in an awed whisper.

Nikki just nodded to her mother's question. "We turned down her offering," she said in a dead voice.

At this, both their parents got looks of confusion, then sadness, and finally back to confusion again. "How? Why?" asked their father.

"We don't know," they said in unison. "But somehow we did," Shade continued. Both he and Nikki were still unable to look at anything properly; the horror of what they had just inadvertently done was causing them to stare off into nothingness.

"OK, let's go eat. The two of you need it; you're paler than Jazabel," their father said, trying to lighten the mood. He put his arm around Nikki as his wife put hers around Shade, and the parents led their children to dinner.

As they were seated, Shade felt his consciousness leave his body. He stared out at the guilt his mind felt; not just about Lilith, but the Mask as well. He tried to fight it, but there was no point; he knew he'd caused this. It was entirely his fault. He'd been warned and had forgotten that warning until it was too late.

He tried to close himself off from everything; he didn't want to feel anything. He longed for an emptiness he'd once cursed. No sight, no sound, no thought. Just empty, alone in that void.

But before he could close his eyes, he saw one thing. Sitting across from him in her simple grey dress and looking more worried than he'd ever seen her, was Jazabel. He saw that she'd barely touched her food; she was too focused on him. And when he looked into her eyes, he saw that she recognized that he was seeing her. And for the first time that he could remember, he heard a voice in his head that wasn't Nikki. *Fight it! Fight the darkness that even I can't see with your light! Fight, Shade, I believe in you. And we need you.*

And suddenly, Shade found that the guilt was gone. His heart gave a surge and his senses became extremely sensitive to the point of pain. Doubling over, Shade felt the pain fade as quickly as it had come. "Shade?!" he heard Nikki shriek at his side.

Taking a moment to breathe before he answered his sister, Shade tried to collect himself. "I'm alright," he said after a few panted breaths. Turning to look at Nikki, he tried to smile. "Seriously, I'm just fine; just choked on my last bite."

Don't lie to me. You haven't taken a bite in five minutes. So what's wrong?

Nothing you need to worry about now, I'm fine. I'll tell you about it later, OK?

OK, just as long as you're alright.

I am. And to prove his point, Shade kissed her gently in her special spot, right behind her ear at the hinge of her jaw. He heard and felt her sigh at this as he sat back up. Looking over to Jazabel, he saw that she was smiling at him, though her eyes contained an eternity of sadness.

But before he could do anything to comfort her, he felt Nikki take his hand. Looking to her, she gave him a weak smile as she squeezed his hand lightly. He returned both the smile and hand squeeze before turning back to Jazabel. The sadness in her eyes had disappeared and only love shone in them now as she smiled at him.

Knowing Alix would be personally offended if he didn't finish at least one plateful of food, Shade took his fork in hand and started to eat in earnest.

Chapter 59:

Greater Regrets

Shade couldn't put his finger on it, though he knew he was dreaming. But this was different than any dream he'd ever had, for Nikki was nowhere to be found. He was in their chambers. He just knew something was off, but no matter how hard he tried, he couldn't figure out what. He walked over to the window opposite the bed and opened it to reveal the full moon.

Stepping out onto the small ledge outside the window, he looked up at the moon. It seemed bigger to him, like it was closer to him somehow. Looking out over Terang and the surrounding countryside, Shade felt calmer than he ever had before. He also experienced a great swell in how protective he felt about his homeland.

"I hope you're feeling better," a voice said behind him. Turning around, Shade saw Jazabel lying on his bed where Nikki was supposed to be. "Come to me, White Knight, for I don't have much time." The formality in her voice startled Shade.

It had been a long time since Shade had dreamed of

Jazabel, so long that he couldn't remember the last time it had happened. But despite his confusion, he went to her without hesitation. "I don't understand; why are you here?"

Jazabel simply smiled. "To explain myself. My being a Lady of the Night has caused you problems that you don't even know of yet, my love; but tonight it helped you. For through that magic and the nature of our relationship, I was able to siphon away the crippling guilt you felt tonight at dinner and take it within myself. I knew that the weight was too great for you, and so I sacrificed the last dredges of my heart to give you a fighting chance against the Beast that comes for you." Shade was about to protest this when Jazabel stood and put a hand to his mouth to silence him. Taking his hand, she led him out to the balcony, where she gazed up at the full moon. Still holding his hand and not looking at him, Jazabel continued, "I'm sorry, Shade. I never wanted to have your heart heavy because of me, for it pains me to see you so heartbroken. Please know that I had no choice." And without looking at him, Jazabel jumped over the ledge.

Shade made to reach for her, but it was too late. Rather than feeling saddened by her leaving, or confused by her words or presence, Shade felt oddly calm. And then he felt it again, the wrongness of the dream. As this uneasy feeling washed over him, he saw millions upon millions of bats take wing and block the light of the moon. And then, one by one, the bats fell to the ground. As each one fell, he could hear them scream his name in pain. Each scream pierced his heart as each bat had its own unique voice. As they fell, the light of the moon returned, and its light wasn't white, but blood red.

There were only three bats left now in the sky. As they flew ever closer to him, Shade could see that they were clearly injured. By the time they were circling his head, he thought he recognized them, and he wondered if bats could look familiar. "Help her!" they screeched as they fell to his feet, dead.

Shade knew then where he'd seen these bats.

Shade woke with a start, sitting up straight. Looking to his side, he saw Nikki was still asleep. Sliding himself out of bed, he rushed to the window from his dream. Throwing it open, he looked to the moon to find that it wasn't full, bigger than usual, or red. It looked the same as it had when he had gone to sleep a few hours ago. But he couldn't shake the feeling that his dream was a call for help.

Turning back to his bed, Shade knew he had to get some sleep. What Nikki had said the previous morning was right; he'd barely got any sleep since they were married. But just as he was climbing under the blanket, he heard a thud against the bedroom door.

Before he could move to see who it was, the door flew open and Jazabel stumbled into the room. Even in the little light from the window, Shade saw that she only wore her Lady of the Night attire, and that the leather had been cut in many places.

"Jazabel!" he cried as he ran to catch her before she fell. But she pushed him away and grabbed onto the chair at the desk to steady herself. "What happened?" he demanded in a voice that was higher than his own.

"The inevitable," she said, smiling through the discomfort she clearly felt. "I don't have much time, Shade, so please just listen. My leather has been torn; I'm dying."

Shade fell back onto the bed as he absorbed this piece of information. The force of his fall seemed to stir Nikki, as she groggily sought him out. And then, he knew she saw

Jazabel as he heard her gasp out and felt her sit up at once.

Jazabel just smiled another pained smile at seeing that Nikki was awake. "Before you ask who did this to me, let me explain. It was Brudas; he is the one who longs to kill you. And I've helped him. I've told him to torture you in ways you would have gladly taken before realizing what they were.

"You know that I can see the darkness in people, that I'm drawn to it like nothing else in this world. And from the moment I laid eyes on Brudas three years ago, I've known that he came here to destroy you. And even though I knew how wrong it was to not only help him, but keep his darkest of secrets, I couldn't help myself. You asked me yesterday what we said at my wedding; I said how I've known all along who Brudas was and how cruel it was for me to have never even hinted at the fact that I was keeping such a deadly secret.

"I've betrayed the two of you for nearly as long as we've lived under the same roof. It's slowly killed me to do this, but it's in my nature to serve the Dark. Now my servitude is over, and I can tell you everything. But be careful, he's the son of Lilith and she will do nearly anything to help him win. He seeks to kill one of you while the other is left to live with the agony of that loss. He feels nothing but hatred for the two of you, a hatred that has grown for the last six thousand years. Nothing will get in his way as he takes revenge for his Anilla, the Soul Twin who was raped and murdered right in front of him."

"Soul Twin?" both he and Nikki asked. Did they really have to fight one of their own?

"Yes, he's a Soul Twin; driven insane a thousand times over with the loss of his Twin. For whatever reason, he's chosen the two of you as the ones responsible for her death and will stop at nothing until you feel his pain.

"I never wanted to have to do this to you; I love you both more than I can say. I know that my actions and words greatly contradict each other. I have no right to ask after what I've done, but I want to die in your arms, Shade." As she said this, she let go of the chair she was leaning against and started to stumble towards them on the bed.

Shade knew he had every right to deny her, and that he should, but he just couldn't. He stood up and caught her in his arms as she fell into them. Looking into her eyes, Shade could see the same sadness he'd seen at dinner. She'd known this day would come for a long time and had still embraced it openly; she was far braver than he could ever be. "I'm sorry that I can't help you, Jazabel. I knew that you were in trouble and I did nothing to help you."

"You heard them? My babies, you heard them cry out for you to help me?" she asked in a shocked tone. Shade just nodded as his tears fell from his face onto hers. "Take care of them; they need a gentle hand to raise them."

Again Shade could only nod. "I forgive you," he whispered in a choked voice.

Smiling as she brought a hand up to stroke his cheek, Jazabel nodded. "I know. I love you," she said as she pulled his head to hers, allowing their lips to meet.

Shade held her so tight to himself that he felt her go limp in his hands as he inhaled her last breath. Releasing her ever so slightly, he saw her eyes were closed. "No! Jazabel, no! Please, come back; I need you!" he shouted at her lifeless body.

He felt Nikki kneel behind him. She wrapped him in her

arms as they cried over the death of their friend. Though Jazabel had betrayed them, she was still family. But for Shade, she was more. She was his *deaur sange*, and now he would never see her again in this world.

As Nikki held her brother who cried out his heart, she saw a shift in the shadows. They'd formed in the middle of the moonlit floor with no apparent source until she saw the body rise from them. The form was tall, looking like he'd just escaped the underworld, and with black eyes and hair that was slicked back tight to his skull. Nikki knew that when he spoke it would be with a slow, deep voice. She watched with anger in her eyes as Hados approached her and her brother.

Letting go of Shade, Nikki glared at the Lord of the Underworld and stood up straight. "Bring her back. You bring her back right now!" she demanded of him in her most authoritative voice. This caused her brother to finally look away from Jazabel's body to see who she was commanding.

But Hados only looked at her with a blank face. "Do you not think that if I could bring the dead back to life, I would've done it a long time ago? I'm so sorry, sweet queen, but I can't bring her back." His voice, however, was quite pained.

"You're also not supposed to be able to be here only twenty-one years after your last visit. So if you can break Lilith's curse, you should be able to bring her back. Give him Jazabel back!" Nikki demanded as tears stung her eyes.

"That is beside the point; the two are not related in terms, you understand. And why would you want a traitor, one who will continue to do so for him, to come back anyway?" The curiosity in his voice was impossible to miss; he really didn't know why she would demand such a thing so strongly.

"Because Shade loves her, and so do I. She is our best friend and is as important to us as each other." She saw Shade look to her with a look of deep gratitude as she said this. "Now, I won't tell you again; bring back Jazabel to us. NOW!"

Despite the fierceness and rage in her voice, Hados didn't flinch at Nikki's order. He simply knelt down to Shade and put a hand on his shoulder. Looking him in the eye, he said, "Believe me, young one, when I say that if I could I would in a heartbeat. But that is something that I cannot do.

"That's not why I'm here. As I'm sure you've guessed, your war has just begun. There is one piece of good news: it will not last long. And the only prophecy that matters now is this," he said, as their prophecy book appeared in his hand. "*A secret kept to keep love safe, will a house divide. Return to find a forgotten tale play before you that victory demands you abide. Tell truth and see differences set aside.*"

"I'm sorry about Jazabel; she really was unique. I'll watch over her spirit and she will be hailed as the queen among women that she was." And before either Shade or Nikki could say anything, Hados had melted into the shadows.

Nikki ran to the spot where he had disappeared in some vain attempt to see if he was still there. When she realized that he wasn't, she cried out in anger. "HADOS! You said anything was to be ours; we need only ask! We've never asked for anything, ever! Answer me!" she raged, but there was no answer.

"Nikki," Shade said in a dead voice, making her turn to him. "Forget it, it can't be done."

"Shade...?"

"Thank you for understanding, sister. I need you to be calm right now, so that I can be as well. Jazabel would not want us to go out into the night and chase Brudas; she'd want us to outsmart him at his own plan for vengeance! And that is exactly what we are going to do. Before we do, we need to tell Mom and Dad what's happened," he said in a voice that was closer to his own. Nikki knew the pain he felt would never truly go away.

But she also knew that what he said was true, so she took a calm breath before nodding. Giving him her hand to help him off the floor, she gave one last look to Jazabel before she led her brother to their parents' chambers.

Shade's heart felt empty as he and Nikki walked to their parents' chambers in the middle of the night. He could barely move his feet, as his whole body was consumed by the utter heartache he felt. Nikki had her arms around his shoulders from the moment they'd left their room, allowing him to set the pace of their march.

But despite the slow pace at which he walked, Shade soon found himself at his parents' door. Taking a deep breath to try and prepare himself for what he now had to do, Shade raised his hand to knock. Before he did, he turned to his sister. *Will you promise me something?*

Anything, anything at all.

Can we not tell them about how she helped Brudas? I don't want her to be remembered as a traitor, but as the sister she was to us.

In lieu of a response, she sent him her feelings of sadness at having Jazabel dead because of them. She then nodded before giving him a brief kiss. "Thank you," Shade answered before knocking on his parents' door. He waited about thirty seconds before knocking again, figuring they were asleep.

Before he could knock a third time, the door opened to reveal their mother wiping the sleep from her eyes. When she saw the looks on their faces, she started to silently cry as she opened her arms for them to seek her comfort. Shade went to her immediately with Nikki not far behind. As the three of them cried, their mother led them inside. Their father shut the door and lit a few candles to illuminate the room.

As one, the four sat themselves on the bed. His mother held Shade while Nikki was being held by their father. "Who?" their father asked. The simple question made it seem like he knew why his children had come to him and their mother in the middle of the night.

Nikki turned to him, silently allowing him to tell the events the way he wanted them told. "Jazabel," he said to the gasps of his parents. His mother held him tighter as he gave a sob. "And if that isn't awful enough, it was Brudas who killed her. Brudas is the Beast that seeks to destroy us; he's a Soul Twin and the son of Lilith." Shade felt his mother stiffen as this was revealed and his father gave him an intense look.

"That's horrible. How did we not see this; how did Jazabel not see it? I thought she could see the darkness in people.

Isn't that what she said a Lady of the Night could do?" their mother asked.

"She said that she thought Brudas was lighter than he was; he fooled her somehow," Nikki said. Shade noticed her eyes were closed so that they wouldn't betray the lie she'd just told for him. "As for how we didn't see it, we were so bewitched by his sword technique and trusted in Jazabel's opinion of him that it never entered our thoughts that he would betray us. We thought he was our friend, and the love of Jazabel's life. You never suspect those closest to you." Everyone nodded as she said this.

Shade noticed his father shift away from Nikki as he stood up and walked to a wardrobe behind the desk at the other end of the room. Everyone watched as he opened it, keeping his back to them. Shade wondered what he was doing, until he turned around with two glass goblets in his hands and another two floating behind him. Walking back to the bed, he handed the two in his hands to his children, before handing one from the air to his wife. "It's whisky," he explained to everyone. "I haven't had any of this since your mother was taken by Korena, and before that when my mother died. It's a small ritual I've developed for myself whenever sadness has so overcome me that I can't do anything but feel its burn.

"I know how much Jazabel meant to you two. And to be honest, I'd come to think of her as an adopted daughter. She will be missed more than I can put into adequate words. To Jazabel, our family's Lady of the Night!" he said with pride as he raised a glass.

"She was a queen among women," Nikki said, raising her own glass.

"She had a strong heart, which allowed her to be braver than most," his mother said.

After a moment's pause, they all looked to Shade; the wonder of why he wasn't saying anything on their faces. But what could he say? Everything that came to his mind seemed unfitting and unrepresentative of how he felt. Finally, he settled on just telling the truth. "She was Jazabel, and that was enough for me, the one who loved her like nobody else could." Shade raised his goblet and swallowed its contents without as much as a shake.

Everyone followed his lead in drinking their whisky, with his mother and sister making sour faces. He looked to his mother and saw the sadness in her eyes - sadness for him, as well as for Jazabel, but it was mostly for him. She took his hand, giving it a long, light squeeze. "We'll announce her death in the morning and allow for her friends and any who will mourn her to come. She will be honoured, by all of Braria. But for now, you need to try and sleep. It won't help much, but you're going to need as much sleep as you can get these next few weeks." The way she never took her saddened eyes off him made Shade feel that she was only speaking to him.

But then she turned to Nikki, while still holding his hand. "You do anything he wants or needs you to do. This will be extremely hard for him to get over and anything you do to help will go a long way." Nikki just nodded at her mother's instructions on how to take care of Shade. "Ok then, back to bed."

The twins rose and gave their parents one last hug as they made their way back to their room. But before Shade left, he walked over to the wardrobe and took the whisky.

Once they were back in their room, Shade knelt down beside Jazabel's corpse. In a flash, Nikki was at his side as they looked down at the woman they'd loved so much. Shade opened the bottle of whisky and took a long sip from it, before offering to Nikki. When she declined, he took an even longer sip.

He was about to take his third, when Nikki took the bottle from him. "Go easy on this stuff, Shade. You said that Jazabel would want us to outsmart Brudas at his own plan. Well, to do that, you can't be drunk on liquor or sadness. Don't dishonour her by becoming undisciplined now."

Setting the bottle down behind him, Shade nodded sadly. "Thanks for the reminder. I wouldn't be able to get through this without you. You're my everything and I don't know what I'd do if I lost you again, for real this time. If I knew that you would agree, I'd tell you not to go up against Brudas; that you should leave him to me." Nikki was already shaking her head as he uttered this last sentence.

"No. I'll do no such thing. We will take him together; that way he has to kill both of us if he wants to get out alive. We trusted him with the life of the one we loved most, and he killed her just to make us mad. Well, he failed; for I am not mad, I'm furious. And I can feel the hatred that is rolling off of you, my love. The time for being nice is over, Shade; Brudas has made it clear that he will not show us mercy, nor will we show him any. Jazabel never was one for a fair fight." The passion with which she spoke made Shade smile despite himself.

"And that is why I love you," he said. "You give me strength when I need it most and motivate me to do the right thing, even if it's a very wrong thing. Thank you, Nikki, for being everything I need you to be." She gave him a smile as he came back to his regular self. "Now, I have something to do with Jazabel that I need to be alone for."

Without looking to Nikki, he picked up Jazabel's body and walked out the door. While teaching him the wedding rites, she'd told him of a funeral rite that he could perform on the night of her death. And that was what he now was going to do. *Be careful* he heard Nikki think to him as he left the room to go to the caves.

Since he'd last looked at the moon an hour before, the night had become cloudy. Despite the clouds, Shade was still able to make his way to the caves. As he made his way into the clearing just outside the caves, the moon peaked out from the clouds and allowed Shade to see the scorched and ripped earth where the Star of Death had been two nights previous. And it was in the centre that he laid down Jazabel's body.

"I didn't think that I'd have to do this so soon. And I'm so sorry for dragging you into my conflict, Jazabel; you didn't deserve to die. But I promise you, either you will be avenged or we will see each other sooner than we should hope for," he vowed as he cupped her cold face in his hand.

Standing up, he looked down at her as he whispered, "I hope I'm doing this right." Then he looked to the sky, throwing his hands up. "*Oh dark Night, let loose your tears. For your faithful servant, Lady Jazabel Nyx, has died this night. On leather wings carry her spirit to the darkest of resting places. Oh cruel Night, take her to her fallen sisters, your servants.*"

Lowering his hands, Shade drew the dagger at his back: the dagger that had drawn the Star of Death he now stood in. Holding it to his forehead, he closed his eyes as he shoved every negative feeling over Jazabel's death into the blade. All his sadness, guilt, and anger flowed into the dagger, making it grow unnaturally cold in his hands. And once the cold was too much for him to bear, he opened his eyes and whispered, "*Dark spirits I call you forth. Accept your sister with open arms and send the dark fire to my blade. Let it consume all my pain at Lady Nyx's death. Let it also carry Lady Nyx's power to she who is most deserving of it.*"

Holding the dagger before his face, Shade didn't even flinch as its blade was enveloped in the same black fire that had outlined the Star of Death two nights previous. The blade did not heat up, even though it started to glow orange, then blackish purple, and finally so black it was as if it was absorbing the little light in the clearing. Kneeling back down beside Jazabel's body, Shade raised the dagger above his head. "*With this blade, I steal your power so that your successor may better serve the Night than you did.*" And he plunged the blade into the centre of the bat whose wings had concealed Jazabel's breasts.

Where he had stabbed her was a jewel. As he stabbed her, the jewel shattered. And once it had shattered, the leather and mesh that had for so long been fused to Jazabel's skin came loose and drew itself into the black flames of his dagger. Removing the dagger, Shade noticed that he hadn't left a mark on her skin; it was still flawless as ever.

But Shade knew the ritual was not over, for the blade of the dagger was still engulfed in the nightfire flames. Standing back up, Shade called out, *"Pandora, Bruce, and Adriana, come bid farewell to your mistress, and drink of her power."* No sooner had Shade finished calling for them, he heard the flutter of bat wings as Jazabel's most loyal companions - the three from his dream that had blessed her marriage to Brudas - descended to say goodbye to their loving mistress. Each bat took its turn to land on Jazabel's chest before licking and nudging her cheeks. As the last one finished, the three started to circle Shade's raised hand and the dagger he held before scooping up the nightfire with their wings. Shade was surprised to see that they were not burned as they seemed to be eating the flames.

Once they were finished and his dagger was no longer consumed by nightfire, Shade figured that the ritual was over. Looking up from his knees beside the naked body of his dead *deaur sange*, he saw the three bats were still circling his head. Their presence made him feel like he had to explain. "I heard you in my dream, but I didn't understand until it was too late. I appreciate your trusting me enough to try and warn me about what was happening to her. I'm sorrier than I can say that I wasn't able to help her. I guess you know that. I don't know how close she was with other Ladies of the Night, but could I request that the three of you send word to them and let them know that Terang will be holding a funeral service for Jazabel in a few days? If they wish to pay their respects, they are welcome and will be protected for their stay."

Shade didn't expect to get an answer from them, but when one, the medium sized one that had sliver-grey fur, flew down and licked the tears off his cheek lightly, he took it to mean they would. "Thank you. I'll see you soon," he said with a smile as the three bats rose in the air before taking off in opposite directions. Picking up Jazabel's body, Shade left the clearing for his room for the second time in the past eight hours.

Chapter 60:

Queen Eva Amaranth

Three days later, Shade stood upon the raised dais in the throne room looking out to a sea of black. Behind him, the thrones had been removed and only a small, rectangular marble table was in their place. On the table was Jazabel's body, now wearing her grey dress from the day she was killed and a black rose in her folded hands.

As Shade looked out at the gathered masses that had come to honour Jazabel, he searched constantly for Brudas. He didn't expect Brudas to come to Jazabel's funeral, but Shade was by no means an expert on Brudas' tactics. With a brief look back at Jazabel's shrouded face, Shade turned back to address the crowd. "Thank you everyone for coming to this most tragic of events. Your support is greatly appreciated.

"To those who knew her, Jazabel was kind, loving, and generous with anything she could give you. For those who didn't know her, she was a quiet, beautiful woman who worked as an archivist here at the castle. I'd like to think that she was a friend to everyone. As for me, I was closer to Jazabel than nearly anyone.

"I first met Jazabel when I was four years old, on the first Reunion Day. It was only for a few hours, but I never forgot her, nor she me. And then eighteen years later, fate intervened and had us meet again. It was then that she came to live here in Terang and we all grew to love her.

"Jazabel was my best friend and one of my closest confidants and I loved her nearly as much as I love my sister. And it is my fault she is dead." As Shade revealed this the crowd gave a collective gasp. "She was killed to deliver a blow to my heart by a most insidious enemy. And what a blow it was. For the rest of my life, I will miss Jazabel and wish we had more time together. Forevermore there will always be an empty spot in my heart where this unique woman once lived." Turning back to Jazabel's body, Shade walked to her.

Bending down, he kissed her forehead. "Goodbye, Jazabel. I'll always love you," he whispered. Turning back to the gathered mass, he said, "I'd like to invite everyone to come up and say your final goodbyes, one at a time, starting with Queen Nikki. While you wait, please console each other; for grief is that much harder when you grieve alone."

As Nikki made her way to Jazabel's body, everyone else got into small groups and tried to give support to each other. Shade waited for Nikki to reach him before he let loose his tears and they held each other close. "When you came back to Terang, the first thing I told you was that I'd kill you if you ever hurt Shade. I never thought that this was how you'd hurt him, or that it would hurt me so much, sister. It's not only Shade's heart that will be empty with you gone, mine will be too. I miss you so much - laughing with you, crying with you, talking with you. I never realized how much time we spent together, and now I don't know what to do with all that time. I'm so sorry that it was you who had to die. I love you, Jazabel; my friend, my sister," Nikki whispered as she leaned down and kissed Jazabel's chest, right where her heart would be.

And then Nikki was crying, like Shade had never seen her cry before. Pulling her to him, he held her tight as he rubbed her back. He had no other way to help her feel better, for he felt the same way as she: lost and heartbroken. But Shade knew that they needed to leave Jazabel's side.

As they walked away from the dais, Shade led them to a corner of the room. while the people started to go and pay their respects. For a long while they just held each other and silently cried. But soon Shade saw their mother make her way to them. "Nikki," she said when she got to them, "why don't you go tell your father that his real daughter is still here. I think he could really use your help in overcoming this right now."

"Sure Mom," she said with a sniffle and final squeeze to Shade.

When she was gone, his mother pulled Shade into her arms. "I'm so sorry, sweetheart. I know how much you loved Jazabel, and how good you think you need to be to her. But she betrayed you to Brudas."

Shade pulled away from his mother as she said this; he and Nikki were the only ones who knew of the betrayal. "No she didn't; she loved him and he killed her for loving me! She would never betray me."

"You can't lie to me. I know you may not want to hear it, but she did. And I know you don't want people to know that, but you can't deny it didn't happen. Tragedy found her here by bringing to her the one person she would do anything for and made her love him and then had her do things for him to the ones she cared the most about, things she would never do to them but for his love. Life indeed interfered cruelly to you and your *deaur sange*. I won't say anything to anyone, if that is your wish, but you should at least tell your father."

"Fine, you can tell him; I'll not add insult to injury by spitting on her grave for something she couldn't help. I cannot fault her for being who she was; I can only fault myself for not thinking things through earlier. I was just happy to see that she was happy. But right now I'm not worried about people thinking me to favour traitors more than them; I'm focused only on finding Brudas and making him pay for what he did to Jazabel, and what he intends to do to Nikki." Shade couldn't believe his mother was making him this angry, especially today. She should have left things as they were.

He stormed away from her and tried to find Nikki. But before he could reach her, his path was blocked by an older woman with long hair the colour of ashes wearing a black cloak that concealed her entire body from view. With a slight bow of her head, she whispered softly, "Forgive me, your highness, but I believe we need to talk. Lady Nyx left you in possession of some things that were not hers to bequeath." The woman's voice was quite smooth and carried great authority. And the fact that she had referred to Jazabel as Lady Nyx told Shade that his invitation to the Ladies of the Night had been received.

"Yes, I guess we do, Dark Lady." His voice was his official voice and his posture became rigid as soon as he gave her a slight bow. "If you'll allow me to get my sister, the three of us shall talk outside. There's a balcony at the top of the stairs; you may wait for us there and we shall be there in a few moments," Shade said, pointing to the staircase behind the dais. Nodding her head, the woman left him to retrieve Nikki while she made her way to the staircase.

When he got to Nikki she was hugging herself to their father as he stroked her back. "We have a guest waiting for us outside on the balcony. She's a friend of Jazabel's from out of town," Shade said to Nikki cryptically.

She turned right around at hearing him and understanding his thoughts. "I didn't think that any had come. What does she want?"

"To have some things returned to her, I think; but I'm not sure. I'd rather we didn't keep her waiting; I don't want her angry."

"Good idea; let's go." Turning to their father, Nikki said, "Thanks Dad; I'll see you later." And with a kiss to his cheek, she turned to her husband and they left for the balcony.

※

As Nikki made her way up the staircase that led up to the balcony with Shade, she became nervous. To meet one Lady of the Night was a rare occurrence; meeting a second was unheard of. She didn't know what to expect and that made her scared.

But when they reached the balcony and she saw the woman, Nikki had to hold back a laugh. The way the woman was wearing her black cloak so that only her long ashen hair and mouth were visible reminded Nikki so much of how Jazabel had first arrived in Terang. This reminder of Jazabel then quickly served to sadden Nikki.

Turning at the sound of their footsteps, the woman was able to keep herself concealed. Bowing her head slightly, she said, "Thank you for seeing me on such short notice, your majesties. I realize these are not the best circumstances for us to meet, but from what Lady Nyx told me, you are strong in the face of adversity. And from what I saw down there, she was right. Allow me to introduce myself: I am Eva Amaranth, queen of the Ladies of the Night." As she introduced herself, Queen Amaranth shook her head loose of the hood that concealed it. She looked to be about as old as Nikki's parents, as the lines of age were starting to scar her skin. But the most intriguing aspect of the woman's appearance was her eyes; they were a yellowish orange that reminded Nikki of a wolf's.

Upon hearing who they were talking to, both Shade and Nikki fell to a knee. As one they said, "It is a great honour to have you here in our city, Queen Amaranth. If we had known that you were coming, we'd have made better arrangements. Please forgive our lack of knowledge."

At their apology, she just laughed. "It's ok; I'm not some foreign dignitary that needs to be given the greatest of everything to not feel offended. Please stand; this is your home, not mine." And when they had stood up, she continued. "I'd first like to say that what you just did for Lady Nyx was very beautiful. Not once has a Lady of the Night been honoured and loved like Jazabel was here; it is an act that our society will not soon forget.

"Second, and I know this is most unpleasant, I need the

book that Jazabel brought back here. It is full of the secrets of our society and we do not wish to have them be more revealed than they already have been to the two of you. I am aware that while you know what to say, you don't understand it. But we can deal with all this later.

"Lastly, I carry a message to the two of you from Jazabel." The use of Jazabel's name caught Shade and Nikki off guard, as did the tear that fell from the queen's eyes at her mentioning it. "When she came to Pandora's tomb seven months ago, she told me of the two of you and how much she loved you. She also told me that the one she was to marry was your enemy, though you didn't know that yet. She said that her death was not soon far off, and that she would have to reveal her treachery. She wanted you to know that she tried to resist his orders to tell him your secrets for as long as she could, but that it was too much in the end. She said that for the few things that she told him, he told her things of himself. She said that his pain and anger are his driving forces, and that he never thinks anything fully through. He isn't too bright either, though he has seen everything in the way of battle strategies for the past six thousand years, so don't think that he'll be fooled by these tactics." Wiping away the tears that were coming freely, Queen Amaranth took a moment to compose herself before continuing. "Lady Nyx broke the most sacred of oaths of our kind to tell you these things; do not let that be for nothing," Queen Amaranth said fiercely.

But this completely shocked both Shade and Nikki. Jazabel had broken an oath to help them kill Brudas. Nikki wondered which betrayal had been harder for her; she hoped it was betraying her and Shade. "We won't," Nikki whispered.

"But if she broke an oath this sacred, why did you give her the book; why are you even telling us?" she asked.

"Because I, like you, loved Jazabel. I was the one who taught her everything about our culture; I've never seen anyone take to the language of Darkness so quickly. She was a natural at everything, and more powerful than me. But with that power came the draw to Darkness at a strength never felt before. The fact that she was able to resist at all is a credit to her strength and love for the two of you. The world is a darker place with her not in it," she said sadly. "Jazabel knew that what she was doing was wrong, and so to redeem herself in both our eyes, she betrayed both her Dark and White Knights." The look she gave Shade as she said 'White Knight', made Nikki feel like she was both happy and sad that Shade was one.

But then she turned to Nikki with a small smile. "And now, my dear, I must ask you to do something you won't like to do. I must ask that you go and get the book that Jazabel returned here with. I must speak with Jazabel's White Knight in private, if that is alright."

Nikki turned to Shade, searching his eyes for any resistance. *You sure you'll be ok?*

Yes, she won't harm me, not intentionally at least.

It's the unintentional I'm worried about.

I'll be fine. Go and get the book; it's on the shelf in her office. He leaned down to kiss her gently as she turned and left the two of them alone.

Shade watched as Nikki descended the stairs back inside before he turned back to Queen Amaranth and her lupine eyes. "So, what is so private that Jazabel felt the need to tell only me, and not my Soul's Twin? Or is it something that you want to tell me?" he asked as he leaned himself on the stone railing, looking to the new moon.

"It's nothing that I need to tell you, but something I must ask for: the blade with which you stabbed Lady Nyx to make her simply Jazabel once again. If it's not too much trouble," she said as she joined him at the railing.

From beneath his floor-length cape, Shade drew the dagger. The blade was very thin, thinner than most daggers, and had a serpentine pattern close to its polished onyx hilt. Twirling it in his hand, he said, "There's no trouble; but if it's alright with you, I'd like to keep it for a while longer. There is one thing that I must still do with it."

"And what is that?"

"Plunge its blade into the heart of the one who killed Jazabel. She was my *deaur sange* and I'll not let her murder be unavenged." Shade gave her a look that he hoped conveyed the seriousness of this remark.

Breathing a heavy sigh, Queen Amaranth leveled her sad eyes upon his. "Don't be too eager to blacken your heart, Shade Kanta. While he does deserve to die for what he's done and plans to do, you should not kill him in the name of vengeance - especially with that blade. That is the blade that Cadel Thymab used to kill her king with; it's a Dark object that should only be in the possession of those who understand its history. You'll forgive me when I say that you should have never touched that blade, that you could never understand it properly. You're too-"

"-Too pure of heart. Yes, so I've been told. But Jazabel gave this to me to help in her marriage to that Beast I once called friend. This dagger may be a Dark object, but it will perform one last dark act before I give it to you. You'll forgive me when I say that that's the end of it. Before Jazabel placed this dagger in my hand, she told me of what it had done; I'm well aware of why you want this dagger back, your highness. But if you loved Jazabel as you say, then you'd let me do this. I promise you that you'll get it back when I'm finished with it."

She just stood there as she judged him and his word. And with a heavy sigh, she said, "Very well. The bats that served Jazabel will watch over you, and when your task is complete, they will tell me. Then I shall come and will expect no hassle with my demands."

Before Shade could reply, he heard the sound of Nikki's footsteps on the stairs that led to the balcony. Turning to see her at the top, he saw the book in her hands. The *Codex Nocturna* Jazabel had called it, the laws and codes of the Ladies of the Night that governed their actions in every aspect of life. The book was so thick that Nikki needed both hands at its bottom to carry it. The covers and binding were leather, but according to Jazabel the pages within were the dried pieces of Cadel Thymab's skin. She also said that every indecipherable word on those pages of skin was written in the blood of Pandora herself. When Jazabel had first told him all this, Shade had nearly lost his stomach, but he was able to control himself in a feat of mental strength that had impressed both of them.

Shade went to his sister and took the book from her. Turning back to the queen of the Ladies of the Night, he held the book and bowed his head as he said, "Dark Queen Eva Amaranth, I return to you the *Codex Nocturna*. And in so doing, I hope to bridge our societies to a time when we can coexist, where everyone knows who we are."

"Maybe one day," she whispered as she took the book, allowing for both Shade and Nikki to see her for the first time. She wore the same leather and mesh as Jazabel once had, but where the mesh at Jazabel's breasts was shaped like a bat, hers was shaped like a leaping wolf.

"Perhaps if our bloodlines ever mix," she continued. "But I must be going; my Sisters will want to hear of this beautiful funeral and memorial. It just may inspire them to open up to others as Jazabel did. Goodbye your majesties, and good luck with your war." As she made her way to the stairs, she drew her cloak closed again, the bulk of the book unseen.

"Wait!" Nikki called to her. When she'd turned back to his sister, Shade saw a faint smile on her lips. "Please, Queen Amaranth, I beg a favour."

"And what would that be, your highness?" she asked with that smile growing on her lips.

"Jazabel always spoke fondly of the beauty of the Night, and, like my brother with Gothtor, I wish to see your homeland. If we survive, I'd very much like to see the home my sister always spoke so highly of. I'd make any oath of secrecy you want and hide everything, even from my brother. I'd come alone, if you so wished it. Just please, let me walk the halls of Pandora's tomb." Shade was completely stunned by this revelation; he didn't know she'd become so enamoured with Jazabel's life. But he knew the passion in both her eyes and voice, for he saw and heard it whenever they were together.

Queen Amaranth's smile, however, had faded as Nikki spoke. "If you survive this war you're in, I shall consider the possibility of letting you see within our walls. It is not something that I can decide on my own, for there are others who must allow it as well. I shall take your request to the others and tell them of the passion with which you begged me for this and the sacrifices you were willing to make. If you survive, I shall personally return to give you their answer."

Nikki just bowed her head. "Thank you," she said as she straightened. Turning to Shade, she said, "Everyone seems to have cleared out downstairs. And Mom and Dad want to talk to us when we're done here." The way she said it so lightly conveyed to Shade that she didn't know why they wanted to talk to them.

He just nodded. "If everyone's gone, would you like to say your final goodbye to Jazabel?" he asked Queen Amaranth.

With tear-filled eyes, she nodded. "I'd like that very much, thank you." And so Shade took Nikki's hand, drawing her into himself, and led the three of them back down into the throne room.

When they got there, Shade and Nikki let Eva go ahead alone so that she could have some privacy. But they didn't stop until they were within earshot of her, and as they listened to the chilling beauty of the language of Darkness, they held each other tight.

"*My darkest Jazabel, I'm sorry it had to end this way. You were the best and strongest of us and even you were overcome by the Darkness. But perhaps Lilith's son wasn't the best choice.*

"*You were like my daughter, Jazabel. You were so young when I found you trying to outrun the Night, here to Terang. I taught you everything that I know and as I watched you grow, there was only love in my heart for you. I shouldn't be at your funeral; you should be at mine. But this life is never fair, is it.*

"*I'm sorry I scolded you for always thinking of this place and of your White Knight. Both he and his sister are quite beautiful and you were right about his light; it does shine brighter than any I've seen. I'm sorry to say that your death at the hands of his enemy has seemed to darken it, but I'm sure that you figured it would.*

"*I hope you were happy with the way your final days played out, dear daughter. I'm happy that I got to see you again one last time. I've delivered your messages and even agreed to grant them liberties that I wouldn't usually give, if I didn't know they loved you so. They do love you, and miss you greatly. I can see why you so enjoyed living here, even with the constant threat of discovery.*

"*For that you will be remembered. You will be remembered for the courage to try and reintegrate yourself into society, and having people know who you really were. Your White Knight hopes for a day when we don't have to hide; perhaps there is hope for the world after all. We all know what you did, and we still applaud your sacrifice. You showed us that while we serve the Dark, we can still be Light; and that we can be loved for that. And that's something we will never forget.*

"*Goodbye Queen Nyx, for you are the rightful queen. I shall love and miss you fiercely.*" As she finished, Shade saw her kiss the wedding ring that he'd had made for Jazabel, as tears fell from her eyes.

Chapter 61:
Pregnant

As Nikki ate breakfast with her mother, she couldn't help but feel nervous. It seemed as though she was always nervous now. In the month that had passed since Jazabel's funeral, Shade had become obsessed to the point of recklessness with having Brudas captured. He had the entire army stretched thin as they searched every crack in Braria to find Brudas. He'd also called in many favours - even promised some new ones - to all surrounding countries in an attempt to have them help out in the search.

No report had ever come back with any sign of him.

As Nikki thought of all these things, she noticed her mother was trying to talk to her. "Hello? Have you listened to a word I've said since we sat down?" she was asking while waving a hand in front of Nikki's face.

"Wha-Sorry Mom; I was worrying about Shade."

"That's understandable. It doesn't take a Soul's Twin to realize that he's stressed about finding Brudas; I think the birds have even noticed." This made Nikki smile faintly, something that was becoming less frequent of late. "But what about you; how are you feeling, sweetheart?" her mother asked with concern etched in every wrinkle on her face.

"Worried; I'm worried about everything, but mostly Shade: he's become closed off to everything that isn't a scouting report, even me. He barely sleeps or eats; he's shocked to find me at his side after I've been there for an hour. Me - you know, the woman who is supposed to be his world! He's barely touched me since Jazabel's funeral. The hunt for Brudas has become everything to him." As Nikki explained her worries, tears started to fall from her eyes.

Seeing her cry, her mother moved seats so she was at Nikki's side and put her arms around her daughter, stroking her back. After crying for a minute, Nikki realized that her mother was humming Shade's lullaby to her. And at hearing the soothing rhythm of the melody, Nikki calmed down. Her mother couldn't know that Shade still hummed that to himself every night before going to sleep. As she finished, Nikki joined her for the last verse as Shade had always done when he was young. "Feel better?" her mother asked with a smile at seeing Nikki's serene face.

Nikki simply nodded. "Thanks Mom; I don't know why, but that song always makes me feel better. I've heard it all my life, though I've never sung it to anyone, not even myself. I am grateful for you singing it to me when I've needed it most."

"Of course, sweetheart. Its what mothers do. Now, eat something; Alix always says that worrying is made easier on a full stomach," her mother said, indicating the eggs in front of Nikki and pulling her own plate to her new seat.

Giving a nod, Nikki took her fork and loaded it up with scrambled eggs before shoving it in her mouth. But when she put them in her mouth, she couldn't stand the taste and spat them back out before her stomach forced more than just eggs out her mouth. She had to cover her mouth to prevent more from escaping.

Seeing her spit out the eggs, her mother got a puzzled look on her face, as did some of the cooks and stewards who were nearby. "Since when do you not like scrambled eggs?" she asked.

"I do like them, but something's wrong with those. They taste awful; it was like I'd put a steel rod in my mouth, it tasted like metal," Nikki explained.

Taking her own fork, her mother tasted the eggs. "They taste fine to me," she said, looking down at Nikki with a quizzical look. "Try another forkful."

Taking her mother's fork, Nikki again filled it with a slightly smaller amount this time. Before she could put it in her mouth, Nikki smelled the eggs and nearly dropped the fork. Covering her nose and mouth, Nikki pushed herself away from the wooden table and ran to the area of the kitchen where the staff threw all the waste before emptying her stomach. Her mother came running over and held back her hair so it didn't get anything on it. Now the entire kitchen staff seemed to be watching the movements of the former and current queen.

"Is my cooking really that bad and you're only just telling me now?" her mother asked when Nikki had finished.

Shaking her head, Nikki said, "You're a great cook, Mom. But those eggs smell worse than the lake did that summer when all the fish died when Shade and I were twelve."

Her mother just laughed a tiny bit at the comparison. Then she looked at Nikki strangely, back to the table with the questionable eggs, and finally back to Nikki. As she looked at Nikki, a smile was slowly forming on her face. "Nikki," she asked slowly, "when was your last time of the moon?"

Not understanding where her mother's question was heading, Nikki simply answered, "It was supposed to be two days ago; but I've been a couple of days late before." As she answered the two of them walked back over to the table they'd been eating at.

"But have you ever been sick like this on those occasions?" her mother asked with a look in her eyes that Nikki felt was meant to urge her to understand.

"No, I've nev-" Nikki started before realizing what her mother was hinting at. "Am I really?" Feeling the waves of happiness that were tentatively rolling off her mother, Nikki felt her own spirits start to rise.

Taking her hand, her mother smiled at Nikki. "There's only one way to know for sure. Let's find your father and find out."

"Find out what?" her father asked with a puzzled look on his face as he entered the kitchen.

Running to her husband with an infectious smile, Nikki's mother pulled her father back to where she was waiting. "We were just discussing how Nikki seems to have this glow about her, even though she's constantly worrying about Shade. Can't you see it, darling?" she asked with a nudge to her husband to look at their daughter.

Like Nikki herself, her father didn't get what his wife was saying. "She looks the same to me: a little paler and more stressed, but basically the same as always."

Heaving a sigh of exasperation, her mother took her husband's hand and placed it on Nikki's stomach. "Does she look different now?" she asked him while rolling her eyes at Nikki.

Giving a brief look to his hand on Nikki's stomach and then to his wife, her father finally seemed to clue in. Turning back to Nikki, he looked serious as he concentrated on her stomach. Within thirty seconds, he was smiling and nodding his head. And as the affirmation registered in all their minds, Nikki could literally see the explosion of pure joy they released.

But before her father could say anything, his wife was pushing him out of the way as she pulled Nikki into a tight hug. "CONGRATULATIONS!" she shouted as she and Nikki jumped up and down. When they finally stopped jumping, both of them had tears in their eyes. "I can't believe I'm going to be a grandmother!" her mother loudly whispered.

Smiling as big a smile as she'd ever seen on his face, her father gave Nikki the biggest hug he'd ever given her. "Congratulations, sweetheart! You and your brother needed this," he whispered in her ear.

Releasing herself from the hug, Nikki smiled. "Not a word until I tell Shade, to anyone. And I mean anyone, Mother," Nikki said, pointing a finger at both of them. Her mother seemed a little upset at this, but they both nodded with understanding. "I'm going to tell Shade, and then we can all talk." Not waiting for their answer, Nikki headed for the door, unable to wait to tell her brother the good news.

Nikki found her brother in their chambers, looking over

some reports at the desk. Nikki had always been used to the fact that when she entered a room, he would immediately look to her, but he seemed to be taking less and less notice of her lately. Even knowing that he was stressed didn't make her feel any better about Shade not even looking at her.

But her good mood wasn't dampened much. And seeing as Shade was in need of some stress release, she sneaked into her closet to change. Pulling the dress and jacket down that she'd worn to Jazabel's wedding, Nikki paused for the slightest moment at the thought of Jazabel. But then she decided that she couldn't be sad today; she'd only feel the joy of discovered parenthood.

Ten minutes later, she peaked out her closet doors to find Shade hadn't moved; he still stood over the desk studying the scouting reports. Turning to the mirror that was at the far end of the closet, Nikki made sure that she looked just as she had the last time she wore this outfit, minus the extended hair. Smiling at the perfection in the mirror, Nikki turned back to the doors. Taking a deep breath as she drew the dark authority she felt this dress gave her, Nikki shoved the closet doors open so they banged against the outside walls.

Her entrance had the desired effect as Shade looked up at the loud noise with a startled expression. Nikki took the briefest of seconds to enjoy his shock before snapping her fingers and pointing to her side. "Come here, NOW, Shade Leo Kanta!" she playfully snarled at him. It was clear Shade didn't think she was being playful; she could hear him gulp in fear across the room.

But it was also clear that his curiosity greatly outweighed his fear, for he was soon at her side. "Yes?" he asked with a sly smile on his lips.

"Wipe that smirk off your face," Nikki whispered with menace. She continued as she started to slowly circle her husband. "You're in big trouble." And before he could do anything else, she started to drag him to their bed.

"Nikki? What are you doing?" he protested just before she threw him onto the bed, where he stayed.

"Nice to see you still know my name, or recognize me for that matter." While Nikki didn't really feel this way, these two statements weren't an unfair assessment of late.

"What-What are you talking about? How could I ever forget a single thing about you? You're my everything, Nikki."

She could feel the fear that was pouring out of him; he didn't think this was a game anymore, he really thought she was mad at him. And while she was, she didn't want him to think that. And so, she allowed her face to show some of the pain she'd been feeling lately. "Then would you mind showing that? Did you even see me come in ten minutes ago?" At this question, Shade turned his head away in shame.

Sitting down at his side, she gave him a small smile. "I'm not mad; I just miss you. We haven't spent any time together since Jazabel's funeral. And I know you want to have Brudas found, as do I, but if you don't even notice my presence I think you have a problem. Ok?"

Heaving a sigh, he nodded. "I'm sorry; I realize now how much I've neglected you. And I'm sorry you had to resort to such lengths to get me to realize that. Can you forgive me?"

"I already have; just make sure it doesn't happen again," she said as she opened her arms and he pulled her in tight. At having him so close, Nikki let out a sigh and was very tempted to show him just how bad she could be. But she had more to talk to him about; more happy things.

"I didn't come here to yell at you. I don't think even your depressing obsession could ruin the good mood I'm in," she said with a smile as he released her from the hug.

"And what could have brought about such a strong good mood?" he asked as he looked deep into her eyes with all the love he hadn't given her in a month.

Smiling at finally seeing this look on his face, Nikki kissed him. "I just finished talking with Mom and Dad. They seemed to think that I looked different, they said I had this glow about me that they couldn't put words to. What do you think; am I glowing?" she asked as she stood and turned once for him to see.

Shade got a puzzled look on his face as he tried to pick up on what she was talking about. "You do seem different," he agreed. "I can't put my finger on what it is, though. Won't you tell me so I can be as happy as you are?"

"Besides all this to be over and us to be victorious, what do you want most from your future?"

"To know that you're happy, and that I'm the reason for that happiness. That's all I've ever wanted, to be the source of your happiness."

"Good, because that's exactly what you've done. But it's more than happiness I feel: I feel joy. And it's all thanks to you, brother," she said as she kissed him with all the love she felt for him. Before either of them could be consumed by the kiss, Nikki pushed herself away. "I'm pregnant, Shade."

It took him a moment to comprehend this, but when he did, Shade had the biggest smile she'd seen on anyone. And then he was holding her, kissing her, showing his love for her like he never had before.

Chapter 62:

Strategies

For the last month and a half, Shade had stayed by Nikki's side, making sure nothing happened to her or their child growing within. They had agreed to keep the knowledge that she was with child a secret for as long as they could. Naturally they told their extended family, who were ecstatic; but other than them, no one else knew. Shade feared what Brudas would do to Nikki if he found out she was pregnant.

But he still hadn't heard any word of Brudas, except that there was no word. And with the fact that Nikki was pregnant soon to spread throughout the country, Shade feared the worst. He'd become restless to the point of nearly ignoring Nikki; but that was one mistake he'd never make again.

They were sitting having lunch with their parents. Like any other day, they ate in the kitchen talking of everything but what was on their minds: the baby and Brudas.

"I hear that the trade ring expansion the two of you made with Ichmensch is becoming quite productive," their mother was saying. "But what I don't understand is how you got them to agree to it all. What was it that was included in that deal?"

Shade just looked at Nikki and rolled his eyes, for his mother had asked them this question at least a half dozen times since they'd told her about it. "In exchange for free trade, a copy of *Magic's Legends*, and their help with the war effort, we gave them free access through Braria for their troops, as long as they didn't harm our citizens, as well as sword training with one of our best swordsmen," Nikki answered as she tried to avoid mentioning Brudas by name.

But before more than a second of awkward silence could be observed, Shade noticed Romulus run into the room. When he had spotted the four of them, he made as direct a route to them as he could in the crowded kitchen. Snapping a fist to his heart as he bowed his head, Romulus turned to Shade. "Forgive me, your majesties, but I bring urgent news from Lieutenant Shaw. We've found him, sire; he's created a small hideout in the Sharedwood Forest. Upon your earlier command, we haven't engaged him but we do have him surrounded. At least we did a day ago when I left," he reported. "How should we proceed, your highness?"

Looking to Nikki, Shade silently judged the look in her eyes. She trusted his judgement, but he wondered if she would if she knew his plan. He noticed that his parents were also looking to him with stifled anxieties. "It's good to hear those words. Romulus, get yourself something to eat and take a rest for the next two hours, because you're going to need it. The two of us aren't going to stop until we get back to your father and bring Brudas back here for execution."

Shade then tried to stand so as to avoid Nikki's protests, but he should've known better. "No! You'll do no such thing," she told him. Then turning to Romulus, she said in a nicer tone, "You are free to do as your king recommended, Romulus: get some rest and food. But my brother will not be accompanying you back." At her words, Romulus looked to her with the love Shade knew he still felt for Nikki as well as a look of concern before he went to the nearest cook and requested some lunch.

"What are you thinking? I thought we were going to take him together. You're not going anywhere near him without me!" Nikki whispered to him angrily. "Isn't that right, Mom?" she asked, turning to look to their parents.

His mother just shook her head. "No, you shouldn't do this alone or so far away from home. The Sharedwood Forest is the southernmost point of Braria, on the borders of Pitag and Ichmensch where all three meet. You may have Ichmensch's support, but you don't have Pitag's. Not to mention the forest is too dense to pursue anyone successfully, let alone someone like Brudas who can blend into any surrounding. You know he could be right in front of you and you wouldn't even notice him until it was too late. No one wants you to die out there, when there's so much here worth living for." The look in his mother's eyes as she pleaded with him not to go was the look she got right before she was about to cry. Shade didn't want to see her cry.

And then he, Nikki, and their mother all turned to his father, as if they'd all decided that this was going to be a family decision. Heaving a sigh, his father looked to him. "They're right; it will be very dangerous if you go out there alone. But I think that Brudas will evade capture until you go to meet him on his terms. I also know that you want your sister to stay here so you know she's safe. You are the only person I know to have defeated Brudas in combat: whether he let you win or not, I don't know. But if you want to end this now, I suggest you go, and that you take Nikki with you. She's just as capable with a sword as you, and you'd be able to know that you're both safe. The two of you together are much stronger than if you're separated. But the decision is ultimately yours to make; you are the king." His father's eyes were locked on his as they judged his resolve.

Turning to Nikki, Shade saw the amount of love she had for him, as well as the fear that she'd lose him. *Dad's right; I'm the only one who can defeat Brudas, and I want you to stay here so I know you're safe.*

What about the part where we're stronger together than apart? Or the fact that I won't know if you're safe or not, or if I'll ever see you again? You promised you'd never do this to us again, that you'd never leave my side! You can't do that to me again, Shade, I won't let you!

Do you think I want to leave your side? It causes me pain too, not to mention it could be the last time I'm going to see you alive. I hate breaking my promises to you more than I hate Brudas. But what about our child? If I go out and never come back, Brudas will have had his revenge and he won't come for you, thus leaving you to have our child and raise it. Even though I'd be dead and your world would be empty, there is that one light. But if you come with me, and Brudas kills you, I will have nothing left here in this world but my pain. I'd kill myself just to see you again, and that would completely destroy our parents and all of Braria. For as much as I want you to come with me, I won't risk that outcome; it's too high of a price to pay.

And how do you know I won't kill myself to see you again? How do you know that you going out there alone and dying won't produce that same outcome?

Because you're stronger than I am; you always have been. When Mom left, my Reckoning, all this, you've always pulled me through it. You can push through your pain and do what's right, regardless of how much it hurts. I'm not saying it won't be difficult to face every day knowing that I'm gone; I'm only saying that you can do it and that our child will help you through it all.

I've only been able to pull through because I knew you would help me every step of the way. I need you, Shade, to raise our child, to give me more, and to help me through every painful part of our life. You can't leave me!

I'm trying not to look at it that way; I'm trying to look at it as I'm protecting you. Brudas has probably slipped past them by now, and I'll be in no more danger than you would be here. And then I can come right back and we'd know that we're both OK.

If you're so sure he's gotten away, then why are you going out there and not letting me come with you?

On the off chance I'm wrong. I won't risk your life and the life of our unborn child like that. When I took this crown, I swore that I'd give my life if necessary for Braria to prosper, before I let one innocent life be harmed by Brudas' brutality. Our child is the most innocent being that I know of, just like its mother. I lost you once; I can't lose you again.

I was unable to say a proper goodbye once. I'd never forgive myself if I failed to give you one again. And I made those same vows, and you are just as innocent as I am - you're the White Knight! And what happens if Brudas doesn't stop with just you? What if he comes back for me once he kills you? How will I protect myself if the only person who can defeat him is dead?

You'll have a castle full of guards, not to mention Dad. That should be enough to overwhelm him, don't you think? But do you really think that he will kill me, without me giving him some form of injury? Do you have so little faith in my combat abilities that you're automatically assuming the worst?

No, not assuming, fearing. I believe with all my heart that you can kill Brudas out there in the woods. But I watched the two of you every day as you battled in the courtyard, and I know that he is better than you with a sword; no matter how much we wish the contrary. I fear what will happen if you go out there and face off against him.

While I was trying, I wasn't properly motivated during those sessions. I am now; I'm overflowing with motivation. As they had silently discussed the situation, Shade and Nikki had walked closer together until they were in each other's arms. With closed eyes and his forehead resting against hers, Shade whispered, "I can defeat him. And then we can be happy again. Let me do this my way, and I swear on any and everything you want that I will return to you, alive and whole; that our family will grow and be happy. And if I should fail to keep this promise, let my soul forever be tortured in the Pits of the underworld, as I'll never see your face again. That is how confident I am in myself and this course of action." He opened his eyes as he looked to see how she would react to this.

But as his eyes opened, hers closed. Pulling herself in closer to him, Nikki laid her head on his chest and then let out a frustrated sigh. "If you die out there," she said without looking at him, "I will personally bring you back to life and kill you with my bare hands for not fulfilling your promise and leaving me here. Do you understand me Shade Leo

Kanta?" She finally looked in his eyes as she sought his understanding. Shade nodded as he looked into the beautiful blue eyes he'd loved since he first saw them. "You have five days to bring yourself and that Beast back to this castle," she said as she turned away from him.

Shade knew there were tears in her eyes, and that this was one of the hardest decisions that she'd ever made. He saw his parents' eyes widen at Nikki's acceptance of his plan. But he just turned Nikki around, and before she could say anything he had his lips on hers in the most passionate kiss his lips could give. She at first resisted, but soon gave in, as she couldn't contain the feelings that he himself was trying to release.

When he finally pulled away for air, she pushed him away. "Four days," she corrected, once again turning her back on him. Shade took this to mean that she wouldn't, or couldn't, watch him go. So he silently stole away to prepare for the journey to the south and Sharedwood Forest.

Nikki both heard and felt Shade leave as her heart and composure began to break. Turning back to the table, she sought out the comfort of her mother's arms. Once she was in them, she felt another pair wrap themselves around her. Lifting her head, she saw that her father had joined her mother in consoling her. The fact that he had tears in his eyes showed her how much both her parents were worried about her decision to let Shade go alone.

"You... let him go alone...?" her mother asked as her

tears slowed.

Nikki shook her head as she released herself from the hug. "No, I put faith in my husband and his promises. Now, I need to be alone." And she walked away, leaving her parents confused and grieving.

But before she could leave the kitchen, she saw Romulus, sitting atop a wooden table used for cutting vegetables, watching her leave her parents from the corner of his eye. Walking over to him, she took his hands into her own and pulled him off the table. Looking up into his hazel eyes, Nikki took a moment to soothe her emotional pain in the love she saw in his eyes. "What is it, my queen?" he asked her in a gentle whisper.

"You're a good friend, Romulus, one of my oldest and best friends."

"Thank you, your majesty," he said with a proud smile and curt nod of his head.

"And in all our years as friends, has there been anything that I asked of you, save for you to be my friend?"

"Nothing that compares to what you're about to ask me, your highness; no."

The look of resolve in his eyes always gave Nikki pause, but this time was different. This time, his eyes offered her his life. And that's exactly what she was demanding. "Protect my brother, at any cost. I do not want to have to ask this of you, Romulus, but if it should come down to it, please swear to me that you'll give your life for his." Nikki wanted so much to not have to look into his eyes as she asked him this, but knew she had to.

But the resolve she saw in his eyes only strengthened at her request. "As a soldier in this country, I have sworn to give my life, if necessary, in battle. As a friend to his highness, I would sacrifice myself for him, knowing he is needed more than I. But for you, Nikki," he said, causing her to gasp at his using her name in public, "my queen and the woman I love, I would do anything you ask. To the best of my abilities, I will keep your brother safe, and if need be, give my life for his."

"Thank you, Romulus," Nikki whispered with closed eyes. When she felt his lips gently brush against her own, her eyes shot open. But just as quickly as they came, his lips were gone and his smile and eyes requested her forgiveness for the great liberty he'd just taken. From the corner of her eyes, she could see the looks of people who'd seen Romulus kiss her, but she ignored them. "Safe journey, Captain." And upon seeing his salute of a fist to his heart, Nikki turned and left for the place she knew her solitude would be given.

She took the service stairs as she made her way up to her old bedroom. Since Jazabel had died, her and Shade had tried to avoid this room as much as possible. This is why she was heading there now; nobody would look for her here. Twenty-five years of wonderful memories, all tarnished by one act.

As she walked through the door, she felt her heart catch as all those memories came flooding back to her. Her and Shade's first steps; all their sneaking around and learning about magic; telling their father, Aunt Kailee, and Aunt Sabrina they had magic and were Soul Twins; the night Shade had returned from his Reckoning; she remembered them all. She tried to remember the wonderful past so as to lighten the pain in the present.

But nothing would ever be able to dull the

heart-wrenching ache that was building within her at the knowledge that she might never see Shade again.

And like the last time Shade had left her here while he went in search of something, she walked over to the empty bed. Even though he hadn't slept on it in a few months, Nikki was still able to discern the dent in the mattress that was where Shade had once slept. Lying down in the imprint of her brother, Nikki did something that she'd never done before: she hummed Shade's lullaby to herself, hoping that it would help her feel better.

When it occurred to her that Jazabel had probably spent her final sleeping moments in this spot, Nikki felt tears come to her eyes. How she missed Jazabel, even if she had betrayed her and Shade. She hoped that the child growing within her was a girl so that she could honour her dead sister. She just wished Jazabel could watch her niece or nephew grow, as Nikki wished she could have watched Jazabel's child grow.

As Nikki lay on her old bed thinking about the better times in her life, she felt Shade trying to talk to her. Allowing herself to relax even though she knew it would hurt more later, Nikki opened her mind to her brother. *I don't want you to go, but I know that you feel you must - not just for me and our child, but for Jazabel as well. He ripped our hearts open when he killed her, so let's stop his.*

You know me too well. That is why I am going, to stop his heart. I'll do everything I can to get back to you as soon as I can. Do you want the honour of taking his head, or can I bring it back for you to admire?

You do whatever you need to do to make sure you get back alive. I'd be lying if I said that I didn't want to see him die personally. But your safety is first priority. If you need help, ask for it; don't try to take him on your own to try and prove something. You already have the most important thing here: a loving wife who's expecting her first child. So just make sure you get back to us unharmed.

I'll do everything in my power to make sure I do. You make sure that you're healthy for when I do return.

I will. Remember, if you're not back in four days, I'm going out there looking for you. Don't keep us waiting. You're my everything and I love you; I want you to know that.

That was the first thing I ever knew, because it is exactly how I feel about you. I'll see you in four days. Keep an open mind, ever listening for my return.

And then he was gone. As she knew he had left the castle to go find their enemy, Nikki couldn't help but cry out her pain. She knew that he, too, was letting loose the tears of pain at their separating.

Shade clutched his hand to his heart as he saw the scene before him. All the men who had congregated to Sharedwood Forest lay on the ground, slowly dying. Their injuries weren't immediately fatal, but left unattended - as Shade knew most would be - they would become so. Romulus had instantly run to Lieutenant Shaw, his father, to see if he was alright. Shade followed him to get a report of what had happened.

When Shaw saw his son approach, he gave a sigh of relief. "Romulus, thank the spirits you're alright. I feared that you would run into Brudas as you returned." He and his son clutched at each other's hands when they were close enough. Shade saw that the lieutenant's injuries were less grievous than most and was silently thankful for this.

"What happened, Lieutenant? Surely Brudas didn't do all this?" Shade asked in his official voice.

"That is exactly what happened. He came crashing through the trees this morning and managed to evade every one of our attacks; we didn't even scratch him. He didn't kill anyone, but most of us will most likely die from the injuries. Forgive us, your highness, we tried our best." Shaw looked like he was in pain as he revealed this; the lines on his face looked more defined with his paleness.

Shade just nodded his understanding. "Do you have any idea which way he went?"

At this question, it seemed as if he paled even more as he was suddenly overcome with a fit of coughs. But when they died down, Shaw bowed his head. "I know exactly where he's going. He's going back to Terang; he told me so himself. He said he knew the queen is pregnant and that you'd never let her leave the 'security' of the castle with him on the loose. He told me to tell you that he'll be waiting for you where his mother was. I hope I'm right in assuming that you know where that is."

Shade had gone numb when he heard that he'd played right into Brudas' hands. His mother had been right; he shouldn't have come this far. He should have never left Nikki's side. Turning to his travelling companion, he said, "Romulus, I know you promised Nikki to protect me with your life, but as your king, I'm ordering you to stay here and help as many men as you can, starting with your father and the most grievously injured. Find anyone with any knowledge of healing these types of wounds and get them to teach you, if you don't know yourself. I must return to Terang." He knew the captain wanted to protest, but he saw Romulus snap a fist to his heart as he set about trying to heal everyone's injuries. Shade returned to Isabelle and climbed onto her back as he kicked his heels into her sides, urging her to run home.

Nikki sat in her throne looking out to the empty room. Three days had passed since Shade had left to confront Brudas, and she knew that any minute now she could feel the unbearable pain of having forever lost her most beloved. But she refused to think that she would lose her brother this day, or any for the foreseeable future. He would come back to her; he had to.

So engrossed in her own thoughts and worries, Nikki didn't notice the commotion that was gripping the castle until it was right outside the throne room doors. But before she could go to them to see what was going on, the doors burst open to reveal the tall and menacing figure of Brudas. Behind him, she could see that everyone seemed to be frozen in place, unable to move and help their beloved queen.

Nikki stood and drew a small dagger from the side of her throne as Brudas calmly strolled towards her. "Not one more step, Brudas, or I'll drive this knife through your heart right now, and not wait for my brother to get back to see your life leave you," she snarled at him.

He stopped for only a second to smile at her. The most

twisted smile Nikki had ever conceived was positively peaceful compared to the scar that was Brudas' mouth. It alone made her courage falter, but the harsh laugh he gave at hearing her made it disappear. "So, he dreams of watching me die. That's not very White Knightly of him, now is it?" he teased her as he marched up the dais to her side. "It's good to see that the two of you act so much like your Babomoran ancestors. They, too, loved watching others die by their hands. But I know your father told you all about that back when you were just a little girl. Speaking of fathers, I hear that you're pregnant, nearly three months if I'm not mistaken." He smiled that disturbing smile at her as he circled her.

"How did you know?" Nikki's voice was steady, but she certainly wasn't. She turned with him, constantly re-gripping the dagger in her hand. "We haven't told anyone but family."

"You forget I'm the son of Lilith, and that nothing happens in this world without her allowing it. You and your brother owe a great debt to my mother for all that she has done for you."

"If she's your mother, then why hasn't she killed us for you? Why does she grant us favours if we are her son's greatest enemies? Does she favour us more than she favours you?" Nikki asked in a taunting voice, trying to bolster her courage.

But at the sound of Brudas' inhumane laughter, her courage once again left her. "No, she doesn't favour you more than me; quite the opposite in fact. Mother has given you and Shade everything so that I could take it away, just as your family took away my everything to make that insidious Mask!"

"That's what all this is about?! The Mask of Babomorah? That was your Soul's Twin?" Nikki asked in befuddlement.

"DO NOT SPEAK OF ANILLA! YOU AREN'T EVEN GOOD ENOUGH TO KNEEL AT HER FEET!" Was the look of pain and hatred upon his face the same look Shade had given Jazabel when he'd watched her stab his Soul's Twin?

"What do you want from us, Brudas? Surely through all your hatred and pain you can see that my family has changed since the Mask was created. We wish to help everyone, not watch them die!"

But Brudas seemed to not hear her. "Six thousand years: that's how long I've waited for Soul Twins to be born to this family. SIX THOUSAND YEARS! You cannot conceive of the pain and hatred I feel towards you and your family."

"If you're going to kill me, do it already."

"All in good time, your highness," he responded in a mocking tone. "We have to wait for your brother to arrive. But until then," he continued as he stepped in front of her and removed the dagger from her hand, "I think you need to sleep."

And as he waved his hand in front of Nikki's eyes, she felt them close as she fell into oblivion.

Chapter 63:

Prophecies Fulfilled

As Shade raced towards his castle, he saw the dark purple clouds above it. As fast and hard as Isabelle was galloping, she seemed to be making little headway against the ferocious winds. Seeing red lightning cut across the darkness of the clouds, Shade knew that these clouds were not natural. Brudas had already arrived, despite his not stopping at a break-neck pace. But the clouds weren't the only unnatural thing happening around him. He saw that everyone was frozen in place: Brudas had ensured their fight would remain private.

As Isabelle rushed through the castle gate, Shade jumped off her, the wind nearly blowing him away, and then he saw her collapse; he'd clearly pushed her to her limit. He hoped she would be ok, but he had bigger problems than his horse's health. He ran to the large doors that had been blown open in the fierce storm and saw that everyone in the castle was frozen, just like the townspeople.

As he entered the throne room, he saw Nikki's body lying on the dais. Running to her, he jumped the stairs three at a time, before holding her in his arms. "NIKKI?! NO! You can't be dead; please Nikki, don't be dead!" Fearing the worst, Shade leaned down to kiss his world goodbye.

Just before his lips met hers, he saw her eyes open. But rather than the blue he loved so much, her eyes were as dark as night. Stunned, Shade didn't even react as Nikki drew his sword and pushed him away. He couldn't believe his eyes as her body started to float above his head. "Oh, don't worry Shade, she's not dead." The voice was clearly Nikki's, but Shade could hear the undertones of Brudas' voice in hers.

"What have you done to her?!"

"Nothing yet." A flash of red lightning washed the throne room in blood and thunder rumbled so powerfully that the castle shook beneath Shade's feet. "But what plans I have for her," Brudas said in Nikki's voice with a twisted smile marring her perfect face.

"If you hurt one hair on her head, I-"

"You'll what, kill me? To do that you need to have me leave this body, and to do that you need to kill it. But you can't do that, now can you?" He gave a vicious laugh as he circled Shade from above. "Kills, doesn't it? Being physically able to help your Soul's Twin, but knowing that you really can't. Now just imagine having to listen to her scream and cry out for your help as she's being raped and her bones are being ripped from her body to make some insidious Mask that looks into your head whenever it's used. Now imagine having to hear those screams and cries every moment of every day for six thousand years while you waited and prepared for the moment that you could finally take your revenge. You think you felt pain when she died in the Star of Death? You have no idea what pain is until you've felt my pain!"

"But I have felt your pain, Brudas. When I found myself wearing that infernal Mask, I felt the chaos within you: all that hatred and pain and guilt. I felt it for a few hours and was unable to bear it past the first few seconds. The fact that you've endured it for six thousand years proves that you're a stronger man than me. I understand why you want to kill me and Nikki, but it won't bring Anilla back. No-"

"DO NOT SPEAK HER NAME! Like your sister, you are not good enough to kneel at her feet. I'm going to kill you now, Vigmece spawn, with your own sword. And when it's too late to stop herself, I'll release Nikki so she can see it was her who killed you!"

And he raised the sword he'd stolen from Shade above his head before swooping down upon him. Shade just stood tall to what he knew was to come. And when he saw Nikki's eyes return to their perfect blue, he could only smile as he felt the blade of *Peacemaker* pierce his heart for the second time. "I love you," he whispered in her ear as the force of the blow brought them together.

Nikki woke up from the dream to find Shade smiling at her, and her hand pushing his sword through his chest. She heard him whisper "I love you," as his lips found themselves at her ear. The emotional explosion of what she had done jarred loose a nearly forgotten memory. And then she felt him slump into her arms.

Clutching him as they fell to the floor under his dead

weight, Nikki realized what she'd just done. "NOOOOOO! SHADE! No, no, no! I couldn't stop myself, I didn't know! You can't die, Shade! I love you and I need you; please don't die!" she yelled at him as he just smiled up at her. She looked into his eyes and saw they had dimmed; her world was dead. "Shade…? SHADE! NOOOOOO!" The emptiness she felt as she held her dead brother was more than Nikki could handle; the hatred she felt towards herself for being the one to kill him nearly made her heart stop.

Turning at the sound of cruel laughter behind her, Nikki saw Brudas sitting in her brother's throne with that hideous smile on his face. The red flash of the storm that howled outside did nothing to her vision as it was bathed in anger already. She couldn't even comprehend how much she hated the man in front of her; he'd taken everything from her. When he saw her glaring at him in hatred, his smile became slightly empathizing and he bowed his head slightly. "Try living with that feeling for six thousand years and then come and find me," he said to her in an intimate whisper. Standing, he walked over to her. "Do not fret, for you will not have to wait that long. For I shall reunite you in the underworld - a courtesy that was never given to me."

Nikki turned away from him, refusing to give him the satisfaction of looking in her eyes as she died. As she looked to the limp body that was her brother, she saw his sword still lodged in his heart. Looking upon the sword, Nikki knew what she had to do.

With a cry of fury, the likes of which she'd never known she was capable of, Nikki pulled Shade's sword from his chest as she spun around to face Brudas. The look on his face was one of paralysing fear, as she knew it would be.

Kicking her leg up at his face, Nikki saw Brudas' feet leave the floor as he flew back from her attack. Jumping at the only chance she knew she'd need or get, Nikki launched herself at Brudas and climbed up his falling body. Raising the sword above her head, she cried out as she plunged it down into Brudas' screaming mouth. And when she felt his body hit the floor beneath him, she turned the blade and sliced up, cutting the rest of his face in half. An ear-splitting clap of thunder sounded as the storm outside ceased and dissipated to reveal the calm deep indigo of the natural twilight sky.

Nikki smiled a vengeful smile as she saw Brudas' body burst into tiny pieces of shadow and disappear. But then there was a blinding flash of light from behind her; how Nikki hoped this part of the story was to be true as well. When the light had faded, she turned around to find Shade smiling at her. Feeling the greatest relief she had ever felt, Nikki jumped into his arms. *I love you* they thought as they clung to each other, never wanting to let go.

You figured it out, the forgotten tale. I was afraid you wouldn't until it was too late.

When did you figure it out?

As soon as I entered the throne room and saw you lying there. But I should have never left you; I'm so sorry.

It's ok; it had to be this way. I didn't want to kill you, but that's how it had to be done. It's over and we won; and we didn't even get a scratch. And then she was kissing him, or was he kissing her? She didn't care; he was alive and Brudas was dead, and that was all that mattered. She just wanted this moment to last forever.

But when the doors to the room slammed open to reveal both her parents as well as nearly every soldier left at the castle rushing into the room, she knew her moment was over. Every one of them had weapons drawn, except her father who had a ball of nightfire ignited in each hand. Turning herself and Shade towards them all, Nikki gave a big smile. Upon seeing the smile, the small army cheered as they knew it meant that their king and queen were victorious.

Nikki saw her parents run up the dais as they embraced both their children in a four-way hug. All four of them were openly crying as they made sure that they all were indeed alive. Once they had finished, Shade turned to their parents. "I need you two to go to Sharedwood Forest; Lieutenant Shaw and his men were badly injured as they tried to stop Brudas, and only Romulus is there to help heal them. Unfortunately, most of them are probably dead, but I want you to go and help as best you can. They're on our side of the forest just a few leagues in."

"Of course," both of their parents said with a bow and giving a fist to their hearts.

"And once you've healed the survivors, send word to all that I'm calling a Heritage to be held in a month's time. And I hope all can make it." Nikki looked at her brother in confusion, the same confusion as her parents looked at him with. There hadn't been a Heritage called since the Kanta family had taken the throne, and they'd always brought great change.

But their parents once again gave a fist to their hearts as they said, "Yes, your highness." And they watched as their parents rushed to complete the tasks their son had set for them.

Shade then turned to the gathered soldiers. "You all can help in spreading the word: there will be a Heritage in a month's time. And whichever one of you finds himself in OJA, please extend an invitation to our aunts; I want them there too. Now, please, off you go; I need to spend some time with my wife." The room echoed with the sounds of the soldiers snapping fists to their hearts before turning to go about their tasks.

Nikki held herself tight to her brother as he watched the soldiers leave. She still could hardly believe that they were victorious against the seemingly impossible odds. As the last soldier left and closed the doors, Nikki expected Shade to lean in and kiss her once again, but he didn't. Instead, he turned to the ceiling, raised a hand, and beckoned something to him.

Looking up, Nikki saw three bats descend from the hidden heights. She thought she recognized them from Jazabel's wedding as the bats that had stroked her cheek so lovingly. She was surprised when she saw them land on Shade and he stroked their fur lovingly. "The only remaining physical proof that Jazabel was a Lady of the Night," he explained to her unasked question. "Pandora, Bruce, and Adriana," he said as he pointed to each bat in turn. Nikki lovingly pet each as he named them. "My Dark friends, the time has come. Tell Queen Amaranth that Nikki and I have survived our war and anxiously await her return. But I ask that she wait so that she can be a part of the Heritage I just called. Tell her that I still want our societies to be able to coexist peacefully. Now, fly to the Dark Queen," he said to the bats, throwing his hands into the air as they took off towards the ceiling.

When she could no longer see or hear the bats, Nikki looked to Shade. She saw him smiling at her with such love that her heart swelled to the point of pain. "I love you," he said as he looked deep into her eyes.

Upon seeing the unmistakeable truth of those three words in his eyes, Nikki just smiled at him. "And I love you," she said as she pulled him into a passionate kiss.

※

Shade looked out to the filled throne room, seeing all the representatives from every town in Braria; as well as his parents, aunts, and uncle; and even Queen Amaranth, who was hiding in the back of the room. Taking Nikki's hand, he rose from in his throne as every eye locked onto him. "Thank you, everyone, for coming. I'd like to acknowledge that this is the first Heritage to be called in nearly twelve generations. Unlike Heritages of the past, I've called this one to tell you all of what has happened.

"Since me and Nikki were four years old, we've known that we'd face a powerful enemy in a conflict that would decide the fate of the known lands. We've trained, formed alliances, and made every preparation we could think of for the past twenty-one years. Four months ago, that conflict began with the death of our dearest friend Jazabel. But the truth is," he paused at the thought of declaring her a traitor, "the truth is that Jazabel had, reluctantly, betrayed us to this enemy, her own husband Brudas Smiledoilt." Sensing the commotion that he saw stirring at this statement, Shade raised his hands and voice. "But before you all go cursing them; you should know their actions were not without reason.

"Jazabel was a Lady of the Night; for those of you who don't know what that means, it means she was a woman who dedicated her life to bringing about more Darkness into this world. I knew this before I invited her to come and live in this castle; my love for her blinded me to the potential dangers she could unleash upon our beloved country. But I also knew her better than nearly anyone. I knew that she would never hurt anyone willingly, for she felt that being a Lady of the Night was a curse and not a blessing. At her funeral, we met the queen of this secret society and found out that this view was shared by most of their society.

"And Brudas was a broken-hearted man. My family doesn't even know this, but before we came to Braria we lived in Babomorah, the capital city of Nefas, as its rulers. Back then, our name wasn't Kanta but Vigmece, and our way of ruling wasn't like it is now. The Vigmece clan were completely heartless and only served themselves. They once raped and ripped the bones out of a woman right in front of her Soul's Twin. As you can imagine, that would drive even the most forgiving of people to the point of murderous rage. Brudas had to watch as the woman he loved with every fibre of his being was tortured right in front of him, and he couldn't do anything to help her. He made a deal with the goddess Lilith to allow him the opportunity for revenge on a set of Soul Twins born to our family, so that those who had had caused his pain would feel it.

"I have forgiven both Jazabel and Brudas for their crimes against me and Nikki. But the fact that Brudas' actions resulted in the deaths of over fifty of our soldiers, including the long serving Lieutenant Remus Shaw who was my friend, I cannot forgive. Those men didn't have to die for the sins that my ancestors committed. My heart goes out to all their families as I sympathize with their loss.

"And now, I open the floor to you. Your opinions will be highly valued, even if they are to have my family removed from power. You represent all of the towns of Braria as their elders and leaders, and we are your servants." He sat back down as he awaited the judgement of all those present.

The room was silent as it digested Shade's revelation. Shade looked to his father to see how he'd react to having the family's darkest secret revealed to all. If he had expected him to be mad or upset, Shade was to be disappointed. His father was looking at him with a prideful smile that made Shade sure that his father agreed with all he'd just done. His mother, on the other hand, was giving him a look that told him she thought that he shouldn't have told everyone all this, but that she was also proud of him for doing it. Honesty to all, about all.

Suddenly, Shade saw a man he believed to be in his forties in the middle of the room stand and start to clap. Everyone turned to look at him, and slowly everybody joined in with their own applause. Shade even saw Queen Amaranth clapping in the back. There seemed to be no end to their clapping.

Finally, Nikki stood and commanded silence. Pointing to the middle of the room, she asked, "Will you please come forward?" Everyone cleared a path for the man who'd first stood to come to the front of the room. When he got there, he bowed deeply. "And what, good sir, is your name? And why is it you clap?" Nikki asked him once he'd straightened up.

"My name is Thomas Howard, your highness. And I clap

because I believe you and your brother are still more than capable and worthy of leading our people. You are honest people and I know you love this country with as much of your hearts that is taken in loving those around you. You probably don't remember, but the day that you came rushing into this very room and told everyone that your mother was finally coming home, I'd come as a petitioner. I saw even then that you two had a connection to each other that I'd never seen before; I saw that you loved each other very much. I also saw that you just wanted everyone to be happy; that you'd give up nearly everything to make some random stranger happy. It was then that I realized that you and the king were the best things to happen to this country in a long time. Braria is a near paradise, and with you as our leaders, it can only get better. We all have ghosts in our past that still haunt us, but I trust that we all can deal with them in a cathartic manner. ALL HAIL THE HOUSE OF KANTA!" he finished with a fist raised in cheer.

Within seconds, the entire throne room was raising their fists in a similar fashion as they all chanted, "HAIL KANTA! HAIL KANTA!" Shade could only smile at the love his people had for his family. When after a minute he stood to command silence, the chant only grew stronger.

But as he lifted his hands up, Shade was finally able to get everyone to be quiet so he could speak. "I'll take that to mean you all agree with Thomas's words. If there is anyone who doesn't, I request he or she come forward; you're all meant to have a say in this. Does anyone feel that jeers and revolution are in order?" When not one person came forward, Shade's pride leaped into the air. Finally, Shade turned to his parents and aunts and uncle. "And what of our family? What do you have to say at all that has been revealed?"

The six of them just looked back and forth at each other as if trying to silently communicate with the others how they felt. Finally, his mother stepped forward with a big smile on her face. "Not a day goes by that we aren't proud of you two. We all love you so much; we could never speak of you in a negative way. We will never have to, for there is nothing that you would ever do that isn't in the best interest of this country. We all have total faith in you, as do your people." Behind her, Shade could see them all nod in agreement, causing tears to come to his eyes.

Taking his hand in hers, Nikki smiled at him. But it was to the gathered masses that she spoke. "Thank you everyone. Your love and support are what keep us going when we feel we have nothing left. That is all we have to say to you. If nobody else has anything they wish to discuss, then this Heritage is over." When they didn't say anything, she continued, "Thank you all. I just have one more thing to say before you all leave, but I do not wish to discuss it at length just at this moment. I'd like you all to know that I am four months pregnant; Braria will soon have a new princess!"

Everyone cheered at this joyous announcement, but Shade and Nikki ignored it. Instead they made their way to the staircase behind their thrones and out to the balcony for some privacy.

Chapter 64:
Names, Favours, and Forgiveness

Nikki held herself into the empty space created by Shade's body, moulding herself to him. Caressing her slightly swelled belly, she looked out over the stone railing to the full moon just barely visible in the twilight sky. Their father had just told them earlier that day that the child growing within her was to be a girl, and she couldn't stop smiling because of that piece of information. "What should we name our daughter?" she asked Shade as they held each other tight.

"Zelda has yet to be honoured with our generation, and I do think it's a very pretty name. Then there's also Marina, Iselda, and the ever beautiful Nikki," he said as he smiled at her with so much love.

She just kissed him gently for that remark. "All wonderful suggestions, though I think Mom's name is too unique to be given to someone else, even her own granddaughter. And as for my name, I don't want her to get confused when you call for me and she's right there. That leaves Zelda and Marina." She paused for a moment, thinking he might say which he liked better, but then she remembered her other aunts. "Oh!

What about Kailee or Sabrina? How did we forget them?"

"I don't know, but we can never tell them; Mom would never let us forget it," he said as they both laughed at the truthful joke Shade had made at their mother's expense. "But I still like Zelda the best. What about you; what names were you thinking of?"

Nikki turned away from him at this question, and looked back to the full moon as the tears filled her eyes. "Jazabel; even before she died I thought that if we ever had a daughter, we'd name her Jazabel. I miss her so much and I just wish I could see her again. But you can't tell me you never thought we wouldn't name one of our children after her."

Shade gave a weighted sigh at hearing of her longing for their closest friend. Pulling her closer to him, he rubbed her shoulder in an attempt to comfort her with one hand while the other wiped her tears away. "I miss her too; and I wish she was still here. You're right; I always thought I'd name my daughter after her. We loved her more than anyone else, as we will love our daughter. I think it's very fitting, and the ultimate honour we could give her."

Nikki nodded as she turned back to him. "It's settled then: her name will be Jazabel Zelda Kanta. And she will have her father's love and compassion."

"And her mother's laugh and strength. Not to mention her eyes and smile, which stop my heart with their beauty every time I see them."

Nikki blushed and smiled at him for this praise. "If she has all that, she'll need her father's way with words and his commanding presence. And the way his nose twitches whenever he smells something he doesn't like, a nose that makes me laugh at how cute it is." For nearly twenty minutes the two of them offered the traits they most loved in the other as something their daughter would possess.

They would have continued all night long, if they weren't interrupted. "The two of you are nearly exactly the same; what more could you find different in each other that you don't have in yourselves?" a voice asked from behind them, startling them.

Turning to see who had spoken, they saw Queen Amaranth. As one they bowed to her and said, "We were honoured that you would attend such a historical event for us. Not many people get to say they're friends with such a powerful woman, but we'd like to think that we are friends, and we are thankful that you indulge our friendship."

Queen Amaranth returned their bow as she smiled at their praising of her. Nikki wondered how often she was praised by her people, and figured it wasn't often enough. "Thank you," she said, "but the honour is all mine at having been called your friend. And I offer my sincerest congratulations at the fact that you are expecting your first child, as well as your victory. I must say I was more than slightly surprised that you survived, but I'm glad you did; the world is better off for it." Nikki and Shade gave their thanks at Eva's support. "But now I must get down to business. I believe, King Shade, that you have something of mine. I would like it back now that you've finished with it."

Nikki looked to Shade in confusion, but he just nodded at Queen Amaranth. "Of course, your Darkness. It's in my chambers; please excuse me while I go retrieve it." And with a quick kiss to Nikki's cheek he was gone, leaving the two of them alone.

"Do not think that I've forgotten your request, your

majesty. I have spoken with the others who hold your fate, and they have agreed to allow you entry to Pandora's tomb. But for this great liberty, we ask that you make a sacrifice. Fear not, for there will be no pain to you or your loved ones," Queen Amaranth said as Shade disappeared down the stairs.

"Really? What must I do?" Nikki asked, excited at the prospect of being granted this request.

"There is a ritual we'd like to perform while you are still pregnant. Your daughter will not be harmed, but this ritual must be performed within our walls. It will allow us to determine whether or not our bloodlines will ever mix - that is to say if a Kanta will ever become a Lady of the Night. I understand if you wish to discuss this with your husband, as it is an odd ritual. The council has also allowed for him to accompany you to the tomb, but he may not enter. We understand the pain it gives you two to separate, and don't wish to have our allies in such a state."

"Thank you; we are very grateful for that. And I do not need to discuss anything with Shade, for this is my wish and he knows that I will have to pay some form of price. You may perform your ritual on me when I arrive," Nikki said solemnly.

Queen Amaranth just smiled. "Of course, you'll also not be allowed to speak of what you see inside to anyone, not even Shade. No male has ever seen the inside of Pandora's tomb, and we would like it to stay that way." Nikki nodded her understanding just as they heard Shade's return. "Ah, King Shade; I hope my gift served you well in your war."

Shade smiled at her as he held out a sheathed dagger in both hands to Eva. Nikki thought she recognized it as the dagger she'd used to carve the Star of Death for Jazabel's wedding. "I actually never got to use it as I wanted to; Nikki had that honour, but with my sword."

Taking the dagger from him, Eva put it behind her back, using the leather cord that ran down her back as a hold. "That's too bad for you, but also a good thing. This dagger has enough blood on its blade. Thank you for returning it. I just finished telling your sister that her request has been granted. You will be allowed to accompany her to our gate, but you may go no further."

"That's excellent, thank you for allowing this. We've been anxiously awaiting that verdict. When can we see it?" Shade asked with a smile.

"Whenever you like; if you wish, I can stay a few days and guide you to the tomb. But if you need a while longer, I can provide you with a map and a few guides to make sure you don't get lost." Queen Amaranth had a small smile as she said this, as if telling a joke only she understood.

Turning to her, Shade smiled as he asked, "When would you like to go? We only have to tell Mom and Dad we're taking a much needed break, and that we'll only be gone a few days."

Returning his smile, she said, "Let's leave tomorrow. I can't wait anymore; and we have our own personal guide."

Shade just nodded. "I couldn't agree more." Turning back to Queen Amaranth, he added, "Thank you again, for this great offer. We'll be ready tomorrow afternoon. If my memory serves correctly, you sleep from dawn until a little after noon." When she nodded with a shocked smile, he continued, "Allow us to show you to a room for the night. We have something that we need to do."

"Of course, your highness. But I do not need a room; I

prefer to stay with those who serve me: my wolves. We've found a nice clearing on the other side of the lake to rest. I'll see you tomorrow, goodnight." And with that, she descended the stairs without looking back.

Taking her hand, Shade turned to Nikki as he got a saddened expression on his face. Heaving a sigh, he said, "Let's go put Brudas to rest." Nodding, Nikki allowed him to lead the way back inside and out to the caves that had always had a hold on the men in her family.

As Shade unveiled the Mask of Babomorah, he flinched away in disgust; disgust that he'd actually used this infernal thing and not destroyed it the moment his father showed it to him. Now knowing that his usage of the Mask had been the last thing Brudas had waited for before revealing himself would always burden Shade. He heard Nikki gasp in disgust at his side.

"All this pain over such an ugly thing; it's a disgrace to the beauty it was created from," she said.

"I just hope Brudas and Anilla find what we're about to do a form of closure." Lifting the Mask into the air with both hands, Shade continued in his official voice, "Brudas, I hope that you and Anilla find peace in what I now do, and not more anger. I'll make it so that this thing will never be used again." And with that, Shade snapped the Mask in two, and as he did, he felt the draw that had always pulled him to it fade.

Dropping the two halves into the two holes he and Nikki

had dug minutes early, Shade looked down on them with a hint of sadness. "I hope you were reunited with your love in death, as your death reunited me with mine. I'm so sorry for the pain we caused you."

"We both are, Brudas. And we wish that we had met under different circumstances. We would have liked to known the real you, and your true love," Nikki added.

And with a one-armed hug of each other, they started to bury the two halves of the Mask of Babomorah, the bones that had once been Anilla.

Chapter 65:

Chronicle Epilogue

Shade and Nikki are led by Queen Amaranth to Pandora's tomb. Queen Amaranth's ritual is performed and it is learned that a Kanta shall be born to lead not only Braria but the Ladies of the Night as well, as their true queen. She will be the strongest since Pandora herself, and the only Raven Lady of the Night in their history. The Ladies of the Night keep all this from Nikki, as she is unconscious for the ritual. While at Pandora's tomb, Nikki is granted the opportunity to speak with Jazabel's spirit, where she tells her how much she misses her and loves her, revealing the name of her daughter in the process. Jazabel is greatly honoured and says she is sorry she won't know the child, as well as expresses her love for both Shade and Nikki.

Nikki gives birth to Jazabel Zelda at midnight the morning of the winter solstice, the darkest time of the year. All of Braria rejoices at her birth. It rejoices again two years later when Nikki gives birth to a boy, Cassiel Daris. But tragedy strikes five years later when Pan dies at age 67. Iselda dies two years later, and is finally not reborn as she is reunited with her loved ones in the underworld.

Six years later, Nikki realizes that Jazabel, now fifteen, is going through the same phases the original Jazabel went through when she became a Lady of the Night. Worried that her daughter will try to kill someone if she isn't told what is happening to her, Nikki confronts Jazabel and tells her the truth. Jazabel, however, claims to have complete knowledge of what is happening to her and tells her mother that it must happen: the Darkness is calling her to the Night.

Nikki then decides to take Jazabel to Pandora's tomb to help her with the transition of becoming a Lady of the Night. Along the way, however, it happens: Jazabel gives into the Night, killing a thief in the process. Upon arrival at Pandora's tomb, Nikki is shocked to see every Lady of the Night bow at Jazabel's feet as they lead her to the tomb's throne room. There she is hailed as the true queen.

Nikki returns to Terang alone, knowing that she will hardly ever see her daughter again, and dreading the fact that she has to tell Shade this as well. Shade and Cassiel are saddened by this news, but come to accept it. Braria is told the truth of Jazabel, and a wave of sympathy is sent to the Royal Family.

Over time, Cassiel grows to become king and eventually marries his childhood love, Cassandra. Jazabel, now twenty-six, returns for the first time to Terang to attend the wedding, wearing only her Lady of the Night attire, and is accompanied by another Lady. Much joy erupts for having Jazabel return, and the city celebrates in a grand fashion.

A year later Braria is again celebrating: this time for the birth of the new prince, Luxzefer. And with the help of his Aunt Jazabel, Luxzefer would usher in a new age where everyone is equal, bringing the Ladies of the Night back into society.

Bolfodier